George Joseph Williamson

The Ship's Career

And other Poems. Third Edition

George Joseph Williamson

The Ship's Career
And other Poems. Third Edition

ISBN/EAN: 9783337401566

Printed in Europe, USA, Canada, Australia, Japan

Cover: Foto ©Andreas Hilbeck / pixelio.de

More available books at **www.hansebooks.com**

Yours Faithfully
Geo J Williamson

THE

SHIP'S CAREER

AND

OTHER POEMS.

BY

G. J. WILLIAMSON.

THIRD EDITION.

London:

THOMAS MURBY, BOUVERIE STREET, FLEET STREET.

1867.

CONTENTS.

PREFACE.

Dedicated to the Friends of Wesleyan Methodists

EAR CHRISTAIN FRIENDS,

In introducing the Third Edition of my humble work, the only apology I can offer is, that I have received such encouragement from the public and kind friends, as to induce me to write many new pieces, which are added to the work, and the whole have undergone careful revision with a view to render the work as acceptable as possible, and I trust it may be as favourably received as the former editions. I will take this opportunity of tendering my gratitude to my kind friends and the public, for the patronage and encouragement they have given me; and I humbly hope that the present edition will become a source of good to all who read it, for this is my first and greatest desire in publishing, and not pecuniary recompence. I will venture to say that the sentiments will be found of a beneficial tendency: though perhaps roughly written, they point to the paths of Truth, Honour, and Virtue.

Believing that the chief blessings I have received on earth have flowed to me through the channels of Wesleyan Methodism, to that body I feel I owe a large debt of gratitude,—indeed a much larger debt than I can ever repay; and as a recognition of the benefits I have received, I dedicate my literary efforts to the members of the Wesleyan body, who are spreading themselves and their doctrine through all parts of the world, and are champions of the truth as it is in Jesus.

I may be asked, "Are you not afraid to launch your small craft on the great sea of literature where so many have been wrecked?" I boldly answer, "No!" Another question may be asked, "Are you not afraid of critics, and that the waves of public opinion dashing over your little boat will overwhelm it?" I again reply, "No!" for I believe that when they see the author has done his best, and that in a good cause, they will not attempt to sink his frail bark, however much they may differ from him.

With this belief I launch it without fear, for many small vessels have weathered a storm in which larger ones have been wrecked. Yet another question may be asked, "Will you put it before the world in a meek and humble manner?" I should wish to do so; but to profess humility when we feel proud is false modesty; and as I believe there is now far too much hypocrisy in the world, I shall be candid, and acknowledge that I am proud of my little work, when I consider the limited education I have received, and throw myself with my pride and all my other failings upon the generosity of the public, with an anxious desire that it may be read, and favourably received.

Though I am conscious the following pages still have many defects, yet I fondly hope they have not been written in vain, but that the work may be kindly taken by the hand by many, and meet with success. But oh, glorious thought! should it dry up the tears of some mourner, or be useful in giving consolation in the smallest degree to the afflicted, or should some straying Christian find in it a line to cheer him on his journey through life, directing his affections toward the better land to which he is journeying, promised by his Lord, then my end would be answered, and I would humbly desire to shake the hand of that Christian in the spirit, for we are all pilgrims to the same Heaven, and in our Father's house are many mansions.

In conclusion, I would add that there will be found in the work several pieces of a loyal and patriotic character. It has been my desire in these effusions to express my deep sense of the inestimable value of the Constitution under which we live, my love and veneration of the exalted virtues and example of the Royal Family, and the fullest amount of Religious Liberty enjoyed by every class of the community.

That we may all meet in a better world, where sin and sorrow are unknown, and happiness reigns supreme for ever, is the fervent prayer of your faithful friend,

THE AUTHOR.

THE HISTORY OF MY LIFE.

The following sketch of the history of my life is from memory, consequently it is in many parts very imperfect; but the reader may be assured that I shall write nothing but the plain truth, which is stamped upon my remembrance.

I was born of poor parents in the city of Rochester; my father was a fisherman, and had to labour hard for the bread that perisheth, and my mother helped to support us by binding shoes, but still it was a hard struggle to keep the wolf from the door. I remember having a kind grandmother; who, I have heard my mother say, was greatly persecuted on account of her religious principles, being locked out of doors, and having to walk about the yard on many a bitter cold night, because she would continue to go to Meeting, being a Wesleyan—for persecution was carried on openly to a much greater extent at that time (upwards of fifty years ago) than at the present. But Methodism is fast outliving the prejudices once raised against it. All honor to those Christian heroes, both churchmen and dissenters, who have so nobly upheld the sacred banner of the Cross, and transmitted it to posterity unsullied; such men as Ridley and Latimer, champions of the truth, who could exclaim, when bound to the stake,—"None but Christ! None but Christ!"

My first days were spent at an infant school kept by a woman, who inspired our little minds with awe under the title of "governess." And I still have it firmly impressed upon my mind, that very often a piece of whalebone (part of a lady's dress, I believe,) came in contact with my hand, and I also remember that these two parties were never on the best of terms, and I doubt very much whether such chastisement in the slightest degree assisted my progress in learning. When I was six or seven years of age, I remember going down the river Medway on board the frigate "Phaeton," of which ship my uncle, George Knowles, was boatswain; she was lying off Sheerness for the Admiralty to try the experiment of using cast-iron masts; they could not make them answer then, although in the present day we have iron ships, iron ropes, iron houses, iron churches, and so many other things made of iron, that this may be termed the iron age of the world.

After I had been some time with the governess, I was sent to a commercial school for a short time, but as my parents could not afford to pay eighteen-pence a-week for my schooling, I was taken from that one and sent to a charity school, where the payment was only one penny a-week, I was there nearly twelve months, and made some progress in reading, but very little in writing or arithmetic. I well remember the fights the several schools had with each other, at which we were drawn up in regular armies with leaders, and fought regular pitched battles; and when a prisoner was taken we formed ourselves into two rows, and he had to run the gauntlet between us, assisted in his progress by smart cracks from all within whose reach he came.

Being taken from school, a situation was procured for me at a milliner and dressmaker's, and, of all the places in life for a boy to obtain, I feel this must be the worst; I was continually on my feet from seven in the morning, till eleven and twelve o'clock at night, and this I should not have minded could I have given satisfaction, but that seemed impossible, for I got a crack from one and a slap from another, until I was almost weary of my life, but being out one day I received a finishing stroke to my connexion with the millinery business. A boy much larger than myself, whom I had offended, wreaked his vengeance upon the band-box I was carrying and smashed it to pieces, and completely spoilt two bonnets I was taking home to a lady; the boy's father had to pay for the bonnets, and I received my discharge and a severe reprimand and went home. My parents thought me incorrigible, and the only good to be done with me was to send me to sea, as they could not afford to keep me idle. I was sent on board the ship of a notorious smuggler belonging to the city of Rochester, who had lost five vessels in the practice of smuggling; I did not stay long with him, as my father wanted me in a small vessel of his own, into which I was installed.

As we were sailing down the Medway one cold November morning just before daylight, we saw a boat belonging to H.M.S. "Prince Regent," which had upset, and five men were clinging to it; we were fortunate enough to rescue them, and not a minute too soon, for we had scarcely got them on board, when the boat went down, and they would all have surely perished, as they were so benumbed with cold that they could hardly move.

I will relate an incident that occured to me during my stay on board the smuggling vessel:—We had taken a load of oysters to Billingsgate Market, and after sailing all night we arrived off Greenwich early in the morning, when I was sent to keep watch; being very tired I though that the best place to keep watch was to get up into the truss of the mainsail. I accordingly got up there, and soon fell fast a-sleep and rolled down into the wet mainsail; I laid there till it was low-water, and the boat was about to proceed to Billingsgate. I was soon missed, and a great search was made for me, but I was not to be found; after a long time, when I had been given up as lost or drowned, on the men letting go the truss of the sail to get the vessel under weigh, I fell down right across the boom fortunately much more freightened than hurt, greatly to the satisfaction of myself and all on board.

I had at that time a wen growing on my right eye. It became so large, that it was feared I should lose the sight of the eye. I went to St. Thomas's Hospital with a friend of my father, and having been examined by some of the doctors I was told by a white-haired old gentleman that unless I had it cut I should very soon lose the sight of that eye. This gentleman spoke so kindly to me, that I told him I thought I had courage enough to go through the operation, and I expressed a wish that he would do it himself. He instantly took me at my word, but when I was bound to the chair I felt my courage fast oozing away; yet as I had gone so far, I was ashamed to retreat, and therefore submitted with the best grace I possibly could. I must own that the cutting caused me so little pain, that I scarcely felt it; but when the roots were extracted the pain was so excruciating that I fainted away, and remained insensible for some time. When I came to myself, I found I had my head bound up, and was then very glad to think that I had had the courage to go through the operation. It left a scar over my eye, but I have felt no pain since. I must not let this opportunity pass without offering my warm tribute of praise to those valuable Samaritan Institutions—the hospitals of our country. All honour to their noble and benevolent founders; all honour to the memory of their past supporters and friends, and also to those worthy men who are still generously using a large share of their means annually to cheer the spirits and ease the pain of their suffering fellow-creatures and provide an asylum for the afflicted, however poor, free of expense.

From what I have seen, heard, and read I do not believe there is a country in the world where poor afflicted humanity is so well cared for as in England, thanks to the noble generosity of the more wealthy and benevolent citizens.

But to return to my father's little vessel. She was a very old one, and having once belonged to a painter, she was nicknamed the "Paint-pot."

After it had been raining all night, we got up one morning completely wet through, in consequence of the deck leaking so much. This reminds me of an incident that occurred to my grandfather's brother Frank. He was owner of just such an old boat as my father's; he had directed his son James to put the bed out to dry on the stern part of the boat, for it had rained the night before, and not only soaked the sleepers, but likewise the bed, upon which they were lying. After the bed had lain there some time, the rain began to pour as it had done the night before, and, fearing that the bed would become soaked again, the boy asked his father what he should do with it. "Oh!" replied he, joking, "if you can't find any other place for it, throw it overboard." The boy thought it a strange order, but after consideration he concluded that a bag of wet straw was of no great value, and accordingly threw it overboard. When the father saw that he had been taken at his word, he very coolly took the boy in his arms and threw him in after it. The boy being a good swimmer, was soon picked up by one of the other boats, but he did not dare to come into his father's presence again that day. The manner in which these fisher-boys are treated is in general shameful, and requires a law to alter it. We have laws for the prevention of cruelty to animals, and surely there ought to be a law to protect these poor fisher-boys from the inhuman usage inflicted by their unfeeling masters whilst out at sea.

My father's only brother perished in a snow-storm: his little vessel being sunk by the violence of the gale, he wrapped himself up in the mainsail, to protect him from the snow, and was found next morning frozen to death. My grandfather was more fortunate; for after the vessel went down, he was washed on shore nearly dead, but being picked up by a fisherman, who took him to his home and nourished him, he recovered. He served in one of Nelson's ships after this, and though he fought in several battles, he was never wounded. On coming home, however, he was superintending the slinging of a butt of rum, which was being hoisted from the hold of the vessel, when the slings broke, and he fell head foremost down the hold, and fractured his skull. He had it trepanned and a plate of silver fixed in it, which remained there till the day of his death. While I was in the "Paint-pot," my father had an appointment to sell oysters in London for the Rochester Oyster Company, and my grandfather was left in charge of the vessel. The old gentleman frequently promised me a liberal supply of ropes-endings and pitchings overboard, but luckily for me he never kept his promises; but he gave me regularly sixpence a week for myself, not, as he said, because I deserved it, but with a view to encourage me to become a better boy.

My father had an apprentice, who occasionally was very fond of bestowing a kick or a cuff upon me, which would call forth the interference of my grandfather, who seemed to consider it his sole privilege to knock me about, although he seldom exercised it. When I had grown to nearly the size of the apprentice, I challenged him to a fight, and notwithstanding his superior strength, and the bruising I got, it was declared a drawn battle. Soon after this he went on board a man of war, and is now in Geenwich Hospital. Whilst dredging for oysters off Sharfleet, in the beds of the Rochester Oyster Company, I was in the act of throwing the dredge overboard, when it caught in my Guernsey shirt and dragged me with it. I was some time under water before I could clear myself from the dredge, and what was most surprising to those on board, I threw the dredge over on the weather side, and I came up on the lee side, which showed that I had gone quite under the vessel's keel—a dredge is a large iron machine with a net attached to it. During the time we were dredging about this place, three whales came into the river Medway, and staid for two days. Several persons tried to shoot them, but without success. About three days afterwards a large one was taken ashore at Gray's, and from the description that was given of it, I considered it to be the largest of the three I had seen in the Medway. I was now about thirteen years of age, when my grandfather died, and left me in charge of the vessel. I have said she was a very old vessel, but she was now usually so bad as to be nearly always half full of water. During an easterly gale she sprung a leak, which gained so fast that we were obliged to run her ashore. She did not require much breaking up, for the bottom nearly dropped out the moment we got her ashore. After this I went on board the "Diamond," for the mackerel season, with Mr. A. Smith, now pilot, of Gravesend. What money I earned, I carried home to assist my father in the purchase of another vessel. He bought one for six pounds—a very old one of course; but after he had got it into repair, it proved the best he ever possessed.

After it was fitted out, which cost nearly seventy pounds, I went on board as master, with my two brothers, William and Henry; and in one season by dint of working hard, we cleared off the debt that was upon the vessel, but met with a heavy misfortune. We were blown away from our anchors during a heavy gale of wind, and despite all our efforts, we drifted towards the shore. Here the waves broke over the vessel so furiously that she very soon sunk; we had to scramble as well as we could to the highest part of the marsh, and pile the hatches one upon another to keep us out of the reach of the tide. Here we remained for some time almost benumbed, for the weather was extremely cold, and saw no other prospect but drowning; when, just as our courage began to droop, we saw a small vessel running into a creek, to escape the fury of the storm. We hailed her, and were overjoyed when she came and took us off from our perilous situation; had she been a short time later we should certainly have been lost, as the hatches began rising beneath us from the force of the tide; and this very tide rose so high that the fields and gardens of Rochester were overflowed, and a poor school-master's wife was drowned in her bed on Rochester common; her name was Leader. We were all very kindly treated by our rescuers, and after we had eaten and drank, we fell asleep and forgot our troubles.

The next day being fine, we went to see the state of our sunken vessel; she was deeply imbedded in the marsh, but not so much damaged as we expected; we set to work at once, and by digging her out and stopping the leaks, we succeeded in floating her out the second day after the storm. We took her to Rochester, and put her into the hands of a shipwright and I went to sea again to earn more money to assist my father in defraying the expenses of repairing. I finished my term of apprenticeship, but being too young to take up my freedom, I went on board the "Gazelle," the property of Mr. Guston, one of the elder brethren of Trinity House. She was a new vessel and was launched one Saturday from Mr. Meckiff's yard, at the entrance of the canal, Rochester, and on the following Saturday she sailed in a match of the Thames Yacht Club, and won by a considerable distance. About this time a considerable impression was made upon my mind by reading some stray leaves that fell into my hands; they were leaves from that epitome of piety entitled, "The whole Duty of Man" I read them, and trembled for the future; but the impression did not last long, for when I sailed on a Sunday in our yacht, I laid the flattering unction to my soul that it was no sin for me to do so, but that the whole of the sin rested with the master of the vessel. I much improved myself in writing about this time, by taking copy-books on board, and imitating the written copy at the top of the page. I am very sorry to say that I was also much addicted to gambling, particularly playing bagatelle for money, at which I was rather expert. One night I won a young man's gold watch by play, and he was so overcome by despondency, that I returned his watch to him, and vowed I would never gamble again.

After I had been a season on board the yacht, I left her to go on board a brig, on whose books I was first placed as half-man, but I soon get the pay of a full man. I was not long in the brig before I accepted an offer of a better situation, as mate of the "Aboyne." During my stay in this ship I got married, and that very economically, for ours being the first marriage the clergyman had performed he did it without any charge. I had a very narrow escape from drowning while in this vessel; through the violence of the wind, a huge wave dashed over the deck and swept everything away before it; but we were luckily all in the rigging at the time, and so escaped an almost certain death. We had a flowing tide at the time and succeeded in forcing the ship into deep water at the expense of springing a leak; but as we had good pumps, we very soon got the leak under.

After this voyage I left the ship, being tired of the coal trade, and my place was taken by my cousin James. The captain had a favorite dog on board, which my cousin delighted in teasing; but by some mishap the dog fell overboard, and my cousin plunged in after it; and although he was a good swimmer he sank and was drowned, but the dog was picked up about a mile astern of the ship, having been carried that distance by the tide. So many were the accidents about this time, that out of twelve apprentices with whom I was acquainted, eight were drowned.

My wife had some little property left her after I had been on my last-mentioned voyage, with which I purchased a vessel. All went on prosperously, and I was able to purchase others, and soon increased my stock of vessels, through the goodness of God, to whose divine mercy and protection I thankfully attribute all my prosperity.

Whilst running along the shore at Deal in one of my vessels (I had three at that time), we struck on Deal Rocks, and were advised by the Deal people to quit the vessel, but we did not think their advice good, and therefore remained. Our boat was soon swamped alongside of us, and the vessel half filled with water; the wind dropping, however, we were able to get her off the rocks into Ramsgate Harbour, very thankful to God for His merciful goodness in preserving us. An incident occurred on board this same vessel which I will narrate, vouching entirely for the truth of the circumstance.

While crossing the Channel one beautiful moonlight night, my apprentice said, "Master, there is my mother sitting on the windlass." I looked, but saw nothing, and quite rediculed the idea, but he still persisted in his assertion, and I then told him to see what time it was When we arrived at Rochester, he received intelligence of his mother's death, and on enquiry it proved to have occurred exactly the same night and hour that he declared he saw her sitting on the windlass.

I now come to an important phase in my life, namely, my conversion. My wife was a constant attendant at chapel, and it was my usual custom to accompany her thither, although I did not benefit by it, until the light burst I prayed very earnestly to be forgiven, but was still very miserable. Going down the river with a coast-guardsman, he noticed my despondency, and earnestly inquired the cause; as I knew him to be a pious man, I unreservedly told him, and proposed prayer. He prayed long and earnestly for me, but I did not feel any better when he left me. The thought then struck me that my own prayers might accomplish my end, and I resolved at once to pray. Acting upon this resolution I knelt down in my boat and began the Lord's Prayer, when light burst upon my soul, and I rose up and shouted "My Father!" This was the happiest moment of my life, for I felt that my sins were pardoned, and my soul was filled with joy.

I connected myself with the Wesleyans, and became a Sunday-school teacher and tract distributor. After I had joined them about twelve months, I took the Bethel flag on board my little vessel, and, when opportunity offered, had prayer-meetings and services on board.

I was much annoyed at being called a hypocrite, and also at the statement that I had joined the people of God for the purpose of gain. While painting and repairing my vessel, I was often told that it was all gained through joining the chapel I resented these insults, and I am afraid sometimes I used intemperate language, but the more they saw it annoyed me, the more they persisted in doing it. I next tried another course, and when they annoyed me, I quietly allowed that the chapel was a great benefit to me, and I gave them to understand that the same course was open to them, and that they might all partake of its benefits. By thus reasoning with them, and endeavouring to act as consistently as possible in my profession, I soon effectually stopped their annoyance.

It was my custom when we could not work to collect as many men as I possibly could from the vessels about us, many of which carried the Bethel flag, and have divine service performed. I shall never forget the first time I conducted the service. There were seventy vessels in the harbour, and we mustered about sixty men to the service. I am sure that any Reverend Divine could not have restrained a smile if he had seen me at my pulpit (which was an inverted oyster-tub covered over with a clean white sail), dressed in my Guernsey frock, expounding the Scriptures to a congregation, who were accommodated with baskets and boards for seats We sang together greatly to our own satisfaction, more especially as we had a young man amongst us who played a clarionet. Although our harmony made no pretensions to rival the choirs of St. Paul's, or Westminster Abbey, it was conducted with earnestness and zeal, and afforded us a degree of holy pleasure, such as is not often surpassed by the more pretentious bodies of religionists. One of our congregation has since departed this life, and, we hope, has gone to heaven, leaving behind him a glorious testimony of his righteousness. Another is now a fisherman preacher at Colchester, and is labouring very acceptable in the Wesleyan Society. Others are members of various churches, and I rejoice to find them still looking Zionward, longing for the better home, and though time hath wrinkled their brows and whitened their locks, their chief regret is that they have not served their Master better, whom they have found ever good, ever just, ever loving, and ever merciful.

While at Dunkirk I saw a very beautiful piece of sculpture representing Christ upon the cross; a great many people kissed the feet of the piece of sculpture, and an irresistable impulse induced me to do the same; immediately an indescriable feeling of joy took possession of me. The people seeing a rough fisherman kiss the feet of their Lord, came and shook hands with me very kindly, and though I did not understand a single word of French, nor they a single word of English, yet we understood each other, being servants of the same God; and I doubt not that, should I ever reach heaven, I shall meet many good Catholics there. It is a custom in France to place flowers on the graves of the dead; and on most of the crosses and tombs are glass boxes containing wreaths of small "Immortelles" While sauntering about the churchyard of Basville, a small town about a mile from Calais, I saw two girls decking the grave of some lately departed one; one girl was about eight years of age, and the other about eleven; and as they placed their wreaths of "Immortelles" upon the grave and wept, I felt that I should have been glad to have known the French language, that I might offer them some consolation; and as I heard them weep, I could not help weeping myself, and thought, Oh! if that departed mother were able to see the affection of her offspring, it would repay her for all the pains and cares she had bestowed upon them while on earth. But alas! how few children seem to know the value of a kind parent until they are taken from them by death, and then how many a prodigal son has mourned over the corpse of an affectionate father, "whose grey hairs he has brought with sorrow to the grave." How many a gay and thoughtless daughter has had to shed bitter tears over the grave of an affectionate mother, who taught her the infant prayer, and strove to lead her in the path of virtue! and when friends are laid in their last resting place, then we remember all their acts of kindness to us; and if it be a fond mother, whose heart we have caused to thrill with anguish by our ingratitude, how our busy mind will recall the scene, and make us wish we had acted differently; or should it be a father or a wife, how sorrowfully we look back to the time when we caused them pain by our unkindness.

Out of twelve young men who were my acquaintances when I was apprentice, I believe there are but three now living; six of them were drowned, and the other three met with sad and fearful ends; one, a very wicked man, was crushed between two ships; another I visited just before his death and found him in a fearful state, for he was covered with virmin and totally unconscious of everything around him. I merely relate these incidents to show what a debtor I am to God, who has prospered me, and kept me out of the paths of sin and wickedness. I have tried in my humble way ever since I gave my heart to God, to labour in His cause, as Sunday-school teacher, and tract distributer, and I have preached in the Workhouse to the poor. I have been Society Steward at Southwark Chapel, Long Lane, Bermondsey, for three years, and I declare, from the bottom of my heart, in language of Scripture, that "I would rather be a door-keeper in the House of God, then dwell in the tents of wickedness."

I now come to the cause of my first attempt at writing poetry. A young Lady of my acquaintance was about to celebrate her birth-day, and solicited all her friends to send her a piece of poetry as a birth-day present and I was asked among the number. I declined at first, as, although I was forty-two years of age, I had never attempted to write a line of poetry in my life. However, as the young lady would accept of no denial, I was obliged to comply, and with the idea that my attempt would effectually cure her of asking me again. Judge then my surprise when I was told that mine was the best of the pieces sent. When my wife heard of this she told me that we had been married twenty years, and she thought she was entitled to some, so I wrote her the second piece. Since that time I have occasionly written pieces, sometimes on board my vessel, sometimes in my counting-house, and also when travelling. It is my custom to carry a small book and pencil in my pocket, so that when anything strikes my mind I may note it down on the spot. I cannot say I am desirous of becoming a poet, but I have laboured hard to write the pieces I now present to the public. I sincerely hope that, if they serve no other purpose, they may be the means of saving some immortal soul from perishing. The pieces have all been written since I have been connected with Billingsgate, and I feel that this fact must tend rather to enhance their value than to create any prejudice against them. It has been my privilege to meet with gentlemen connected with that market, who I boldly affirm, would be a valuable acquisition to any company, however high it might be. I am proud to own the many advantages I have derived from the association and conversation of such men; it has tended very much to rub off that roughness of demeanour, which generally characterises men of a seafaring life, which would otherwise have attached itself to me. It would be invidious to select individuals, for I have met with respect from every one, except in one or two instances, which have occurred when the parties have been drinking. Experience has shown me that if you treat a man like a dog, he will hate you; but if you treat him like a man, he will respect you. I do not think we should have so many strikes among the working classes as we have if employers, would condescend to reason with their workmen, and show them they feel an interest in their welfare, and recognize as men those whose muscular frames and sinewy arms are hourly building them up immense fortunes. I say we ought not, and should not, lose the goodwill of any man, no matter how poor he may be. What a deathbed that would be, when, after living three score years and ten, we could not say with truth that we had done a single good deed or action towards our fellow creatures. It is assuredly the imperative duty of every man and woman to leave the world better than they found it. The man who professes to love his country, and does nothing to benefit his fellow-countrymen, is a hypocrite. If we, in this little sea-girt isle, are blessed with the gospel, it is our privilege—nay, it is our duty—to propagate the glorious gospel to the most remote and distant parts of the globe, that the savage and heathen may be brought to partake of the life-giving fountain of mercy, and raise their voices in shouts of gladness for the nation that brought them the glad tidings of everlasting salvation. Thus England will become the life-boat of saving grace, and God with His mighty arm will ever protect us.

From one of the steam vessels crossing the Atlantic was seen a man floating on a piece of wreck; a boat was dispatched and he was saved. When he recovered he said, "There's another man on the wreck;" the boat returned and saved him also. Such ought to be the feeling of every man saved through Christ; he ought to say, "There's another still on the wreck." I believe I am the first fisherman who has written poetry, and therefore claim something in the shape of originality in this respect. I do not know why a fisherman should not write poetry, unless it is that his employment is not calculated to engender poetic ideas. But still the fisherman has been stamped with dignity by our Saviour choosing the Galilean fishermen for his disciples, and even now He sometimes chooses humble fishermen to preach His gospel, and though they are generally rough men, they are very earnest, and often accomplish a large amount of good. Our captains and sailors too seem to have become a different class of men to what they were—more thoughtful and provident; many captains carry the Bethel flag, and are doing great good for their fellow men by having service on board. May God, in His infinite mercy, grant that every ship may soon become a Bethel, and every sailor's heart His temple! May they carry abroad the Christianity of England, and thus propagate the gospel all over the world! I once sailed in a barge with one of the most wicked captains I ever knew; he was a most awful swearer and drunkard. When I became a visitor of the sick, one of the first persons I had to visit was my old friend the captain, who was so ill that there were little hopes of his recovery. I trembled when I knew I was to visit him but was determined not to flinch from my duty; so I went with a trembling heart, but with a firm conviction that I was to be made a blessing to him. When I reached his door, my heart failed me, and my knees almost knocked together. I took courage, and knocked. The door was opened by his wife, who, thinking I was visiting him as an old acquaintance, said, "Ah! poor Jack is sadly altered, you will scarcely know him." When I told her the object of my visit, she looked amazed, and called her husband, saying, "Jack, here is your old friend George come to pray with you." He told me to come up stairs; I went up, and if I ever prayed in earnest, it was then. I sincerely trust he was pardoned, and hope to see him in the better world, where we shall join in songs to the Redeemer, who has rescued us from everlasting destruction.

When I was a Ragged School teacher, I was rather fond of dress. One evening I went to the school, wearing a pair of light-coloured Angola trousers, which made me, in my own opinion, look very smart. It happened that I had in my class that evening, about sixteen boys, four or five of whom were chimney-sweeps; and while speaking to them about the love of Christ, they where so interested that they kept drawing closer and closer around me. Excited by this best of subjects, I did not observe how close they had come; but when I had done speaking, I chanced to glance down, and saw that my Angola trousers looked as if they had been used to sweep a chimney with. My first impulse was one of anger; but when I looked at the sooty face of one of the boys, and saw a line where a tear had trickled down while I had been speaking of the love of Christ, I felt that if I had had all the trousers in the world, I would have given them up to have rescued a soul from eternal death

The first time I went to the Wesleyan Theological Institute, I was introduced to Mr. George Harwood, then the Governor of the Institute, by a student who told him I had been the instrument of his conversion. It appeared that I had been his teacher for four years in Bethel Sunday-school; he is now a minister in the Wesleyan Connection, and I believe a very useful and acceptable one. Another one, who was in my class at the same school for nearly three years, stated on a chapel platform that I had also been the means of his conversion; and he has now gone out to China as a medical Missionary. To benefit both body and soul, he has been studying medically; his attention has been principally directed to "diseases of the eye." May He who opened the eyes of blind Bartimeus, assist him by His Holy Spirit to enlighten the Chinese! What an encouragement to Sunday-school teachers! for if they convert one, that one may be the means of the conversion of a hundred, or even a thousand. It is my belief that if every converted sinner would set about converting another *one*, they would in nearly every instance be successful. What large numbers would then be added to our Church! The work of soul-saving would go on gloriously. But most of us are for leaving too much for our ministers to do, while we ought to strengthen their hands by bringing all we can under their ministry. It is the small streams flowing from various sources that form the mighty river; so must it be with different members of our Churches. They must be like the small streams that run into great rivers; they must use their influence both in public and private, until the Wesleyan river becomes a mighty ocean—cleansing with its waters every part of the habitable globe.

They must their standard raise,
  On every clime and shore;
Till the sons of Adam's race,
  Their Saviour Christ adore.

For His kingdom they must fight,
  Like soldiers good and brave;
Must spread the Gospel's light,
  And all men try to save.

They must their colours show,
  And scorn all shame and fear;
And let all others know,
  They'll do their duty here.

Christ's banner of the Cross,
  They must display to all:
Count earthly things as dross—
  Set men on Christ to call.

His standard they must hoist,
  Whilst there's a soul to save;
A pledge of love to Christ—
  Till they shall reach the grave.

Then they their Lord will meet,
  When victory here is gained;
With love He will them greet,
  For truth they have maintained.

He then to them will say,
  "Come, of My Father blest!
You've nobly gained the day,
  Receive the promised rest!"

In the month of May, in the year 1861, his Grace Algernon Percy, Duke of Northumberland, honoured me with an invitation to see him, through the recommendation of Thomas Groves, Esq., his Grace's fishmonger. His Grace's desire was to improve the condition of the fishermen along his own coast, and to furnish them with the means to improve their own condition. Complaints had reached the ears of his Grace, that the fishermen had often to lie still, and could not fish from want of mussels for bait, which caused them great loss, and this his Grace was desirous of remedying, and desired to consult some person who understood the nature and training of mussels and oysters, and to go and make beds on the coast of Northumberland, to carry out the object his Grace had in view. I accordingly went, and at the first interview I had with his Grace, the map of the coast of Northumberland was brought in, and his Grace went through it in a thorough seaman-like and business manner, and pointed out the most suitable places for the establishment of mussel and oyster beds. I was highly pleased with the courteous and kindly manner with which his Grace received and treated me. After asking me a few questions he instructed Thomas Williams, Esq., the steward of Northumberland House, to place one thousand pounds at my disposal, to use in the manner I thought most advantageous to make oyster and mussel beds for the benefit of the fishermen. After the interview with his Grace, I immediately set to work, and sent my vessel, "The Perseverance," with dredges and nets, to procure mussels and oysters. I also sent agents to different places to procure them, and sent them on to Alnmouth, the place I had visited and chosen to commence operations, and this being a central position on the coast of Northumberland, I thought would be the best place for the fishermen to get their bait from. Another reason why I chose Alnmouth was, I thought it the quietest place I could lay them in to grow and breed, as their were few ships that went into the harbour to disturb them, and the sea could not come in to wash them away, as it had done on the coast where the fishermen had laid some before. Another reason that prompted me to lay them there was, that the place is opposite the residence of W. Dickson, Esq , the gentleman who has done a great deal for the benefit of Alnmouth, by building gas-works to supply the town with gas, and fitted up baths in a beautiful manner for the inhabitants and visitors, and erected other buildings for the benefit of the town. And I must say. that should the oyster and mussel beds succeed, it will be owing in a great measure to the kind assistance I received from this gentleman, who took a very great interest in it, and rendered all the assistance in his power to carry out the design. I had previously informed his Grace that I could not be answerable for the success of the undertaking, but that I would do my utmost to make it succeed. I had considered the difficulty of getting oysters and mussels to Alnmouth, as the fishermen had cleared them all away, both small and large, everywhere near the river Aln, so that I could see there would be great difficulty in the undertaking, but as his Grace was anxious to benefit the fishermen, he was willing to risk its success or failure.

The Northumbrian fishermen are a fine race of men, and looking at these fisheries in a national point of view, I feel that should the Government at any time be in want of men for the defence of the liberty of our country, and safty of our shores, there is not a better set of men then the seamen and fishermen of the northern coast of England. And I believe it to be to the interest of the legislature, as well as its duty, to encourage all fisheries, not alone for the enormous amount of food they produce for the people of all our inland towns; there is also this very important consideration: what excellent nurseries they form for our navy, from which true British hearts of oak can be procured in times of extremity and peril, to uphold our National Standard triumphant on the main.

The first voyage of mussels was sent from Lynn, in Norfolk, but owing to calms, when they arrived at Alnmouth they were nearly all dead. The next voyage was a schooner load from Scotland, and of these nearly half died, but the next load by the vessel was in good condition. I had some sent from Belgium by steam ship, and forwarded by rail to Alnmouth, but I found it too expensive to have them that way, and was consequently obliged to discontinue having them from Belgium I proceeded to Stockton-on-Tees, from whence we had some good voyages of mussels, which have formed a large bed at Alnmouth, and are going on prosperously, under the care and management of W. Dickson, Esq.

The oyster ponds required a great deal more labour in constructing than the mussel beds, consequently they were longer in making, and more expensive.

As soon as they were finished, we began to place oysters in the different ponds, of various sorts; we had natives from Colchester, oysters from the Isle of Wight, Falmouth, Jersey, and the Channel. We had some also from Portsmouth Harbour, Scotland, and Wales. We made twelve ponds, and built a large oyster house over one of the ponds; and after stocking the ponds with oysters, we then, by his Grace the Duke's desire, and under the superintendence of W. Dickson, Esq, tried the French system of breeding, oysters, and succeeded far enough to find the heathwood we had placed to catch the spawn, nearly covered with small oysters; but whether it was from the lateness of the season, or the difference in climate, we could not tell, but they did not come to perfection. My own ideas on the subject are, that owing to the climate being so much warmer in the south coast of France, it would be far easier to produce oysters there artificially, than it can ever be on the coast of Northumberland; the coldness of the north coast did not give the oysters a chance of coming to perfection. There was another thing that did great injury to the oyster beds at Alnmouth, and this was the river flood that broke over the banks of the ponds, and filled them all over with mud and sand, destroying a large quantity of the oysters, and caused so much labour to be done a second time, that in my opinion, drove a great many oysters out into Alnmouth Bay. And if in a few years any should be found in the bay, or round about where the tide could carry the spawn from Alnmouth river, I should attribute the same to our laying down oysters there.

As we tried day after day in the vessel with the dredges at different parts of the bay, and off by the Coquet island, and could not find the least sign of the presence of a single oyster, or even an oyster shell, should oysters be discovered in a few years anywhere in the locality, I should at once say that it was owing to the efforts of his Grace the Duke of Northumberland, in trying the scheme of breeding on the Northumbrian coast, and to the assistance received from W. Dickson, Esq., who manifested the greatest concern about it, and did all in his power to promote its interest. On Thursday, July 11, 1862, we took a party on board the vessel, consisting of Dr. Bruce, his wife and daughter, Mr. Brow, his wife and family, Rev J. Stevens and wife, Mr. Burnett and two sons, Capts. Clementson and Hickley, Wm. Purvis, and others.

We took also a pilot on board, and had a day of inspection to try to find oysters or mussels or any other shell-fish in the bay. We caught a few swimming-fish, but no shell-fish of any kind, although it appeared a very nice clean bay, and one where oysters and mussels would grow well. The oyster-house was made so that oysters might be taken from the sea-water, and eaten on the spot, and also to keep the stores required to work with in the ponds. The oyster grounds have not succeeded at present as a commercial speculation, but there have been, and still are, plenty of mussels, and, if left to increase without removing the small ones, there will in time be a very large supply.

I have written this, that it might he known that his Grace the Duke of Northumberland was the first person to introduce the artificial system of breeding oysters on the French plan into England. This was done at Alnmouth, in Northumberland, in the year 1861, since that time others have tried the plan, but have met with little or no success up to 1864; thus I consider the French system of raising oysters artificially in England has been a failure up to the present time.

During the last four years I have been engaged in delivering Lectures, for Ragged-schools and Sabbath-schools, and Young Mens' Christian Associations I have twenty lectures written, some of which I have given several times, and which have been generally well received, I have also found it delightful employment to preach as well as I was able, to the poor in our workhouses. and when I have looked upon them have thought their souls as much worth saving, and bringing to the Saviour, as a King's, Queen's, or an Emperor's. If the poor seem to be in a sad condition here as regards their temporal state, they may have a rich inheritance in heaven for ever; God being no respecter of persons has provided a crown of glory, in the everlasting mansions for the poor as well as the rich, and it is their own fault if they will not accept it.

THE SHIP'S CAREER AND OTHER POEMS.

THE SHIP'S CAREER.

How noble the structure is that which I view!
  How fair the proportion and form
Of the beautiful vessel, so graceful, and new—
  She's erected to weather each storm!

What tongue can foretell her a destiny bright,
  As she floats on the boisterous main?
Though she flies o'er the waves like a sea-bird so light,
  Who can say she'll return home again?

It seems as if art had exhausted its store
  In a form so enchantingly grand:
How proudly she looks, as she rests in her power,
  And waits to be launched from the strand!

Old England's fair ensign waves o'er her stern,
  And the Union-Jack over her bow;
The Standard of Royalty's hoisted in turn,
  Shows all is in readiness now.

"Knock the dog shores away!" the builder hath cried,
And lo! now the mighty mass moves,—
Sliding downward majestically into the tide,
Like a swan to the water she loves

Soon thro' her own element nobly she'll ride,
See her masts are all ready to rear;
The rigging is also brought up alongside,
And her large heavy cannons are near.

The masts are put up, the caps fitted strong,
The rigging goes forward with speed—
The yards are all strung, so tapering and long,
All must be a-taut they're agreed.

The seamen the sails are beginning to bend,
The riggers heave all taugh in place;
And to sea the great vessel is soon fit to send,
As a bulwark of Albion's race.

The ship is in trim, and the stores are aboard,
And now she is ready for sea;
The sails are all up, and the anchor is stowed,
And the land is far under the lee.

The glorious old colour that flies at the peak,
With dishonour shall never be stained;
While freedom to all! is the voice it shall speak—
Man's freedom it ever maintained.

The poor negro slaves that are stolen from home,
And sold like the cattle on shore,
How dreadful their fate, if a ship never come
To give them their freedom once more!

"A sail! Ho! to leeward!" the look-out now cries,
From the topmost the place of the tar;
A large slaver schooner from thence he descries,
With its Yankee flag looming afar.

"Bear down, now, my boys! bear down on that craft!
Hoist aloft the true colours we wear!
Show that England's brave hearts are prepared, fore and aft,
To free slaves wherever they are!"

But the schooner flies fast o'er the white foaming main,
While the groans from on board are distressing;
The slaves are shut up in the hold once again,
And more sail on the ship they are pressing.

Hark! hark! to that gun, as it sounds o'er the sea—
See the shot as it bounds o'er the wave;
'Tis a voice to the slave, to bid him be free,
And tell him they're coming to save!

And now the shot strikes the mast with a crash,
Which overboard goes with the sails;
The vessel in chase comes on with a dash,
And her captain the slaver ship hails.

"Ship a-hoy!" he cries with the trumpet in hand,
"Didn't you mark the signal to back
Your sails to the mast, before reaching the land,
And your speed on the ocean to slack?"

"Now lower our boat!" the captain cries out:
"This trim looking vessel now board;
His papers examine, and look well about,
See what in his hold he has stored!"

He lowers his flag, they step upon deck,
And search all his papers with care,
From South Carolina, with rice loaded, back;
And all seems straighforward and fair.

But a sickening stench from the hold doth arise,
  When the hatches are moved from their place;
O God! what a horrible sight meets their eyes,
  Which years can never efface!

There, chained fast together, the helpless slaves lie,
  Death marking them off for his prey;
How shocking the scene as for water they cry,
  While they one by one wither away!

Alas! that mankind should e'er be so base,
  As to trade in the blood of a brother!
That mammon should bring so vile a disgrace,
  And God's creatures to torture each other!

The Redeemer He died to purchase us all,
  No matter what colour of face;
And the Gospel of love has bidden us call
  All brothers—of every race.

Oh! when shall this horrible trafficking cease,
  The blood of the slave washed away?
When America lives out the Gospel of peace,
  There will soon come a happier day.

America's sons, wipe away this disgrace;
  From you let it ever be hurled:
'Neath the sway of old England no slave can ye trace
  When the banner of Freedom's unfurled,

See the slaver now being towed to the strand,
  And hark! to the groans on the way:
While many have died, and gone to that land
  Where oppressors can never hold sway.

What wonderful sights will meet their eyes there,
  As heaven's gates ope to their view!
Those poor wretched slaves, despised so much here,
  With glorified bodies made new!

But where the oppressors when *they* leave the world,
  And their souls are called from the strife?
Like Dives, alas! into hell they are hurled,
  For the woes of an impious life.

Now the ship's work is done, for which she did sail,
  And the slaver is sold or destroyed;
And again she starts on with a favouring gale,
  All hands to make sail are employed.

The joke is passed round, as she skims o'er the sea,
  The tars think of loved ones at home;
The land is left far away under the lee,
  And on she flies through the white foam.

But see that small cloud rising far in the sky,
  Coming on like a treacherous friend;
In the deepest repose does the azure sea lie,
  Hushed and silent the terrible wind.

But list! how the thunder booms over the main,
  And the winds waken up with dread moan;
The lightning darts over the watery plain,
  Flashing round as the ship saileth on.

And see! the red lightning has struck the lone ship,
  As she ploughs through the merciless waves;
The gale in rude gusts driving her thro' the deep,
  While a foaming broad furrow she leaves.

The topmast is shivered and split by the flash,
  And the wild waves break over the deck;
While all apprehending the finishing crash,
  Prepare to abandon the wreck.

The waters are raging and swelling around,
With a terribly threatening roar,
While the poor cabin boy sadly kneeling is found,
He bewails that he ever left shore

He thinks of his home with its peace-giving scenes,
Of a mother who pillowed his head,
Of a father so good, who laboured for means,
Of daily supplying their bread

Now he offers to Heaven the long forgot prayer,
Taught him in his earlier days—
"Our Father in Heaven." he cries, "O me spare!
And my life I'll devote to Thy praise."

And the sailor ofttimes, at the coming of death,
With a swelling and penitent heart,
Breathes the prayer of his childhood with soft saddened breath,
When about from this world call'd to part.

He thinks of the Bible that lies in his chest,—
That Bible his mother has given;
Though often neglected, he now will protest,
It shall hence be his guide unto heaven.

But the storm has increased as the sun has gone down,
With darkness of dreariest night;
While the skies are portending with threat'ning frown,
They re lit with a deep lurid light.

O could we have seen that morning so fair,
With a breeze scarcely rippling the sea;
We could not have thought such a danger was near,
As the sun rose in bright majesty!

How fair has life's morning too often began,
And our path seemed all smiling with peace;
With youth's fondest ardour we laid out our plan,
Nor dreamt that our pleasures would cease.

The castle illusive was built in the air,
  Fancy tinged with a gorgeous glow;
Till life's sterner lessons that came to our share,
  Taught us happiness was not below!

And the bright'ning hopes of childhood's first years,
  Like bubbles, with dazzling hue.
We blew from our pipes, with hopes and with fears,
  Saw them rising, then vanish from view!

And as years have rolled on in life's rugged ways,
  And storms have o'ershadowed our course,
Fond memory brings back our childhood's bright days,
  Rushing on us with fresh vivid force.

Our lives seem a span, and our memories die;
  Oblivion covers our fame;
Our deeds on the marble attract not an eye;
  Forgotten as 't were but a dream.

I covet no monument, marble, or shrine,
  That time shall crumble to dust;
The sculptor's fine emblem, the poet's chaste line—
  Or the praise—that on earth I was just.

Much rather in heaven's bless'd book be enroll'd,
  Having souls to the good Shepherd led;
Rejoicing redemption's grand tale to unfold—
  How His life blood for them He shed.

To be but an instrument in the bless'd place
  Of God's precious grace to us all,
And the means of redeeming our poor fallen race,
  Are monuments never to fall.

The crash of all ages, the wreckage of years,
  Cannot crumble the working divine;
Each soul that the image of Jesus Christ bears,
  In His kingdom for ever shall shine.

On monuments ever undying—on these
 Would I humbly decipher my name;
Religion upholding with all its decrees,
 Which elevates nations to fame,

But here I have wandered away from the plan
 Of my writing the vessel's career;
Your pardon I crave, and return once again
 To mark life as its quicksands appear.

O how our life's voyage with storms is beset,
 Ever tossing mankind to and fro,
While trials and cares often cause him to fret,
 How to steer. oft he scarcely doth know.

And thus the fine vessel she lurched and she rolled,
 While the waves mounted over her side;
Tinged by the lightning like shining bright gold,
 As their radiance shone on the tide.

But the gale it still strengthens, the ship rushes on,
 The storm sails are needed all now;
Each moment more dang'rous it grows thus to run,
 And all hands must be heaving her to.

The trysail is set—it has weathered the gale,
 All headsail is stowed and secure;
To the winds point the yards with tightly furled sail,
 The helm's hard-a-lee to make sure.

The captain now watches the waves as they spend
 Their strength on the bark as they break;
And the mariners all are at their wits' end,—
 And the ship (to make worse) springs a leak.

The pumps are all manned, but the leaking increase,
 Their lives they work hard now to save;
They think of the loved ones they last saw in peace,
 Each expecting a watery grave.

Hark! hark to that cry, causing hope to expire,
Death seems now awaiting his prey;
An alarm is now given, "The ship is on fire!"
As they lay-to in Biscay's rough bay.

How many brave hearts in those waters sleep!
Biscay's bay their last sorrows could tell,—
Of loved ones that rest in its bosom so deep,
Who of home and of life took farewell!

Peace, peace to their bones, where'er they are laid!
Some coral cave hides them from sight;
But for them the widows and fatherless prayed,—
Hope to meet them in Heaven's bright light.

Some upon Christ with their last ebbing breath,
Like the self-abased publican cried
For mercy, free mercy to save them from death,
And Jesus spake peace as they died.

And they have gone where storms can ne'er come,
On angel's bright wings soared on high:
To live with archangels in that blessed home,
Of glory beyond the blue sky.

But my muse seems determined to wander on high,
From earth to divine things above;
Leaving all things below, in fancy to fly,
Where angels and saints sing and love

Say, who can describe the horrors of fire
On board with deep water around!
All hope from frail men seems there to expire,
And help from God only be found.

But "Nil desperandum" the motto should be
Of the sailor such scenes passing through;
How often in life he deliverance may see,
When nought but death seemed in full view.

The captain cries "Courage!" and bravely the crew
With redoubled energy try
To quench the fierce flames, with hopes rising new
That the storm may give place to bright sky.

And they labour on hard and soon heave to shore;
But the fire, that once threatened to be
Their speedy destruction, is burning no more,
And they their deliverance see.

The winds too are hushed and sunk into rest,
And the ship safely holds on her ways;
Again is relieved the late terrified breast,
And they shout their Deliverer's praise.

And sailors so brave, do the wonders all see
Of that God whom all nature controls
But how strange it appears that many should be
So careless concerning their souls

How mad a thing surely they ever should dare,
With a plank only 'tween them and death,
To break God's holy laws, without the least fear
He should stop their presumptuous breath.

The Psalmist declares they should all praise the Lord,
That oft see His works in the deep;
And the power and the goodness exalt, that afford
Sweet protection awake or asleep.

Oh, may the time speedily come that's foretold,
When the fruits of the sea shall be given;
And God shall have saved our sailors so bold,
And each ship be a Bethel to live in.

Then, wherever they go, they will loudly proclaim
God's mercy to poor fallen man;
And sound with glad singing their Jesus' name,
To accomplish salvation's great plan.

But see what's the land that now bursts on their sight!
  The white cliffs of old England they view;
And home-joys to them that do so invite,
  They think of with sympathy true.

And when they're all safe, to their children they'll tell,
  How oft they deliverance have found;
How God in His love hath done everything well—
  For they're back on old England's ground.

If every blade of grass that is displayed
In the green fields, in every nook and glade—
If every leaf in nature's lovely scene
Decking each tree and flower in hue of green—
Were into emeralds turned, even the whole
Would be as nothing to the deathless soul!

If every sparkling dew-drop seen at morn
Glittering in hedge, on flower, or spreading thorn
Like pendant brilliants—on each leaf or bough,
Like purest crystal they with sunlight glow—
Were to bright diamonds turned, then the whole
Would be as nothing to the deathless soul!

If every grain of sand round every shore,
Washed by the ocean, vast as is the store—
Though infinite in number round each isle,
Could all be gathered up in one vast pile,
And to gold ingots turned,—even then the whole
Would be as nothing to the deathless soul!

If every drop of every genial shower
That falls on hills, or plains, or lovely bower—
That with it rich fertility doth bring,
Till plenteous harvests from its blessings spring—
Were into rich pearls turned, even then the whole
Would be in value nothing to the soul!

If every star or planet seen by night,
Studding the skies above with beams so bright—
Or all we ever heard of—great and grand,
From pole to pole, from skies of every land.
Were all together placed, even then the whole
Would fail to purchase one immortal soul!

The soul will live when all has passed away,
And time o'er worlds has ceased his mighty sway;
Scripture declares these orbs shall all expire,
And earth dissolve in elements of fire:
As long as ages ceaselessly shall roll,
God's breath in man shall live—his deathless soul!

Then let us aim and do the best we can
To save the immortal soul of every man;
If others mock and God's great boon despise,
And will not try to gain the glorious prize,
But will be fools, rejecting God's control,
We will His favour seek, and save the soul.

CHRIST CRUCIFIED.

I often gaze upwards in stillness of night
Beholding the planets, so glorious and bright,
And think of their grandeur and size:
And my soul is filled with wonder and fear,
As I think of Him who created the sphere,—
And to Him my spirit would rise.

And I ask, "Can it be, that He who all made,
Calling things into being by a single word said,
Can e'er look with kindness on me—

Weak, simple, and low, rebellious and wild,
Oft spurning His love and mercy, so mild,
Nor wishing his glory to see?"

I think of the wonders attending His birth,
When angels sung peace and goodwill to earth,
And how that he laboured for all;
I think of redemption—the glorious plan,
Stamping God's own image again upon man,
To raise him from sin's dreadful fall.

I think of the wondrous and great name of old,
By saints and by prophets so often foretold,—
O, Wonderful Counsellor He!
The omnipotent God, and the eternal Sire,
The great Prince of Peace, the foretold Messiah,
In Jesus the man we all see.

I think of the wonders He here did perform,
With stilling the waves, and calming the storm:
While the devils away from Him fled;]
Of the lepers He cleansed, and the myriads healed,
Sight gave to the blind, the Gospel revealed,
And Lazarus raised from the dead!

I think of the prophecies now all revealed,
And how that in Christ they all are fulfilled,
And astonished, I stand at the plan;
That He who created the earth and the skies,—
Wonder of wonders! in mercy He dies—
On Calvary for lost guilty man.

I think of the sun that in darkness was veiled,
Of the cross on which He was cruelly nailed,
When in death He bowed His head;
I think of the temple's veil rent down in twain,
Of the dear Son of God then dying in pain,
And of some rising up from the dead.

I think of His love to the rabble and rout,
Who repaid it again with their impious shout—
"Away with Him, let Him not live!"
And amid all their scorn, their hellish disdain,
He did not of that one moment complain,
But prayed thus: "Oh! Father, forgive."

I think of the Roman centurion's fear,
As he gazed on the wonders exhibited there,
Exclaiming, "This must be God's Son!"
I think of the power divine there displayed,
Enough to make sin-living men all afraid;
And of the great victory won.

With stern indignation my heart ever burns,
That His goodness should meet with such cruel returns—
O could I have e'er done the same?
But alas still for me! against Him I sin,
Opposed to His Spirit the working within,
And this ever fills me with shame.

I think of myself through sin all undone
And how utterly helpless I am to atone,
As the law now demands that I die;
But looking to Calvary, joyful I see
God's only Son died and suffered for me,
And by faith now for pardon I fly.

Humble, and yet by faith I'm made bold,
On the Saviour's dear cross I fix my firm hold,—
If I die it still shall be there;
And as there I gaze, and my Saviour I view,
Saying "Poor sinner, this is all for you!"
Faith banishes all of my fear.

I think of those mansions oft promised above,
Purchased by His beneficent love,
And my life seems nobly grand;

His friendship I have while dwelling on earth,
And that makes my life of far greater worth,—
As in Himself perfect I stand.

Oh, Jesus, dear Saviour, now reigning above,
Oh draw me to Thee by Thy merciful love
In an endless communion divine;
In all my works may I lean upon Thee,
A humble and penitant sinner to be,
And pure in Thy righteousness shine.

And when I have done Thy work here below,
Oh call me to Thee, Thy treasures to know,
And in Thy bright kingdom to rest
With all the host ransomed, who love and adore,
Ever praising Thy name on the heavenly shore,
For ever to dwell with the blest.

THE PEARL OF DAYS.

When first Almighty Power with wondrous skill
Called on the earth to demonstrate His will,
The mass, then shrouded deep in void chaotic night,
Leapt by His command to pure and marvellous light:
As each day newly dawned, in beauteous order stood,
Each work performed, by Him was fair and good,
The earth in six days made, the seventh blest,
And ceased upon His holy day of rest.

O gracious boon to man! this day so freely given,
From labours called to rest, and then prepare for heaven;
For this great gift, O God! accept our humble praise,
That Thou of goodness gave this blessed pearl of days.

May every one by faith, and prayer's ascending wings,
Realise the blessings every Sabbath brings;
In communion holy with Thee our time employ,
In soul and body blest on this great day of joy.

O wondrous condescension! that Thou should'st deign to bend
To be unto a sinner, Father, Guide, and Friend;
When within Thy courts his earnest vows he pays,
And praise Thy gracious goodness for this the pearl of days.
Our spirit's strength renewing throughout life's weary road,
Still nearer bringing us towards Thy blest abode,
When we shall then for ever grateful homage pay,
And live in joy with Thee an endless Sabbath day.

AN ACROSTIC.

BY MR. J. CARR, OF IPSWICH, TO MR. G. J. WILLIAMSON.

G ood fellowship reigneth wherever thou art,
E ver ready thy council and aid to impart;
O n the platform thy presence is welcomed with pride,
R evered with warm feelings by friends far and wide,
G iving words of calm solace to mankind oppressed,
E ver pointing the road to the haven of rest.

J ustice and truth in thy nature abide,
O 'er life's rugged path so cheerful to glide;
S orrow ne'er daunts thee, no care on thy brow
E ver checks the warm streams in thy bosom that flow,
P erseverance has raised thee, aye thousands above,
H eaven smiles on thy efforts with bright rays of love.

W henever thy presence can banish a sigh,
I mprove a sad heart—thou art ever nigh:
L ike a beacon of hope 'midst the sea of dispair,
L ight'ning the burden of sorrow and care.
I n humanity's cause 'tis thy pleasure to speak
A mong every class, young, aged, and weak;
M ercy proclaiming the glad tidings of grace,
S ends a halo of peace and despondency chase;
O h! may thy blest works meet a lasting reward,
N earer each day bringing souls to the Lord.

LINES ON THE DEATH OF PRINCE ALBERT.

O mourn, England ! mourn, for death assails thy great,
A noble one hath fallen from his lofty state ;
Loved Albert, now laid low by death's cold icy hand,
He's passed away and left us for the better land.

Thou Prince of truth and worth, we wished thee long to live,
To thy adopted nation thou didst blessings give ;
Pure charity and love with thee their names enrolled,
And noble institutions will long thy fame unfold.
Through all the time thou dwelt among us here,
Thy warmth of heart made all thy name revere;
Cherished and beloved alike by great and small,
A household word thy name, endeared to one and all.

Were it a first stone for some charity to lay,
Thy hand was ever near, apart from proud display;
For many an asylum o'er its peaceful door,
Proclaim thee benefactor to the old and poor.

Our numerous Ragged Schools in thee have lost a friend,
Thy love was ever ready, thy constant aid to lend;
And when the World's Palace of Industry we see,
It awakens in our hearts the memory of thee.

Our handsome Coal Exchange, with noble motto stored.—
" The earth and its fulness belongeth to the Lord;"
Recalls thy form to mind in health and vigour's glow,
And bids the saddened tear of gratitude to flow.

But thou hast passed away, and mourners' broken sighs
Arise from every heart, and tears bedim their eyes;
We feel thy absence still, and grieve thy early doom,
Our loving aspirations ascend above thy tomb.

Our noble Nation weep so soon with thee to part,
And for our Queen's bereavement with almost broken heart;
In sadness grieve for him who caused her heart to glow,
But now struck down by death to the cold tomb below.

They think upon that home where thou didst once preside,
With happy wife and children loving by thy side;
But now bowed by grief and widowed mother's care.
And for our Queen, O God! accept our earnest prayer.

And though we mourn thee, Prince; yet still thy God in love,
Hath taken thee from earth to thy blest home above;
Now thou art far removed from evils yet to come,
And landed with the blest in thy eternal home.

A worthy noble father! 'twas thy manly pride
In holy virtue's path to be thy children's guide;
The whole wide world will yet their lofty influence feel,
As kings and queens devoted to their country's weal.

It oft hath been fair Albion's dreary lot to mourn.
For loss of lofty ones whom death hath from her torn;
But ne'er has England's people shewn more real grief,
O'er monarch, prince, or statesman, or noble warrior chief.

O thou great God of mercy ? who hath thus bereaved
Our Queen, which has our Nation deep and sorely grieved
Beneath this heavy stroke we all most humbly bend,
And crave Thy loving mercy for the Queen our friend,

Be husband to the widow in her great distress,
Father to her children, who now are fatherless;
O Thou most gracious God ! on Thee we humbly call,
That Thou would'st send Thy blessing on the heads of all.

O, our dearest Queen, this is thy people's prayer,—
That God for many years, thy life will deign to spare,
To live to bless us all with thy talents given,
Then join thy loving husband in the bliss of Heaven.

MY MUCH LOVED PRIZE,

Be still, fond heart, nor let thy throbbing tell
How warm ye beat for her I love so well;
The sigh subdued, the tear and blushing cheek
Discover thoughts the tongue can never speak.
Why is it thus? 'Tis honour stills my voice,—
I'm yet too poor for her I'd make my choice,
Yet I'm resolved with manly zeal to rise,
And gain her maiden heart—my much loved prize.

When fortune gilds my now aspiring name,
With others blazoned on the scroll of fame,
I'll then declare how oft my heart has beat
To lay myself, though humble, at her feet.
I'll tell her then how ardently I strove
To subdue the flame, the mighty power of love;
'Twas loving her that caused me thus to rise,
And then I'll fondly ask my much loved prize.

The boon is granted: like music is her voice,
It has the power to make my heart rejoice;
My love's returned with pure affection fraught.
Her blushes tell how oft of me she thought.
She now rejoices in love's transcendant bloom,
To be the darling helpmate of my home:
What gratitude! I feel my star of hope did rise
To send me this life's joy—my much loved prize.

THE LOST SOUL'S LAMENTATION.

What would I give were life's probation,
Allowed once more to me again;
I would not then slight my salvation,
Nor treat my Saviour with disdain.
For life's allurements I would never
Barter my soul—no worlds could buy,
I would count loss all things else ever,
To gain that mansion in the sky.

No more should worldly pleasures blind me
In vice to cast my soul away;
Life's nothingness should e'er remind me
To make the most of life's short day.
No more should Satan make me sever
From my salvation and the Lord;
I'd hourly strive to gain for ever
That mansion promised in His Word.

Life's course has past and I am lost,
Alas! in torment doomed to dwell;
Call'd by His Holy Spirit's voice,
I scorned to hear, am now in hell.
And here for ever must remain,
No hope to cheer my woes, no end,
For ever waiting rack'd with pain,
For slighting thus the sinner's friend.

O sinner! think before too late;
Life back you never can recall;
The next life is an eternal state,
Oh! now on Christ for mercy call.
Then when before the judgment seat,
With nations at His bar appear,
Bright endless joys you then shall meet,
By serving God while dwelling here.

THE RETURNED PRODIGAL.

See, the Prodigal home is returning,
  Long fed on the husks of the earth ;
On his brow shame and sorrow are burning.
  As he's seeking the home of his birth.

Yet over his soul there is beaming,
  A light shed from calvary's brow ;
Though tears o'er his features are streaming,
  And the tide of his grief overflow.

A penitent spirit comes o'er him,
  Now softening his heart, once of steel,
And he looks with a new light before him,
  With a conscience awakened to feel.

In the dark gloomy silence of night,
  A voice has broke in on his ears,
Which he heard with enraptured delight,
  And he thinks 'tis some seraph he hea s.

His soul thrills with trembling and awe
  "God, save the poor sinner!" he cries,
"Though often I've broken Thy law,
  Yet mercy still dwells in the skies."

A blest welcome! now banish thy sadness:
  A glorious light from above,
Now brings consolation and gladness,
  From the mansions of heavenly love.

Thy petition is heard, and thy fears,
  Which thy sinning have caused, shall depart;
Thy sorrows, repentance, and tears,
  Through Christ shall bring peace to thy heart.

Thou art weighed and found wanting, but though
  Thy sins as bright scarlet appear,
Jesus' blood washes whiter than snow,
  Redemption through Him we have here,

The Prodigal, once sinful and wild,
  Through His blood now made spotless and clean,
Is adop'ed once more as His child,
  At His feet a true Christian is seen.

LINES TO THE CHRISTIAN CHURCHES ON THE GRAND EXHIBITION OF 1862.

"We do hear them speak in our tongues the wonderful works of God."—Acts ii. ver. 11.

Awake, Christian churches! arouse from your slumbers!
Many strangers are coming to visit this land;
Up then, and be doing, to add to the numbers

Of those who've enlisted in Christ's happy band.
Up Christians, and at them, till every false system
Before the truth falls. like false Dagon of old
Fell down 'fore the ark,—boasted God of Philistine,—
Was broken in dust and before the ark rolled.

Let no Christian shrink from the battle now raging,
But firm for the truth may each boldly stand ;
And not be ashamed, in Christ's cause engaging,
To chase sin and error away from our land.
Haste now to the rescue in your day of living,
Death's night will soon come ; when you cannot tell
About Christ your Redeemer, on the cross giving
His own life to rescue poor sinners from hell.

Old England, thy destiny is grand, if revealing,
The blest Gospel of Christ—His own hallowed Word !
To thy Saviour be faithful, with Christian love feeling,
And plant through each land the cross of our Lord.
Work on till all nations His sceptre brought under,
Till empires and colonies bow to His sway ;
Let thy zeal in Christ's cause be a blessing and wonder,
And hasten the glorious millenial day.

Old England's the life-boat for all men's salvation,
Her language is spoken in every clime,
Her religion is best for each generation.
Present light of the age and glory of time.
Why should we fear in this day of probation,
To man this life-boat, and our bright colours hoist ?
Undaunted to show them to each tribe and nation,
For salvation of man, and glory of Christ.

English pastors and people now all join together,
The blest Bible distribute to every one,
In their own language, as here they all gather,

From out of all nations under the sun.
While science and art are here each combining,
To exalt this great palace in annals of fame,
Work nobly for Christ, with true love entwining,
And bring all you can to call on His name.

Let not this great gathering pass by unheeded,
Such may never occur in Old England again;
Show forth the blest Gospel, by this world so needed,
Never let it be said your religion is vain.
Tis your bounden duty, and if you neglect it—
And your talents are hid in a napkin away,
Souls sureley will perish—you may not expect it—
Of you be required in God's judgment day.

May all Christians in faith, their standards appearing,
Now publish with joy the truths of his Word!
And all those who long for His kingdom appearing,
Proclaim free salvation through Jesus our Lord.
Christians put on your robes,—radiant and glorious,
From thy Saviour received, His righteous robe bright;
Then pray for His spirit, which will prove victorious,
To show to all people how Christ is their light.

Awake from your slumber put on Christian armour,
Let all join together His standard unfurled;
Fight for the truth in the ranks of your Saviour,
To bring under His cross the whole of the world.
This world shall be His, the Scriptures declare it,
Subdued to His scepter all nations shall be;
His truth shall shine forth, in rays so refulgent,
Filling earth as the waters and sands of the sea.

Fight on the side which will sure prove victorious!
Press forward with truth, let it be in the van!
Raise high the blest Cross and show it forth glorious,

Preach Christ as the only redemption for man,
Do not hang in the rear, but be valiant and true,
Undaunted as saints refreshed by His love,
And ne'er let your talents be hiden from view,
But labour to fill His bright Heaven above.

A Pentecost time the blest Spirit invoking,
That every stranger may hear the glad sound,
Of the grand Gospel truth in his own language spoken,
At the feet of the Saviour be penitent found.
Then as they all listen to hear the glad story,
What Jesus hath done, each and all being blest,
Will return to their homes all filled with His glory,
With the new beams of life His love hath imprest.

Then when He comes with His angels surrounding,
With all heaven's host in His power supreme,
His faithful shall find His love all abounding,
To repay them for all their labours for Him.
He will say, "Come ye blest of my father inherit
The mansions prepared for those that I love,
Take thy robe and thy crown a reward for thy merit,
And enter for ever my kingdom above."

MY REDEEMER.

See, there my Lord upon the tree!
I hear, I feel, He died for me;
Oh, love divine! how can this be?
Say, dear Redeemer,

Oh, say and speak it to my heart,
That from Thy love I ne'er depart,
But of Thy fold e'er form a part,—
Thou great Redeemer!

In Thy fond heart soft pity dwells,
The gospel Thy compassion tells,
My heart with loving rapture swells
To our Redeemer!

Upon the cross He bore my load,
And for my sins He shed His blood,
And thus disarmed the wrath of God,—
Did my Redeemer!

For me His head was crowned with thorn,
For me His side was pierced and torn;
He hath my sins and sorrows borne,—
My kind Redeemer!

On me He hath compassion shown,
For me He breathed the dying groan,
For me He pleads before the throne,—
My blest Redeemer!

My Advocate and Priest above,
Shows there the tokens of His love
And this my truest friend doth prove,—
My good Redeemer!

My Saviour, now I trust in Thee,
For now my guilty soul is free;
Jesus, I know Thou lovest me,—
My own Redeemer!

And when Death comes to seize his prey,
And I from earth am called away,
May I behold, in endless day,—
My dear Redeemer!

LINES TO MY FRIEND MR. JOHN BAXTER.

ON HIS FIFTY-SECOND BIRTHDAY, 1858.

Accept, dear friend, this tributary lay
Called forth by friendship on thy natal day;
And let the effusions of my mind now raise
Affection's tribute in a Baxter's praise.

In social life how oft we try to find
A friend indeed just suited to our mind!
One sure and firm in bitter times of trial,
To cheer our hours of gloom with friendly smile.

If honest worth can claim a note of praise.
Accept, dear friend, from me these humble lays;
And let my muse with earnest candour pen
The genuine virtues of the best of men.

No pomp surrounds him with the breath of fame,
Nor trumpets to the world a victor's name;
Nor deeds of valour on the battle field,
Where right to might is often made to yield.

Religion guides his way and rules his heart,
His lofties aim to act the good man's part,
To soften every woe that he may find,
And be the generous friend of all mankind.

Years fifty-two have gone and passed away,
Since Leigh, in Essex, heard thy infant lay;
Unto thy parents then a child was sent,
To bless their hearts with joy and sweet content.

And in thy future journey on through life,
May piety within dispel all strife;
While always feeling thy acceptance sure
For that blest mansion Christ died to procure.

The poor in thee have often found a friend.
To tell them of the joys that never end;
With liberal hand bestowing clothes and food,
And leading them to seek the Sheperd good.

And as old Time in his resistless flight,
Brings thee still nearer to the realms of light,
May God's own promised staff thy comfort be—
And all through life may'st thou His mercy see.

May smiling Peace, with Plenty by her side,
Long o'or thy house with happiness preside;
Religion with her glorious truths impart
Her virtue still to adorn thy manly heart.

And still long years may'st thou be spared to live,
To crown thy home with excellence, and give
Thy dearest wife love's generous faithful care,
And keep her on her way to Heaven with prayer!

Thus while thou sailest through life's boisttrous seas,
Each striving how the other most shall please;
Bound for the haven of eternal rest—
To be with Jesus there for ever blest.

But should misfortune, with its fiery dart,
Pursue thee on through life and pain thy heart,
'Tis done, remember, by parental love,
To fit thy spirit for His courts above.

Or should prosperity attend thee here,
Place not upon it too much thought or care;
Though worldly trifles may the heart allure,
Let thy salvation's state be made most sure.

May'st thou have faith Pisgah's top to view
The Promised Land as Moses looked it through,
And see the Lamb in His beauties there,
The object mind of holy faith and prayer.

And may'st thou oft to Calvary turn thine eye,
And cry, "Alas! and did my Saviour die?
My sins, with thorns, then crowned my Saviour's head,
For me He died, for me His blood was shed."

Then when in angel-choir thou lift'st thy voice,
And with the ransomed blood-bought throng rejoice.
This shall thy hallelujah chorus be,
"My Lord has bought this fadeless crown for me."

There shalt thou meet the friends that went before,
Now singing their new songs on Canaan's shore;
'Mid heaven's high arches shall thy joy notes rise,
And grateful praises echo through the skies.

Nor shall thy time of praises o'er be past,
But long as an eternity shall last,
With God shut in for ever to be blest,
And with His saints enjoy the heavenly rest.

And when thou thus shalt join the host above,
And sing with rapture thy Redeemer's love,
Thou will't acknowledge God dose all things well,
And through eternity His wonders tell.

May this dear friend, be thy most happy state
When life is ended here with joy elate,
To tread heaven's realms, and all thy powers employ
In praise, in love, in extacy, and joy.

HOME SWEET HOME.

There is a little spot on earth.
  Hallowed by strong affection's tie—
It is the home that gave our birth,
  Where all our choicest treasures lie

How sweet that place at close day,
  When twilight throws its shades around,
To see the children there at play.
  Their childish toys strewn on the ground.

The traveller as he journeys far,
  Through foreign climes compelled to roam,
He thinks of scenes where parents are,
  And dwells with rapture on his home.

How memory lingers o'er each scene
  Made precious by the loved ones there,
Where growing hearts and smiles have been,—
  'Tis thoughts like this his bosom cheer.

Of friends he thinks, now passed away,
Gone to more better realms above—
Shining with everlasting ray—
Made happy through a Saviour's love.

Their ransomed spirits though at rest,
With joy beholding Jesus' face.
Though far away in glory blest,
Seem hovering o'er the hallowed place.

But there's a home that never fades,
A mansion blest for ever sure,
Where sin or sorrow never shades,
And bliss for ever shall endure.

There is a home where all, unite—
Saved from a fading world like this—
Shall live and love, with souls delight,
In an eternal age of bliss.

ODE ON THE MARRIAGE OF THE PRINCE OF WALES.

Hail! noble Prince, son of a sire so dear,
Whose memory England ever will revere;
Hail! noble son of our beloved Queen,
The greatest monarch earth has ever seen.
To thee our homage we desire to pay,
We greet thee with love on this auspicious day;
We hail thee Prince, as old England's pride,
And wish thee happy with thy lovely bride.
Lord! hear Thy people's voice,
Through England far and wide,
Bless Albert and his choice—
His lovely Danish bride.

O God of goodness! we will Thee implore
From heaven on them Thy choicest gifts to pour.
Deign, we beseech Thee, this union here to bless,
Crowning their lives with health and happiness.
Beloved Prince, may thy father's pattern lead,
Old England then will be blest indeed;
With gratidude will hail thee England's pride,
Having cause to bless thee and thy loverly bride.

Lord! hear Thy people's voice,
Through England far and wide,
Bless Albert and his choice—
His lovely Danish bride.

For thousands will be looking up to thee,
Through England's realms their pattern here to be;
And thousands more will elevate their voice
To bless thee and the Princess of thy choice.
The English and the Danes will together bear
Their voices to heaven in humble, fervent prayer,
That God through life will bless Old England's pride,
With Alexandra, his beloved bride.

Lord! hear Thy people's voice,
Through England far and wide.
Bless Albert and his choice—
His lovely Danish bride.

ODE TO THE PRINCESS ALEXANDRA.

Bright star of the Danes! we hail thy appearance
With rapturous joy on our free English shore;
Sons and daughters of Albion greet thee with welcome,
And blessings abundant on thy head they pour.

We know thou hast left thy home and thy kindred,
The land of thy birth, among strangers to come;
But right is the faith thou has placed in old England,
And in Albert's true love, the Prince of our home.

Thou hast come to the heart of a Prince great and noble,
The hope of our land in its glory and pride,
Whose care through this life will be for thy comfort,
Who'll rejoice to make happy his own lovely bride.

Thou art come to the heart of our virtuous Queen,
To our Sovereign, thy mother, who ever will prove
A kind parent and friend like those thou hast left,
Who will gain thy esteem, veneration, and love.

Thou art come to the hearts of a brave loyal people,
To the greatest free nation e'er known upon earth,
Who welcome thee to them with love's best affection,
And rejoice to approve and acknowledge thy worth.

And though like a flower from thine own land transplanted,
We will cherish and prize thee with true English love,
In our own land will tend thee with kindest affection,
Till thou art transplanted to thy home above.

SABBATH MEDITATIONS.

'Tis Sabath day. How calm, how chaste
Seems all around, with reverence graced
Approach the toil-worn artizan
To bless the day God gave to man;

To serve Him in His house of prayer,
His Precious flowing grace to share,
His Word to hear, His peace to prove,
To taste the rich manna of His love.

Delightful, blissful, glorious day,
How grateful to our feeble clay,
When souls in pure devotion meet
To lay their sins at Jesus' feet;
In meekness bent to supplicate
For mercy on man's fallen state,
Inspired by Christian faith alone,
Before the high eternal Throne.

All nature seems to share the charm,
The solace of the Sabbath's calm:
What comfort to the heart opprest
Is this great boon this day of rest.
Oh! that man should live so base,
To turn aside from mercy's face,
And tread a guilty, headlong way,
And desecrate the Sababath Day.

Alas! alas! how much we see
Of human vice and misery,
By worldly gain and folly made,
Of those engaged in Sabbath trade;
Whose lives no thoughts of heaven control
And thus falls many a youthful soul,
Who else had sought the better way,
And blest God's own great Sabbath Day.

MY NATIVE LAND.

Old England, my native land, what shall I speak of thee
Thou art above all nations, land of the brave and free.
The waves that wash thy shores loudly lift their voice,
And sparkle in the sunbeams, so freely they rejoice.
On the cliffs that guard thy coast around our happy isle,
I see bright Freedom's beacon flame, with fadeless splendour smile,
To cheer the hardy labourer's lot, and the more successful home
And sweeten all with happiness where'er its beamings come.

Old England thou art greatly famed in the annals of the world;
And art renowned for enterprise where'er thy flag's unfurled.
The voice of fame exalts thee high through every distant clime;
A world thou art within thyself—thy triumphs swell with time!

The freedom of thy Press and speech sheds mightest influence round,
Is fast dispelling ignorance from thy glorious ground ;
The tree of knowledge flourishes upon thy happy shore,
And shall dispenseits healing leaves when time shall be no more
Old England boasts her heroes great in many a battle famed
And long as this dear isle shall last, a Nelson shall be named
With honour as the nation's pride, who served his country well
And in the hour of victory, he for that country fell !
" England expects each man to do his duty !" loud he cried,
Then fought the foe, and victory gained, but in that victory died,
He nobly did his duty then, and England morned her son,
For with such a hero's loss the victory's dearly won.
Old England mourns her Wellington, whose noble deeds of arms
Abased Napoleon's vaunted pride, and stayed his war's alarms
That eagle-crested hero great, who many a battle won,
Yet struck his flag at Waterloo to Britian's valiant son ;
"Up, Guards, and at them !' was the charge our noble soldier gave,
And gallantly was he obeyed. for the Guards were nobly brave
The grand Old Guard of France, so brave, that ne'er had feared a foe,
Before Old England's sons gave way, fled from the field of woe!
Old England's mourns her Havelock, and posterity will tell
Of many glorious heroes' fame, who for their country fell ;
But we hope the day will shortly come, when commerce shall be found
Bringing peace, and joy, and plenty to all the world around ;
While true religion's glorious laws shall bind the tribes of man
In golden links of friendship true, each other's good to plan.
Then, then the world shall soon become a family of love,
And having done their work on earth shall meet in Heaven above

TEMPUS FUGIT.

From Heaven the great Archangel's trump shall sound,
  Proclaiming far and wide the dirge of time,
And all shall hear, amid the awe profound,
  The solemn call to earth's remotest clime.

The fiat of Omnipotence goes forth—
  "Perish all nations!"—stern, imperious fate.
The soul of man, that only gem of worth,
  Survives the wreck of works and cities great.

Where are those towers, those battlements so high,
  That seemed to bid defiance to the world?
Time's all-destroying hand hath bid them fly,
  And all their glory to oblivion hurled.

Where are those cities on the scroll of fame?
  Where those monuments, each sculptur'd bust?
Where the great men, and their long glorious name?
  All, all are fallen, silent in the dust!

Alas! how sad to think that all must die!
  Those, too, we love, who make us cling to life;
Youth, glory, riches, all life's joys must fly,
  And death, with its own darkness, end the strife?

But thoughts arise that gild this theme of woe,
And bid us look for higher joys above:—
Joys our great Saviour purchased here below,
And made for ever sure by dying love.

Religion, as with angel hands, points up,
And drives away the fear that makes us sigh;
Our dear Redeemer drank death's bitter cup,
And ope'd the way for us to mount on high.

The pearly gates of heaven shall ne'er decay;
And if through Christ we once have entered there,
The golden light of God's eternal day
Shall bid us all His heavenly joys to share.

EARTHLY PLEASURES.

Earthly pleasures! earthly pleasures!
Vanishing and fading treasures;
Sparkling, fleeting, fast they fly,
Though to hold them still we try;
They shine like dew-drops on the rose,
And for a season brief disclose
A transient beauty that decays,
E'en while we on that beauty gaze.
Drawn by the sun's resistless fire,
They droop, they fall, and then expire.

Such are earth's pleasures to our view,
We grasp, and find them only dew;
For still is life beset with snares,
The world is full of anxious cares;
And all its joys are at the best
Foundations false whereon to rest.
Each of its roses has its thorn,
Fades in the holding, soon is gone;
Blest virtue's path is only sure—
Its flowers for ever will endure.

LINES ON THE THEOLOGICAL INSTITUTION, RICHMOND.

Dedicated to the Rev. J. Cunningham, Missionary in India.

Tis not of ancient pile my muse wou'd write,
Of gorgeous palaces that awe the sight.
Nor time-worn temples, calling forth my strain;
Neither of armies on the battle field,
Where the brave warrior scorns to flee or yield,
Shouting, "To Victory or Death!" upon the plain.

'Tis not of forts with many a bristling tower,
Their armoury of cannon, whose dread power
With still repeating echoes shake the earth;
Of kings or queens I here no line indite—
Of sun, nor moon, or stars, or planets bright;
But of a building of the noblest worth.

High upon Richmond Hill the building stands,
And growing fame through all the earth commands:
For thence has come forth many a faithful son
To uphold the sacred banner of the Cross,
Preach Christ, without regard to gain or loss,
And show how heavenly glory may be won.

The sacred lessons they imbibe while there
They treasure up in mind with anxious care,
That they, by faith, this world of ours may raise,
Till the time prophesied shall surely come
When all mankind shall seek their heavenly home,
And with one heart and voice their Saviour praise.

But what devout affections centre there!
Oft for its inmates upraised is the prayer
From fondest mothers, who their sons have given,
As dedicate to God in youthful days,
That they through life might manifest His praise,
By leading sinners in the path to Heaven.

Its missionaries sent unto the heathen world,
With Gospel truth and light, their banner wide unfurled;
Seeking to enlighten the dark and savage race—
As shepherds of Chrirt's flock searching out His fold;
To tell them of His love—that tale so often told—
To make them all the the subjects of His grace.

Deep pain oft rends the mother's heaving breast,
When parting with her son she loves the best,
To go where she may see him ne'er again—
Where oft the fatal climate hath distroyed
The moral hero, who for God employed
His hallowed energies, as if in vain.

Oft little marks the missionary's grave;
Perchance some beauteous wild flowers o'er it wave,
And shows the spot where rests his hallowed dust;
But still his name is written in deep love
On many a heathen's soul, now blest above,
Who, through his preaching' did in Jesus trust.

Such glorious monuments shall ever stand
A portion of heaven's eternal, happy band;
In love to chronicle the name of these
Who parted with their homes and friends so dear—
Ready themselves to offer—to duty clear—
To bring poor sinners to the paths of peace.

The crash of ages, and the wreck of years,
Man's works destroying all his hopes and fears,
Shall on these monuments possess no power;
But in Christ's kingdom they shall ever shine,
And bear the stamp indelibly divine,
Which sin and sorrow shall defile no more.

The pastor there shall see his work again,
That oft discouraged him and gave him pain ;
  There in those glorious realms shall it be found—
As gems in Jesus' crown the souls appear,
He laboured hard to save from hell while here,
While heaven shall with their praises loud resound.

Then who would hinder us to make our boast
Of work like this, and try to raise a host
  Of Godlike, working, self-denying men ?
Wesley's right glorious principles act out,
Shouting, "God is with us!" his last dying shout,
  And help to [illegible] the world again.

Firm may this building stand to latest age,
An honour to our land on history's page !
  And from it oft may Christian men go forth
To uphold pure godliness in all its truth :
While justifying faith be dear to youth,
  And Methodism spread in all its worth.

LINES ON SEEING TWO LITTLE GIRLS WEEPING OVER THEIR MOTHER'S GRAVE.

Hark to that sound of grief
  From children young and fair !
At the grave they seek relief—
  For their fond mother's there.
O'er th' grave their tears are shed
  Around them all is stilled,
All weeping o'er the dead—
  With sobs the air is filled.

The sun withdraws his beams,
  All nature miss his light,
Hills, vales, and flowing streams
  Have lost his glories bright
Sad tears were on my cheek
  As I gazed silent there ;
And upward looked to seek
  Her spirit in the air.

I thought her form I saw,
  Oh! beautifull and bright ;
Her guardian course she bore
  'Midst rays of fadeless light
I thought how much this scene
  Had charmed the children dear,
Could they her form have seen,
  A guardian Angel there !

Shs looked on them with fond love—
  So lovingly repaid ;
In innocence they gazed above,
  She guards them with her shade
A ministering angel bent
  O'er them with loving eye
To salvation's children sent.
  To lead them forth on high

When here their race is run,
  Their spirits soar away—
And when life's toils are done,
  They'll meet in brighter day.
Ne'er more to part again,
  But bless'd with parents sing,
In heaven's bright shining plain,
  The praise of their heavenly King.

THE CHRISTIAN'S CROWN.

There is a crown, most gloriously bright,
  Laid up for those who truly love the Lord—
Who here maintain His holy cause, and fight
  Most nobly, with the Spirit's powerful sword;
These faithful warriors shall His kingdom share,
  Wearing that crown of many fadeless gems,
And gold and pearls, with costly jewels rare,
  Shall glitter in their blood-bought diadems.

Warriors their laurels win, and gain renown
  Through blood and strife, and ghastly victims dead;
While kings and queens, too, wear a fading crown,
  Though gorgeous, to decorate each head.
The Christian's diadem is nobler far
  Than all earth's crowns or glory's wreaths of bay,
Shining more brightly than the morning star.
  And never, never can it fade away.

Ne'er will its lustre tarnish or decline,
  But deck with lustre each true Christian brow;
A glorious wreath laid up by hands divine,
  For all who love and serve the Saviour now.
Press forward, Christians! gain the heavenly prize;
  Conquer the world, tread sin and Satan down;
Press forwerd to the mansion in the skies—
  Fight faith's good fight, secure the promised crown.

The trials we are called to suffer here
  Will help us forward, towards that better land,
In wisdom given to prove our faith sincere,
  Will all be over when in heaven we stand.
O trembling Christian! hence dismiss thy fears,
  Press forward, the infernal host keep down,
And conqueror prove untill your Lord appear,
  Then receive from Him your heavenly crown.

CHRIST OUR INTERCESSOR.

All men are sinners, while on earth
Their hearts to evil are inclined;
Their best works are but little worth,
And poor to God's all perfect mind;
And when we our own doings scan,
And see sin cling to all we do,
It makes us cry, "O, wretched man!
Who will atone for one like you?"

But Christ above hears all our prayers,
Pleads with them at the throne of grace;
He there on our behalf appears—
He knows the frailites of our race.
For he hath borne life's care and grief,
And felt the feebleness of man;
Then died to bring us full relief—
And now He pleads love's gracious plan.

In all life's trials here below,
For us He intercedes on high;
What consolation this to know,
That we though Him may never die!

In all our conflicts and our grief,
The assurance of a Friend above,
To our tried souls should bring relief,
And make us prize our Saviour's love.

O ne'er distrust your Saviour's grace,
Depend on that, 'twill never fail;
If for awhile He hides His face,
He's pleading still within the veil.
He sympathises in distress,
Nor should your griefs your faith remove
From Him who loves your souls to bless,
And ne'er forgets you, though above.

O, think not yours a hopeless state,
As many have thought theirs, before—
Patient for mercy would not wait,
But in complaint their souls would pour.
They only thought upon their woes,
Not of their Advocate above;
Who yet was pleading for all those
Who now are blessed in His love.

We all shall find that Jesus' prayers,
Presented at the Father's throne,
Have saved us from ten thousand snares,
When He His dealings shall make known.
Then myriads shall in Heaven meet,
Who folly morned through half their days,
But now at their Redeemer's feet
Chant their Intercessor's praise.

ON T. C. PEARSON, ESQ , MAYOR OF HULL.

On the occasion of his presenting a Park to the Inhabitants of the Town

True liberal men most liberal things devise,
And blessings to their fellow men arise
When throb their hearts with patriotic glow,
And on their countrymen their gifts bestow.
Thus liberal Pearson, favoured man of heaven,
The Park at Hull so liberally hath given,
That all his townsmen may pure air enjoy,
And their spare hours in pastimes may employ.

His name in honour shall be handed down,
In distant years, a blessing to his town—
With Wilberforce and such, that men may see
Who are old England's true nobility;
Whether they be alas! men who are bent
On self-exalting with no good intent,
Or those who by their merits rise and live,
And wealth and talents to their townsmen give.

Men who are formest in each noble cause,
Upholding England's honour and its laws—
True patriots, whose aim it is to plan
Schemes that will benefit their fellow man;
While labouring in this hive-like world like bees,
Extracting honey from life's flowers are these
Philanthropists, transmitting down to fame
A useful virtuous, and long-honoured name.

Hull's people also may securely boast
That of great men it has produced a host.
First, Andrew Marvel, two centuries ago,
Its honoured member stood, as all men know;
And Hogge. the sheriff—once a sailor boy—
For Hull's welfare his talents did employ;
While others, now long dead, once living there,
Were patriots all to numerous to declare.

But there are some who are misnamed the "great,"
Because. perchance, they own some large estate,—
Though how it came to them but few doth know,
And they perhaps would hardly like to show;
But they have got it, and think life to enjoy
Their means in trifling pleasures oft employ,
And, like the butterfly of summer's day,
In flitting follies waste their lives away.

O, foolish worldlings; life you can't enjoy—
The world's vain pleasures satiate and cloy.
Man's *real* wants in life are very few,
And one must strive to do e'en as the others do—
Must labour to enjoy refreshing sleep,
Use exercise in perfect health to keep;
And if he would be wise in life's short day,
Be useful unto others as time departs away.

Freedom's blessed time is surly coming on,
When offices alone by merit shall be won;
When birth, rank, or family, however high in caste,
Unless with worth and talent link'd will scornfully be pass'd !
And men of mind and honour, however mean their birth,
Shall occupy high places formost through the earth;
And men who wisely will not in folly life debase,
But labour here right manfully to raise their fallen race.

Pearson, the best proof of thy exalted mind,
Is, thy every desire to benefit mankind,
And ever to do good while thou art here in health,
Distributing aright thy great and princely wealth.
Hull well may proudly speak of such a noble friend,
Its rights to entertain, its honour to defend;
And while this splendid Park to pastime shall allure,
Shall Pearson's honoured name in memory endure.

LINES ON THE POOR OUTCAST.

Poor helpless outcast, scorned by almost all,
 From thee both Priest and Levite turn aside,
Yet there are those who contemplate thy fall
 With deep regret as you from virtue glide.

The coldly virtuous from thee turn away,
 And sneer as they thy fading form pass by;
Nor will reflect that, in thy earliest day,
 Thou wert unsullied as the morning sky.

And once the pride wert of thy humble home,
 Watched o'er by parents anxious, kind and true:
With every virtue thou didst seem to bloom,
 And made their loving hearts with pleasure glow.

But since, perchance, thou'st broke'n a mother's heart,
And brought with sorrow to his lowly grave
Thy grey-haired father, who tried every art
From shame his lovely daughter's life to save.

But the vile tempter came, and thee beheld,
Like some fair rose, some beauteous fragrant flower;
With passion his unhallowed bosom swelled,
And how he watched to have you in his power!

He fascinated as with serpent's eye,
Till he had drawn you to his cursed embrace;
Then left you, like a villain, lost, to sigh,—
A monument of guilt and sad disgrace!

That was not dream't of when thou gavest in faith
Thyself, and all thy virtue had to give;
Thou only thoughtest of the joy till death
With him as his beloved wife to live.

Who would have thought that he could so deceive,
Or in thy breast plant such a bitter thorn;
Or crush so sweet a flower, now left to grieve,
Heart-brok'n and blighted, for the proud to scorn?

And there are moments when thy thoughts survey
The past, that now seems like some fever'd dream,
Shocked that from virtue thou shouldst ever stray,
And guilty live in life's tempestuous stream.

And how it grieves the virtuous, when they hear
Thy language, which their modesty doth shame,
And see thee cast th' insidious, lustful leer
On youth and age, their passions to inflame.

Thy end perchance the suicide's sad grave,
To plunge in some dark stream, and end thy woe:
Dread thought! shall no good creature try to save,
But let thy soul thus to perdition go?

Poor profligate! for thee we shed the tear,
And beg thou wilt the precious Saviour try,
Who ne'er cast out a penitent, while here,
That for His mercy humbly did apply.

O! go to Him, whose blood was shed for thee,
And you shall find a Friend both kind and true,
Who died for outcasts, although bad they be,
His loving mercy ever doth renew.

And you, self righteous ones that pass her by,
Gazing with anger in your breast alone,
The Saviour's test to your own selves apply—
"If without sin, then cast ye the first stone!"

A TRIBUTE OF AFFECTION TO THE MEMORY OF MISS L. M.

Lovely flower! chaste, transient, and bright,
She was early called home to her rest;
To those heavenly regions of light,
For ever to dwell with the blest.

For a time to her dear parents lent,
The joy of their lives she was given;
Till God's holy angels were sent,
To bear her to glory in heaven.

But what hand can picture the stroke,
That like a sad blight seemed to come,
And the heart of the parents most broke,
When they missed her loved presence from home.

As each little momento they view,
Of one to their hearts very dear,
Its remberance their sorrows renew,
They silently oft shed a tear.

Yet they hope, free from sorrow and pain
Their spirits shall one day arise,
To meet their dear daughter again,
United to dwell in the skies.

LINES ON TIME.

"Life let us enjoy," some recklessly say,
"We know it is short and will soon pass away;
Let us eat then and drink, and banish all sorrow,
And live well to day, we may die to morrow."

This is what the gay and the worldling oft say,
As life's generations pass quickly away;
Only cumbering the earth as onward time flies,—
In uselessness lives and unhonoured dies.

But the Christian says always, "I will work to-day.
Improve every moment that's passing away;
Probationers here while dwelling below,
The seed of the gospel delighting to sow.

The world by our lives something better should be,
For all our actions our Master will see;
Endeavouring the good of our fellows to prove,
Laying up for ourselves a rich treasure above.

If we labour in love for God and for man,
While living do always all good that we can,
Working hard in the vineyard laid out by our Lord,
He will give us a bright and a lasting reward."

To make the world better is the duty of man,
Each one in his sphere to do all that he can,
And those who do nothing as on the hours fly,
Like fools only live, and like the brute die.

THE DYING CHRISTIAN'S FAREWELL TO HIS WIFE.

The time is come for me, dear wife,
To pass by death from thee away;
From this cold earth of care and strife,
To brighter realms of endless day.
But ere we part, my own true wife,
My dying tongue to thee shall tell,
That thou hast proved my joy of life,
And shown to me thy love full well.

I am passing away to a better home,
My Saviour calls and bids me come;
I am going above in heaven to roam,
I am passing away! passing away!

Thou hast been a fond and faithful wife,
And thou hast kindly borne with me!
Thou'st crowned my days with blessings rife,
Life's sweetest joys I owe to thee.

But now to die I hear the call,
My soul through death above shall rise ;
And I must leave my wife, my all,
To join the ransomed in the skies.
I soon shall join the holy band,
Before the throne for ever stand,
Singing the hyms of the better land,
I am passing away ; passing away !

Now let me hold thy hand, dear wife,
Long as my beating pulse shall last,
Till death comes in to end the strife,
Untill life's battle's o'er and past.
Let my last look be on thee, love,
Thy voice the last on earth I hear;
Then join the heavenly host above,
To sing with saints and seraphs there.
I am passing away to my Saviour's breast.
Where my soul for ever shall rest,
Rejoicing still in the home of the blest,
I am passing away ! passing away !

Then banish all thy tears, dear wife,
Ere long in heaven we meet again ;
To live for ever the endless life,
And sing a pure melodious strain.
Soon as you die I will you meet.
Go hand in hand to realms of light ;
And kneel at our Redeemer's feet,
To receive a crown of glory bright.
I am passing away, O happy state !
To heaven's bright and pearly gate,
Angels now at my bedside wait,
I am passing away ! passing away

LINES ON THE DEATH OF THE DAUGHTER OF A FRIEND.

She is gone from our sight ! our loved one's departed,
And we weep for her loss almost broken-hearted ;
Thus link after link in life's chain we sever,
Earthly unions are broken to be blended for ever.

She is gone from our sight ! the delight of our eyes,
Severed from us by death to her home in the skies ;
Prayed as the purest in raiment so bright,
She shines like an angel in that world of light.

Though our loved ones before us often are taken,
Our heavenward thoughts it but tends to awaken,
Adding still to our treasures stored up by God's love
In the blest realms of glory, the bright world above.

They are transplanted flowers removed from earth's sod,
And will blossom for ever in the garden of God ;
And though on earth we may ne'er meet again,
We once more shall meet her in heaven's bright plain.

Yet her voice and her features in memory will last,
Recalling to mind those happy days past ;
The joy of our home, and the pride of our life
Is taken for ever from this world of strife.

Though her body now rests within the cold tomb,
She has gone to a better—a heavenly home;
She dwels now in peace having gained the rich prize,
Like a blossom all pure where love never dies.

Like an angel of light she looks down from above
On friends left behind, with feelings of love;
Our hopes become bright when we think of her rest,
Our spirits mount up to the home of the blest.

Then dry up your tears, ye fond parents, awhile,
Yield your treasure to Christ, He has taken your child;
Though heavy the loss, view it all for the best,
Thy loved one now dwells in His promised rest.

O mourn not nor sigh, but comfort receive
From God's blessed word, which all Christians beleive;
Have faith, strong and sure, in His promises given,
Though here you have pain, you will have joy in heaven.

O sweet consolation! O life giving balm;
To think of thy loved one now freed from all harm;
From Satan's temptations and sins luring snares,
Now the glories of Jesus her Saviour she shares.

Then let us improve each bereavement we meet,
And bow with submission at Jesus' feet;
When heavily laden, with sorrow oppre se'd,
He invites us to Him and has promised us rest.

"Come to me." there's a volume of love in that word,
"Come to me, and your burden I'll bear," said the Lord;
"Come to me, Come to me," O hear the glad call,
And low at His feet in humility fall.

O, Christ! with glad hearts Thy call we obey,
Still be Thou our guide, our light, and our way;
We bless Thy compassion which calls us to prove
Thy glorious salvation, Thy fullness of love.

Fade then, our beloved ones, from earth fade away,
Lay them low in the tomb in the dust to decay;
But remember, Christ's victory o'er death and the tomb,
He shall raise us to heaven for ever to bloom.

LINES ON THE ORDINATION OF MISSIONARIES AT LAMBETH CHAPEL.

In Lambeth Chapel solemn silence reigned,
When at communion young men meekly knelt
As missionaries there to be ordained,
Their grave responsibility they felt.
Their calling, O how solemn, yet how grand!
In heathen lands the Gospel forth to preach—
Christ's love to magnify unto a foreign land,
His mercy to the savage race to teach.

And now the hands laid on with solemn prayer,
That these young men should firm and faithful prove
To Christ, and work with earnestness and care,
To bring poor souls enlightened to His love.
In solemn song the congregation join,
And tuneful anthems fill the holy place;
Christ's flock around, with voice of praise divine,
And prayer for God's protection and His grace.

Around God's glorious throne of grace on high
Silence there reigneth while the hymns ascend,
And human praise arise unto the sky,
And God in mercy deigns to condescend
To bless these young men with His Spirit's might,
Of grace a double portion to them given,
To be a burning and a shining light,
To lead poor heathens safely home to heaven.

"COME UNTO ME ALL YE THAT ARE WEARY AND HEAVY LADEN AND I WILL GIVE YOU REST."

Amidst scenes of trial and numerous foes,
O where shall I go to seek for repose,
Dear Saviour, I come unto Thee ;
Weary with sadness the sound of Thy voice,
Oft causes my trouble-worn soul to rejoice
That happy with Thee I may be.

Thy voice, dearest Jesus, is oft heard to say,
"On me your cares and your sorrows all lay,
In me find a haven of rest ;
For envy and pain, tribulation and strife,
You'll meet and endure through the course of your life,
In my love you still shall be blest.

Come now to the life-giving waters, O come,
And find in me your peace-giving home,
Your long sought solacing place ;
Drink of the life-giving stream that I give,
Stoop, thirsty soul, drink freely and live,
From the streamlets of God as they flow ;
If the way be as dark and as black as the night,
Look faithfully up to thy guide for the light.
And rest upon me, weary soul.
Draw from the pure living streams from above,
The fountain o'erflowing with thy Saviour's love,
And thou shalt then be made whole."

We certainly know there are many a one,
Have proved Thee often their shield and their sun,
Through this vale of darkness and tears;
They come unto Thee to heal every wound,
And quickly revived their souls they are found,
On Thee they could cast all their cares.

Our great and good Shepherd has promised to keep
In safety His ransomed and purified sheep,
On the bread of His love they may feed ;
His love to them all He daily will show
Throughout all their pilgrimage dwelling below,
Then all to His green pastures lead.

There is nothing can move from the Almighty hand,
Those who on His rock of all ages shall stand,
For in Him their dwelling's secure ;
On this firm foundation strongly they build,
The rock that no storm can loosen to yield,
Their defence and their holding is sure.

O fix me, dear Saviour, on this solid rock,
That I may be free from each earthly shock.
Let me in His sweet image rise ;

Each day help me on to live unto Thee,
From all repining and murmuring free,
To press on for my heavenly prize.

Before Thee in holiness joyous to walk,
Continually anxious of Thy love to talk,
Nor ever Thy Spirit blest grieve;
With what Thou bestowest, O make me content,
My life for Thy church shall ever be spent,
While here upon earth I may live.

And oft I will drink of the heavenly stream,
And feel all my joy come only through Him,
Rich full in the beams of His light;
And glad of the staff of His friendship below,
To lean upon here as forward I go,
Till faith is all changed unto sight.

Feeling earth's affections no pleasure afford.
Like the glories in store for our final reward,
When Christ our Redeemer shall come
To call each weary worn soul to His rest,
To repose in peace upon His holy breast,
In the promised mansion's bright home.

Then let the world move at the Almighty's will,
We're journeying onward to Zion's bright hill,
The glorified saints blest abode;
And soon we shall see that His ways they were best
To lead us by love to the land of the blest,
The promised abode of our God.

For thousands have gained that glorious land,
Though sorely tried here, did firmly withstand,
Made strong through almighty love;
They conquered all through patience and faith,
And victorious proved over sinning and death,
Now reigning in glory above.

LINES ON THE DRUNKARD.

How many men, with talents rare,
Oft plunge into a dangerous snare,
Through insatiate love of drink;
It drowns their senses, and still worse,
It proves to hearth and home a curse—
Can ever drunkards think?

Of all the men on earth accurst
A drunkard surely seems the worst.
Who thus himself degrades;
When drunk what folly he'll commit,
While in his beastly sottish fit
A laughing stock is mode.

His character, his health and time,
Destroyed by this debasing crime,
Death's in the fatal bowl;
The poison lures him from the right—
Whoe'er would seek in it delight
Endangers life and soul.

He in the tempter's snare is cought,
His peace of home is gone to nought,
His life a wretched blight;
Now down destruction's path he goes,
A prey to grief and stung with woes,
Robs wife and children's right.

He still keeps on his fearful course,
And headlong goes from bad to worse,
The gin-fiend drags him on;
Inflaming body, soul, and mind,
To ruin all he seems inclined—
His soul hath Satan won.

Say, who can the joys of the drunkard see
He swallows his vilest enemy,
Is like a bondman led ;
And when th' inflaming spirit dies,
A shaft of agony through him flies,
And racks his throbbing head.
To think of home, and fond wife there,
Lonely and sad in deep despair,
How he performs his part ;
Her at the altar he vowed to love,
Protector and guide through life to prove,
But now he breaks her heart.
Within her home she sits and weeps,
With scalding tears her pillow steeps,
Alas ! her sorrow's vain ;
Her patient care he ll oft abuse,
Her sinking form with blows ill-use
Till life's one scene of pain,
He wallows like a beast in mire,
Drinks till his body seems on fire,
And all his sense is fled ;
Then when his money is all gone,
His looks most abject and forlorn,
With shame he bows his head.

Oh, drunkard ! think before too late
What ! what would be thy awful state,
If a drunkard thou did'st die ?
For such as thee the Scriptures tell,
Shall have their portion low in hell,
Through all eternity

Then turn at once, poor drunkard, turn,
Repent of this thy sin, and mourn,
The wasted life thou'st passed ;

Turn now to Christ without delay,
For He can cleanse thy sins away,
And save thy soul at last.

Haste ! fly to His atoning blood,
And there be washed in mercy's flood,
Ere time shall cease to roll ;
Bid drink, the alluring fiend, depart,
And yield the Saviour all thy heart—
He'll save thy precious soul.

LINES ON MEMORY.

What wondrous powers our memory shows—
Retains the much-loved forms of those
Whose image tells of scenes long past ;
Of childhood's joys, and hopes, and fears.
With youth and manhood's riper years—
Of scenes too bright and fair to last.

How memory still delights to trace
Some by-gone scenes, some well-known face—
Dear relics of our life's joys past—
Which it delights to bring to view,
Again pass life-like in review,
Imprest on memory's tablet fast.

I rejoice that memory will retain
Love-enshrined forms to bring again,
Friends' image stamped upon our breast ;
Restores them with all by-gone joys,
When memory sweet her power employs,
Those who have gained the promised rest.

We call them back, and then pourtray
Their vivid scenes in bright array,
From forth the stores of memory borne ;

What magic power have those wrapt there,
Beyond the scenes each hour so near,
    That all is not to oblivion gone.

Is memory soul's connecting chain
Linking us to earth, scenes to retain,
    In all their powerful form and force?
If so, how careful should we be,
That memory only scenes should see
    To bring delight with our past course.

Let conscience now here have the sway,
Do good in this our life's short day,
    For truth determined e'er to fight.
Like champions bold let us nobly stand,
Chase sin and error from our land
    And fill it with heavenly light.

HYMN OF INVOCATION.

Come, Holy Spirit, with light divine,
On us with beams of mercy shine;
While we with penitence draw near,
With heartfelt love and mind sincere,
And humbly bow before Thy throne,
Great God! to us Thy ove make known,
And while we at Thy footstool bend,
O, show Thyself the sinner's friend.

We do not in our own strength come,
For works of merit we have done:
We come invited, Lord, by Thee,
Through Christ, the sinner's only plea.
We come, because the Saviour died
And ope'd the fount of mercy wide;
We come, because we feel our need
Of pardon for each act and deed.

Lord, we believe Thee just and true,
Thou can'st our stubborn will subdue:
Thy Spirit can bow down our pride,
Bring us to Jesus' wounded side.
Beam on us. Lord, with heavenly light,
And let us feel Thy Spirit's might;
While in Thy house we humbly pray,
Grant us to feel and own Thy sway.

O Father, hear our earnest prayer,
And for the sake of Jesus spare;
In honour of our Great High Priest,
Let us partake of mercy's feast;
And let each feel the atoning blood,
And that we all are born of God;
May we now feel our sins forgiven,
And shout, "This is the gate of heaven."

LINES ON GARIBALDI, FREEDOM'S HERO.

Brave Garibaldi, whose wide-spread name
Throughout the world illumes the scroll of fame;
Brave advocate of liberty, in whom we trace
Desires of freedom for all the human race;
Posterity shall bless thee, thou hero brave.
Who strives to rescue every human slave.
O God of goodness! Garibaldi bless.
His work of freedom crown with great success.

May Italy, that country long opprest,
By his great mind with freedom now be blest,
Religious liberty exert its peaceful sway,
And Italy's children see a brighter day.
May the banner of the cross be wide unfurled,
And wave in beauty o'er this sinful world,
Each child of Adam rescued from sin's thrall,
Find freedom in the Lamb who died for all.

And may the time arrive mankind to free,
Blest with glorious heaven-born liberty,
When not a nation's flag again shall wave
In all the world above a down-trod slave.
When Poland—fettered Poland—breaks her chain
From Russia's yoke and lifts her head again.
O God! for Poland work with power and might.
Chase slavery's darkness—give her freedom's light.

For America, great God! warm our pulses beat,
That Thou wilt give them freedom we entreat,
And may her blood-stained soil peace soon have
War at an end, and freedom to each slave.
Their stars and stripes no more be a disgrace,
To wave so proudly e'er a bondaged race.
In liberty's great cause soon may we find
America a blessing to all the human kind.
O dear Old England, what shall we say of thee,
Who leads the van to bid the world be free?
Thy flag of freedom wherever wide unfurled.
Offers the boon of liberty to the world.
God prosper thee in this thy mission grand,
To break the oppressor's chain in every land;
Blest land, in freedom's cause still lead the van,
Till liberty blesses every race of man.

POOR JACK.

A STORY FOUNDED ON FACTS

In a seaport town, some twenty summers past,
My lot in life for some few months was cast;
Where scenes I saw that filled my heart with pain;
Vice raged around, and following in its train
Were drunken brawls, 'midst loud and fearful oaths,
Made sad each day, and broke each night's repose.
One home I saw destroyed by drunken strife,
Where cheerless sat the pale heart-broken wife;
One pale affrighted boy in terror shrank
To hear his father's tread along the bank,
Whose reeling steps too plainly told the tale
What made both wife and child so deadly pale.

They listening sat one night, no father come ;
"Go child," she said, "persuade your father home,"
For sad experience still had left the trace
Of the drunkard's blows upon her pallid face,
Too well his violence she had often known,
That made her fear to meet his angery frown.
'Twas near midnight, the waves broke o'er the pier,
The darkening sky forebode a storm was near ;
From out the western sky the lightning flashed.
As the sea waves' foam against the breakers dashed,
Large drops of rain fell pattering on the shore
As the child departed from his mother's door.

The rays were shining from the pier-head light,
That darted flickering, through the darkening night,
Forth ran the boy with looks of deep concern,
While his fond mother prayed his quick return ;
His little feet went bounding o'er the sand,
As fast he hastened o'er the shingly strand,
Until at length his drunken father spied,
Along the pier, just by the water side.
High words and cursing met his trembling ear,
That filled his mind with dark forebiding fear,
He found his father staggering to and fro,
His eyes all fire, and dark his angry brow,

"Come home, dear father," said the anxious child,
He spoke in gentle accents calm and mild ;
That would have brought the hardest heart remose,
Had not strong drink polluted reason's course,
Foul imprecations left the father's tongue
As the poor boy persuasive round him clung,

He crying pleaded—fierce was each reply,
Until there rose a sharp heartrending cry,
For with one kick the drunkard spurned his child
Into the raging sea and billows wild;
Remorseless then he turned upon his heel,
And left the spot.—He long had ceased to feel.

At length he sobered, thought what he had done,
How 'neath the waves he'd kicked his only son,
Then wildly raved, and like a madman swore,
His hands he wrung his matted locks he tore;
The wind blew bitter, drenching fell the rain,
The darkness made all hope of searching vain;
He then the alehouse sought his cares to chase,
But oh! at every turn the pleading face
Of his poor boy, now terrified his heart,
He swooning falls with fierce convulsive start;
And thus for hours unconsciously he lay,
They bore him home a drunken lump of clay.

But Gracious God! Thy saving help was near,
The drowning cry, the helpless shreik to hear!
A ship of war was anchored in the bay,
And from the shore a boat's crew made their way,
Saw the poor boy fall helpless from the pier,
And rowing to him, raised a hearty cheer,
They pick him up, though weak and almost dead,
With tender care heap kindness on his head;
They reach the ship, he tells his artless tale,
The vessel spreads her canvas to the gale;
"Poor Jack" they name him from his helpless state,
A tender reed tossed by the storms of fate.

And soon the broad Atlantic meets their view,
Our hero grows, beloved by all the crew,

Though weak and sick in sweet content he lay,
His now lost mother taught his lips to pray,
And now her words sink deeply in his mind,
He turns to God, in Him his peace to find
And soon he feels his sins all cleansed away,
Through Christ our Blessed Saviour, Light and Way;
Smart, faithful, and obedient soon he found
Himself in ties of strong affection bound,
With pious men brave sailors of the Fleet,
Who feared no danger England's foes to meet.

These sailors brave would o'er their Bibles bend,
And love to talk of Christ, the sinner's friend,
They joined each day in humble earnest prayer,
To God to keep them in His Holy care.
Such men as these are ever firm and brave,
They know Christ died, their deathless souls to save.
And they are calm in every danger found,
Because God's love doth in their souls abound,
And thus they pass their useful lives away,
A harbour seeking where there's no decay,
With Christ their Pilot constantly they try
To gain the Port of Heaven, and dwell on high.

But soon again resounds from shore to shore,
All nations' curse, the strife of awful war
Spreads pain and woe, and desolation wide,
And dyes with blood, both land and ocean's tide,
The conflict rages, death stalks o'er the deep,
And many a soul is sent to his last sleep;
The cannons roar amidst the dreadful fray,
And decks are crowded where the wounded lay,
'Midst groans of pain distressing to the ear,
When lo! the signals for a truce appear;
Oh! 'tis a frightful thing at War to be,
When crowds of dead are thrown into the sea.

The battle past, the wounded claim all care,
In which our hero takes a lively share,
For by God's grace Poor Jack from first to last
Through all the conflict almost scathless passed ;
With gentle hand and kindly words he strove
Their pains to ease, their comfort to improve ;
He told of Jesus' love the lost to save,
Faith's balm of consolation freely gave,
All gladly listened to his words of cheer,
Which had the power to dry the bitter tear,
A good Samaritan he proved to all,
And taught them on their Saviour's name to call.

One poor old sailor, seeming dying fast,
Upon Poor Jack a strange expression cast
While praying on his knees beside his bed
For Christ on him His boundless grace to shed,
The old man breathed in heavy choking sighs,
While sorrows' tears were streaming from his eyes ;
" Can sinners black be saved ?" he feebly cried,
" My bygone life in crime is deeply dyed,'
" Be calm," said Jack, " though thou art dyed in shame,
And seek for pardon through thy Saviour's name,
Who suffered on the cross and passed the grave,
The blackest sinner's fallen soul to save

He told that Jesus blood could cleanse from sin,
That Christ was waiting souls like his to win ;
Poor Jack drew near and grasped his feeble hand,
Emotions felt he could not understand.
A link there seemed of sympathy that bound
Their hearts in one, a latent chord seemed found,
He seemed consoled, he closed his eyes awhile,
Some inward thoughts his senses did beguile,

By pangs of bitter conscience sorely torn,
In mind and body crushed he lay forlorn,
At length he raised himself upon his bed,
His features racked with horror, shame and dread.

And then he shreiked, " No murderer can be saved,
No ! no !" he cried, and incoherent raved,
" My child ! my child ! my own, my darling boy !
Oh save him ! a boat ! a rope ! ship ahoy !
Hark he cries for help ! I hear him say
Oh father save me, cast not me away !
He sinks he dies, a murderer now am I,
Reproach me wife, and wring your hands and cry !
Give me my child ! she says, my only joy,
Husband bring back. Oh bring me back my boy ;
But she forgave me with her parting breath
And long ago that voice is hushed in death.

Now vengeance comes Oh ! see his dripping hair
Oh ; God of mercy this I cannot bear ;
Those clammy eyeballs stare at me again"
And so raved on in incoherent strain ;
From sheer exhaustion then he sunk and swooned
My son my son, in anguish then he groaned.
Poor Jack fell weeping on the sailor's breast
His sinking form he tenderly caressed
My Father ; Father here behold your son !
I did not sink for the allseeing One
Was near and saved me from a watery grave.
I was picked up when sinking neath the wave.

And there is mercy for you father dear
Your Lord your Saviour He is ever near
To him for succour now for mercy fly
For him to save you ere you come to die.
What ; cried the trembling man my poor boy here ;

The same I dashed in madness from the pier;
Art thou my boy; my own dear flesh and blood?
A wretch I've been to you a murderer stood;
Yes tis he; my Mary's eyes; oh! grief
My poor poor boy shall bring my heart relief
And though through life I've played a wicked part
O God of Mercy; Purify my heart.

His prayer was heard and grace came from above
He cast himself upon the Saviour's love.
With humble soul he pleaded meek and mild
Shed tears of joy beside his long lost child
Father and son each day engaged in prayer
God's saving grace shone forth resplendent there.
Before the father was removed from earth
His hopes were centered in the brighter birth,
A pardoned sinner soon his hour was come
To pass from earth, and reach his heavenly home
Where thousands once poor sinners here below
With Jesus dwell were endless mercies flow.

Poor Jack still lives, a monument of grace
To faith's great rock he loving turns his face,
He labours in the vineyard of his Lord
And points the way where love and grace are stored
A pious humble saint he grasps faith's spear
Drives sin away and dries the sinner's tear.
Champion of his master firm he stands
To pilot sailors free from vice's sands
The gospel teaching zealous in Christ's cause
Regardless of this sinful worlds applause
Living hourly in Christ's precepts given
'Neath Calvary's Cross advancing towards Heaven.

THE SHIPWRECK.

Hark! how the storm is raging,
 The sea rolls mountains high;
The elements' war seem waging,
 The vivid lightnings fly.

Borne on the winds are heard
 The cries of deep despair;
And from the sinking ship
 Ascends the voice of prayer.

For succour now they look,
 But seem to look in vain;
They cannot see the shore,
 Through storms of drifting rain.

Their sails to atoms torn.
 The ship strikes on the rock;
She surely soon will sink,
 So fearful is each shock.

Now in the waters roll,
  She's bilged and on the strand ;
The sea breaks o'er her deck,
  How can they get to land ?

As hope begins to fail,
  A boat appears in view,
'Tis the gallant Life Boat,
  Manned with her noble crew.

They come to save or die,
  With these poor shipwrecked men
All through the raging waves,
  They pull with might and main.

And through the foaming surf,
  They strive the ship to reach !
Around them roars the storm,
  And wild the sea-birds screech.

Undanted on they pull,
  And reach the ship at last,
And rescue all the crew,
  Despite the roaring blast

To land them now they haste,
  Upon the rocky shore ;
Secure in safety placed,
  The hardy crew once more.

Then up ascends their prayer,
  For the Life Boat's gallant crew ,
' O God ! for ever bless them,
  To them our lives are due,

Had they not come to save us,
  We soon had sunk and died ;

Our bo lies lost and drifting,
About the rolling tide.

Thy blessing give them now,
Let life to them be given,
Numbers more to rescue,
Then land them safe in Heaven.

The sailor perils brave,
Of ocean rough and wide ;
Its wonders and its grandeur,
Its ebb and flowing tide.

Friends he leaves behind him,
His children and his wife,
Who anxious mourn his absence,
And pray God spare his life.

When homeward bound he comes,
With honest joy and pride,
His heart with fervour yearns,
To view his own fire-side.

When landed home he bounds,
And brings his hard earned store,
His perils all he tells,
Since last he left the shore.

Then thankfully they join,
In humble earnest prayer,
To God for His great love,
Their parent's life to spare.

And thus on life's rough sea,
They sail in peace and love,
And brave its every storm,
Til called to Heaven above,

THE DYING CHILD TO ITS MOTHER.

Oh ! mother dear I'm weary, and here I cannot rest,
  Sharp racking pains are on me but all is for the best ;
But soon it will be over, and I shall pass away,
  To that glorious better land, where there is no decay.
But O I would not leave you so very sad behind,
  Without some words of comfort to dwell upon your mind,
That when I go and leave you to soar to realms above,
  You'll think again upon your Child with all a mother's love.

I know I oft have vexed you and pained your mind full sore,
  But now if you forgive me I'll never do it more ;
Come take my hand dear mother, and on my lips impress,
  The sweet kiss of forgiveness, once more your child now bless,
And though my pulse is feeble, and fluttering is my heart,
  Give me but one more token ere I from the depart,
That thrilling pressure tells me that love you still do feel,
  On all my faults forgiven thy kiss hath set the seal.

But mother, dearest mother, pray do not sob and cry,
  I'll be your guardian angel till you shall come to die,
Around your earthly path I'd like an angel wait,
  Till the summons comes for you to quit this earthly state,
Then then my dearest mother Jesus you will save ;
  And he will give the victory over the silent grave,
And to the glorious mansions He has for you prepared,
  These mother you shall enter, and have a rich reward.

O mother, dearest mother, then pass away I must,
  And this frail dying body will mingle with the dust,
And O my dearest mother, you have been kind to me,
  And taught my infant lips to pray as I sat on your knee,
I lisped the word's "Our Father" and now he bids me come,
  He s sent his holy angels to convey me safely home,

There I shall dwell for ever in that glorious better land,
Be crowned with radiant glory before His face to stand

Then open now the window and let me see the sun,
Whose golden beams on earth he shows when His days, course is done
Sure mother, still more beautiful than this that land must be,
I wonder then what heaven is like when here such light I see
And oft before I've seen the clouds all fringed with golden light,
And thought of the Great Maker who dwells where all is bright
And then the glorious rainbow with its vast mighty span,
Showing the blessed covenant that God hath made with men.

But surely mother he will save me sinner though I be,
And I shall when I leave you be a pardoned sinner free,
In leaving those I dearly love it grieves me I confess,
And yet my dearest mother, I am bound for worlds of bliss
Where I shall dwell for ever in my dear Saviour's sight,
In God's own heavenly temple the Lamb to be the light,
There shall he gently lead me to taste of living streams,
The waters of eternal life which though that City gleams.

There robed in whitest garments amoung the blessed throng,
I cast my crown before Him and mingle in their song,
My sorrows changed to gladness, my grief all turned to praise,
With the grand immortal host my voice shall loudly raise.
I there shall dwell in happiness, and love that blessed clime,
And shout how Jesus loved me with all His love sublime,
And this shall be the echo, He has done all things best,
And safely home has brought me to his promised rest.

SONG OF THE FISHERMEN.

We are bound away, at the close of day,
  Far off on the briny sea,
All hearts are brave, as we leap the wave,
  And joyous as mortals can be
With favouring gale, we onward sail,
  And over us flies the spray,
And Zion's song, as we sail along,
  We sing at the close of day.

The stars above, seem heralds of love,
  And the moon with silver light,
Awaken the fire of fond desire,
  To dwell in heaven so bright.
Our sails are spread, no fear or dread,
  Appal each manly breast,
Our songs arise through glittering skies,
  To God our Fountain of rest.

We remember of old how Jesus told,
  The faithfull fishermen then,
Their nets to forsake and he would make
  Them preachers and fishers of men.
They heard His voice, and their hearts rejoice,
  To leave their earthly store,
The message of love, he brought from above,
  To preach it on every shore.

He often had told His disciple fold,
  That trials and sorrows would come,
Though cares should increase, in Him was their peace,
  And this cheered away all their gloom,
Him they believed, and His word they received,
  Did the meek and faithful band.

Then in Christ's praise our songs we will raise,
  As our boats glide far from the land.

How oft we are made, most sorely afraid,
  While viewing some trial to brave,
But to each wave of ill Christ saith be still,
  My power each loved one shall save,
In the darkness of night, when gone is the light,
  With souls bowed heavy with care,
Our voices we've raised, and His love be praised,
  He has answered our supplicant prayer

On the storm crested deep, he knoweth no sleep.
  But peace to our souls doth he send,
This voice soundeth still "fear not any ill,
  I'm your firm unchangeable friend."
Though life may be short, you may reach the high port,
  All your sins by His mercy forgiven,
Here partake of His grace, now see His bright face,
  And gain the bright harbour of Heaven.

We will think of the time, in a happier clime
  In the glorious land of the blest,
We shall sing in the song of the triumphal throng,
  In the heavenly haven of rest,
Looking back on the past, and each stormy blast,
  Shall own that His doings were right,
His mercies repeat, with love at His feet,
  For ever to dwell in his sight.

HYMN OF PRAISE TO JESUS.

Great King who reigns in glory,
  Upon thy dazzling Throne;
We'll come and bow before Thee,
  Our refuge Thee alone.

And though thou art exalted,
Beyond our loftiest thought;
By Thee we are invited,
And by Thy spirit brought.
Then listen dearest Saviour,
While to Thy praise we sing;
O listen we beseech Tho,
Thou glorious heavenly King.

And though all angels praise Thee,
Crying Holy, Holy, Lord!
And by the brightest Seraphim,
Thou art gloriously adored.
Yet when their songs are sweetest,
When sound their harps of gold;
The love thou bear'st thy people,
By tongue can ne'er be told.
For everlasting mansions there,
Thou hast prepared so bright,
For all who love Thy holy name,
To dwell with Thee in light.

And therefore we draw near Thee,
And praise with one accord,
The wondrous love and mercy,
Of our exalted Lord.
He shall like a shepherd lead,
His flock to crystal streams,
To drink of lif's pure waters.
That in His city gleams,
And from those heavenly fountains,
We shall gain fresh supplies,
And God our heavenly Father,
Wipe tears from all our eyes.

With beauty He shall clothe thee,
And set thee by His side,
Crowned with Him then in glory,
There ever to abide
And all that hath been ever
To wondering ears foretold;
His love so good and precious,
Shall excel a thousand fold.
To thee shall all this bliss be given,
With love divine and free;
And thou shalt e'er His goodness praise,
To all eternity.

OUR SABBATHS OF REST.

Ye toiling hearts prize the sweet moments of leisure,
One blest day in seven so needfull to man;
Defend it—uphold it—for O! 'tis a treasure!
The gift of our God when creation began
This divine institution of His great affection,
Decreed as a solace and boon to our race,
A sweet respite gives us for holy reflection.
To pour out our hearts at the fountain of grace,
How sweet are the moments of pious communion,
To engage with the Spirit in prayer and in praise,
When the faithful for worship assemble in union.
And their voices to Heaven in thankfulness raise.
Let pure aspirations ascend from each dwelling,
The fullness of gratitude lighten each breast.
With joyful devotion, and thankfulness swelling,
For our foretaste of Heaven, our Sabbaths of rest

Let not the designing mislead or deceive us,
With winning allurements our senses to blind;
When once we're enslaved and undone they will leave us,
In bondage alike both in body and mind.
Beware of those men who with plausible phrases,
And sophistry preach about "food for the brain,"
Would lead the unwary through sceptical mazes,
To end but in cold desolation and pain.
We have food for our souls in the blest Revelation,
God's word to sustain us our comfort and guide,—
That cheers us with hope of eternal Salvation,
For ever with Jesus in bliss to abide.
Then ne'er let us swerve from the truths of His teaching,
By Satan's dark wiles be enslaved or opprest;
But steadily on to the high calling reaching.
And jealously watch o'er our Sabbaths of Rest.

O yield not an atom, denounce every feature,
That tend to deprive us of God's Holy Day,
Tear away the false mask, and expose the vile creature,
The demon of mammon that lurks in our way,
'Tis a truth, sad tho' real, that many are living,
Who grudge us the rest that our Sabbaths afford,
Who to gain's ruling passion their whole lives are giving,
And scorn the blest precepts of God's Holy Word,
'Tis such who complacently view all the scheming,
To darken the Sabbath with worldly pursuits.
Who vainly let's prove, are delusively dreaming,
Of ignorance and folly to gather the fruits.
Let this be our solace, though destined to labour,
A bright home awaits us to dwell with the blest,
By our lives let us seek for the Heavenly favour,
And reverence as Holy our Sabbath's of rest.

In sabbath amusements where selfishness revels
  And rank desecration pollutes the bright hours;
Man's mind to the tone of the infidel levels,
  And Satan the thoughtless with vice overpowers.
O! is it not piteous that thousands are striving,
  To yield up their birthright so sacred and free,
Of life's greatest treasure their fellows depriving,
  Let us boldly protest that it never shall be!
Let us scorn all attemps to impair or disfigure,
  The sanctified moments we cherish and love;
Our claim to the sabbath defending with vigour,
  The claim that we own from the Father above.
United let's firmly resolve to be doing,
  And grasp the great subject with dignified zest;
Our love for our God and His ordinance showing,
  And bravely let's fight for our Sabbaths of Rest.

O JESUS I AM THINE.

O there are thousands now this day,
  Whose care is for this world alway,
Who cannot join with me and say,
    Oh! Jesus I am thine.

Some who profess great love for Thee,
  This world their idol—may they see
Their error—and cry out with me,
    Oh! Jesus I am thine.

With pilgrims to the better land,
  May I seek Thy directing hand,
And through Thy grace and mercy stand,
    Oh! Jesus I am thine.

O help me now to seek Thy face,
Help me to win the christian's race,
And fill my soul with heavenly grace
Oh! Jesus I am thine.

And when temptation vex my mind,
And troubles through life's path I find,
In Thee I'll trust and be resigned,
Oh! Jesus I am thine.

When I am racked with care and pain,
Oh Saviour, then my soul sustain!
And never of Thy grace complain,
Oh! Jesus I am thine.

No other help have I but Thee,
When troubles press—help me to flee
To mercy's throne, Thy face to see,
Oh! Jesus I am thine.

I once was sinful, wayward, wild,
But through Thy blood am reconciled,
And now Thou own'st me for Thy child,
Oh! Jesus I am thine.

The sinner and the Saviour meet,
In love Thou draw'st me to Thy feet,
O what a gracious mercy seat,
Oh! Jesus I am thine.

And here I taste the sweets of love,
In richest streams from heaven above,
And soon its glories I shall prove,
Oh! Jesus I am thine.

LIVING TO CHRIST, AND ADORNING OUR CHRISTIAN PROFESSION.

Oh may we in our lives express,
  The love of Christ that we possess ;
In Him may every Christian shine,
  And show to all the world the sign.
The sign that rules by grace and love,
  And does its heavenly doctrine prove ;
Here live according to His word,
  Looking to Christ for the great reward.

This living to the Word proclaims,
  The honour of our Saviour's name ;
Tells Christ's Salvation reigns within,
  And grace subdues the power of sin.
Our sinful lusts must be denied,
  With passion, envy, pomp and pride ;
While justice, temperance truth and love,
  Show all the new birth from above.

LINES ON FOREIGN MISSIONS.

Great God what offering shall I bring,
  To aid our missions' righteous cause—
That makes dark heathen lands to ring,
  With joy beneath Thy glorious laws ?
How many an Indian once so wild,
  Have now been taught to read and pray ;
And Thou hast owned him for Thy child,
  And brought him forth the heavenly way.

And many a lost benighted race,
Had sunk in darkness 'neath the sod;
Now own their priceless crowns of grace,
To the Gospel pioneers of God.
Who, braving clime, dissease and pain,
Mid'st burning heat and withering cold;
Salvation for the lost to gain—
A home in Christ's redeemed fold.

Each torrid zone, and frozen pole,
Have heard the blessed Gospel's sound;
Oh may its gladdening tidings roll,
And everywhere with light abound.
And still the glorious Gospel's rays,
Shine forth to bless and cheer the world;
Till every land exult in praise,
Beneath Christ's banner wide unfurled.

For God hath formed the human race,
Of soul and flesh and blood the same;
All free to gain the sovreign grace,
Whate'er their colour, caste or name.
Then let us do our duty here,
And towards the heathen show our love;
Let each one labour in his sphre,
To guide their souls to heaven above.

Great God the offering I would lay,
Low at Thy feet, is one poor heart,
Who humbly seeks from day to day,
The warmth of gladness to impart
To soothe the erring wanderer's breast,
To bring him to the christian fold;
To guide his steps to peace and rest,
When Christ, with Saints communion hold.

"I CAN DO ALL THINGS THROUGH CHRIST, WHICH STRENGTHENETH ME."

Ah! is it so St. Paul? what can you mean?
Strange statement this is, in our earthly scene,
Is it not vanity for you to say,
You can do all things in your pilgrim way?
But stay! I see its not in your own might,
But Christ the living way the Truth and Light.

Ah! Paul! in this with you I will agree,
For in His power the weakest saint can be
Made mighty by His allsufficient grace,
And valiant be in this his earthly race;
By good works here he may in Christ abound,
In fruits of righteousness be ever found.

There we may listen to his loving voice,
And in His strength may evermore rejoice;
And we may always hear Him kindly say,
My strength is given equal to thy day;
And glad may be although in deep distress,
And rest in Him who surely will us bless.

And thus we may, just like St. Paul of old,
Journey on towards the heavenly fold;
Still doing all things with our earnest love,
Till He transplants us to the fold above;
Living to Him we shall find all secure,
This Rock of ages ever shall endure.

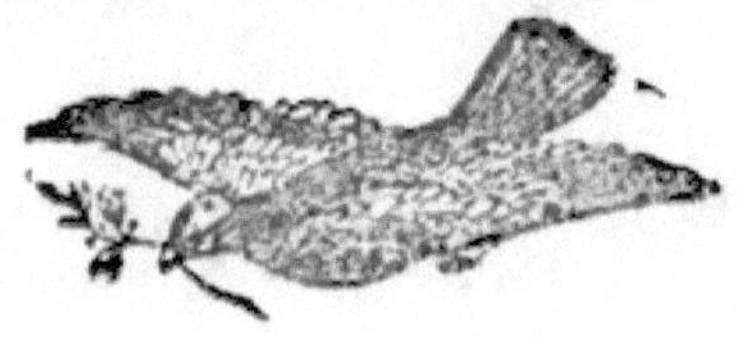

THE LIFE BOAT.

The winds lash the waves, the surge mounts on high,
Still the crew of the life boat the tempest defy ;
The blasts of distruction they brave.
'Neath the thunder's loud roar and the lightning's flash,
With stout british hearts on they fearlessly dash ;
'Midst the cries of distress, and the ship's breaking crash !
The hopeless and drowning to save.
Huzza ! man the Life Boat ! and let the storm rave,
Our watchword is rescue—we'll perish or save !

O'er the white crested billows she manfully sweeps,
Like an angel of mercy she gallantly leaps ;
Rejoicing all terrors to brave.
Now lost to the view and now mounting on high !
As flash after flash ! illumes the dark sky ;
Through the death-dealing torrents and breakers they fly,
As the hapless they hasten to save.
Huzza ! man the Life Boat ! and let the storm rave,
Our watchword is rescue—we'll perish or save.

Hark, hark ! that wild shout—now heard 'mid the blast,
Huzza ! now they board her—the grapnel is cast ;
'Tis joy from the wreck that is heard !

They rescue her crew from the rigging and mast,
Of the ill-fated bark, and on they speed fast;
To the shore the boat fles like a bird.
Huzza! man the Life Boat! and let the storm rave;
Our watchword is rescue—we'll perish or save.

Like sea dogs they shake the wet spray from each vest,
The fears of the rescued are past and at rest;
While a sobbing and heart-touching prayer,
From a fond mother rose, as her sailor boy prest
In safety once more to her joy beating breast;
And a husband again by a fond wife caress'd
And joy takes the place of dispair.
Huzza! man the Life Boat! and let the storm rave;
Our watchward is rescue—we'll perish or save.

Haste hither ye wreathed ones with victory crowned,
Say where in creation rich gems may be found
To sprinkle on honour's bright pile.
All worthy of your's in a wreath to be bound,
What jewels too costly their brows to surround;
What praise is there equal their merits to sound!
The men who dare death for a smile?
Huzza! man the Life Boat! and let the storm rave;
Our watchword is rescue—we'll perish or save.

Then build them a home where old age may glide,
'Twould redound to our country's honour and pride—
Till they reach the confines of the blest.
Where kind mercy hovers, where justice would chide,
And win them a prize oft to greatness denied;
Blotting out all their follies from life's erring tide,
As they journey in peace to their rest.

Huzza! man the Life Boat! and let the storm rave;
Our watchword is rescue—we'll perish or save.

LIFE'S SERMONS.

Our preachers they are always teaching,
That life is subject to decay ;
As bubbles perish they are preaching,
That all shall die and pass away.
Each fragile flower in its decaying,
Each summer's shower that passes by ;
To all of us the truth is saying,
The time will come when you must die.

The fallen leaves in autumn lying,
Bestrew the ground and plainly say ;
O ! let us each while time is flying,
Now make the best of life's short day.
It is a solemn thought—how fleeting,
Is our existance here on earth ;
But Jesus calls us with love's greeting,
Unto a brighter, holier birth.

Yet God—our God—our Father dearest,
A throne on high for all hath made ;
Through all the earth His love appearest,
In lustre true, time ne'er can fade.
His every work our earth adorning,
A sermon teaches to mankind ;
The starry night, the beams of morning
Instruct the calm and thoughtful mind.

And sickness preaches to our hearing,
A sermon bidding all prepare ;
Passing our lives in Heavenly fearing,
That we the promised rest may share.
But let us all each hour improving,
Whilst here on earth time flies away ;
To feel that onward we keep moving,
To heaven above where's no decay.

HYMN FOR BERMONDSEY RAGGED SCHOOL.

(Dedicated to Mr. W. Penny, Secretary.)

We praise Thy name O God our King,
For Thee our grateful songs we sing.
For all Thy care and love,
Though very poor we are on earth,
We know our souls of wondrous worth—
Shall dwell in Heaven above.

O! God of good our praise shall rise,
To Thee whose glory fills the skies,
We raise our youthful songs!
Our teachers show Thy way of truth,
And lead us in our early youth—
To Thee all praise belongs.

We often find we'er prone to stray,
From Christ our Shepherd King and way,
Great God of love forgive!
Let Thy good Spirit lead our mind,
The righteous path in Thee to find—
And to Thy glory live.

May we our Blessed Saviour know,
And in our lives His virtues show,
As children of His fold.
And may we in His image shine,
And bear the stamp of Love Divine—
In Heaven's Blest Book enrolled.

O bless our teachers' labours here,
Prosper their work their hearts to cheer,
Let souls through Him be blest.
And when they've done their work below,
May they, and we Thy glories know—
In Heaven Thy promised rest.

ON THE DEATH OF HIS GRACE ALGERNON PERCY, THE DUKE OF NORTHUMBERLAND.

Alas ! He is gone and left this earthly scene,
His christian virtues shone in rays serene,
Though high exalted in this earthly sphere,
He studied well the poor to bless and cheer ;
His chief delight to form some noble plan,
To benefit and help his fellow man.
No self-love dimmed his calm benignant days,
His generous deeds inspired all hearts with praise !
And countless blessings showered upon his head,
Throughout the land his noble fame was spread ;
And now his mission's done, his spirit flies,
To endless realms of joy beyond the skies.

And though he's gone, yet as we gaze around,
On good and holy works his name is found ;
He passed from earth, his soul hath soared away,
But still he lives in deeds that ne'er decay.
And thousands yet unborn shall laud his name,
While history's page perpetuates his fame ;
And truth's pure words bear record of his worth !
And spreads his fame abroad through all the earth,

Recording how a Percy nobly stood,
A pattern bright to all the just and good;
Inciting peers among the rich and great,
To bless and cherish all of low estate.

His princely wealth he summoned to his aid,
And all the fullness of his heart displayed;
Raised stately temples, dedicate to God,
For in God's fear he ever meekly trod.
The ship-wrecked sailors' stedfast friend was he,
His life-boats braved the perils of the sea;
Glad tidings bearing o'er the furious wave,
Rescuing souls from many a watery grave.
And though his death on all hath cast a gloom,
Yet will his deeds survive beyond the tomb;
His numerous tenents, all, his loss deplore,
And grieve to think they'll find him here no more.

He has passed away to Heaven to meet his King,
There with cherubim and seraphim to sing;
He has landed safely on th' eternal shore,
Joined the redeemed his Saviour to adore.
Ours is the loss and sorrow,—ours the pain,
The change to him is everlasting gain;
From heights of bliss, he can with joy look down,
His Ducal gems resigned for Heaven's bright crown.
With holy joy he joins the glorious throng,
And sings in Heaven the Hallelujah song;
With golden harp before the throne he'll stand,
And sing God's praises in the better land.

LINES TO MR. ISAAC HUNTER CLARK.

On the presentation of a valuable Time Piece bearing the followin inscription. "A Jubilee Testimonial to Mr. Isaac Hunter Clarke, from the Ministers, Trustees, Stewards, Leaders, Members, Friends, Teachers, and Scholars of Southwark Wesleyan Chapel, London, in grateful recognition of Fifty Years of happy membership and useful service, *March* 3rd, 1865."—"To God be all the Praise."

Hail! noble vetran, thy Jubilee we greet,
Thankful that thou art spared with us to meet;
Hail! worthy Clark we give thee hearty cheers,
For labour in Christ's cause for fifty years.
We meet in crowds to celebrate this day,
That God will bless thee everyone will pray;
We give thee honour and are glad to see,
Thee look so well on this thy jubilee.
May God thy useful life still longer spare,
And ever keep thee neath His guardian care.

But in the past what changes thou hast seen,
In half a century—hosts of mighty men
Have gone to their reward! men thou hast known,
Who left the earth to take their heavenly crown.
But God's great goodness kindly leads thee still,
Climbing life's mazy thorny ragged hill;
In every storm He kindly shelters thee,
Beneath the wings of His Benignity,
And here amidst thy friends thou still dost stand,
A pillar of grace kept by His mighty hand.

Still thy heart throbs with warm desires to plan,
Fresh means by which to save thy fellow man;
Thou labourest still in every useful sphere,
A blessing made to all while dwelling here.
With gratitude thy zealous care we trace,

Thy earnest efforts for the rising race ;
Thy labours in the school worth more than gold,
Bringing the tender lambs into the fold,
And for thy patient toil thy Saviour Lord,
Will give to thee a glorious rich reward.

How often at the sick-bed thou'st appeared,
And blest the dying, and their spirits cheered ;
Many dear infants to the font were brought,
By thee first registered and after taught.
Again as Steward faithful to thy trust,
Thy liberal hand bestows where'er'tis just ,
And many will thy righteous labours bless,
For turning them from sin to righteousness,
Many through thee will join the glorious throng
Near the bright crown, and sing the heavenly song.

How many now there are on beds of pain,
While health flows richly through thy every vein,
How many are in want throughout our land,
While thou hast plenty by God's goodness planned,
Thy faltering tongue unable to express,
Thy gratitude and love and thankfulness ;
For mercies far too numerous to count,
While every moment swell the vast amount,
And here thy grateful heart anew would raise,
A fresh memorial to His glorious praise.

Around thee now, how many friends we see,
Rejoicing all in this thy jubilee ;
United with one heart their joy to prove,
By offering thee this token of there love ;
Long may this "Time Piece" as its hands go round,

A token of their true esteem be found;
And every moment as time flies so fast,
Be happier than the one already past,
Till in a better world when Time's no more,
For ever thou thy Saviour Christ adore.

TIME PAST

It is gone, it is gone! it has vanished away,
The time I have spent of my life's fleeting day;
And I look on the past like a feverish dream,
With its quick rushing flight to eternity's stream.
And I start quite aghast at the path I have trod,
And prodigal like I return to my God;
He met me, He kissed me with loving embrace.
While tears of repentance rolled down o'er my face.
And I humbled to think of the love I had slighted,
When he fell on my neck and in mercy delighted;
Is there mercy for me who spurned the love given?
O yes to the penitent! mercy in heaven.

O come now and taste of my bounty so free,
And drink of the life-given stream shed for thee;
I have come and found how mercy still blesses,
And strews our life's path with blissful caresses.
I have come and have found the stream in commotion,
I have come and have drank of love's purest ocean;
Though black in times past was the stain of my sins,
Yet the merit of Jesus for me pardon wins.
I now gaze with joy as on Pisgah I stand,
In my glorious home in the bright promised land;
I perceive now with gladness my sins all forgiven,
And look forward with hope for a bright home in heaven.

ON THE DEATH OF MR. HAWKINS, LEADER OF THE CHOIR, AT SOUTHWARK.

Alas! he's gone, his voice no more he'll raise,
To lead God's people in their hymns of praise;
To thank the Great Supreme for mercies given,
And join with them to seek for peace and heaven.
He sang as Leader, long in Southwark Choir,
His zeal and constancy did all admire;
But now his voice is hushed—his spirit's fled,
And in the grave now lies his weary head.
But though the body's laid in mouldering earth,
We trust his soul hath found a brighter birth;
And dwells on high before the celestial throne,
Where sin and care, and sorrow are unknown!
Upon the brink of death he trembling stood,
And viewed with anxious thoughts death's streaming flood;
Then raised his voice to Heaven in earnest prayer,
He sought for mercy and the Lord was there.
There to impart bright Gilead's healing balm,
To grant him pardon, and his fears to calm;
To sooth his sorrow and to give him rest,
And call him home to dwell among the blest.

From seats of bliss the shining angels come,
And bear him forth to Heaven's eternal home ;
In blood divine washed pure from every sin,
And clothed in raiment white he enters in.
Cheered on by them he passes death's drear flood,
Made pure and clean by Christ's atoning blood ;
And soon he gains the everlasting shore,
Where earthly sorrows shall be known no more.
And now his voice makes Heaven's high arches ring,
With Love adorning towards the Heavenly King ;
Where nought but bliss and bright eternal joy,
In glorious lustre free from earth's alloy !
Resplendent reigns throughout the boundless space
With hosts of angels meeting face to face ;
All journeying clothed in glory's dazzling rays,
Raise lauding anthems in their Maker's praise.
'Tis there again he sings with rapture sweet,
All all the choir his voice and presence greet ;
There meekly bows with thanks for pardon given,
And blesses Christ, through whom he entered Heaven.

TO A FRIEND WHO WAS MUCH CAST DOWN, BY REASON OF HIS AFFLICTION.

Why is your heart so full of grief,
What ! cannot Jesus bring relief—
And ease your troubled mind ?
"Oh yes," methinks I hear you say,
If I had but a heart to pray—
I soon should comfort find.

But now alas! I cannot pray,
Can only just look up and say—
Quicken my simp'e heart.
O make me what Thou'dst have me be,
I would not live so far from Thee,
Nor from Thee more depart.

Jehovah hears when thus you groan,
And when you make the heavy moan—
He knows your every sigh.
Though long His mercy seems to stay,
He'll not forsake, he may delay—
Your faith and p.tience try.

Acknowledge then His tender love,
You soon will meet your Lord above—
. Beyond the reach of fear.
May Jesus's smiles attend your days,
And all your future life be praise—
Until you're landed there.

And when your Spirit takes its flight,
To yonder realms of life and light—
And at the Throne you bow.
Then you'll adore His lovely face,
And doubt no more the power of grace—
Though all is darkness now.

Like some tall ship with crowded sail,
That runs before a prosperous gale—
O may you enter there!
Triumphant may you join the throng,
And join with rapture in the song—
From sorrow freed and care.

"WHAT SHALL I RENDER TO THE LORD, FOR ALL HIS MERCIES TO ME?".

For mercies countless as the sands,
Which daily I receive,
From God's, the bounteous Giver's hands,
My soul what can'st thou give.
Mercies that make my cup run o'er,
For every blessing given ;
Drawn from God's all bounteous store,
And glorious hopes of Heaven.

Alas! from such a heart as mine,
What can I bring Him forth?
My best works stained with deadly sin,
My all is nothing worth.
The best returns for one like me,
So sinful and so poor ;
Is from His gifts to draw the plea,
To ask Him still for more.

And then when I shall see his face,
And bow before His throne ;
I'll sing the wonders of His grace,
And bless the Great Three-One.
I'll tell of mercies gone and past,
That led me in His way ;
This! this will be the song to last,
Through an eternal day.

"OH! EVERY ONE THAT THIRSTETH COME YE UNTO THE WATERS."

Oh! Ye that pant for living streams,
And pine away and die,
Here you may quench your raging thirst,
With streams that never dry;
Rivers of Love and mercy here,
In a rich ocean join,
Salvation in abundance flows,
Like floods of milk and wine.
These streams of bliss shall ever flow.
From Heaven's abundant sea;
Down to the depths of human woe,
Alike for you and me.
"Whoever will," O! gracious word,
Shall of this Stream partake;
Come thirsty souls and bless the Lord,
And drink for Jesus' sake.

THE CHRISTIAN WARRIOR'S WELCOME TO HEAVEN.

(Lines in Remembrance of the late John Vanner, Esq.)

Hail! Hail! valiant soldier of Jesus thy Saviour,
Thou'st fought the good fight for thy Master and King,
Victorious returned to the light of His favour,
All heaven with gladness thy welcome shall ring.
At the portals of heaven a host is in waiting
To greet thee with loving affection divine;
A host thou hast zealously helped in translating
To that blissful abode where in glory they shine.

Hail! Glorious old veteran thy labours and honours
Have shewed thy sincerity holy and true,
And great was our joy to have thee among us,
Iniqnity here found a foeman in you;
And for evermore now in bright Majesty's presence,
In love, peace, and joy, thou shalt ever remin
Sustained in God's grace by the Spirit's blest essence,
Heaven greets thee with welcome again and again.

When sinking to rest there was glory around him,
It was joy on this Christian warrior to gaze,
The angel of Death as in fetters he bound him,
Heard him break forth in accents of praise;
He leaned on that Rock no tempest can shiver,
And relied on the truths of God's holy word,
He drank of the stream that flowed from His river,
And rejoiced in the prospect of seeing his Lord.

God's angels were there around his death pillow,
And seraphs hung over his fluttering breath;
Jesus softened the pains of death's turbulent billow,
And was with him while passing the valley of death.
The chariot was waiting, the angels attending,
His spirit is freed and sings a glad strain,
All heaven is waiting the warrior ascending,
And rings with the welcome he's safe home again.

Around him now gather pure beings of glory,
And loud anthems swell the celestial dome;
While saints fair and lovely and patriarchs hoary,
Peal forth loud hosannas and welcome him home.
O sweet salutation of sanctified greeting
To arise from the whole of that wonderful choir,
Unspeakable joy there was found in the meeting
That filled his brave soul with celestial fire.

He gazes around and sees arms wide extending,
To clasp him in fond recognition's embrace;
Old friends with rapture in their hearts lending
An ecstacy grand to their heavenly face:
While glory to God and the Lamb they are singing,
Hallelujahs peal forth in melodious strain,
The arches of heaven with rapture is ringing,
And welcome re-echoes again and again.

The archangel summons with love all abounding
The saints to appear before the white throne,
In the holy of holies' midst light all surrounding
The great seat of mercy of godhead alone;
The warrior advances with rapture beholding
The brightness of Majesty, glory, and love,
Where Christ at the right hand of God is unfolding
The fulness of grace that is centred above.

A sweet voice is heard of love all inviting
And the warrior trembles with ecstacy sweet,
A pure blaze of light on his form is alighting,
And the Saviour is waiting His servant to greet,
Well done good and faithful and blessed arise
In the joys of thy Lord thou shalt ever remain,
Thou'st fought well and conquered gaining the prize,
Heaven greets thee with welcome again and again.

THE MEDIATOR.

Jesus thou source of Heavenly light,
The image of thy Father bright;
From whom we all derive our might,
On us Thy Spirit send.

Hear Jesus now our humble lay,
While at Thy feet we kneel to pray;
And send from Heaven a glorious ray,
On us Thy Spirit send.

For Thou art full of grace and love,
And all our sins Thou can'st remove;
Our pleader at the Throne above,
On us Thy Spirit send.

Let Thy bright beams around us shine,
The beams of love with light divine;
And prove to us that we are Thine,
On us Thy Spirit send.

And let it all our sins efface,
And fill us with Thy Heavenly grace;
And stir us up to seek Thy face,
On us Thy Spirit send.

And when at last our death is nigh,
O then be near to hear our cry;
And teach us Lord the way to die,
On us Thy Spirit send.

"THE GRASS WITHERETH, THE FLOWER FADETH, BUT THE WORD OF GOD ABIDETH FOR EVER."

All all is fleeting here on earth,
Subjected to continual change;
Their value is of little worth,
With all the things that men arrange.
But those who build their hopes on high,
And seek to lay their treasure there;
On faith's strong pinions upward fly,
And live above this world of care.

On Christ their Blessed Saviour rest,
On this rock they shall build secure;
And with His Spirit here they're blest,
And thus their happiness is sure.
The mansion promised by His Love,
Firm as Eternity shall stand;
The christian's glorious home above,
Jerusalem the better land.

PUBLIC WORSHIP.

What sweet delights, what heavenly joys,
What glories fill the place!
Where Jesus manifests Himself
In streams of flowing grace.

The sweet refreshing streams on earth
His people feel of love,
And onward they rejoicing go,
To see His face above.

And though above in lofty strains,
Archangels sound His praise;
Yet in His mercy still He deigns,
To list to earthly lays.

And thus through life we travel on,
And in His worship join;
Our sou's rejoicing in the hope,
That we in Heaven shall shine.

And when we see our Saviour there,
Whom we unseen adore;
With rapturous joy shall on Him gaze,
And praise Him evermore.

THE CHRISTIAN'S VICTORY OVER DEATH.

Death vanquished they'll sing, despoiled of his sting
Who have conquered through Christ from above;
On the plains of delight, with thousands in white,
They shall walk and converse of His love

How blessed a thing Hallelujah to sing,
When earth's meetings and partings are o'er:
In Jerusalem grand the saints shall all stand,
His goodness behold and adore.

In that wonderful place, in the light of His face,
They for ever in glory shall dwell;
No more the sad tear, on each face shall appear,
When bidding each other farewell

Each harp struck with joy the praise shall employ,
Christ the Saviour each note will be given;
Of Jesus' blest grace, they will sing in that place,
And increase the great glories of Heaven.

THE RICH AND THE POOR MEET TOGETHER. THE LORD IS THE MAKER OF THEM ALL.

I saw the poor beggar while asking for bread,
Unheeded by many passed by;
The chill dews of winter encircled his head,
And a tear trickled down from his eye.
His form told of hunger and withering want,
His visage of sorrow and care;
His heart that groaned under many a taunt,
Seemed breaking with hopeless despair.

He wrapped his old garments his bosom around,
And in speechless but agonized woe!
Looked wishfully up to the mansion he found,
Thought the master might something bestow.

He approached, but was thrust as a thief from the door,
"No vagrants would there be supplied"
He pleaded his cause, he was hungry and poor,
Said O pray do not have me denied.

He pleaded Thy barns may be full to o'erflow,
And fruitful thy flock and each field;
Which God in His bounty on you doth bestow,
That some to the poor you may yield.
Thy clothing the finest, and silver and gold,
Thy goblets all costly and rare;
But I have no clothing my limbs to enfold,
And hunger drives me to despair.

If it be but the crumbs that fall from your board,
E'en to feast with the dogs I would crave!
Then sure thou wilt some of thy plenty afford,
'Nor let me sink into the grave.
If denied then may plenty be loathsome to thee!
Thy wine cup soon poison thy breath;
Thy friends every one prove faithless to thee,
And disease soon strike thee with death

God's mandate perchance may be sent "thou shalt die"
And the messenger stand at thy door;
The voice of the poor might be lifted on high
Against thee, for witholding thy store.
Yet forgive me O Lord, this curse on him here,
He exclaims "I will give unto thee!
Come hither ye needy your hearts I will cheer,
Take a part of my plenty with thee.

For I know that before the great Judge I must stand,
This record He left upon earth;
The souls of the poor and the meek of our land,
He says are of infinite worth.
And whate'er of your treasure on them you bestow,
Its the same as if done unto me;
Then blessings for you up to heaven shall go,
As a treasure from moth and rust free.

THE MOTHER'S CARE.

Hear all kind mothers of our Isle,
Nor scorn my humble homely style;
You judge it of important weight,
To keep your lovely daughters straight,
For this such anxious care you feel,
You almost case them up in steel;
In fashion's style you wish them seen,
In pompous flow—of crinoline.

For them is brougth the foreign cane,
For them the monster whale, is slain;
To the body is your care confined,
You leave the nobler part—the mind.
Why not adorn the better part,
With truth and virtue light their heart;
Deformity of soul I call,
The worst deformity of all.

Bid their young minds in time forego,
The treacherous paths where pleasures flow;
Save their young minds from folly—save,
Bid them in virtues cause be brave.
Bid pleasure cease its evil sway,
That makes pure virtue fade away;
Beneath the alluring snaring chain,
Whose end is everlasting pain.

When virtue leaves a woman's mind,
And honour scorns to stay behind;
All noble principles destroyed.
And vice fills up the empty void,
Like syrens they perform their part,
To weaken and corrupt the heart;
It is a shock to virtue's sight,
Oft proves their everlasting blight.

Then sunk in vice of foulest dye,
With father, mother, no one nigh;
What anguish racks the erring breast,
She night or day can gain no rest.
Till maddened by remorse or shame,
The maniac's thrill strikes through the frame;
Beyond the power of aught to save,
She leaps and finds a watery grave.

Then mothers pray of those take care,
Those tender maidens chast and fair;
With whom thy God hath blest thy life,
The pride of every virtuous wife.
O guard them, tend them, watch them well,
That virtue in their bosoms dwell;
So that with life's last setting sun,
Thou cans't exclaim my duty's done!

WOMAN.

Bright star of our being in sorrow and gladness,
Lovely woman, so precious, so charming and dear;
Thy warm breathing words chase the bleak air of sadness,
Like a message from heaven they fall on the ear.
Thy love like the rock standing firm in mid-ocean,
Brings the richest of bliss man can know upon earth,
And fills all our bosoms with joyous emotion,
We will honour thy virtue thy beauty and worth.

When dark disappointment hath filled us with sorrow,
Who so anxious to buoy up our spirits anew;
And lead us to hope for the beams of to morrow,
With love's melting accents, so cheering and true.

O what would life be were woman not near us,
A cold cheerless wilderness, wretched and drear ;
No smiles, no embraces, no soft words to cheer us,
Man's existance a maze of desponding and fear.

When prostrate we lie on the couch of affliction,
What balm is so potint our pains to assuage ;
As woman's kind tending that wakes the conviction,
That our ease and our comfort her thoughts all engage.
And when ruddy health once again is returning,
From whom doth the prayer of pure thankfulness rise?
'Tis from woman, sweet woman whose bosom was burning,
With anguish while watching with tear flooding eyes.

Alas ! in the world how oft we discover,
What wrongs heaven's creatures are born to endure ;
When libertines foul around innocence hover,
To crush the bright jewel created so fair.
Oh heaven's ! 'tis frightful to know the dark calling,
Of fiends who about in society crawl ;
How grievous to feel how sad and appalling,
The fair mould of woman to vice should e'er fall.

But when her whose life hath been crushed with dishonour,
How firmly she clings to the object she loves ;
Though wrongs upon wrongs are inflicted upon her,
Her quenchless affection she constantly proves.
Alas ! how often remorse overcomes her.
In madness her feelings for death's coming crave ;
The last spark of shame now distracts and benumbs her,
She rushes on wild to a seucide's grave

Stand forth noble ladies, whose graces and beauty,
Both charm and adorn the high ranks of our land ;
To rescue thy sisters O strive as a duty,
Show forth a Samaritan's bosom and hand.

O think of those forms now in infamy dwelling,
Who once were dear innocents pure as the light;
The youthful emotions each bosom was swelling,
Now wanderers lost in the mazes of night.

O think of the time in their life's gayest morning,
When they bloomed in the pride and the hope of their home;
With virtues and graces that home then adorning,
Spread joy and delight whenever they come.
Then Oh! think again on their fallen condition,
Be determined like Jesus your sisters to raise;
And save the frail creatures from lasting perdition,
And saints shall attend thee with honour and praise.

LINES ON HEARING A SERMON, PREACHED BY THE REV. JAMES MAYER

On Peter's denial of Christ. "And the Lord turned and looked upon Peter and Peter remembered the word of the Lord—how He had said unto him before the Cock crow thou shalt deny me thrice; and Peter went out and wept bitterly."—Luke XXII, Chap. 61st & 62nd Verses.

Vain boasting Peter, whose self-righteous cry,
Declared thy master thou would'st ne'er deny;
But on thyself thy faith was fixed strong,
And founded thus, thy faith did not stand long.
In this he showed how weak the faith of man,
Without strength divine how feeble is each plan;
If in this life a man desires to stand,
He must rely on God's Almighty Hand.

Now doubtless Peter loved his master well,
A fervid impulse caused his heart to swell;
He felt the words he uttered were sincere,
On self-faith trusting, saw no cause of fear.

He doubtless felt with Christ he could have died,
But Oh! How weak our faith when sorely tried;
Oh! Weak indeed! as it in Peter proved,
In one short hour, denied the Lord he loved.

But Christ his heart knew well,—and had foretold,
That Peter would deny Him—though so bold;
The Blessed Jesus knew man's best resolve,
Is doomed before temptation to disolve.
And melt away the more when self-esteem,
Throws in its false and proud vain glorious beam;
And Jesus said "before the Cock shall crow,
Thou wilt say that me thou dost not know."

He followed Jesus to the Judgment Hall,
And on him soon were fixed the eyes of all;
A maiden said:—"this man I surly saw,
Thou wert with him in Gallilee before."
But he denied:—O Peter was it so?
And didst thou not thy Lord and Master know?
"He knew Him not:—he said—although he knew—
His conscience heaved—the cock then loudly crew.

Another said—"you with him I have seen,"
Your tongue bespeaks you are a gallilean,
"I know not the man"! He thus denied again,
And falshood dared in Peter's breast to reign.
Oh Simon! was that not thy Saviour—He
Who saved thy life from drowning in the sea?
But at the man a look of scorn he threw,
And now again the cock distinctly crew.

Again being pressed "thou wert with him to day,
I saw thee following talking by he way"
But Peter still denied with angry stare,
And at the man began to curse and swear.
The man declared that he was one of them,
Whose speech and looks would surely now condemn;
But Peter's falshood seemed to be in vain,
He stood aghast—the cock crew shrill again.

Now Jesus turned and look in Peter's face,
A look of mingled pity love and grace ;
And Peter quailed before his master's eye,
His tears fell fast he breathed a bitter sigh.
Grief wrung his heart, he wept now like a child,
And worshipped Him whose truth he had denied ;
His boasting words now rankled in his breast,
With deep remorse, and penitence opprest.

God help thee ! Peter ! send grace to all mankind,
And keep vain boasting from each sinner's mind ;
He searches all our hearts' tries every thought,
And by His mercy on our way we'er brought.
Let's humbly strive with earnest prayerful care,
To serve our God, His precious grace to share ;
Then shall we not deny, but seek His face,
Upheld by God with His preserving grace.

ROME, ANCIENT AND MODERN.

When I think of the glory and grandeur of Rome,
Of her ancient historic renown ;
Where science and liberty found a bright home,
And monarchs all quailed at her frown.
When I think of her senators' wisdom and power,
When the nations all bowed at her feet ;
And her warriors covered the earth like a shower,
And the ocean was swept by her fleet,

I grieve for her mournful decadence and gloom,
The light of her grandeur's decline ;
And mourn her abasement to slavery's doom,
At Popery's idolatrous shrine.
My feelings revolt at the souls of mankind,
By antichrist fettered and bound ;
To the regions of darkness by terror consigned,
Where priestcraft encumbers the ground.

Thou city once hailed by the nations the Queen,
When a Roman was proud of his birth;
When thy temples' and palaces' splendour was seen,
And thy glory spread over the earth.
How changed is thy state, since the Ceasars of old,
Issued mandates to govern the world;
When thy seven-hill'd capitol glistined with gold,
'Neath freedom's broad banner unfurled.

O why art thou fallen thou city so grand?
And why are thy children in chains?
O why are thy dungeons a stain to the land—
A blight to thy once sunny plains?
And why art thou prostrate so low in the dust,
Why cringe to the power of thy foes?
Thou'st forsaken the faithful, the true and the just,
Sunk deep is thy anguish and woes.

'Twas the foul brand of Popery darkened thy fame,
And brought all thy power to decay;
Cast a stain on thy children their honour and name,
And banished thy freedom away
The blood of the martyrs so tortured and slain,
By the black inquisition's decrees;
Shall live unforgot, and confront thee again,
Till the demon of Popery flees.

Rise again noble City! Thy past deeds efface,
Banish all thy corruption from sight;
Of dark superstition renounce every trace,
Grasp the banner of Jesus so bright.
Let the Bible of Truth be your peoples' guide,
True Religion your buckler and shield;
And soon shall you stem false idolitry's tide,
Superstition's dark forces shall yield.

To a crucified Saviour in purity turn,
And gladness shall reign in thy land;
The clear lamp of grace in thy City shall burn,
And freedom return to thy strand.
Thy sons and thy daughters by priesthood opprest,
Shall emerge from their bondage again;
And find in Christ Jesus a heaven of rest,
Papal terror shall haunt them in vain.

Far and wide shall the tidings of gladness be spread,
Every christian shall join in the song;
"For our fetters are burst—false Popery's fled,"
Shall be echod by many a throng.
O bright consummation! to worship and pray,
Unfettered untrammelled to be;
And the nations shall shout in the light of the day,
Brave Italy's Children are free!

GRATITUDE AND DEPENDENCE.

My Father, God, help me to raise,
My soul to Thee in love and praise;
With deeply grateful heart I own,
How constantly Thy help I've known.

Whate'er may be my future course,
Well stayed by Thee I shall rejoice;
And this should set my heart at rest,
Thy will ordains all things for best.

Oh Lord! Had I more faithful proved,
And loved as I have been beloved;
What heights of glorious joys divine,
Throughout this life would have been mine.

O Saviour! by Thy mighty power,
Guard me in fierce temptation's hour;
O let Thy kind and watchful care,
Preserve me safe from every snare.

Oh! let Thy pure refining fire,
Purge me from every low desire;
O let Thy love to me be given,
A foretaste of the joys of Heaven.

Help me to consecrate to Thee,
My time and talents—let them be;
All labouring in thy sovreign plan
To save the fallen race of man.

Let all my now remaining years
Be spent for Thee, all free from fears;
And through the merits of Thy Son,
The welcome sound shall come—Well done.

And when shall come the closing scene,
Let all be tranquil and serene;
And as I sink from earth away,
Soar up to realms of endless day.

Grant me, O Lord, this one request,
Ever on Thee my rock to rest;
And both in life and death to prove,
The comforts of Thy gracious Love.

"HOLD THOU ME UP, AND I SHALL BE SAFE."

Great God! to Thee what gratitude I owe,
For all Thy mercies shown me here below;
Bought by Thy Son's most precious blood divine,
All that I have—O consecrate it thine!
But O how weak are all my vows to Thee,
In myself such sinful weakness I see;
Hold thou me up O God! shall be my cry,
Though weak I am—on Thee I can rely.

For Thou hast power and gracious love to save,
Me from all sin—the power of hell to brave;
And wither should I go, but unto Thee—
O Rock of ages—unto Thee I flee!

Fixed on the Rock I have my faith assured,
Thou hast for me eternal life secured ;
And feel through Faith in the atoning blood,
Thou art my Christ, the Glorious Son of God.

Viewed in the light of heavenly things divine,
How little earthly things appear to shine ;
Riches and fame with all their earthly joys,
The mind of man soon satiates and cloys ;
The pleasures all, that o'er our minds hold sway,
Are fleeting all, and fading fast away ;
For this world holds so many burning snares,
"Dangerous to man,"—the Word of God declares.

Lord help me to find Thee, in thy Gospel Word,
And rest my soul on Thee my gracious Lord ;
Have all my functions by Thy grace renewed.
All sin in me by Thy great love subdued.
May mighty grace in me its power display,
To save me in Thine own appointed way ;
And in my heart delight to rule and reign,
'Nor of Thy absence ever more complain

Hold thou me up by Thy own truth and love,
Send forth Thy powers from out Thy courts above ;
And O in sinful me O deign to show,
What thine Almighty grace can for me do.
Thy Gospel here can all our souls revive,
May I obey its voice, and in Thee live ;
My sins all pardoned clothed by Thee afresh,
My heart of stone, turned to a heart of flesh.

Hold Thou me up, and my whole soul renew,
That all may see and love my Jesus too ;
The love that saveth me doth here engage,
A safe defence for all from Satan's rage ;

Be Thou my pattern, make me here to bear,
Thy gracious image, and Thy love declare;
Then God, my Judge, shall own my humble name,
Among the followers of the glorious Lamb.

Enlighten with thy Spirit's heavenly ray,
My shades and darkness, turn them all to day;
Thy Spirit's whisperings make me ever know,
Be thou my refuge while I'm here below.
And let my conscience hear Thy gracious voice,
And trembling, in its mighty Lord rejoice;
Fix on Thyself, my faithful stedfast mind,
And all my springs of blessings in Thee find.

Enter my soul with all Thy lovely train,
Let it the Master's richest love contain;
For others' souls Thy loving pity feel.
And fill them all with pure and earnest zeal.
Be thou my portion, and my happy choice
Hold thou me up, in Thee may I rejoice;
Help me to bear from Thee each earthly rod,
O fill my soul with Glory Gracious God!.

THE LAW AND THE GOSPEL.

"The Law was given by Moses, but grace and truth came by Jesus Christ."--John: 1st Chap. 17th verse.

To Horeb's Mount God's angel came,
  Where Midian's Shepherds watched their Sheep;
Spake from the Bush of fiery flame,
  High holy words of import deep.
For God had heard from Egypt's land,
  His chosen people's cries and chains;
And came to save with mighty hand,
  And leadthem forth to Canaan's plains.

God sent His servant Moses forth,
  To set His bonded children free;
And Egypt's tyrant felt His wrath,
  And perished in the deep Red Sea.
Soon after God revealed His word,
  To Israel gave His ancient Law;
Which Moses took with trembling hand,
  And to the priests the message bore.

On Sinai rang the tempest loud,
  The lighnting flashed, the thunder pealed;
When God came down mid'st fire and cloud,
  His laws to Israel's tribes revealed.
Well may they stand in awful fear,
  And strongest men in terror quake;
When God to them did thus appear,
  And by His power the mountains shake.

Now ages passed, and time rolled on,
  The earth grew dark with sin and shame;
But still the Father's mercy shone,
  Though men reviled His Holy name.
His promise to Abraham of old,
  To send His Son the world to save;
Was now redeemed as 'twas foretold,
  He now the true Messiah gave.

The Gospel came on wings of Love,
  And angels sang in joyful strain;
"Goodwill to all from Heaven above,"
  Was echoed over Bethlehem's plain.
"Glory to God" their heavenly song,
  And "peace to all who dwell on earth,"
Sound it O Lord the earth along,
  The tribute of Immanuel's worth.

O haste the time so long foretold,
  Of Christ's redeeming gracious sway ;
By holy prophets—men of old,
  And bring to pass that glourious day.
When Christ the Sun of Heavenly Light,
  Shall through this world of darkness shine,
And men shall see—O glorious sight !
  Earth filled with righteousness divine.

THE HEROES OF OUR DAYS.

(The Indian Mutiny Defeated).

Again Great Britian's banner waves,
  Defiant in the breeze ;
New glory crowns her valiant arms,
  Resounding o'er the seas.
Th' inhuman traitors' doom is cast,
  The tide of murder stays ;
Before old England's warriors—
  The Heroes of our days.

The maiden's shreak—the mother's wail,
  The orphan's helpless cry ;
Call loud for vengeance on the foe,
  For crimes of foulest die.
For Havelock—and his noble band,
  Ten thousand blessings raise ;
Their history then with honour crowd—
  The Heroes of our days.

Brave Havelock with his valiant men,
  'Neath honour's standard fell ;
To avenge outraged humanity
  They fought, but O too well.
All loyal hearts shall sound their worth,
  In strains of lofty praise ;
And shout for England's warriors—
  The Heroes of our days.

LINES ON THE DEATH OF A MEDICAL FRIEND, WHO WAS GOOD TO THE POOR.

He is bourne to the tomb, and the tears are now shed,
To hallow the spot where his ashes repose;
Who oft to the poor, and the suffering was led,
When anguish assailed them and bowed down each head,
And their comforts of life seemed to close.

For aided by Heaven he grappled with pain,
Regardless of self—in the fray;
Never fearing disease with its pestilent train—
How oft did his wisdom contagion restrain,
And death was deprived of his prey.

I saw the pale faces and many a tear;
Of those who looked saddened with gloom;
The index of grief—as they stood by the bier,
And thought of the loved ones to memory dear;
He had plucked as it were from the tomb.

The poor man was there, who felt that his friend,
In affliction could visit no more;
The rich man was there lamenting the end,
Of one he esteemed as a brother and friend,
Whose loss they must ever deplore.

His loved wife was there in sorrow to mourn—
Who attended his illness with worth;
She mourned that her husband so soon should be torn,
Down to the dark tomb to leave her forlorn,
And to mix with the dust of the earth

But O there's a chain nought on earth can destroy,
Though the form lies entombed in the sod;
That will oft cause the thought, with joy to take wing,
And oft to the mourner rich comfort will bring,
'Tis the thought that he dwells with his God.

THE MURDERER'S DOOM.

Pause murderer, pause—though 'tis darkness abroad,
And the black veil of night shrouds thy way;
Tho' revenge goad thee on—or gold the reward,
Yet the guilt shall be thine, and a voice from the sward
Shall proclaim thee to justice by day.

Though the storm howls around and stifles the cry,
Of thy victim, who pleads but in vain;
On the wings of the gale shall a messenger fly,
The watchers of justice to rouse with its cry,
And the murderer's crime be made plain.

Though thy blood-besmer'd weapon be cast in the wave,
And corruption disfigure the deed;
A whisper shall steal from the murdered one's grave,
Though hid in a nook, or some desolate cave,
To point out the victim's cold bed.

Where God's beautiful work by thy merciless hand,
Lies marr'd and disfigured in death:
Unshriven, unshrouded a stench to the land,
Till surefooted justice o'ertake and demand,
The wretch who deprived it of breath.

Perchance thy grey head might descend to the tomb,
Where earth's honours and men might applaud;
But the dark pent up crime will gnaw and consume,
Thy hopes of hereafter, and fright with sad gloom,
Thy thoughts, with thy future reward.

It will teach thee 'twere better by justice to die
Repentant in Christ, than to dwell
In agonized fear, and each heartbreaking sigh,
Is wrung with remorse which all comfort deny;
Till thou'st banished for ever to Hell.

THE DIGNITY OF MAN.

How great is man! his intellect sublime!
His traits of greatness known in every clime;
Enduring searching, where christians ne'er had trod,
Sustained and blest in fellowship with God.

Salvation's heir, on him, the angels wait,
To cheer his progress through this earthly state;
A child of God, joint heir of Christ above,
God's choicest work—blest with Almighty Love.

Can walk with God on earth and upward raise,
His grateful powers to celebrate His praise;
Enjoying life, with all its blessings given,
And after death a glorious home in Heaven.

THE CONTRAST.

How shall my feeble muse pourtray,
The end of those who pass away—
Without their sins forgiven.
Of those who waste their time on earth,
And let it pass in sin and mirth—
And never seek for Heaven?

Can mortal man the horrors trace,
Upon that pallid dying face—
Who finds now to his cost,
That from the world he's forced to go,
To sink mid'st anguish pain and woe—
With those for ever lost.

O language fails and is to weak,
Of the impenitent to speak—
Who'r filled with sad dispair.
No ray of hope, now can they gain,
On their past life they look with pain—
The future dreads to dare.

A painful sight, glad would they fly,
To Christ for mercy e're they die—
But fixed now is their doom.
The harvest past their mercies end,
And now their guilty souls descend—
To everlasting gloom.

The judge arrayed in glorious power,
Tho' long delayed th'avenging hour —
Now on each guilty head.
The summons comes without delay,
"Depart to punishment away—
On thee my wrath is shed."

Their sins now stare them in the face,
How they despised God's loving grace—
And pleading now is vain.
For Hell's now open to each eye,
Now racked with dark despair they cry
In anguish and in pain.

And there in deepest misery placed,
Among the lost by fiends embraced—
Yet never to expire
They once would jeer at things divine,
In evil with companions join—
Now dwell with them in fire.

My muse would now a contrast show,
And leave these solemn scenes of woe—
And sing a holier strain.
Of others, saints that graced our earth,
Whose pure religion, truth and worth—
Chased sin, and care and pain.

And thus we leave the fallen throng,
And turn to one whose dying song—
Was Faith and Hope so bright.
Whose sins through Christ were washed away,
Who fought Faith's fight in life's short day—
Then soared to endless Sight.

As his last lingering moments come,
He's waiting to be gathered home—
Just view his radiant smile.
No sting of conscience cause alarms,
Embraced within his Saviour's arms,
He rests now from his toil.

His troubles here for ever cease,
He longs now to depart in peace
According to Christ's word.
I have done with earth and now I feel,
My anchor's cast within the veil,
I'm waiting for my Lord.

Come angels hosts fetch me away,
To brilliant realms of endless day,
To join with you in song.
To chant of Christ's redeeming love,
Amidst triumphant hosts above,
With the holy happy throng.

The summons comes—by death released,
His joys for ever are increased;
He joins the holy band.
While all the saints their voices raise,
He joins with love his Saviour's praise
In the upper—better land.

Loud hallelujahs he will sing,
Before the Throne of Heaven's High King,
In lovely meekness crowned.
His joys will never have an end,
For Christ will ever be his friend,
At his right hand be found.

AUTUMN.

When Autumn comes with golden grain,
And gladness tunes the reaper's strain;
Amid the rich ripe sheaves.
Our barns are filled with bounteous yield,
With produce stored from every field;
But left are withered leaves

But death when he the harvest reaps,
The young and old for sheaves he keeps;
And all to him bow down.
O pray that when death comes for thee,
Thou'lt be prepared from earth to flee,
And waiting for thy crown-

And then with joy thou'lt pass away,
To brighter realms of endless day;
A sheaf for Heaven's floor.
Where comes no blasts or winters cold,
But safe within his heavenly fold,
And gathered to God's store.

With all Thy sheaves O God we'll raise,
Our Hallalujah songs of praise ;
Astonished at Thy Love.
With rapturous joy low at Thy feet,
We'll sing the song so grand and sweet,
And dwell with Thee above.

THE AGES OF WOMAN.

In childhood's tender years,
We love those accents sweet ;
That please our listening ears
With sounds we love to greet.
How be uteous then to hear
The tiny daughter's prayer ;
In words of trust and fear,
She asks for future care.

O little does she know,
The pits and snares of life ;
What crime the world doth show—
What cares what pains and strife !
O well it were that all
Should early pray for aid ;
To shun each sinful fall,
And vice's dreary shade.

At school her mind expands,
And learning's treasures gain ;
To virtue true she stands,
Her prayers are not in vain.
Then home from school returns,
A blooming maiden fair ;
Where fond affection burns,
To greet her welcome there.

In woman's brightest hour,
With joyous feelings bright;
A sweet uprising flower,
With hearts all pure and light.
Ere marriage her hopes all gay,
Rejoicing in maiden pride;
She gives herself away
A beauteous blushing bride.

How happy are those days!
Alas! how soon they're past;
Comes Autumn's fading rays
Her life is gliding fast
Of fancy's charms bereft,
How splendid they appeared;
Have gone and sadly left,
But little to be cheered.

But though time quickly fles,
And onward moves apace;
Her soul with love may rise,
Moved by the power of grace.
Then though her life decay,
Above her soul shall soar;
To a home of endless day.
Happy for evermore.

EPITAPH.

In memorium of my mother, Isabella Williamson.

The frail weary body now rests
Its pains and its sorrows are o'er;
She is gone to the land of the blest,
And safely arrived on its shore.
Through Jesus her Saviour and friend,
Who blest her on earth with His Love;
She was meekly resigned to the end,
Now she reigns with Him ever above.

DEPARTURE OF A BELOVED MINISTER, TO ANOTHER FIELD OF LABOUR.

Farewell beloved Workman, God's blessing be thine,
Into whatever part of Christ's vineyard ye go;
We regret that to leave us has now come the time,
Still pray God may bless all your labours at Bow.

We pray that His Bow may your pathway surround,
That thousands of souls be your seals of reward;
Souls that through you shall in glory be crowned,
In thee you shall hail your triumphant Lord.

Your ministry here have been years of great labour,
And many have been by your preaching imprest;
With penitant hearts they have come to the Saviour,
And sought through His blood Salvation and rest.

Our Circuit has flourished with help from above,
Success hath attended God's all-powerful word;
The Saints have been filled with heavenly love,
And wanderers brought homeward again to the Lord.

God greatly hath blest you, your labours hath crowned,
His Vineyard hath prospered from toil without rest;
Your hands were upheld by true workers around,
A new Chapel is raised all in Peckham to bless.

My pen would endeavour thy Virtues to praise,
For labour which beareth the signet divine;
But surely no muse of mine can o'er raise,
The "Workman" who has in each bosom a shrine.

Go herald of Truth on thy mission of peace,
Thy life e'er be bright with God's covenant bow;
When in thy new Circuit, may His love increase,
Till each heart their Jesus their Saviour shall know.

Go disciple of love, the gosple wide sow,
And souls for thy Master continue to win;
Seek His glory alone in going to Bow,
And souls out of number be saved from sin.

And when Heaven's harvest bright ending shall come.
Your zeal and your labour so cherished and blest;
Shall appear in the hosts of Spirits brought home,
For ever arrainged in the mansions of rest.

"GO YE INTO ALL THE WORLD, AND PREACH THE GOSPEL TO EVERY CREATURE."

The word shall win its widening way,
For God hath said the word;
Then let each one be valiant still,
In fighting for their Lord.
For sure the victory we shall gain,
If for Him we shall fight;
And earth shall shout His praise again,
For sending peace and Light.

Though clouds and darkness o'er our camp,
Hang thick in dread array;
The Sun of Righteousness shall rise,
And make a glorious day.

Lord help thy servant s where they are,
Thy radiance let us see ;
And bless Thy missionary sons,
And give them victory.

The combat of the living truth,
Right well our fathers' fought ;
Though many years have passed and fled,
Since first the Word was taught.
And still we grasp within our hands,
The weapons they used well ;
Armed with the blessed Bible Truth,
We'd beat the hosts of Hell.

Though many years have passed away
Religion's still the same ;
As when the Patriarch Abraham,
Felt Faith's enkindling flame.
And we too by the help of God,
Its living light shall raise !
And plant the Cross in every land,
And labour all our days.

Long lines of Saints are looking down,
A white robed host are they—
Our fathers in the Faith, and lived
To light an evil day.
And we will follow in the track,
Of those who've gone before.
When life is past again we'll meet,
Upon the eternal shore

Then children of the Saints arise
To follow those of old ;
Who now have gained the glorious prize,
And strike their harps of gold.
God calls on us to trample down,
The dragon-monster Sin ;
Heaven's bright gates before us shine,
And the victor's Crown we'll win.

THE CITY WHOSE BUILDER AND FOUNDER IS GOD.

There is a glorious City—O how wondrous bright!
God Himself the Builder,—Christ His Son,—the Light:
It stands unchanged for ever, in beauty to behold,
Its walls of Stone most precious; its Streets of purest gold,
And there the saints for ever, shall in the mansion blest,
With all th' adoring angels enjoy the glorious rest;
There robed in purest lustre, they shall His praise declare,
With cherubim, and seraphim, adore Him ever there.

No sorrow there will meet them, or sound of jarring strife,
For God will wipe all tears away, in that blest land of Life;
To living streams will lead them, and fill them with His Love,
In pastures green will feed them, in the happy home above.
Oh, land of fairest beauty! our souls to Thee aspire,
The thought of Thee enkindles a holy chaste desire;
O Saviour be our Pilot! our strength and holy guide,
Till we are safely seated, in glory by Thy side.

LINES DEDICATED TO S. BEVINGTON, ESQ., ON THE RE-OPENING OF BERMONDSEY RAGGED SCHOOLS.

We hail Great God this bright auspicious day,
And ask Thine aid to help us on our way;
We thank Thee for kind teachers to us given,
To train the young, to seek the path to heaven.

Let blessings on our benefactors flow?
And sanctify the seed they daily sow;
A holy mission theirs to teach the young,
To inspire with truth the helpless wanderer's tongue.

Thou Gracious God! o'er ruling earth and space,
O consecrate this work with thy blest Heavenly grace,
And may this school for many ages stand,
To bless the young of this our favoured land.

Father, we thank Thee for Thy loving grace;
Thou'st helped our friends to gain the better place,
Jesus, we pray, on us Thy blessing send,
Be thou our kind Shepherd, and our constant friend.

Guide us we pray Thee by Thy Spirits might,
Untill we reach the heavenly world of light,
Then with our friends, we shall Thy name adore,
For ever praise Thee, on the eternal shore.

Then we shall sing the glad triumphant song—
And dwell for ever with the angels throng,
Midst hallowed light we shall Thy face behold
With the Good Shepherd in our Father's fold.

THE FOOL HATH SAID IN HIS HEART "THERE IS NO GOD"

Fools may say that my Faith is deception,
"A doctrine of priests—a fable—a lie,
And the sceptic refuses to give it reception.
And says 'tis all folly on such to rely,"

But I envy not them of their boasted opinion,
And laugh at their folly when faith they deny,
In life it gives peace by the sweetest dominion,
And teaches the Christian in triumph to die.

The foul tongue of slander may try defamation,
And seek by injustice each good to revile;
But those who have seen Faith's power and affection,
Will say that no malace its name can defile,

And this is the balm of our sweet consolation,
  That soothes the sad heart when with sorrow distrest;
The hope of the Christian in his contemplation;
  Some day he will dwell in the land of the blest.

Let them say what they will of our glorious foundation,
  The Rock of our safety—despise it who may;
Fixed on this Rock is our certain salvation,
  Secure it shall stand when earth fades away.

Our religion through life we surely may cherish,
  And glorify God, with lives just and pure;
For the sceptic shall in his unbelief perish,
  While the Christian's Salvation shall ever endure.

THE DREAMS OF MANKIND.

What a strange and mysterious state do we find
When slumber encircles the powers of the mind,
What fanciful forms are presented to view,
So vivid and clear, as if real and true.
All ranks and all races and sects are the same—
When sleep hath surrounded and conquered the frame.
How rapid the changes of life's running stream,
What sights are revealed in one single dream!

What a solace doth innocence bring to the heart!
Through the dark shades of sleep the keen piercing dart
Of truth will assert her imperative sway,
Show the blackness of crime in its frightful array.

While calmly reposes the innocent breast,
And its sweet visions picture the land of the blest,
Like celestial existence the bright moments seem
When the angels' soft whispers are heard in a dream.

Though downy the couch where an Emperor lies,
The flitting night prompter incessantly flies
Around the rich tapestry o'er the soft bed,
Where imperial riches and grandeur are spread;
Brilliant Victories' charms, cause his bosom to heave,
In fancy he hastens his sports to receive.
While in glory enthroned as a monarch supreme,
He wakes and finds all is a flattering dream.

The Statesman retires to his chamber each night
After gracing the Senate with wisdom so bright,
Reclines on his pillow, when lo! to his view
Come the years that are past, fresh, vivid and new;
He labours aspiring to win a great name,
To inscribe his renown on the records of fame,
And quick beat the pulses of life's glowing stream,
As the ardour of boyhood comes fresh in a dream.

In the still shades of night, amidst calmness and love,
When all is resigned to the Father above;
The Pastor's meek eyelids droope calmly and close,
Released from the world he is lulled to repose;
But Oh! what a glorious vision is there,
The new land of Edon, and Paradise fair,
Where Christ and His Angels sound forth the blest theme
While the man of God prays in the midst of a dream.

The fond dreams of love, how charming they glide,
As in sleep by the brink of its murmuring tide;
The bright bank of pleasure is wafted along
Midst smiles and caresses, and music and song,
At length love awakes to the stern living truth!
What cares will o'er take us emerging from youth?
Still let us rejoice in loves holy stream,
Preserve all we can of its first happy dream.

When the battle field's covered with wounded and dead,
The brave weary soldier reposes his head,
He dreams of his wife, and dear children at home,
Of the fields where in youth he delighted to roam,
In fancy embraces his wife's darling form,
Feels her breath on his cheek, all glowing and warm;
At length he awakens with a desolate start!
His dreaming hath left but a void in his heart.

When the waves of the ocean are mounting on high,
And the white crested billows shoot up to the sky,
The brave hardy sailor in peace in his berth,
Oft dreams of his love, and his dear native earth,
Of the old folks at home, in the cot by the shore,
Whose beauties perhaps he may never see more,
But O! in that vision how sweet are those ties
That twine round his childhood, so dear to his eyes.

When the hard flinty miser his shrunken limbs stretch,
Where truth could inscribe "Here liveth a wretch,"
He rolls and he tosses throughout the long night
On the cold cellar floor, no food, and no light;
His treasure he clutches, his glassy eyes roll,
He dreams that he's filling a rich jewelled bowl,
With the gold he hath wrung from Mammons dark stream,
But he curses and raves, when he finds its a dream.

The cold hearted libertine, haughty and proud,
Who trumpets his conquests of virtue aloud;
And because he is rich escapes the world's frown,
He is called a gay spark, of the fashion and town,
But follow him home, to his night's solitude,
Where conscience unbidden, will dare to intrude,
He is racked in his sleep by his victims loud scream,
He finds no escape from his harrowing dream.

Through the long hours of night with feverish brain,
While dreaming of suffering horror and pain,
The drunkard's eye lights on some hideous form;
Fancy calls forth a tempest, he quai's at the storm,
While legions of spectres sweep over his bed;
His blood rushes madly distracting his head,
His eyes wildly roll, he utters a scream!
And terrified wakes from his horrible dream.

There is joy in the cottage where labour and love—
And contentment abide, to raise us above;
The vices and follies, disgracing we find
So largly dispersed through the ranks of mankind;
How sweet are the dreams of the labourer's bed?
No craving ambition discomforts his head,
His dreams are contented, he loves the green sod,
His neighbours he loves, while he praises his God.

LINES ON A RAGGED SCHOOL BOY, WHO BECAME A MINISTER AND MISSIONARY.

Our Ragged Schools have bravely stood,
  And rescued souls from sin;
Framed children to be chaste and good,
  To Jesus' fold brought in,
They've been a blessing to mankind,
  To spread the Gospel truth,
To cleanse the heart, and light the mind,
  Of many a ragged youth;
Made many hate the haunts of vice,
  Good Christian's they've become;
Through teachers' prayers, and good advice,
  Have sought their Heavenly home.

LINES ON A RAGGED SCHOOL BOY.

When Ragged urchins throng the Street,
  How little do we know,
The gems there are in some we meet,
  They little care to show,
But speak to them one word of love,
  Ignite the slumbering flame,
The virtues soon will shine above,
  None thought could dwell in them ;
That, cheers the Christian teacher's heart,
  Shows him—his toiling days
Are blest, while here he does his part
  The fallen here to raise.

Poor children reared in dark recess
  Of ignorance and sin,
Where love of parents do not bless,
  And them to virtue win ;
But from the cradle naught is known,
  But precepts sad and vile,
And such examples to them shown,
  Which tend them to defile ;
But ev'en with these, Almighty love,
  Can light the wanderer's breast,
And by His Spirit from above,
  Lead them to seek His rest.

One boy I know, who mischief loved,
  A most unruly lad,
Who often had rebellious proved,
  By conduct always bad ;
I spoke to him, and told him plain
  Such pranks I could not have,
He laughed at me, went on again,
  My rule he dared to brave,
I told him he must leave the school ;
  Nor spoil the other boys,
He stared ! and jeer'd me to my face,
  And revelled in his noise.

I called the School around me then,
And went on to explain
The fate of wanton wicked men,
Their lives of sin, and pain;
My lecture short he did not like,
And vowed he'd scarve me out;
Next day he brought a stick, to strike,
And flourished it about;
I went to him, and kindly told,
If he would order make,
I had a coat which was not old,
He for himself might take.

This kindness won his heart at once,
He was an alter'd boy,
No more a reckless noisy dunce
To learn, his greatest joy.
And blest, by God he forward went—
And spread an honoured name;
To foreign missions he was sent,
And gained a world-wide fame,
And thousands by his righteous life
And fervent words were saved;
They left this land of tears and strife,
Death's terrors meekly braved.

THE GOODNESS OF GOD TO MAN.

Vain are my efforts, and weak is my praise,
When God's goodness to man is my theme,
Yet I wish to acknowledge His goodness, and raise
An offering of love, and my poor muse obeys
With gratitude, in his best scheme.

Upheld by His power, by His tenderest care,
Through this world of temptation and sin,
O Father! Thy love and Thy mercy I share,
Which preserves me from falling in many a snare,
Preserved often, and rescued I've been.

But alas! in return for these mercies all shown,
When my heart should with gratitude swell,
Oft times 'tis as cold and hard as a stone,
My affections seem lost, as I wander alone
From my God, with the worldling to dwell.

But I will not fear, for God's ever nigh,
All things are upheld by His hand,
His mercy that gave the dear Saviour to die
Shall blot out my sins from His record on high;
Jesus died for redemption of man.

And He who controls the world by His word,
Who stilleth the tempest and waves of the sea,
He careth for me, and my prayers are all heard,
Which shows Him to me as a merciful God,
By His kindness and care shown to me.

Then why should I doubt, though the world seemeth dark
With sorrow? O! why should I grieve?
My trust is in Thee, Thou shall pilot my bark
Through the breakers of life, though fearful and dark
To Heaven for ever to live.

AN ACROSTIC.

A round your path life's sweetest joys be spread,
G athering blessings on your youthful head;
N ever evanescent, like some passing dream,
E ver changing through life's fleeting stream—
S olid, sacred happiness ever on you beam.
M ay you be loved by every one around,
A nd prove a blessing wherever you are found;
R ejoicing friends' hearts with affection's tone—
Y ou prove the comfort of your peaceful home.
S trive to be useful through life's fleeting way,
N ever trifle it, like the butterfly, away;
E ver sipping from pleasure's flowers the dew.
L et this never have to be said of you,
"S he lived in vain.' More noble be your aim.
O f past time, if wasted, try some to reclaim,
N or let life pass without honour to his name.

ON THE DISSOLUTION OF THE WORLD.

Shall it be so? Shall this earth ever fall,
With what it now contains? destroyed withal
By its own elements? dissolved by fire,
And into nothing shall it all expire?
Shall all the works so great by man designed,
That show the power of his ingenious mind—
The warlike battlements, and piles so grand—
Cathedrals and temples that rise in every land—
Shall all his works, of which he makes his boast,
To oblivion sink, and be for ever lost?
Worlds and planets, all shall cease their race,
The sun be blotted out from mighty space;
The silvery moon, queen of nature's night,
In darkness quenched, no more shall give her light;
And our bright earth, man's native place below,
Shall be destroyed, and into nothing flow;
And every planet from their spheres shall fall—
Annihilation then shall be the fate of all
Shall the bright sun, with its illuming ray,
That through creation holds it mighty sway—
Shall it through space for ever cease to roll,
And darkness shade again creation's whole?
Shall the moon, with its sweet silvery light,
All orbs and planets, with their grandeur bright,
Be all annihilated with the world—
Into chaotic night again be hurled?
It must be so! God's word hath passed so great—
His imperial fiat hath decreed their fate.
Revolving ages cannot stay their doom—
Darkness again shall cover all with gloom.
Except the soul of man: for that is sure—
It shall through all eternity endure.

Time on that can ne'er exert its power,
To live for ever God hath given its dower,
And though all nature's rent from pole to pole,
And orbs, and planets vanish with the whole,
Yet shall the soul live free from earthly clod,
An emanation from Omnipotence—a part of God!

AN APPEAL TO THE BENEVOLENT.

Dear friends, how noble is it here
The poor and sick to help and cheer,
To bless those hearts who crave your aid,
Help needy souls now wanting bread.
Dreary they sit, their hearthstones cold,
In wretchedness both the young and old;
No food have they, nor table spread,
Their cupboard scant; with scarce a bed;
They're pining cold in sickening gloom—
All onward hastening to the tomb.

How many dwell sunk low in pain
Who call your aid and call in vain?
Poor wandering souls, who can provide
A home, but in our streets abide
In poverty, and cold despair—
O sympathise with kindly care!
While eyes are dimm'd with misery's tear,
Be your delight their hearts to cheer;
While you from hunger and from cold.
Are free; O cheer them with your gold!

May I know, whose hand and voice
Delight to make poor souls rejoice,
Who often on a winter's night,
Leaves comfort, home, and fireside bright;
And wend their way to misery's door,
Resolved to cheer the needy poor,
Who've passed the night in bitter cold.
What scenes of misery they behold:
Worn down with sickness, care, and grief,
They search them out, and bring relief.

These good Samaritans warm each heart,
Oft with the poor their comforts part,
They give them bread their want to stay,
And chase desponding fears away;
Then read aloud God's Holy Word,
And tell of Christ the sinners' Lord;
Oft by their bedsides kneel and pray—
That Jesus will His grace display;
The prayer of hope ascends to Heaven
That all their sins may be forgiven.

And those enjoy their own much more—
Who give as Christians to the poor;
The want and hunger they releive,
Will never cause their hearts to grieve.
Thrice noble those, who daily go
To visit souls in sin and woe;
Who labour in Christ's hallowed cause—
To proclaim the beauty of His laws.
O deign, Great God their works to bless,
Their efforts crown with full success.

Then when the glorious day shall come,
May these poor souls in Heaven their home
Rejoice, and raise salvation's song,
And swell the bright angelic throng;
And bless those hearts whose Christian love
Did lead them to the courts above.
And Christ shall say to all around,
To all who have His mansions found,
Come faithful of my Father's blest,
Rise! enter now, my promised rest.

LINES ON HOPE.

Hope on admidst the storms of life,
 Through all its comforts sever,
And valiant wage the battle strife—
 Hope on and hope for ever.
For if dark clouds to-day appear,
 The bright will dawn to-morrow;
The sunny beams may come to cheer,
 And drive away all sorrow.

For many a care and pain we know,
 While through life's path we tread;
And many a storm as on we go
 Will break around our head;
But if we look for help above,
 To have faith in God endeavour,
We may with confidence and love,
 Trust Him and hope for ever.

Let life's battle never daunt thee,
Be a warrior true and brave;
Show forth a hero's bravery,
In thy march towards the grave.
And when troubles fierce assail thee,
Meet them bravely, falter never;
Though spirits fail, press manfully,
Let hope still cheer your path for ever.

If life's fairest dreams have vanished,
Our friends departed, lost, and gone;
Yet let despair be ever banished,
Let us bravely still hope on.
For if friends and comforts perish,
And each pleasure from us sever,
This hope our hearts shall warmly cherish—
We shall dwell with them for ever.

And when death shall come to free us,
Then our souls shall not despair,
For God's angels shall surround us,
And us to Heaven in triumph bear;
And there our Saviour we shall see,
And sorrow then assail us never;
And happy through eternity,
Shall live and bless His name for ever.

AN ACROSTIC.

G reat and glorious beams of love,
E ach hour shine radiant from above,
O ur course of light to cheer and bless,
R eplete with heavenly tenderness;
G race—the rich balm to hearts oppress'd,
E ternal peace our promised rest.

J oyous and brilliant the rays that shine,
O 'er all creation's works divine;
S uch bliss is found in truth's sweet words,
E ach line inspired such calm affords,
P oor souls delight to hear their sounds,
H igh Heaven's best hope their life surrounds.

W ho can then despise the way
I n which our helpless fallen clay
L ooks upward towards the realms of light,
L amenting sin's distressful sight,
I n pious tranquil grateful mood,
A spiring towards the just and good?
M y friend, I grieve so oft to find,
S atan enthralls the human mind;
O may your efforts firm and bold,
N ew converts bring to Jesus' fold!

ON THE BIRTH-DAY OF HIS GRACE ALGERNON PERCY, THE MOST NOBLE THE DUKE OF NORTHUMBERLAND.

Most noble duke! accept this my humble lay,
As a tribute to commemorate thy natal day;
'Tis a vain effort to record thy worth,
Thy benevolence is so well known to all,
Who pray for blessings on thy head to fall—
Thy bounty has bless'd many on the earth.

"Long live his Grace!" we often hear them say,
"May he live long to bless us through each day,
Loved and revered by high and low around;
May every day his happiness increase,
His happiness and life be spent in peace,
And health's richest blessings to him abound."

May sere old age so gently o'er you steal,
While faith and hope the better world reveal,
That you scarce feel time's decaying hand.
In doing good may each day pass away,
A benefit to others through life's short day,
While on you journey to the better land.

May each sacred church endowed by you,
A blessing prove to thousands, Christians true,
Abiding frail mortals on their road to heaven;
And as they march to Canaan's happy land,
Pray heaven to bless the liberal donor's hand,
Who hath these sacred shrines so kindly given.

May each life-boat by you placed on our coast,
Be the means of rescue to a grateful host
Of Mariners, who but for them would drown.
They trembling watch the life-boat leave the shore,
To bring them save to land again once more,
Ask God the donor with His love to crown.

Then as the sailor's home meets each one's view,
The gift of a noble sailor good and true,
That when once landed they may happy be;
Their hard-earned wages there they will not waste,
But all the sweets of shore they there may taste,
And soon forget the dangers of the sea.

Onward your grace! may your life's every page
Bring blessings unto this, and coming age,
And prosperity have cause to bless your name.
Then as the sculptured tomb thy virtues show,
Thousands who read it will most surely know,
The record of truth showing forth thy name.

And when your grace's work on earth is done,
May the blest voice of God's beloved Son
Say, "Come, faithful servant of my Father blest,
Come, and receive the reward of all thy love,
And share the glories of the realms above,
In my everlasting kingdom now to rest."

There join in happiness with the countless throng,
And sing with the heavenly host the joyful song,
With angels, saints, sud seraphim bow down;
Clothed in spotless white with harps in hand,
And bid thee welcome to the heavenly land,
Exchanging earth's coronet for heaven's crown.

TO HER GRACE THE MOST NOBLE THE DUCHESS, ON THE DUKE'S BIRTHDAY.

Most noble Duchess, may this my humble lay
To greet thy loved husband on his natal day,
Win a welcome from thy generous breast.
Thou kind promoter of thy good lord's plans,
In every good work strengthening his hands,—
May God's choicest blessings ever on thee rest.

For self alone thou dost not care to live,
But the poor do of thy wealth receive,
Blessing with bounteous gifts the peasant's cot;
Thou dost delight to banish pains and cares,
For thou are raised many earnest prayers,
That thou through life may'st have a happy lot.

May heaven preserve thy life for many years,
Thy husband good, to comfort, soothe, and cheer,
And help him use the talents God has given;
Then when thou hast done with earth below,
May he call you home His joys to know,
And then to crown thee both in heaven.

THE DIGNITY OF LABOUR.

There's dignity in the labour of every working man,
His brave and sturdy hand employed in works of every plan
That science brings to light, or architect designs ;
He raises lofty palaces, and borrows in the mines :
The mechanics of our country, they are its greatest pride,
How vast their field of labour spreads, extending far and wide;
Their aid we cannot do without, they help in every way
To raise our country high in fame, in this our glorious day.
How useless would be capital without their active hand,
They break the soil, and sow the seed, and cultivate the land.
God bless their arduous efforts with Thy all-gracious smile,
And grant them all Thy comforts here, these hardy sons of toil.

Both bards and poets write and sing of dignity of race,
And heroes of the battle-field their pages often grace,
But seldom cast a thought towards the toiling busy throng,
Or make the sons of labour the burden of their song ;
But mine shall be the noble task, mine the good design,
To cheer the sons of labour with my poetic line—
To show forth their achievements throughout each passing day,
No difficulties daunt them or hardships o'er dismay ;
But on they plod with patience in every work they try
With persevering energy their talents to employ.
God bless their arduous efforts with Thy all-gracious smile,
And grant them all Thy comforts here, these hardy sons of toil.

The shepherd tends the pastures and labours for the sheep,
And brings them all into his fold in safety there to keep ;
With kindly zeal he watches them and makes them all his care,
And shears their fleeces when they're grown, for raiment that we wear ;
And then the weaver weaves it into cloth of richest hues,
To make our clothes the tailor then his hindiwork persues:
The Prince's costly flowing robe with elegance he'll form,
Or shape the labourer's working suit to keep him dry and warm ;
And thus they work together supplying clothes and food,
In mutual labour joining to work each other's good,
God bless their arduous efforts with Thy all-gracious smile,
And grant them all Thy comforts here, these hardy sons of toil.

'Tis labour moulds the brick and tile, and quarries out the slate.
Cuts out the stone for churches and other buildings great,
And monuments most lofty in gorgeous pride it rears,
Cathedrals most noble too each tapering spire appears,
The merchant's splendid residence with grand and stately domes,

Likewise the dwellings of the poor the cotters' humble homes;
Labour drives down deeply into the solid earth,
And brings to light the coal we burn, that hidden store of worth,
To feed our thousand fires and keep us from the cold,
And heat our many furnaces producing wealth untold.
God bless their arduous efforts with Thy all-gracious smile,
And grant them all Thy comforts here, these hardy sons of toil.

Labour smelts the iron ore, the silver, and the gold,
And turns them to a thousand shapes delightful to behold;
The ponderous, massive anchor, and shafts of mighty size,
With the powerful steam engine along the rail that flies,
With its strong and whirling wheels, its fine and threadlike wire,
Likewise the molten furnace with fiercely roaring fire;
Driving on so rapidly it draws its heavy load,
With luggage cars, and goods, and grain, along the iron road;
Goods despatched at wonderous speed, all by the power of steam,
What multitudes of blessings now to every quarter stream.
God bless their arduous efforts with Thy all-gracious smile,
And grant them all Thy comforts here, these hardy sons of toil.
Labour hews the lofty oak, and builds the noble ship,
And fits it up with sail or steam to bear it o'er the deep,
To wrestle with the tempest throughout its loudest roar,
To bear the produce of each clime towards our peaceful shore;
From India, the richest silks, with stores of corn and rice
And precious other merchandise, most costly in their price;
From China it conveys unto our shores the teas,
With all the choicest spices every one to please:
And sugar from the islands of the sunny distant west,
Supplying us with what we need of quality the best.
God bless their arduous efforts with Thy all-gracious smile,
And grant them all Thy comforts here, these hardy sons of toil.

Labour from the flint-stone produces brilliant glass,
And moulds it into ornaments that nothing can surpass;
And melts it into plates and sheets to admit the light,
Or places it in spectacles to improve the sight.
Labour spans the river, likewise the valley green,
And builds the massive bridge o'er the deepest rivers seen;
It hollows out the tunnel beneath the mountain strong,
While millions travel through it borne by steam along;
It links together by the rail the nations of the earth,
And brings to light in every place the hidden stores of worth.
God bless their arduous efforts with Thy all-gracious smile,
And grant them all Thy comforts here, these hardy sons of toil.

Labour sends its messages along the electric wire,
Coursing o'er its journey with wings of brilliant fire;
A mighty chain of network running through the world,
The grandest scheme that science ever yet unfurled;
'Tis labour takes the thought, commits it to the page,
Man's intellect to keep alive through every coming age,
The dignity of labour our time would fail to tell,
Yet shall its daily triumphs our history's pages swell,
And monuments of genius reared by labour stand,
As ornaments and blessings around our native land.
God bless their arduous efforts with Thy all-gracious smile,
And grant them all Thy comforts here, these hardy sons of toil.

ON THE DEATH OF AGNES PEARSON.

She has gone to her rest by bright angels surrounded,
All tears from her eyes are banished and gone;
All sorrow is vanished that here much abounded,
Now bright is her robe, and radiant her crown.

She has joined the blest band who proved here victorious,
Through much tribulation and sorrow they came;
Now, free from all trials with the spirit made glorious,
She rejoices for ever through the blood of the Lamb.

No more her fond heart shall with sorrow be swelling,
No more shall her eyes be with tears dimmed again;
She has gained the bright mansions, and now she is dwelling,
With her Saviour for ever in heaven's bright plain.

Then let us rejoice that her crown was gained early,
Removed from earth soon and all sorrows to come;
Let us think of her waiting at the gates bright and pearly,
To welcome her friends to their heavenly home.

COLEORTON HALL, THE SEAT OF SIR GEORGE BEAUMONT.

Oh, lovely Coleorton! thy fine hall is seen,
Midst glowing rich verdue and woodlands so green;
Here nature shines lovely in scenery so bright,
That fills each beholder with nameless delight.
Here bloom the rich flowers, their blossoms so neat,
The air around filled with their odours so sweet;
New beauties each moment arise into birth,
It seems like a paradise here upon earth.

The sun now illumes with its radiant light,
All tinged are the clouds so golden and bright;
How merrily carols the bird's cheerful voice,
All nature in harmony seems to rejoice,
The sky a rich arch of celestial blue,
As the bright orb of day his brilliant rays threw.
Variegating each object, each landscape, and flower,
With gorgeous hues by its dazzling power.

Gaze whither we will o'er mountain or plain,
O'er hill or o'er valley, we'd fain gaze again;
Each scene that we view seems again to invite,
And as we behold them increase our delight.
Coleorton was decked like a lovely young bride,
Majestic and grand in its glory and pride;
So Ancient, so fine, no dwelling for gloom,
Amidst the most choice and richest perfume.

The roses so gay with their bright crimson hue,
All floral creation so fair to the view;
The fruit rich and luscious inviting the taste,
With clusters of grapes the hothouse was graced;
Competition or rivals they seemed to defy,
In colour so splendid, in flavour so high,
There's nought could surpass them, so rich and so fine,
As they gracefully drooped from each bearing vine

At Coleorton we tread upon high classic ground,
And view the mementoes displayed here around,
Of men of great genius who in their own day
O'er the mind of mankind held wonderful sway.
With Wordsworth the poet we here live again,
And wander with him o'er the flower-studded plain;
We view the fine trees as stately they stand,
Planted many years since by the Poet's own hand.

If we go on to Wordsworth's rock sculptur'd seat.
What celebrities of fame there often did meet—
Mrs. Siddons, the actress, who played well her parts
So much as to please all ears and all hearts,
With Coleridge and Hastings who here we may find,
Once met and disclosed to each other his mind;
Whilst Wilkie and Constable painted each scene
Of the loveliest picture that ever was seen.

Here Reynolds the painter lies silent and low,
At his monument here we respectfully bow ;
And the tribute we read of his worth from a friend—
Sir George Beaumont, the author, by him it was penned—
Who with warm kindly feelings here gushing forth,
This tribute hath left of his genius and worth ;
And here midst the lime trees' silent still shade,
Uprears the stone pillar by his friendship made.

And here midst the waving trees' shady green bowers;
On all sides surrounded with fragrant flowers,
Sir Walter Scott here mediated, and wrote
His Ivanhoe, famed as a great work of note
He wrote here of knights all fierce for the fray,
Near this place they would meet in battle array,
And urge on their steeds to the tournament field,
Determined to conquer but never to yield.

Here is Shakespeare's bust ! no praises of mine
Can add to his fame that ever will shine ;
And Michael Angelo, that sculptor of fame,
Whose works seem to throw o' a life-breathing flame.
And Raphael the painter, whose exquisite art,
Sent a mirror of nature direct to the heart ;
These to the memory such emotions will give,
That each seems again among us to live.

Though great are the beauties that here doth abound.
'Tis very well known the whole country round,
The Hall is the son's of a fine noble race,
Whose father the pages of history grace.
One was with Exmouth in front of Algiers,
His ship into action undaunted he steers ;
By his courage so brave on the boisterous main,
He greately assisted the victory to gain.

Another, whose paintings the people oft view
As they traverse the National Gallery through;
Of the fine arts a patron, to the poet a friend,
His assistance was ever most ready to lend;
To genius distress'd in the time of their need,
A friend he was always—a friend too indeed;
A genius himself on the bright scroll of fame,
He rich laurels earned, and a much honoured name.

Giver of all good, let Thy gifts now abound,
About this fine mansion let peace still be found;
Let Thy choicest love on its inmates e'er rest
In blessings of others may be doubly blest.
May peace, joy, and plenty their portion be here,
Every blessing attend them, life's pathway to cheer;
May they ever live in their people's love,
Till called by God to His blest home above.

THE DYING CHRISTIAN.

The sun that sinks in the far distant west.
Tinting the sky with golden radiance fired;
Fit emblem of the dying Christian blest,
Who laboured for Christ, and in His cause expired.

Go visit his room, see life ebbing out,
With sickness his powers enfeebled decay;
While strong in the faith, I hear him now shout—
"The victory's won, I am soaring away!"

Come, infidels, come, and see one Christian die;
What safety could he now find in your creed?
If now he was from his loved Lord to fly,
Would it support him in death's hour of need?

I have heard of infidels when in death's grasp,
Crying to Christ with despair in their sight;
But never of Christians returning to clasp
Infidelity in his life's latest flight.

But Christian sought truth in God's blessed book,
And searched for treasures in that glorious mine!
The Holy Spirit's light for guidance he took
To unveil the gems in the Volume divine.

Soon he found gems and pearls of greatest price,
Which made him rejoice in that glorious plan—
A full salvation through the blood of Christ,
Given to fallen degenerate man.

The miner digs in the bowels of the earth,
Hard he labours to find the bright precious gem;
Others for gold dig, as though nothing was worth
A thought besiees it,—it is all to them.

There is joy that fills the Christian's warm breast,
Gold could not purchase with its mighty power—
An udying peace, a sweet hallowed rest.—
Gold is as nought to the true Christian mower.

Though oft the good man in the fire is sore tried,
The tempter's fierce darts oft at him are thrown;
The foe hath had him down; but Christian hath cried,
"Rejoice not Satan! Christ his murcy hath shown."

And then in powerful prayer he hath sought
The precious blood that cleanse from all sin,
That wondrous fountain Christ the Lamb hath brought
From heaven, to pardon and make pure within.

There was a time he ran the giddy round,
And pleasure he sought in this sinful earth;
But in this broken vase no joys hath he found,
But in repentance found his second birth.

And when the love of Christ thus filleth the heart,
How earnest to fill the Shepherd's pure fold;
As a good faithful preacher performing his part,
In saving souls unpurchased by gold.

And after living years threescore and ten,
And age with hoary locks hath whitened his brow,
Both in and out of season still labouring then,
Anxious his fellow men his Saviour should know.

Oh glorious warrior! who hath borne the Cross,
The fight of faith fought to serve thy great King,
And counted all the earthly things as but dross,
That thou might'est sinners to thy Saviour bring.

But there's a heavenly voice that beckons him higher.
"Come, and receive the reward for thy toil!"
He hears the solemn call, his heart is on fire,
He longs to behold his sweet Saviour's smile.

Look upward now, the promised land is in view,
That happy realm, the Christian's beauteous home;
The mansions tho Lord hath purchased for you,
And you calls to his rest—" My loved one come!

And what a holy influence filleth the place,
It seems none other than the gate of heaven.
Where Jesus' standard-bearer endeth his race,
Conquering grim death, this grace by Jesus given.

The pearly gates of heaven are al opened wide,
To welcome this true heir of glory in there;
See, angels' pinions wait at his bedside,
To waft away the valiant pilgrim of prayer.

Angels convey him to that heavenly home,
And saints and seraphs welcome him to bliss;
All heaven is moved to see the good man come,
O wondrous glory! toils that end like this!

But O! what form is that now meets his view,
On which he gazes with such joyous glee?
I know him now, Jesus who suffered for you,
And shows His honoured scars received for me.

I see the mark upon that honoured brow,
Where thorns were placed, that I might wear a crown;
The side they pierced, the hands and feet see now,
In rapture lost at His feet I fall down.

And now we think of Christian walking there,
In streets of gold like brilliant burnished glass;
And hear him say, 'Enough of bliss is here,
To make amends for all I had to pass"

And then he sees som there that died before,
Sharing that joy in that blest world so bright,
To whome he preached on earth, and loved more
Than all earth's pleasuresthat allured the sight.

And then he looks upon himself and says,
"Can this be me, with harp and crown of gold,—
Me wtih this robe of white that ne'er decays?
What wondrous glory now my eyes behold!

And as he gazes on his Saviour King,
He joins the exultant song with saints above;
And there with the Redeemer will ever sing,
Loud hallelujahs for redeeming love.

ON THE BOUNTIFUL HARVEST OF 1858.

O bounteous Donor! whose kind goodness sends
  The plenteous harvest of bright golden grain,
That staple food upon which life depends
  Waves rich in plenty over dale, and plain.

Here every want the soil's best fruit supplies,
  While Ceres holds her rich and glorious reign,
Man's labour cheers and every pain defies,
  To cheer his heart, and banish all his pain.

'Mid rich fruitful boughs Pomona is found,
  Bedecked with the season's rich store,
To clothe with sweet plenty fair England's ground,
  On the husbandman blessings to prour.

O, how shall my pencil pourtray the rich space,
Or picture our now smiling lands;
Nature's richest dress is seen in each place,
Each sheaf like a gem of gold stands.

With plenty our granaries soon shall be stored,
And the crops that our fields now adorn,
Shall form in our barns a luxuriant hoard
Of ripe and well harvested corn.

Kind nature's great bounty's a sacred theme,
That our eyes with delight may survey;
As we offer our thanks to the Author Supreme,
For the goodness He loves to display.

Can e'er it be found that thus favoured man,
On whom all these bounties shower down,
With frozen cold hearts all these blessings will scan,
And fail the Benefactor to own?

Gratitude will forbid that such things should e'er be,
But together all mankind shall join
To shout loud the praise of the Great Giver free,
Glorifying the Almighty divine.

How pleasing are those joyous sounds
That fall upon the ear,
When pleasure's voice our path surrounds,
And happy hearts are near ;
When mirth and laughter fill the air,
And naught their peace alloys ;
Whilst all seem summer, bright and fair,
With merry little boys.

It sends a pleasure through my mind
To hear each hearty shout
Amidst the ills of life we find,
And anxious hours of doubt ;
And takes us back, again we see,
With all their mirth and noise,
The time returned once more when we
Were merry little boys.

No stoic e'er can pass unmoved,
For memory still we cling
Around the childhood's home he loved,
And bygone pleasures bring :
I love to hear the laughter free,
Their frolics and their joys,
And all the happy pleasures see
Of merry litt'e boys.

The churl may bluster and complain,
  Who feels no kindly flame,
Who treats all pleasure with disdain,
  And scoffs at childhood's name;
The child-like mind displays the man,
  Whom romping ne'er annoys,
Who loves to join the happy van
  Of merry little boys.

LINES ON THE RE-OPENING OF SOUTHWARK CHAPEL, AFTER REPAIR.

What sounds are those that greet my ear,
  As on the air they hallowed rise—
In notes of praise and earnest prayer,
  In anthems loud ascend the skies?

From Southwark Chapel once again,
  Arise the grateful joyous song;
Its members join in thankful strain,
  And mingle with the heavenly throng.

From grateful hearts and songs of praise
  Ascend from this fine house of God;
With holy joy His children raise
  Love's tribute in that blest abode.

With one accord His people kneel,
  United to each other there;
The Holy Spirit now they feel,
  God hears and answers to their prayer.

They've proved like Jacob did of old,
  To them the gate of Heaven was nigh:
Whilst G[illegible] in His love [illegible],
  And loud they sing His praise with joy.

O God! we humbly Thee adore,
  Thou'st loved us in our low estate;
Help us to love and serve Thee more,—
  Thy love to us we own is great.

What hallowed feelings seem to swell,
  Weave round our hearts, as now we view
The dust of those we bid farewell,
  Till our intercourse in heaven renew.

A testimony they've left here,
  That they through faith the victory won;
Let's follow them to that blest sphere,
  The victory gained through God's own Son.

Full many here could show the place
  Where first they shook to hear the Word;
They turned at once and sought God's face,
  And mercy through the Atoning Blood.

While wrestling in the house of prayer,
  In earnest sought to be forgiven;
They met their blessed Saviour there,
  Forgave them all, as heirs of Heaven.

Affection fond cling round this place,
  Where our fathers prayed with holy love;
Ebenezers here with joy we'll raise,
  Till we join them in that heaven above.

May many sons and daughters there
  To God come while this temple stands;
His people join, Christ's standard bear,
  Join after death the heavenly bands

LINES ON SABBATH SCHOOLS.

Come to the Sabbath School, children—we seek you ;
Come, for the Saviour hath died you to rescue ;
Come to the shepherd for comfort and peace,
　　Children press forward the battle is raging,
　　Hoist up the blest banner of Christ and His cross,
　　Join with the noble host now who are waging
　　War with all Satan's host, causing his loss.

Love to dear children He showed while on earth,
Laid His hands on their heads, well knowing their worth ;
Rebuked those who hindered their coming to Him,
And His heavenly blessings He gave unto them.
　　　　Children press forward &c.

Range on Immanuel's side, hell's power defy,
Enlist all you can and with each other vie ;
Give Him your early days, lambs of His fold,
Join His blest church before you grow old.
　　　　Children press forward &c.

Fear not the contest, God is your friend,
Sure victory must your progress attend ;
His power protects, He His children will save,
Enlist, then, for Christ in the ranks of the brave.
　　　　Children press forward &c.

Come then, dear children, your love to Him show ;
Accept of His love, it will make your hearts glow ;
Fight under His standard, He died you to save,
And victory through Christ you surely shall have.
　　　　Children press forward &c.

ON THE DEATH OF GEORGE J. WILLIAMSON,

AGED EIGHTEEN MONTHS.

Another lovely boy is snatched away,
Leaving his sorrowing friends to mourn him here;
Angels the innocent did safe convey,
To a far brighter—a celestial sphere.

How many lovely flowers thus early come
Into existence, nipped in the opening bud,
Seem born to glad their parents' hearts and home,
But death is sent to call them to their God.

The parents watch with ever anxious cares,
With fondest love their infant son they view:
Son of his father's hopes, his mother's cares,
How beautiful to see such love so true.

But thoughts of one loved so from his birth,
Will venture in and mark his mother's brow;
She thinks of his sweet dear caress and mirth,
Re-calling thoughts of anguish even now.

The time of infancy, when once he leant
Against her breast, or sat upon her knee,
And lisped his little prayer, while down she bent
Her ear to list with kindest sympathy.

There is no love like a dear mother's love,
  Throughout the earth a greater love's not known;
The infant, nestling like some gentle dove
  Upon his mother's breast, lies calmly down.

Yea, language fails with all its powers sublime,
  To express the feelings of the mother's mind,
As watching o'er her child she sees the time
  When in the grave an early rest he'll find.

How hard it seems for death to take away
  The infant voice that was her happiness;
She felt immensely rich, without alloy,
  When to her heart she could her dear boy press.

Like to some beauteous flow'ret filled with dew,
  Was this dear boy; short with us was his stay;
Death cropped the faultless bloom when fresh and new,
  And called this lovely one to heaven away.

Then, father, mourn not your departed child;
  Fond mother, dry your tears and weep no more;
O, calm your grief by resignation mild—
  Your son is rich, he might have here been poor.

Thus link by link the earthly chain is broken,
  And friends and children vanish from our sight,
And time, like some kind monitor hath spoken—
  "Get ready for those glorious realms of light."

And soon you'll leave too this terrestial ball,
  And haste to meet the young immortal there,
Where grief and sorrow are not know at all,
  But happiness supreme dispels all care.

Could you behold him in that better land,
  Arrayed in white, with golden harp and crown,
With cherubim and angels see him stand
  For ever blest,—you could not wish him down.

The harp he strikes the sounding notes vibrate,
  He's free from sickness now, and restless pain;
Sorrow is banished from that realm so great,—
  He sings with rapture in the heavenly train.

LINES ON DR. JABEZ BUNTING,

ONE OF THE GREATEST CHAMPIONS OF METHODISM AND MISSIONARY ENTERPRISE.

Descend, poetic muse, with hallowed fire,
  Into my heart with sacred love descend;
Help me with judgment sound to strike my lyre
  In praise to him, the Wesleyans' true friend.

'Tis Jabez Bunting—noble-minded man,
  The friend of all who truly loved our Lord;
Well worked he in the Methodistic plan,
  And well therewith did his pure life accord.

In freedom's cause he lifted up his voice,
  That sacred source whence all rich blessings flow,
To free the slave and make his heart rejoice,
  Employed his time and labour while below.

Around his brow the wreath of pious fame
  Shall like a beauteous evergreen be placed,
And many souls shall bless his honoured name,
  And think of him who every virtue graced.

The record now is borne away on high,
How hard he for his sacred Master toiled,
With heavenly love and warmest sympathy,
And loving-kindness like a little child.

To such a man 'tis real joy to raise
The voice of friendship, so that it may sound
A grateful tribute in this hero's praise,
Who ever in his Master's work was found.

His highest joy to elevate mankind,
With judgment sound and earnest love sincere;
With energetic zeal and thought refined,
The good of all he sought while dwelling here.

The fight of faith he manfully hath fought,
And conquered boldly with his valiant heart;
Christ's honour conscientiously he sought,
And when called hence was ready to depart.

Pastor and friend, thy loss we all deplore,
The Lord on high beheld thy truth and love;
Thou art not dead, but only gone before,
And now art blest eternally above.

Taught by thy life may we from sin refrain,
And honoured Him who took thee to that shore,
And grateful own that Christ alone is gain,
Till life is past and sin can stain no more.

Shall we then mourn when God's great heroes die—
Shall naught but sorrow fill the tender heart—
Shall only tears be seen, and heard the sigh—
When from such honoured ones we're forced to part?

Forbid it, faith ! though memory holds them dear,
And shrines their image fondly in our breast,
We should not mourn, although we drop a tear,
For they have gained the everlasting rest.

This our Elijah is gone forth on high,
And passed the bourne that leaves the world behind,
To th' blest abode where sin and sorrow die,
And love, and peace, and holy joy's entwined.

The righteous crown he's summoned to receive,
The glorious crown that ne'er shall fade away,
Laid by those for who in their Lord believe,
In that blest world where there is no decay.

But, praise to God ! his mantle falls on those
Who still are left, in zeal to labour here,
Who the blessed portion of the spirit chose,
To keep them in the cause of Christ so dear.

We see not now his well beloved face,
But still rejoice with holy joy to know,
He has gone home to that delightful place,
Where there is neither grief, nor pain, nor woe.

But still there stands the same, his old arm chair,
And the Holy Bible which he used to read,
Where oft has risen his spirit's earnest prayer
For help to come from God in greatest need.

We can no longer hear his well-known voice,
Now heard amidst the joyous host of heaven,
For with that noble throng he doth rejoice,
In the bright mansion that his Lord hath given.

His mortal frame will very soon decay,
Soon from the bones the withering flesh must sever;
But the last trump shall call to glorious day,
Where th' immortal soul shall bloom for ever.

O, what would life and all its joys be worth,
If perished here the body and the soul;
If blank annihilation reigned henceforth,
And foul corruption seized upon the whole?

Thanks to our Father, such is not the case—
The immortal spirit boldly death defies;
The changeful body, in that narrow place,
When we give up the spirit, only dies.

Though "Tempus Fugit" s' stamped on all below,
And the swift minutes from us quickly fly,
Yet loving God we may rejoice to know,
He has prepared eternal homes on high.

Faith whispers to our souls that we shall rise,
And soon our hearts with holy joy shall glow;
The starry crown shall gain, O, glorious prize!
Unfailing bliss on us shall God bestow.

Then let that faith be ours, that scatters wide
All fear or doubt of Jesus whom we love;
For soon the veil between He'll draw aside,
And saints shall view their glorious home above.

And so, although we deeply mourn his loss,
And sleeps his body in its earthly bed;
As Christ hath conquered death upon the Cross,
We are assured his spirit is not dead.

No, he has only gone awhile before,
And looks down from his blest abode above,
On those whose minds he filled with gospel store,
To see if they still worked with God in love.

O, what would he now say to those still left,
Could but his voice speak to us from the sky;
How would he urge them to improve each gift.
By winning souls each day for Christ on high.

How would he urge to labour in the cause.
And the pure seed of Gospel truth now sow;
To pluck from ruin those who break God's laws,
For whom the Saviour suffered while below.

And if in faith they sow the holy seed,
O may it e'er a hundredfold bring forth,
Of souls from whom in mercy Christ did bleed,
That priceles are, beyond all things on earth.

And soon the ear shall hear the gladdening sound,
"Well done, thou servant true, thou faithful friend:
With Bunting come, and at thy home be crowned,
Where rest, and joy, and glory ne'er shall end."

LINES ON A MISER.

What form is that which walks along,
With head bent down amidst the throng,
And shuns each gaze he meets,
Of busy men who're labouring on,
From rising moon to setting sun,
At work in crowded Streets?

What anxious cares seem on his face,
No joys are in his earthly race,
He lives to hoard up gold.
'Tis the miser—yes, that wretched elf,
Who thinks of no one but himself,
And want will not behold.

The starving child he passes by,
Holds out her hand in vain to try
To move his heart of stone
He passes on, heeds not her prayer,
Although in accents of despair,
Nor e'en her dying groan.

The blind appears with hat in hand,
And begs an alms where he may stand;
He's dead to each appeal;
Dead to all sense of others' woe,
And when from hence is forced to go,
No friends around him kneel.

Once feasted Dives in regal state,
Who spurned the beggar at his gate
Denied the crumbs that fell.
How soon his days of joy were past,
And from his splendour he was cast
To tortures low in hell.

And there in torment lift his eyes,
And Lazarus saw above the skies,
On Abraham's bosom lay;
"O Father Abraham, Lazarus send,
In water to dip his finger end,
And cool my tongue I pray."

But Abraham told him when on earth,
Of good things he'd received from birth,
  And Lazarus nought but bad;
No more the dogs shall lick his sores,
No more he'll lie at rich men's doors,
  His heart is now made glad.

Ye tyrants! why oppress the poor,
And load them with such burdens sore,
  And grind them in the dust?
The reckoning day must surely come,
And vengance sure will be your doom,
  With all your mammon's lust.

O what in history shall be said
Of one who ne'er would lend his aid,
  Or fellows' woes assuage;
Methinks his history soon is told,
There on his tombstone you'll behold,
  His date of birth and age.

A wretched tale he leaves behind—
Likewise the curse of all mankind,
  That near around him live.
Doing good's a joy he never knew,
And passed his life in mis'ry too,
  No heart had he to give.

And when he stands at the Judge's bar,
His trembling soul will fly afar,
  And shun his Maker's frown.
Mercy from God he can't expect,
The poor's appeal he did reject,
  And ne'er had mercy shown.

Many, once poor, will then receive
The welcome glad, "Come ye and live
With your Eternal King;
You had but little when below,
But still with that did mercy show,
Which caused sad hearts to sing."

But O! a different sound you'll hear,
As you stand before the Judge severe;
"Depart to endless fire,
With fallen angels there to be,
In racking pain eternally,
Your soul will ne'er expire."

If I have, reader, told thy case,
Thank God thou art not in that place,
There's time still to repent.
O, let the horrors of that state,
Reform thy heart before too late,
Thy life be wholly spent.

O turn at once, put off no more,
God's Holy Spirit; and adore
His wondrous saving love.
Though hard thou'st been, now mercy show,
And humbly walk with God below,
That thou may'st rest above.

"PRAY WITHOUT CEASING."

What is prayer? 'tis the soul's desiring:
It is the spirit's commune rare,
In wishes to our God aspiring,—
A tear is oft the loveliest prayer.

What is prayer? 'tis converse with Heaven;
Wings to soar from earth away;
Most precious boon to mortals given;
Christ charged us all to watch and pray.

Oft hath grief my heart been rending,
For it knew not what to say;
Mind strove to rise, but swift descending,
I groaned to feel I could not pray.

But my trembling soul that fluttered,
Dark, disconsolate, dismayed,
O'ercame and conquered as it uttered,
For in that sharp deep groan it prayed.

Then Satan fled, the Spirit entered,
Gloom and doubt were chased away;
And all my soul on Christ was centred—
Then 'twas pleasing work to pray.

Thus praying, we resist the devil,
Near praying breath he cannot stay:
It keeps and guards the soul from evil—
O think on this and ever pray.

When vain and worldly cold professors
With stumbling blocks shall bar thy way,
Heed not their words—become professors,
But look to Jesus—watch and pray.

In him feel all your consolation,
Look up to Him to clear thy way;
Select Him for your great salvation,
Love to go through Him to pray.

When in waves of sorrow sinking,
When your brightest hopes decay,
Still on former mercies thinking,
In spite of feelings strive to pray.

Oft in hours of fierce temptation
  Satan triumphs, faith gives way,
Search what cause for condemnation,
  Look to Christ, believe and pray.

When a selfish world is frowning,
  When its threats would cause dismay,
And its cares your thoughts are drowning,
  Close your hearts to all and pray;
When near death your fabric sinking,
  The spirit parting from the clay;
When you feel life's bowl is breaking,
  Oh in that solemn moment pray.

LINES ON THE BIBLE.

Blest book divine! of old wert thou inspired,
  A light to all in each succeeding age;
With holy love thy sacred lines are fired,
  And sacred wisdom fills thy heavenly page.

His comfort from thee every Christian draws,
  And steers through life by thy unerring chart:
Thrice happy they who keep thy happy laws,
  And love their Maker with a perfect heart.

Though infidels, a fable they may call—
  A priestly fabrication made for gain;
If it were so, it must be clear to all
  Its rules are good— who can of them complain?

Surely they'll own that men who could devise
  A book for others with so good a plan,
Must beyond all have been men truly wise,
  And general benefactors been to man.

If men are only to be known by fruits,
  Where can the infidel, so boastful, show
The benefit to man of his pursuits?—
  What has he done to lessen human woe?

But Christianity may take its stand,
  For the great blessing it has ever been:
Its institutions ornament our land,
  And homes of mercy everywhere are seen.

Then ought not Christians, who feel fully sure
  It is God's word, to save and bless the land,
Hardships for it like soldiers good endure,
  And of the cross of Christ true champions stand!

Christ's colours nail they boldly to their mast,
  And of their Saviour never be ashamed,
But fight His battles long as life shall last,
  And not draw back till victory is gained.

If we pursue the Bible's straight good way,
  Traced by the loving hand of mercy there,
Rugged the road may be, but truth's bright ray
  Our path of life is ever sure to cheer.

Though dark and narrow oft that pathway be,
  If faithful we victorious shall prove
Unto the end, when we shall surely see
  All was directed by our God through love.

Then let us nobely hold our course and brave
  The world's temptations, every snare and frown,
And never strike our colours till the grave
  Bring colours, mast and hull together down.

POPE DAY.

'Twas pope day, 'twas pope day, huzza! for its mirth,
    Was the wildest our hearts ever knew,
And though but a mite to the great ones of earth,
Was the trifle we owned, yet, 'twas of great worth;
To joy unalloyed in our young hearts gave birth,
    For our sorrows were short-lived and few.

We paused not to ask why so named was the day,
    Nor what our dead idol pourtrayed,
'Twas joy as we puffed at the noisy old horn,
And shouted our speech, with a yelling huzza,
At some well-known door in our ogred array,
    Till our toils by their hands were repaid.

The rich and the poor assembled to gaze,
    The child and the grey-hair'd old man;
As the fiery-mounted serpent illumined the haze,
Or the wild hissing rocket sped forth in its blaze
To toy with the clouds, and lend them its rays,
    Our glorious pastime to scan

What was honour to us and the garland of fame,
    Or the glittering garments of pride,
The deeds of the hero or patriot name?
Our old swords, like their owners, discarded in shame,
Held a charm o'er our hearts in young life's giddy game.
    Worth the world and its baubles beside.

And where are those forms whose hearts with mine own
    Hail this day as their flood-tide of joy,
And know not the anguish which gnawed to the bone
In the bosoms of those who battled alone
For us in life's conflict, uncheered and unknown,
    While we danced round our ogred toy?

O that time had not changed, and the curtain where care
    Hid its lean haggard form, ne'er been drawn,
To tempt our young hearts, and lure with the glare
Of its poor painted pleasures, each armed with a snare.
By want, grief, misfortune, or gloomy despair,
    All strangers to boyhood's loved morn.

And what are the great ones of earth but the boys?
    They toil for the charms of a day,
To build them an idol a breath may destroy,
And gloat with delight o'er their poor tinsel toy,
Which to-morrow some other as a curse may employ
    To embitter life's dark checquered way.

LINES TO THE REV. R. M. WILCOX,

ON HIS LEAVING SOUTHWARK CIRCUIT, AFTER A STAY OF THREE YEARS.

Beloved Pastor! must we now say adieu?
Have three years gone, for ever passed away,
That each must take a fond farewell of you,
And with us now you can no longer stay?
It must be so: the rapid flight of time
Compels us now to breathe the word farewell;
Though we at your removal may repine,
For you our hearts with pure affection swell.

But there are scenes that memory brings to view,
Scenes on which the mind will love to rest;
Of holy hours we've oft enjoyed with you,
In which our spirits have been greatly blest.
And there are those who'll one day join the throng,
Through arduous labours you have had while here,
Shall raise their voices in th' immortal song,
With blood-washed saints they shall in Heaven appear.

With grateful hearts we have our offering brought,
To record our sense and honour of your worth;
But to souls compared it is a thing of nought,—
Souls you have won for Christ while here on earth.
Our prayers for you, they shall to heaven ascend,
A blessing to each circuit may you prove;
Where'er you go our blessings shall attend,
For God to bless you with almighty love.

And may you, by His Holy Spirit's sway
With earnest loving zeal perform your part,
Upraising mankind in your life's short day,
Directing Heaven-ward many a drooping heart.

May God's best blessing ever on you flow,
And in His Church may you have great success,
Spend many a year of usefulness below,
And thousands more have cause your name to bless.

Though other scenes your labours now invite,
And other flocks require your watchful care;
Yet Southwark's flock will oft think with delight,
Of your love to them, your zeal and earnest prayer.
And when your labours here on earth are o'er,
And God shall call you to your heavenly rest,
May all your flocks join with you on that shore,
And with your Saviour evermore be blest.

LINES ON THE PAST, PRESENT, AND FUTURE.

I asked the aged man, whose head is bald and grey.
Whose fading form is bent with hoary age,
About his time for ever passed away,
And what concerns should most his life engage?

He parts aside his snowy whitened locks,
And mildly, earnestly looks in my face,
And says; "If you would wish to shun the rocks
That often bring to others sad disgrace.

You must avoid the evil paths of sin,
And in your own strength never put your trust;
But trust in God, and in this earthly scene
Resolve in all things to be true and just.

Let all your actions be correct and good.
To bear reflection, chaste as morning dew,
As you would wish they should be if they stood
In heaven's pure light before you in full view.

And like a traveller take the unerring chart
  Of God's most holy word—that heavenly guide—
And bind its noble precepts to your heart,
  And from its laws of truth ne'er turn aside.

Have faith in Christ, and follow after those
  Who now possess the glorious promised land;
They while on earth had very many woes,
  But now before His throne they happy stand.

If called to suffer while on earth below,
  With patience suffer—'tis God's holy plan
The vanity of earthly things to show,
  Make you a good, a holy happy man.

But do not rush along life's road to meet
  Troubles that haply ne'er may come to you;
But fight life's battles like a man discreet,
  And conquer sin and keep thy end in view,

Like Moses try and mount to Pisgah's top,
  And there by faith behold the promised land,
And never in your heavenly progress stop,
  Till near Christ's throne you ever take your stand."

I asked the young man in the prime of life,
  Whose hardy vigorous frame and healthy look,
Seemed truly formed for every pleasure rife,
  And he bade proud defiance to the Book.

That speaks of earthly changes and his end,
  And tells him time will quickly pass away;
He looks not at it as a faithful friend,
  Because it warns him life's joys all decay.

With vigorour step he seems to spurn the foe,
  That steals on man unknown and unperceived ;
And seldom thinks of Death who deals the blow,
  Glad by a treacherous world to be deceived.

As health sits glowing on his manly brow,
  I ask him what should best my life engage ;
"Enjoy," says he, "life's pleasures here and now,
  And leave all serious thoughts for riper age.

'Quaff the o'erflowing bowl of ruby wine,
  And join the merry dance and festive throng,
With jocund mirth in the gay circle join,
  And sing with them the bacchanalian song.

Let all your life be like the flowers in May,
  That deck the earth and beautify the spring—
Like a fair garland with its hues so gay,
  For this to you will present pleasure bring."

I turn, and ask the future if in truth
  It can reveal aught good that I have done ?
Or will it prove I have misspent my youth,
  When for all this there must a judgment come ?

And as a part of time's already gone,
  On me bestow as sojourner below,
Whether that future bids me to atone,
  Nor trifle longer with the subtle foe ?

He says, "Put off ; for time enough there's yet,
  You can repent and seek for mercy here ;"
Satan, depart ! me you shall never get ;
  Come Saviour, then, and be for ever near.

Come Thou, and guide my erring feet that stray
  Away from paths of righteousness and truth ;
O Thou who art the light, the truth, the way,
  Lead me aright and guide my early youth !

Thou glorious pattern of what man should be,
  Direct my steps and path with love divine
Help me with humble love to follow Thee,
  And all my lifetime in Thy lustre shine.

When old age comes, Thou wilt not me forsake,
  Nor let the King of Terrors me affright ;
But angels send my happy soul to take,
  Ever with Thee to live in realms of light.

ON THE WORLDLY MAN OF BUSINESS.

Can it be fully true what preachers say,
That life is but a probationary day,
  Given for trial to each mortal here ;
And that each moment spent will surely prove
Great with importance while on earth we move,
  To fit our souls for an eternal sphere ?

And do the Holy Scriptures tell the truth—
Man's heart is evil ev'en from earliest youth,
  And only tends to lead his feet astray ?
He bows to mammon as to a sacred shrine,
Only for riches does his heart incline,
  For these he labours hard both night and day.

Unheeded is reason's voice, his head and brain
Are full of plans how he can get most gain,
  And thinks but little of the end of life.
For his soul's safety seemeth not to care,
And if perchance he utters words of prayer,
  'Tis for more gains in this our worldly strife.

It is a fearful thought, how chained to earth.
Are men of business, while their souls are worth
 More riches far than this old world can buy;
And never seem they conscious of their state,
Unless o'ertaken by afflictions great,
 Or told by their physician they must die.

Then, O how vain do all their gains appear,
When on a sick bed laid they're made to bear
 The constant racking pain, the throbbing brow.
The pearl of greatest price they have despised,
Have quenched the Spirit and have never prized
 The Gospel, they'd give all they have for now.

The mart and the exchange engrossed each thought.
With studious care his goods were ever bought.
 His greatest joy has been to store up wealth;
And while he made it thus his greatest care,
Each faculty of mind it would ensnare,
 Alike regardless of his ease or wealth

O man of business! what would it be to thee
If thou couldest gain the world, or owner be—
 Or part, thou ne'er could'st gain the whole,—
And found, when all thy earthly race was run,
Thou hast a shadow grasped and wert undone,
 And lost for ever thy immortal soul?

Dear reader, have I here described thy case?
If so, look up, I pray thee, now for grace
 Ere 'tis too late, and ere God's Spirit leaves,
Saying, "He is to idols joined, let him alone,
In him no more shall Jesus' blood atone,
 Who often thus the Holy Spirit grieves."

I cannot think of a more fearful state,
Then he who on his death-bed cries too late,
"I've trifled all my precious life away;
For when God called and warned I would not hear,
And now He grieves, and sorrows for my fear;
My heart is hard, I cannot, cannot pray."

It is a fearful thing God's love to grieve,
And all our life without its influence live:
God surely will in time give up that man.
Turn sinner, turn, His mercy now implore.
Strive ne'er to grieve His Holy Spirit more,
Resolve to love and serve Him all you can.

LINES
TO A
SISTER.
ON
GIVING
HER A
BIBLE.

Dear Sister, accept this inspired book of old,
A book of more value than rubies or gold;
A volume most precious, in rich mercy given,
By God sent to man to prepare him for heaven.

Then sister, dear sister, dig deep in the mine,
Made blest by its precepts may you ever shine;
May you find the pearl, that one of great price,—
Salvation for you through the mercy of Christ.

When this life is over may you and I meet,
Rejoicing for ever at our loved Saviour's feet;
May this Bible through life your best comfort prove,
And lead you safe home to His glory above.

LINES ON FRIENDSHIP.

Friendship! what is it? is it an idle word,
Oft in the mouth of those who would deceive?
A thing of hollow meaning, which has oft deterred
Others from forming it, lest they should after grieve
That they had such a union sought with those
Whose constant aim seemed how they best could get
All that they had, and that whene'er they chose,
Leaving at last just cause for deep regret?

Frienship! what is it? is it the flatter's voice,
The lying tongue of him who seeks for gain?
Who would your downfall p'an and then rejoice
That he had been the cause of all your pain?
One that would have signed a bond for him,
With earnest pleading would assail your heart
Until you have signed it—would surely seem
The best of friends, yet act the villain's part.

Friendship! what is it? it is the spurious thing
Of fiend-like men that, entering a happy home,
With the seducer's subtility would bring
Deep wretchedness and woe where'er they come?

One that would grasp the hand of trusting friend
And plot to ensnare his daughter or his wife,
And, like a cunning serpant, to gain his end
Would sting the hand that warmed him into life?

A friend—who is he? not the man who fails
To tell his friend if he discern a fault,
Or him who suffered others to assail,
And with vile calumny his name assault.
I hate the man whose tongue is ever found
Slandering his neighbour's character and fame;
But love the man whose friendly words abound,
Who ne'er speaks evil of another's name.

A friend, who is he? is it he who clings
Fast to his friend while he's with plenty blest,
But quits him soon as dire misfortune brings
Its troubles, and he is with woe opprest?
Counterfeits these of what a friend should be,
And like base coin they never stand the test,
Are soon detected: soon may others see,
Of all mankind they love themselves the best.

True friendship is a bright and holy flame,
Which all might have if they were so inclined;
Even a cup of water in Christ's name
Given to the needy a sure reward shall find.
It is adversity that tries one's friends,
And no prosperity, when all is peace:
The true man faithfully his friend defends,
And happy should he feel to give release.

True friendship is to dry the mourner's tears,
To alleviate the sorrows of the poor,
To have compassion on the orphan here,
And heavenly comfort bring to the sick ones' door;

To help the widow in her time of need,
And all console who feel affliction's rod,
The beggar that is starving haste to feed,
And mercy love, and be the friend of God.

Him thou canst have as friend, to whom
Thou canst make known the secrets of thy heart;
One that is tried and true. O to him come,
And fully all thy joys and fears impart.
He will uphold thee through life's chequered scene,
And lead thy pilgrim steps in the right way,
Help by His power to fight life's battle keen,
And when 'tis o'er take thee to endless day.

ASHBY-DE-LA-ZOUCH.

In Leicestershire there stands a town,
An ancient place of great renown,
As chronicles still vouch;
Old manuscripts record the same,
That "Ash trees" to the place gave name,
Called "Ashby-de-la-Zouch."

First settled there some Saxons bold,
And Danish men in search of gold,—
Fierce norsemen from the north ;
With stockades first they fenced their ground,
Dug moats that ran their dwellings round,
O'er which they sallied forth.

Rough warlike chiefs, whose hardy hands
Would till and cultivate their lands,
In rude unlettered state ;
Gurths and Beowulphs they were named,
For tilling ground these men were famed,
Although of ancient date.

In Edward the Confessor's reign
Fourteen yardlands was the plain
Of this quiet ancient place ;
Here herds of swine would search for food,
Their forage the acorns in the wood,
And flocks of sheep would graze.

The cattle on the hills and plains,
Attended by the rustic swains,
Would browse their time away ;
Till William came—the Norman lord
Conquering with his powerful sword,
Gained everywhere the sway.

'Twas then these men, before so free,
Submitted now the serfs to be,
Of De Grentemaisnel ;
These bondmem laboured on his land,
And sallied forth at his command,
And fought his battles well.

The population then was small.
But scarce a hundred men in all,
"Bordars and Socmen" named:
Whose rent was always paid in kind,
Poultry and eggs were bound to find,
Both which their masters claimed.

In Ivo's time they much increased,
We find they had a parish priest,
St Helen's Church and Hall;
At morning called by priest to prayers,
And "Vespers" closed their evening cares;
Such was the life of all.

Then Phillip de Beaumais had the sway,
And to some priests he gave away
A large extent of land;
And the lands of Smart cliffe he gave,
Hoping his parents' souls to save.
By charity's open hand.

He left no son to hand his name,
Down future history's scroll of fame,
But left one daughter fair:
She wedded with the first la-Zouch—
This fact historians all avouch—
And made him master there.

And in those ancient feudal days
Were witness'd chivalrous displays,
And prowess of gallant knight:
Who'd bravely herald far and wide,
Battle to all on every side,
That should their ladies slight.

And oft amidst those lovely dales,
Were whispered love's enchanting tales,
Down through the flowery dells :
O'er beds of violets oft they stray'd,
Whose perfume scented all the glade,
Bedeck'd with hyacinth bells.

These knights their ladies did adore,
And on their armes rich scarves they wore,
The work of their lady-love ;
And often valiant knights have their
Contested for trifles light as air,
And dropt the challening glove.

His love looks on with anxious eyes,
Her bosom heaves with fluttering sighs ;
As her knight to the combat goes :
Now sadness rests upon her brow,
Alas ! she is unhappy now,
Her heart is filled with woes.

Now see them meet upon the plain,
Their falchions soon with blood they stain,
To uphold their lady's fame ;
But one soon sinks, no more to rise,
His blood the grass with crimson dyes,
While death surrounds his fame.

And in the records of this place,
A fearful deed of arms we trace,
Of vengeance and of blood ;
"Folville" and "Roger Beller" strong—
The one had done the other wrong—
In deadly combat stood.

From hour to hour they fiercely fought,
With rage and hate they madly sought
Each one his foe to slay;
But wounded they together fell,
A wretched sight for those to tell,
Who saw this dreadful fray.

Their effigies e'en now remain,
The sword and daggers of the slain,
With the helmets of these braves;
One in the lady's chapel sleeps,
Kirby churchyard the other keeps,
At peace in seperate graves.

And Smesby's village still doth show
The fields upon whose verdant brow,
The tournament was fought;
While further up on higher ground,
The fight was viewed by those around,
With dread and anxious thought.

A market near this time was gained—
By Hugh la Zouch it was obtained—
For husbandmen and trade;
Farmers and merchants there did meet,
Each other there would warmly greet,
Where bargaining was made.

On Wednesday there in every week,
The farmers would the market seek,
With produce of their lands;
With corn and cattle brought for sale,
And fruit from orchard, hill, and dale,
From the labour of their hands.

The Great Lord Hastings now held sway,
A valiant knight, both brave and gay,
King Edward's favoured lord;
His bosom friend he soon became,
And rose to rank of highest fame.
In England and abroad.

The king and knight were near of age,
In friendly games they'd oft engage,
Each other's trusty friend;
Both confidants in stately cares,
Consulted on all grave affairs,
To succour or defend.

For Hastings' zeal in works of state,
King Edward made him rich and great,
A baron of great might,
And showered high favours on his head—
In all designs great Hastings led,
And shone with honours bright.

Whene'er for pleasure Edward sighed,
The baron was ever at his side,
To tend his monarch's call;
In dalliance with the young and fair,
The favourite, he was ever there,
In town or stately hall.

He still bore Ashby in his mind,
As near about this time we find
Two fairs by him obtained:
He rode in state like king or prince,
As seldom seen before or since,
He like a monarch reigned.

His fame resounded far and wide,
Whate'er he asked was ne'er denied,
Of worldly grandeur vain.
To him was granted power to raise
The Noblest castle in those days,
Whose ruins still remain.

But all this show and grandeur gay,
Was destined soon to pass away
In misery and in gloom ;
At Edward's death his fame declined,
To treachery's clutch he was consigned,
And found an early tomb

For Gloster's minions all conspired,
By haste and jealousy inspired,
To work great Hastings' end ;
Of treason high he was accused,
All law and Justice were abused,
He'd scarce a single friend.

So great and fierce was Richard's hate,
To dine he vowed he would not wait
Till he saw Hastings dead.
They bore him quickly to the ground,
Where soon a block of wood was found,
On which he lost his head.

Thus this great man who'd fought and bled,
And hosts and armies proudly led,
And foreign foes defied,
Though almost worshipped in his time,
In favour pass'd his earthly prime,
In ignominy died.

But Hastings' name revived again;
Although the first great lord was slain,
It rose again to might.
Distinguished much his race became,
And left a noble honour'd name,
As champions of the right.

And when the war of France came on,
When Theroanne's and Tourney's fields were won,
And Hastings rose to fame;
For his great service to the crown,
He gained much honour and renown—
An Earl he then became.

As Earls of Huntingdon, for years
Their name in highest ranks appears,
Wise counsellors of state.
Some more obscurely passed their days,
And revelled in gay pleasure's ways,
Right hearty and elate.

When Ashby Castle loud would ring
With entertainment for the king,
And lords and ladies fair;
Whilst all the nobles in the land
Sat at the board where plenty's hand
Gave every luxury there.

With feudal pomp and grand array,
In dignity through blithe and gay,
They lightly tripped the hall;
While troubadours with harp and song,
Would charm the glittering fairy throng,
As they led of the ball.

Whilst each brave knight and lovely girl
In the gay waltz's giddy whirl,
Joyous in heart and hand,
With nimble feet and sylph-like air,
Would smile with eyes and lips so fair,
The beauteous of the land.

When ended is th' enchanting dance,
To the banquet hall they all advance,
Where feast and mirth go round;
Where blaze the chandeliers so bright,
And gaily pass the live-long night,
'Midst music's raptured sound.

Whilst rapture fills the brilliant throng,
And sweetly sounds the minstrel's song
Of the deeds of days of yore;
Of heroes bold who'd fought and bled,
The Crusades 'neath the red cross led,
And songs of olden lore.

And many a needy soul hath felt,
That charity in Ashby dwelt,
In ages passed away;
Where food and raiment were bestowed,
And institutions there endowed,
That since have ceased their pay.

And often do these works decline—
Are sunk and lost through ages' line—
The donors all forgot;
When poverty oft doth lose its dole,
The young their once free-granted school,
And find a pauper's lot.

But such in Ashby's not the case,
For numerous bequests we trace,
Of donors wise and good ;
Which time hath hidden not away.
But hold their good and useful sway,
And have for ages stood.

The schools of Ashby stand renown'd,
They've education spread around
To men of lowly birth,
Who by the help of learning's aid,
Have honour won and fortunes made,
Good men of truth and worth.

Whichever way we turn, we find
Rich food to cheer and please the mind,
On Ashby's ancient ground ;
Its church, its parks, its scenery bright,
Refreshing to the stranger's sight,
With interest all abound.

The old castle is in ruins now,
And on its walls green ivies grow,
But still it looks sublime;
Though roofless now, its rare old towers
Still stand the fiercest tempest's showers,
And mock the flight of time.

And though the grass grows in the aisle,
And ivy-wreaths surround the pile,
With sad and sombre ray ;
Still through each niche the sun's bright beams
Of mellow light in genial streams
Sends rays of glorious day.

It tells of ages now no more,
When all the crimes of civil war
Drenched England's plains with blood;
When York and Lancaster laid claim
To England's crown and kingly name,
Through many a crimson flood.

But happily such days are o'er,
We feel no fearful shocks of war;
Our country's peaceful home:
No feudal serfdom do we know—
A free and open heart we show,
With no desire to roam.

Our England is our boasted land,
Where all may live with honest hand,
And love both God and man;
Where all may strive to reach the goal,
That sweet salvation of the soul,
Free from oppression's ban.

Most gracious God! we pray to Thee,
That having made our country free,
Thou wilt protect the slave;
And stay the fearful rage of war,
That now disgrace the western shore,
On land and on the wave.

LINES ON LUTHER.

Reformer great! thy name shall honoured stand
Among the annals of those mighty men
Who were pre-eminent in their native land,
And in great deeds have always foremost been.

With noble courage for the truth didst stand,
  With might unwavering didst denounce the creed
That sold indulgences throughout the land—
  Wolves in sheep's clothing thus their flocks to feed.

Whilst Papal gloom was lowering all around,
  And martyrs died for Jesus and His truth;
Christ's heroes to the fiery stake were bound,
  And not a few whi'st in their early youth,—

Then boldly cam'st thou forward in His cause,
  His standard bearing with a spirit bold,
Against the Pope's anathemas and his laws—
  A valiant protest thou didst ever hold.

And when at Spires before the priests and king,
  That protest famed, of which our boast we make,
Thou didst not fear before them all to bring;
  Which caused the Pope and papal power to shake.

Still does that protest like a beacon shine,
  Dispensing blessings o'er the human race,
Entwines round England like a beauteous vine,
  With holy fruits our noble country grace.

What blessings to us have this time come down
  By thee, thou champion of rights so dear;
And ages yet unborn thy faith shall own,
  And o'er thy dust shall shed the hallowed tear.

There was a time when our forefathers paid
  Dire penalties for faith—their blood was shed;
But now we worship, and are not afraid
  Of our religion bringing evil on our head.

Time past the Bible was a sealed book,—
  Was chained to altars, or in Latin read,—
And artful priests alone could at it look :
  The people learning only what they said :

But now, thank God! it is sent everywhere—
  Published in every tongue is now the plan
Of God's salvation ; sent to every sphere,
  Showing His love to helpless fallen man.

And England's called by providential love
  To spread the gospel o'er the whole wide world,
That fits believers for the home above,
  Where its glorious doctrines are unfurled.

Luther! thy name shall ever honoured be
  'Mid freedom's sons shall shine with glory bright,
While our posperity have cause to see
  Thy protest with a cheering ray of light.

Long as the life-blood through our hearts shall flow,
  We'll think of blessings that through thee came,
We'll bless thy memory while our bosoms glow,
  And deck thee with a deathless wreath of fame.

Though centuries with rapid wing have passed,
  Since thou wert laid within thy grave's low bed ;
Yet long as memory o'er this earth shall last,
  Shall men esteem thee one of the mighty dead.

THE CRUCIFIXION.

'Twas the dawning of day
And the morn in splendour broke over Jerusalem,
And busy men pursued their labours.
But there were vast masses of men, women, and children
Pursuing their way to Mount Calvary.
The mighty God was on His way to suffer for the redemption of the world He had made.
The ungrateful people who had seen His miracles in Jerusalem and round about its environs,
Were shouting, "Away with Him—crucify Him!"
Those who had seen Him give eyesight to the blind,
And cause the lame to walk;

Who heard Him at the grave of Lazarus wake the dead to life;
Who had heard of His stilling the tempest
And the wonderful miracles He performed,
Were crying out, "His blood be upon us, and on our children."
And thus amidst the execrations of the people whom He had loved,
And whom He had come on earth to die for,
He went on His way bearing the rugged Cross.
He that had wept over Jerusalem.
And who would have gathered her children together, as a hen gathereth her chickens under her wings,
Was now toiling and sweating up Calvary's height.
Guarded by Roman soldiers, the God Man who could have annihilated the world with His word,
Was guarded like a guilty felon to die a criminal's death.
He who with His voice had stilled the tempest into a calm,
Now suffered Himself to be led away to execution by the vile rabble!
They gained Calvary's summit;
The Cross is reared;
The God Man is buffeted, and scourged, and spit upon;
He is nailed to the Cross and His head crowned with thorns.
The sins of a guilty world are on His shoulders.
His quivering limbs, and racking joints,
And painful thirst, all tell the agony He suffered!
He is reviled by the people, forsaken by His Father,
And in the midst of His agonies cries out,
"My God, my God! why hast Thou forsaken me?"
Fainting under the weight of His sufferings,
He drank the cup of agony to its last dregs.
How astonishing His great love that would allow Him thus to suffer!

He who is to be the grand Judge and arbiter of the eternal destiny of millions,
Suffered between two malefactors;
He who was in the bosom of the Father, and the King of eternal glory,
Had the tinsel robe of an earthly king placed on Him;
He who swayed the sceptre of the universe, had a reed placed in His hand,
Whilst the mockers cried, "Hail, King of the Jews!"
He who shall come again in glorious majesty,
With all His holy angels with Him, as a Judge of quick and dead,
Was taunted by them, saying, "Save Thyself, come down from the Cross and we will believe on Thee;"
And the Eternal Word through all ages, decreed by infinite wisdom to be our Saviour,
Now was paying penalty of the world's transgressions.
The pure unspotted Lamb of God, who knew no sin, was made sin for us,
That we might be made the righteousness of God through Him;
The Victim was now fulfilling the prophecies;
The Lamb of God was now, in the sacrifice of Himself, carrying out the designs of His heavenly Father,
And, on the blood-stained, hallowed Cross was completing the typical ceremonies of the Jews,
Who offered for their sins the lamb without blemish and without spot,
Who was taken to the altar and slain, and whose blood sprinkled the mercy-seat.
Surely on that day the burning tongue of the seraphim was hushed, and the angelic choir, whose golden harps made melody in Heaven, were silent.

It might be that tears fell from their eyes upon the strings of the harps and stopped them from sounding, as they gazed on the sufferings of their Lord and Master ;

For one day it might have been that there were mourning cherubims in Heaven,

As they beheld Immanuel expiring on the Cross.

But O! what wonders took place on earth :

The veil of the splendid temple rent ;

The graves were opened : a great earthquake shook the foundation of Jerusalem,

And darkness covered the face of the earth.

Well might the Centurion exclaim on seeing these wonders, "Truly this was the Son of God!"

O Spirit of wisdom, come from above and teach us how to appreciate the great gift ;

O eternal Spirit of truth, open our minds to understand the mystery of the Cross ;

O Thou, who on Mount Sinai gave the law, and fulfilled the prophecies by Thy death on the Cross,

And who orderest all things, speak to our hearts with Thy mighty love, and say,

"Be not faithless, but believing."

O Son of the living God, the brightness of Thy Father's glory,

Hasten the time when the benefits Thou didst purchase for mankind on the Cross,

Shall be fully realized in the salvation of the whole human race, and Thy own glory.

Thy mighty arm shall surely accomplish the great work.

For Thou hast said, "If I be lifted up I will draw all men unto Me."

But earth's time is passing,

And whole generations are passing away with it,

And we fear the greater part unsaved,
As we only see, here and there, a few rays of light from Thy Cross beaming on our earth.
O hasten the time when the benefits of Thy death shall fill the whole earth with light,
And all shall call Thee blessed, and Thou shalt see the travail of Thy soul and be satisfied :
Gird Thy sword on Thy thigh, O glorious King.
And ride on till the whole world is subdued to Thy sceptre.
The apostles, the prophets, and the martyrs and saints,
Have all gained heaven through the Cross of Christ,
And now sing the song of the heavenly choir, of
"Unto Him that loved us and washed us in His own blood.
To Him be glory and dominion for ever."
The Cross is to them the blest emblem of love,
And it ought to be of our gratitude.
O man, lay thine hand upon thy breast, and ask thyself,
"What have I to do with the crucifixion?"
And if thou hast found Him precious to thy soul,
And realized in thy heart the blessings Christ came to purchase for thee,
Be thankful, and go on thy way rejoicing to the mansion He has prepared in Heaven for you.
If not, tremble, sinner, for thou must appear before Him as thy judge.

THE RESURRECTION.

The tragic scene of Calvary was over.
The body of Christ, taken from the Cross, and wrapped in fine linen and spices by His faithful and devoted servants,
He was borne to the rock-cut tomb—
A new tomb in which man had never lain.

A great stone was brought to cover it,
And a seal was placed upon it:
The Roman Soldiers were there to guard it,
And they watched it with a vigilance that defied mortals to rob it of its sacred treasure.
All was silent till the third morning.
On that eventful morning they were startled by a visit of the Angel of God,
And for fear of him the keepers did shake and became as dead men;
They fell to the ground lost in astonishment;
Terror seized them as the bright dazzling robes of the Angel flashed before their vision,
And they fell and hid their faces in the dust,
Not daring to look on the glorious Messenger from on high;
Then the seal of death was broken,
The stone rolled away,
And our Jesus came forth the triumphant victor!
In the garden the faithful Mary was weeping;
And a voice spoke to her and said,
"Woman, why weepest thou? whom seekest thou?"
How astonishing she did not know that voice!
But though the stranger was the gardener;
And with tones of thrilling anguish replied,
'Because they have taken away my Lord, and I know not where they have laid Him."
"Sir, if thou hast borne Him hence, tell me where thou hast laid Him, and I will take Him away."
Poor Mary, weak in faith, yet filled with love!
But the voice comes again, and now she is called by her name,—
Now she recognizes the voice she had often heard,
And which thrilled through her heart like beautiful music,

Causing every nerve and faculty she possessed to vibrate when she saw the Lord:

And with a tearful eye, and quivering lip, and faltering tongue,

And heart overflowing with love,

All she could utter was, "Master!"

And sunk at His feet to embrace Him.

But He said, "Touch Me not," but go tell My disciples; which she did.

But her words were as idle tears to them, until He afterwards appeared in their midst,

And glad enough were the disciples when they saw the Lord

Thomas not being then present, all the others with one accord told him they had seen the Lord;

But Thomas would not have believed if it had been a thousand that told him.

Not he: nothing would make him believe, unless he put his fingers into the holes the nails had made in His hands,

And thrust his hand into the hole in His side made by the spear,

He would not believe—not he; and during the week the disciples tried to convince him, but all in vain.

But see, on the first day of the week they are assembled again,

And Thomas with them, and they are again fastened in:

How, then, does this stranger appear among them?

He looks upon Thomas and says to him,

"Reach hither thy hand, and thrust it into My side; and be not faithless, but believing."

Well might poor Thomas, overwhelmed with shame, and love, and gratitude, cry out, "My Lord and my God!"

And hear the Saviour's answer: "Because thou hast seen Me, thou hast believed: blessed are they that have not seen, and yet have believed."

Faith, mighty faith, grasps the risen Lord, and believes the promise,

"Where I am there shall ye be also."

He has led captivity captive, ascended on high, and receives gifts for men :

Heralded by the pomp and splendour of the host,

And surrounded by majesty and glory such as the men of earth have no conception of,

And such as the Angels themselves, though accustomed to celestial scenes of brightness,

Had never viewed before.

How different His position now to what it had been on the Cross !

Here He trod the wine-press alone, and all His disciples forsook Him ;

But now millions of Angels, Cherubim and Seraphim, await His command.

On that glorious head where the crown of thorns had been placed,

There now glitters with the brightest radiance a crown of wonderful glory.

The Cross, once so despised, is now exalted ;

And its victory so great, that it forms a theme vast and mighty for the choirs of Heaven to celebrate through all eternity.

And well it might ;

For it was a love worthy of a God to die for His rebellious creatures,—

A love the fullness of which no angel mind can fathom ;

It was a love that passeth all knowledge ;

It was a love of immeasurable dimensions,—

A love whose subjects were innumerable :

For they consist of a multitude which no man can number, redeemed out of every tribe and nation.

One blaze of stainless white flashes from the garments of that happy company.

They did not purchase those robes with money.

They were given as the reward of faith:

For the wearers of those garments came out of great tribulation;

They washed their robes and made them white in the blood of the Lamb.

All Heaven rejoiceth to meet the Conqueror;

The angelic host sang, "Glory, honour, praise, and power, be unto the Lamb for ever!"

And the host of the redeemed answered, with sublime acclamation,

"Jesus Christ is our Redeemer! Hallelujah! Praise ye the Lord!"

O the solemn grandeur of that scene, when the Almighty Father welcomed the beloved Son again to His kingdom,

Covered with honourable scars gained in the great battle against sin, hell, and death!

Well might all the redeemed strike their golden harps, and shout,

"Unto Him that loved us and washed us in His own blood, and hast made us kings and priests unto the Father, to Him be glory and dominion for ever!"

Methinks it must have been a glorious sight

When the Conqueror of death and hell returned to His glory again.

All Heaven was ready to receive the Conqueror.

Methinks the gates of Heaven, in their pearly brightness,

Were eclipsed by the host who stood ready to shout,

"Lift up your heads, O ye gates;

And be ye lift up, ye everlasting doors; and the King of glory shall come in."

And then the multitude of the choirs of the blessed shouted back,

"Who is the King of glory?"

Again the shout was heard.

"The Lord of hosts, He is the King of glory."

And again was heard,

"Lift up your heads, O ye gates; and be ye lift up, ye everlasting doors; and the King of glory shall come in."

And from the wall of precious stones,

Whose tops were covered with Heaven's host;

And splendid banners, emblems of the Cross, waved over them.

Again the shout was heard,

"The Lord of hosts, He is the King of glory; the Conqueror of sin, hell, and death:"

And as He entered in, all the harps of Heaven united with the triumphant song of the redeemed, who sung,

"Worthy is the Lamb that was slain to receive glory, honour, and power;

For He hath redeemed us out of every tribe and kindred of the nations of the earth:"

And they cast their crowns before Him and shout,

"Glory, honour, praise, and power, be unto the Lamb for ever!"

O the long cloud of witnesses that have gone before!

But they have been ready; for they have longed to depart;

They have met death triumphant;

They have gone down like the sun, leaving a light on the mountain top of death that has made them appear lovely.

The chamber where the Christian meets death is a hallowed place.

Hark what he says:

"I have fought the good fight; I have finished the faith; and henceforth there is laid up for me a crown of righteousness."

He has nought to do now but to clap his glad wings, and tower away, and hasten to the blaze of day.

O the difference between Christians and infidels dying!

So sure as there is a resurrection of all nature,

And Spring comes forth in its loveliness and beautiful flowers,

So sure shall our vile bodies be raised from the dust.

Though that dust shall be left in the different parts of the earth,

Yet it shall be raised and stand before the judgment bar of the Almighty God,

And myriads of assembled Angels,

And the innumerable company of the spirits of the just made perfect.

Sinner, ask thyself the question, the most important that can be asked in this life,—

"What sentence shall I hear at the Resurrection?"

THE JOURNEY TO EMMAUS.

The shades of evening were gathering around Jerusalem.

The setting Sun was gilding with a fiery gold-like refulgence the riven Veil of the Temple.

And throwing its departing radiance on Mount Calvary—

The light on that mountain-top was beautiful then,

Far different from the scenes that had lately taken place there, when all nature seemed in convulsion;

Now all was calm and serene, and the Sun was fast sinking to rest beneath the horizon.

On that evening two of the disciples were returning from the City of Jerusalem to the Village of Emmaus,

They were travelling along slowly and pensively, a deep grief appeared to be settled upon the countenances of both :

They were engaged in deep and earnest conversation it was a most astonishing subject that formed the theme.

They had placed Jesus the wonderful Prophet of Nazareth in the Tomb, but he was not to be found where they had lain him,

His body was gone, and some of the disciples who had been early at the tomb had told them of the vision of angels they had seen there, but they did not understand of His rising from the dead.

And they were exceeding sorrowful, they trusted He was to redeem Israel,

But where now was the Great Prophet, where now was the wonderful Miracle Worker ?

Who had performed such feats in Jerusalem—

Alas ! they said he is dead.

The sick no more will feel His healing power,

The tempest no more be calmed at His word,

The dead no more will be raised at His call !

Where now is the Great Sin Forgiver who could speak peace to the most troubled heart ?

And as they ask where ? the tears course down their cheeks.

Revealing their grief.

But suddenly a stranger draws near and asks them why they are sad ?

And why care seems to set so heavily on their brows,—

Surprised they answer,—

Art thou a stranger in Jerusalem and know nothing of the deeds done there ?

How one Jesus of Nazareth a Prophet went about doing good to all?

A man of such wonderful power that could cure all manner of diseases, and ever raise the dead to life—

But alas! He is gone for ever,—

And we shall never see his like again!

And then the tears flowed afresh, it was then the traveller looked upon them with awful and majestic dignity, and with eloquence and power that would have made a seraph's heart thrill with emotion:—

He unfolded to them the plan of Salvation, and the prophecies concerning Himself.

But their eyes were so blinded by tears that they did not know Him.

Although he showed them how the Scriptures told with their prophetic utterance how one must die to atone for the sins of man.

How Moses the great law-giver had said,

"God would rise them up a prophet from among their brethren."

How David the sweet psalmist sung of the Messiah's conquering glory, and everlasting reign—

How Isaiah with lofty poetic strain told of His birth—and with holy rapture sung

"Unto us a child is born,--unto us a son is given, and the government shall be upon His shoulders,"

And His name shall be called wonderful counsellor,

The mighty God.

The everlasting Father,

The prince of peace of the increase of His government, and peace there shall be no end.

And all the prophets have fortold His life and deeds.

And brought before the Nation.

Jesus offers, as Prophet, Priest, and King,

Offering Himself as a willing sacrifice for the sins of the people.

Descendant He of Judah's favoured tribe,—

From Abraham the friend of God,—the branch,—the stone, —the shiloh of your race has come with power of language, but blind unbelief fails to discern in Him the Sun of God and man.

But this same Jesus—late of Nazareth, whom ye termed a prophet,

He is the prophets' God ;

Behold in Him the slaughtered paschal lamb, whose blood shall sprinkle the soul of man and cleanse it from its iniquity ;

And He shall rise again according to prophecy, and shall judge the world in Righteousness.

Oh ! foolish man why cannot ye believe the Truths of Holy Writ and its prophecies ?

For know assuredly that He whom thy people have crucified is both Lord and Christ !

They listen to His sublime discourse on the depths of revelation,—almost breathless they hang upon His every word, and their hearts are now burning.

His words have been so very sweet they would like to know more,

They constrain Him to abide with them,

He enters their humble habitation, he breaks the bread,—in that act he makes himself known ; prostrate they fall before Him, and would have clasped His feet, but he was gone ;

They look upon each other and both exclaim with reverented love, awe and gratitude—

It was our Jesus !

He is risen !

We have seen Him again !
He is gone to glory and reigns a King for ever, and says to each of His followers,
" Be thou faithful unto death, and I will give thee the Crown of Life."
" Amen, even so, our Lord Jesus "

LINES ON THE TRANSFIGURATION.

One splendid evening, the sun going down
Was tinging the earth as with a radiant crown,
Completing his wonted daily race ;
When near a high mountain some travellers strayed,
And with them was One, of whom oft they'd sought aid
And glad were they to see Jesus' face.

He said to them, " Let us to that mound repair,
There will I wrestle in all-powerful prayer,
And my Father in earnest will seek ;
Men's sins have fallen on me with terrible weight,
And the burden of human transgressions so great,
To the Father in Spirit I'll speak.

And whilst He was praying His features became
More radiant far than the sun's brilliant flame,
His raiment effulgently gleamed :
While both, two shining forms to Him now appear,
Clothed in white, from the heavenly sphere,
Moses and Elias—men highly esteemed.

On the errand of mercy they came from above,
To talk with Him of His redeeming love,
And that the sufferings he must endure :
How on the cross He must be lifted up,
And drink the dregs of death's fearful cup,
Salvation for men to procure.

But while they were talking, sleep overcame
The disciples, Peter, John, and James,
For a time they sank into repose.
But what a bright vision over them broke,
When from their slumbers they were awoke,
And their eyelids in wonder unclose.

What a scene it was that met their gaze,
Filling their wondering souls with amaze—
It was an enrapturing sight
To behold their Lord in glory there shine,
Beautified radiance with light divine—
The mountain was covered with light.

The glories of Heaven appear to come down,
As Christ appeared on that mountain crown,
And the saints of old with Him talked
About men's redemption, that glorious plan,—
God giving His Son as a ransom for man ;
So discoursed they on as they walked.

But transient short was their visit, and transient their stay,
Their mission done they ascended away
To join in the songs of the skies.
And with their dear Lord no longer did stay,
But leaving the sacred mountain upward away
To the portals of heaven did rise.

But hark to the voice that sounds on the ear—
"This is My Beloved, and Him ye must hear
Before ye descend to the grave.
This alone is Messiah, Priest, Prophet and King,
With His loved name heaven's high arches ring,
Your souls He is pleading to save.

'Tis Jesus of whom the old prophets spoke,
He is come to break asunder the yoke
Of Satan from souls that are bound :
This is the bright and fair morning star,
That was to come, as the Scriptures declare,
In no other salvation is found."

The disciples trembled nor knew what to say,
Though Peter said, "Lord let us build straightway
Three tabernacles to be ever here ;
For O ! how delightful for us it would be,
And with Thee ever be near.
Glories like these for ever to see.

But the Master said, "Here must we not stay ;
To the lost busy world we must hasten away,
With the people to mingle below,
I've a work to accomplish, an end to fulfil,
A chalice to drink ; 'tis my Father's will,
That He justice and mercy may show."

How often Christians on Faith's mountain top
Would be glad if they for ever could stop,
But stern duty calls to the world;
Though desirous with Christ their Lord to stay there.
Family and business their time claim to share,
And their hopes again to earth hurled.

But fight on, good Christian, the battle of faith,
And conquer, for thy Lord and thy Master saith,
"Thou must the world tread down."
Hold fast, then, that which thou hast attained—
The heavenly wisdom, so nobly gained,
And press on for thy heavenly crown.

Soon will this short life of ours be done,
And Heaven for ever be lost or won—
How precious our time, then, here;
For we shall either our souls destroy,
Or fit them to live with Christ in joy,
When we at His bar must appear.

Then, however others may hate God's cause,
And set at defiance His righteous laws,
Let us determined for Heaven prepare;
Be that our chief desire to gain,
That we from our Saviour may hear the blest strain
Of "Come, ye blessed, my kingdom share."

LINES ON THE BIBLE.

DEDICATED TO THE JUVENILE BIBLE SOCIETY.

Glorious old Bible! The Best Book on earth,
It showeth how great is the soul's precious worth;
'Tis a gracious charter where we may all see
God's mercy and goodness to all men are free;

A lever whereby man is helped to arise
And seek for a mansion of bliss in the skies;
For a patriot band are those noble youths,
Who seek by all means to publish its truths.

This is the book that has made England great,
Dispelling our ignorance, raising our state;
Given to England to spread through the world,
Diffusing its truths where our flag is unfurled;
And if we desire true freedom for man,
We shall give all our aid to this glorious plan
For a patriot band are those noble youths,
Who seek by all means to publish its truths.

Sometimes we hear enemies talk of this land,—
They tell us that armies will come on our strand;
But true to the Bible we at them may laugh,
With God our protector we'd beat them to chaff;
If faithful to Him, we'd invaders defy,
Yet will send them our Bible—to save them we'll try.
For a patriot band are those noble youths,
Who seek by all means to publish its truths.

Go on then, young friends, in this work engage
For the glory of God and the light of the age;
Do all that you can God's love to reveal,
Make your lives glorious, and labour with zeal
To spread the blest Bible wherever you can,
And be benefactors to perishing man.
For a patriot band are those noble youths,
Who seek by all means to publish its truths

And be well assured if you work for the Lord,
Your labour and zeal He will early reward;
And He'll be your guide through all the world's strife
Will bless you with favour through this earthly life:
And after you've done with the mission of love,
Will call you all home to His glory above.
For a patriot band are those noble youths,
Who seek by all means to publish its truths.

FAREWELL TO THE REV. R. SELLERS.

MISSIONARY TO AUSTRALIA

Farewell, friend Sellors! we grieve to part with thee.
Thy form on earth we never more may see;
But yet our earnest prayers shall still ascend
For God's protection, till thy missions end.
Thy home and friends in zeal thou'st left behind,
A more extended sphere of work to find;
A new and rising land thy voice demands
To preach the Gospel through Australia's lands.

Though hard it is to part from those we love,
Thy solace and reward are stored above;
That God hath called thee to a better part
Shall bring the rays of gladness to thy heart.
Ordained by Him to swell His courts above,
And thousands bringing to partake His love,
May God's high hand surround thee all thy days,
And shower the beams of bliss through all thy ways.

May fire from His high altar touch thy tongue,
Converting sinners all, both old and young,
Till thousands feel the Gospel's purest flame,
And bow their knees, and praise His Holy Name
Proclaim the Saviour's love with Christian fear,
And shout salvation's glory far and near;
And may that land thou art approaching now,
Before the light of truth with grateful spirit bow.

Go forth as did the holy men of old,
Redemption's tidings to the world unfold,
Till all those trackless regions loudly ring
With loud hosannahs raised for Zion's King.
May countless blessings rest upon thy head,
And peace and love around thy path be shed;
And when thou'st ended life's short fleeting day,
Thou'lt find a home that passeth not away.

"ALL THESE THINGS ARE AGAINST ME,"

When over life's path shadows gloomily fall,
And Affliction and sorrow attend on our steps,
How cheering to think One's above ruling all,
Who over His children a constant watch keeps!

And works, too, in wonders, for their good He loves,
And controls every thing by His almighty power;
And a well-tried friend He constantly proves,
Dispensing His love in a glorious shower.

"All things are against me," the patriarch said,
When from Egypt his ten sons again had returned;
"My Joseph is gone; I know that he's dead,"
And all consolation from them he thus spurned.

"And you would take away Benjamin too,
My youngest, best comfort, and joy of my life—
The dear cherished boy of life's short day of woe,
All that's left me of Rachel, my best belov'd wife.

O! do not of him my sad soul bereave,
Or let him from me, his father, be torn;
Nor leave me for him in lone sorrow to grieve,
Lest in sorrow my grey hairs to the grave shall be borne."

He little thought, then, he his Joseph should see,
  Or that Providence had him ordained to be sent
Into Egypt, the family preserver to be—
  There fixed by his God with the kindest intent

He little knew either, the ruler who spake
  To his sons so roughly as spies, when they came,
Was the son, for whom his heart did ache—
  The second in Egypt, and Joseph that same.

But the corn was soon gone, and they must go again
  To Egypt's full store-house, to purchase some more ;
To let Benjamin go caused their father great pain,
  As fearing they never his son would restore.

" But, if he must go, then a present you take
  Of spices and fruits, for the governor there ;
And God grant you favour, and me ne'er forsake ;"
  So bowed he his spirit in reverent prayer.

Nor thought he the governor's sternness would melt,
  When into his house his brethren were brought
Nor ever thought he what his son Joseph felt,
  When, melting to tears, his chamber he sought.

But the brethren before him began not to fear,
  As conscience to memory brought the black deed.
When they Joseph's pleading refused to hear,
  Nor cared how they made his fond bosom to bleed,

They thought of the time when his raiment they took
  To their sorrowing sire, as his clothing he rent ,
"Some beast hath devoured him," they said with sad look,
  When bold with this falsehood, they unto him went.

He never thought Joseph again he should see,
Or that God had him sent, his own life to preserve ;
And had any one said that his son e'er would be
A ruler, the nation of Egypt would serve.

He'd have said that it could not possibly be,
Nor anything of it could he have believed ;
The ways of his God he could not then see,
Or he would not so hardly for Joseph have grieved.

The waggons are sent, they make him revive,
And he longs to go down from Canaan's land ;
"I will go," he said, "And while yet I live,
The goodness will own of God's mighty hand."

How weak is our faith when to trouble we're brought
And on a sick bed in sorrow are laid ;
Think, when we're cast down, that we serve God for nought.
And of being abandoned are sadly afraid.

In many a case this, alas ! is the way,
And we cry, "All this now is against me ;"
But it is to bring low to His feet, and to say,
"O God ! our help and our trust be in Thee !"

Then let us break off that harrising chain,
That burdens our mind so oft with despair ;
And ne'er at His ways with us pining complain,
But cast, all through life, on Him every care;

LINES ON THE BRIG "GEM,"

Which was nearly lost in Robin Hood Bay, on her passage from Hamburg, getting almost on shore on the rocks, when a friend of mine Mr. W. Storm, was the means of saving the ship and crew.

Loud roared the winds as the ship "Gem" lay
Near the great south rocks of Robin Hood Bay:
From Hamburg they'd sailed, and mistook the land,
And were near being lost on that rocky strand.

William Storm was up on the heights, and saw
The ship's fearful danger, as near she did draw
To that rocky shore where scores have been lost,
And to Whitby for help away did he post.

But when he got there the pilots did say,
"It blows so heavy, we can't go to-day;"
But he pleaded hard that some should e'en try,
And not these poor sailors abandon to die.

Then on they went to that fine noble pier
Of Whitby—famed for miles far and near;
There saw the captain of a steam-boat afloat,
Who offered to go with Storm in their boat.

He determined to go, and they got up the steam,
And loosed from the pier and into the stream;
With brave valliant hearts, they long much to save
Those poor sailors bold from a watery grave.

Out bravely they went, but the sea it ran high,
And broke o'er the steamer, and seemed very nigh
To overwhelm her and sink them while going out;
But well they all knew what they were about.

And soon from the harbour they got clear away,
And steered to the rocky and dangerous bay;
And glad were the sailors when watching them come
To save them from shipwreck's deplorable doom.

They steer to the ship, and a hawser they take—
The anchors are weighed, and now in the wake
Of the steamer are towed to a safe harbour near,
And grateful they're left at Scarborough pier.

Then, success to Storm and the other brave men,
Who adventured their lives for their fellows then;
And every danger and hardship they braved,
That the noble ship from wreck might be saved.

Long may they live, and their time thus employed
In doing others good, and still more employed;
And always be ready to venture and save
All that they can from a watery grave.

LINES ON THE DEATH OF ADMIRAL LYONS.

The gallant old Admiral's gone,
   Who the guns of a foe never feared;
A sailor who victories won,
   No matter to what point he steered.
From Westminster School he set out
   On board the "Royal Charlotte" he went;
At eleven years old, or about,
   As midshipman forth he was sent.

A sailor's life there he began,
  That called into action this boy;
His courage had honoured a man,
  When serving his country with joy.
When after a twelvemonth he'd served
  On the ship "Royal Charlotte" at sea,
His practical skill was observed,
  And then to the "Maidstone" went he.

Nearly five years in her he remained,
  Beloved by each one he knew;
He the friendship of officers gained,—
  Was the idol beloved by the crew.
Next to the frigate "Action" removed,
  By the Dardanelles' passage so famed,
Where Duckworth so eminent proved,
  With honour young Lyons he named.

His promotion he soon here obtained,
  To the "Baracouta" lieutenant was sent:
In this little brig honour he gained,
  Prized and welcomed wherever he went.
Here success first rewarded his skill,
  When the Castle of Belgic was stormed;
To succeed he dashed on with a will,
  And feats of bright daring performed.

In this great exploit he displayed
  A true sailor's courage so bold;
Though the channel was bad, haste he made,
  And took the foe's wily stronghold.
O'er the Castle a flag was soon waved,
  Placed there by England's brave son;
Cried "Come on!" while all danger he braved,
  And soon showed the victory was won.

The news soon reached his native land,
His bravely met a quick reward ;
Warm greetings showed on every hand,
A braver youth ne'er drew the sword.
With Admiral Drury next set sail
To Java, in the "Minden" bound,
As flag lieutenant ne'er did fail
To make it honoured wherever found.

As the ship at Java was lying off,
From a prisoner on board he learned
They thought an action would come off,
And then with ardour's fire he burned.
With action prompt in midnight hours,
He planned his scheme to carry out ;
Two boats and five and thirty tars,
Soon put the foreign foe to rout

He saw fort Marrack with its guns
For battle, fifty-four arrayed ;
Though the moon showed England's gallant sons,
They were not daunted or afraid.
The sea was rolling up the shore,
As they were landing on the beach ;
Undaunted firmly under fire,
They pressed and nobly scaled the breach.

Thus onward went the gallant tar,
And charged the foe and gained the fort ;
At dawn of day was seen afar
Old England's colours o'er the port.
With victory, commander he was made,
In the ship "Renald" was sent away,
And o'er to France a king conveyed,
A monarch's sceptre there to sway

Then back to England he returned,
To bear the allied Sovereigns here,
And for this service honours earned—
The treaty of peace did also bear.
In eighteen hundred and fourteen, he
Received Post Captain's rank; his fame
A terror proved to foes at sea,—
Like Nelson's they feared to hear is name.

A time then came—he stayed on shore—
A time of peace—e'er ready he
To fight, and in the "Blonde" once more
On active service went to sea;
And soon his mind was called to play
In the "Morea" an active part;
Allied to France he won the day,
And caused the Turks with fear to start.

Twelve nights in trenches was exposed
To the Turk's great guns and muskets' fire;
His bravery the French disclosed,
And St. Louis' order gave him to admire;
To reward his merit Greece then gave
The order of the Redeemer rare
That many a Grecian great would crave,
The much-loved honour for to share.

For the many services performed
He knighted was in "thirty five,"
In "forty" then he was informed
Forth with a baronet would live
Again he hears his country's call,
A lofty office of the state
He takes, and on his shoulders fall
A foreign mission high and great.

When ambassador at Athens, he
Upheld his country with his voice,
Of England's glory speaking free,
It made his countrymen rejoice.
At Berne he still upheld the praise
Of Briton's virtues, and her laws;
At Stockholm too, his voice did raise,
Which gained his country's loud applause.

Again he braves the azure main,
He then the British fleet command,
And to the Black Sea sails again,
From Russia justice to demand:
In the "Agamemnon" led the way,
And with the fleet the foe defied;
The Russian fleet all hid away
Behind stone walls, the coward tried.

To get them out, he tried each scheme;
Behind Sebastapol's stone walls
Sent shells, all pouring in a stream,
Which sorely then their fleet appals
For country always did his best,
Its rights and honours to maintain;
He sacrificed his health and rest,
For the laurels of the watery main.

Brave Lyons upheld England's fame,
Attack'd Sebastapol so strong,
In that good ship of glorious name
He fought with courage firm and long;
Accomplished all that head and heart
Could do against such walls of stone,
And played a dauntless sailor's part,
With brilliant skill, as all must own.

'Twas by this skill, and knowledge too,
That many a thousand lives were saved,
And sheltered many a valliant crew,
The raging storm could ne'er have braved;
In Balaclava's harbour they
Securely rode throughout the gale,
While those without, for miles away,
Could tell a frighful mournful tale

Some store-ships foundered in the roads,
And all on board were sunk and lost;
The beach was strewn with stores in loads;
And many lives of priceless cost;
But Lyons' wisdom there was praised,
By those who lay in harbour safe;
When outside other's cries were raised,
For succour, shelter, and relief.

But that fine youth his gallant son
Young Mowbray Lyons he was named,
Was struck ere Sebastapol was won,
And died a youth for ever famed
And after peace had been proclaimed,
Our queen across the Channel went,
To Cherbourg fortress now so famed,
The French alliance to cement

And here Lord Lyons held command,
And honours freely crowned his worth:
With every good from fortune's hand,
That men can know or feel on earth;
But England has this hero lost,
All in the blossom of his fame;
But while she can a navy boast,
Shall honour blazon o'er his name.

LINES ON LOVE.

Love! mighty love! Ah! who can tell
Its powers; 'tis known on earth to dwell;
It mocks all language to unfold;
Its full delight can ne'er be told.

It dwells in glances of the eye;
Is borne on zephyrs from a sigh;
It penetrates the guarded heart,
And gladness to the Soul impart.

Love works its wonders on mankind,
Exaults us and refines the mind;
The star of hope to our fond youth,
And maidens' guiding star of truth.

A feeling chaste, when used aright,
To worthy hearts it brings delight:
With pure emotions ever rife,
It decks with flowers the path of life.

Its hallowed joys, its anxious fears,
Hope's richest boon our life endears;
Bright gems of feeling o'er us cast,
Holy the flame that life-long last

And after death immortal given,
As foretaste of the joys of heaven;
Then let us enjoy the full of this love
To improve us on earth, to partake it above.

ON SEEING A MAJESTIC ELM TORN UP BY THE ROOTS BY THE WIND.

I saw it uprooted and torn to the ground,
With its leaves and its branches all scattered around,
The majestic fine elm brought low by the storm,
Its foliage all withered, and shattered its form.

This tree had stood centuries by the roadside—
Ages—year after year in its beauty and pride:
Through numberless storms it still had stood fast,
Sheltering its kind from the power of the blast.

And oft in the storm it hath bowed down its head,
When the hurricane came and the gale through it sped;
But the more the tree shook—the more the wind blew—
The wider it spread, and the stronger it grew.

A mysterious power of mightier strength,
Humbled its greatness and verdure at length;
'Twas the power of the wind—by mankind unseen,
Rushing on in its might– the destroyer had been.

Thus man seemeth firm in the flower of his age,
And earth seems the most of his thoughts to engage,
Allured by its follies—his roots wildly spread,
Says "Take now thy ease, joys round thee are spread,

JACOB'S DREAM.

A traveller once did leave his home,
And journeyed on his dreary way;
Wearied and fatigued he'd come,
Close to the eve of that spent day.

The sun in solemn grandeur set,
  Tinging the earth with splendid rays
Of golden hue, its beauties met
  That lonely wearied traveller's gaze.

'Twas Jacob: with his journey tired
  He for his pillow took a stone,
And fell asleep, and was inspired
  By vision of the Holy One.

He dreamt a ladder to the skies—
  Up from the earth whereon he lay—
To heaven above did brightly rise,
  With angels up and down its way.

And there above that ladder's height,
  Stood Heaven's great Almighty king,
Encircled round with beams of light,
  And seraphs on their azure wing.

Swift to perform His bidding they
  Flew unto this sleeper blest;
For though he on a hard stone lay,
  Yet sweetly he reposed to rest.

Bright guardian angels watched him round,
  Whilst God His promise did reveal;
As long he lay upon the ground,
  God's presence holy did he feel.

He little thought when down he lay,
  That God to him would deign to show
His love in such a gracious way,
  And let him thus His goodness know.

He heard His voice in silent night,
These promises to him did give;
His seed should be as stars of night,
And on that very spot should live.

And he believed God's promise given,
In faithful Abraham's fo tsteps trod;
He felt there was the gate of heaven,
And to him the house of God

The pilgrim then awoke from sleep,
And said, "How dreadful is this place;"
And vowed if God his soul would keep
He would for ever seek His face.

And on that spot a temple raise,
And this he would the Bethel name,
To celebrate his Maker's praise,
And show to all mankind His fame.

He vowed that each year he would bring
A tenth part of his worldly store,
A present to his heavenly King,
And His great goodness there adore.

And it is right for all Christ's fold
Their grateful offerings to bring;
Their talents, health, and gifts and gold,
With free will to their glorious King.

This earth is God's and all therein;
And He can give to whom He will;
To the righteous, or to those who sin,
That His intents they may fulfil.

Earth's greatest monarch on the throne,
Likewise the poorest in the land ;
He guides and leads them every one.
By His All-great, Almighty hand.

And Jacob, when he had to meet
Esau with an armed band,
In prayer went to the mercy seat,
For favour with Esau to stand.

And when they met with fond embrace,
Each to the other thus did tell,
How God had bless'd them with His grace,
And guided both so safe and well.

He'd wrestled with his God in prayer
And after would not let Him go ;
Though weak in body held Him there,
Till he God's gracious love did know.

What wondrous power thus Jacob had,
Over his Maker to prevail ;
Now, Christians. let your hearts be glad
That earnest prayer can never fail.

Lift up your heads, and bend your knees,
You cannot ever pray in vain ;
God listens when a child He sees,
Pour fourth its wailing piteous strain.

His great arm is not shortened now,
Dull nor closed His loving ear ;
Pray on, and feel His Spirit glow,
Meek, humble, lowly and sincere,

Pray on! pray on! now your God hears,
He answers promptly from above,
To banish all thy feeble fears,
And fill thy soul with righteous love

Prayers' blessings holy shall flow down
To every flock He sees in need,
Until they gain a heavenly crown,
And in rich heavenly pastures feed.

And God there altered Jacob's name
To "Israel"—which means a Prince—
The blessings which he then did gain,
Have flowed to mankind ever since.

And all the family of man,
In Jesus shall find peaceful rest;
Fulfilling God's own gracious plan—
Through Jacob's seed be ever blest.

And Christ shall be adored by all,
And all the nation of the earth
Before His sceptre low shall fall,
And glorify his wondrous worth,

Thus Pagan, Turk, Hindoo, and Jew,
Of every tribe and race and clime,
Shall worship the only God and true,
Till the remotest bounds of time.

THE EXILE.

Ye scenes of my childhood, O nought can dissever
The bond that embraces thy charms to my heart,
Though early life's moments are vanished for ever,
There's nought from my memory thy beauties can part.

Long absence but strengthens the tide of my yearning,
And summons each picture in freshness to view;
Old scenes and old faces and friendships returning,
In cherished remembrance, warm, welcome, and new.

Full oft passing objects recall to my senses,
Rich gladdening thoughts of some happiness past;
In those seasons of life ere its trial commences,
Those unalloyed seasons too fleeting to last.
The mignonette's fragrance, the lilac's chaste blossom,
Awaken the charm of past innocent joy;
While soft soothing rapture creeps over by bosom,
And calmly I wish I were yet but a boy,

In silence I wander, as night closes o'er me,
When the sun sinks away in the far distant west;
With no hope of peace on the morrow before me—
No prospect of Fatherland's solace and rest.
Enchanted, I pause, as sweet tones meet my hearing;
Whilst a glow of affection swells full my each vein,
As distant bells chiming bring feelings endearing,
Of home and its joys all returning again.

I reverence as holy those treasured reflections
That bring to my vision the features of yore;
That twine like the ivy o'er mind's recollections
Of loved ones departed from life's busy shore.
O call it not weakness of age unbefitting,
That thus to the scenes of my childhood I cling;
Each hour I prize dearer through life's wane is flitting
The emotions that by-gones to memory bring.

The cold-hearted stoic may laugh in derision,
Who knows not the warmth of humanity's bloom;
In whose chilly slumbers ne'er comes the sweet vision
Of paradise passed in sweet infancy's home.
Oh! could I but feel that when life had departed,
And peace with my God and the world I had made,
What solace 'twould bring the exile lone-hearted,
That my dust would repose where my fathers are laid.

LINES.

Written upon the occasion of going Pilot in the "Victoria" Steamer to Ramsgate, with a party of Wesleyans for a pleasure trip.

Some Wesleyan friends agreed one day
Forth from their native town to stray.
All on a trip of pleasure bent,
On board the boat 'Victoria" went ;
And all was joy 'tween friend and friend,
To Ramsgate steered the day to spend.

The steamer lay at Chatham pier,
Friends flocked on board with hearty cheer :
To see provisions come on board
In hampers large so nicely stored.
You would have thought our friends, at least,
Were going a voyage to the East.

The hampers stored with beef and hams,
Mince pies, and tarts, and lots of jams,
With piles of cake, and fruit, and wine,

On which a king would like to dine ;
And the whole party seemed to be
Determined they would pleasure see.

And then to see how all were drest,
Sure every one were in their best :
The sun shone out in bright array,
All sparkling on the waves so gay,
Which threw a gladness o'er each scene,
Filled every heart with joy serene.

With smiles our friends each other greet,
Warm salutations as they meet ;
But time flies fast—the clock points eight,
Our captain can no longer wait ;
Sure some will be too late to-day,
For time and tide will never stay.

So after they a hymn had sung,
Off from the pier the steamer swung,
And with fair wind and favouring tide,
They down the river Medway glide ;
In social friendship close they sat,
Engaged in lively friendly chat.

Said Mrs. A—— to her friend Miss B——
"A nice man is our preacher C——
He's ever in the path of duty—
My dear I think him quite a beauty !
He tends his flock with anxious care,
To God he offers earnest prayer.

But there's Miss G—— she cuts such capers,
Enough to give a friend the vapours ;
To see her dress and mincing walk—

No wonder that some people talk,
To see her crinoline and flounces,
As she into the chapel bounces.

But still in her there is some good,
For the children she did all she could;
When our Sunday School was raised,
Her conduct good was highly praised,
Collecting money from her friends,
To carry out good Christian ends

And Mrs. M——, who there you see—
I'm told a termagant is she,
And leads her husband such a life,
He wishes oft he had no wife;
But all I hear I don't believe,
I think she would not so deceive"

Such words as these, and other matters,
Each friend unto the other chatters;
The steamer now is going fast,
And very soon Sheerness is past;
But as they drew towards the Nore,
Old Boreas loud began to roar.

The rain began in drops to fall;
Into the cabin one and all
For shelter ran, but sad to tell,
Found everything below pell-mell,
For as the steamer rolled and tumbled,
The hampers all got sadly jumbled.

Poor S——sat in some apple pies,
With others there were heard loud cries;
One for the bucket loud did call
Who wished he'd never come at all,
And promised he would next time fast,
Or else this trip should be his last

Said Mrs. J——to J——, "My dear,
Pray hold my head—I feel so queer,
I know, in spite of all my wishes,
My breakfast must—O!—feed the fishes;
O, husband dear, pray be my nurse—
O dear! I'm getting worse and worse."

Poor J——was in the self-same plight,
Could nothing do, poor helpless wight,
To help his kind and loving spouse—
Both wished they had not left their house;
For stern old Neptune never wavers,
But shares to all his briny favours.

The steamer now took such a lurch,
That sent poor J——from off his perch,
And there were such shrieks and bawling
As 'midst the crockery he lay sprawling.
The sailors cried, "O, what's the matter?"
On hearing such a noise and clatter.

The weather now began to clear,
As near we came to Herne Bay pier;
The glorious sun began to shine,
Inviting all on board to dine.
The sailors up the awning got,
And soon all troubles were forgot.

The hampers from below were brought,
All fell to work as quick as thought;
Their breakfasts lost, as I'm a sinner,
They took a double lot for dinner,
With weather fine became quite jolly,
And bid adieu to melancholy.

With freshening wind and favouring tide,
The steamer on did gently glide,
And very soon Herne Bay was passed,
Likewise the buoy they call " West I ast ;"
Next the Reculvers soon were seen,
About which so much talk has been.

This church was by two sisters founded
Where near a brother dear was drowned ;
The ship, all hands, and all things in it,
Went down and vanished in a minute.
To hold in memory his sad lot,
They built this church upon the spot.

We steamed away now through the " Gore,"
And kept our distance from the shore ;
And here some porpoises did play,
And gambolled, throwing up the spray ;
Some time our company they did keep,
Sporting about on the briny deep.

And thus we went the passage down,
Passing by fair Margate town,
We kept in closely to the pier,
To see the company walking there ;
And soon came to that headland famed,
The extreme of Kent, " North Foreland named."

This place is known through many lands,
For on the cliff a lighthouse stands ;
'Tis seen by sailors when at sea,
Though twenty miles from land they be ;
They're ever anxious first to sight,
This well known welcome beacon light.

And as the Foreland we went round,
The wind was getting high we found,
For hats and caps were blown away —
We saw them roll along the spray;
"What flats," said they, whose hats were gone,
"To think we did not tie them on."

Proceeding, off, Broadstairs we came,
A fishing place of note and fame;
Soon as this place we'd quickly past,
Then Ramsgate came in sight at last.
The Goodwin Sands are seen from here,
Where ships are wrecked—aye, every year.

And many a gallant sailor brave,
Has found therein a watery grave;
When after a prosperous trip hath come
Towards these sands, so near his home;
And ofttimes been his fatal lot
To meet his death upon this spot.

And many a gallant ship lies there,
Been wrecked upon these sands so drear,
And many a cargo has been lost,
Though purchased at enormous cost.
I have no doubt these treacherous sands
Are richer far than many lands.

Into the harbour now they came,
And all were bound to have a game;
Some went on to the bather Foat,
In Ramsgate waves to have a float;
Some of the party walked the sands,
Whilst others went to hear the bands.

Some into the bazaars did stray,
Some went up Jacob's Ladder way;
Whilst others on the cliffs did stride—
Some on the sands the donkeys ride:
And every one was blithe and gay,
It turned out such a pleasant day.

But time, that never will stand still,
The sun going down behind the hill
Told all, on board their way must find,
If they'd no wish to stay behind:
Now on the steamer's deck they stand,
Ready once more to leave the land.

The sun was quickly going down,
When we left fair Ramsgate town,
The people on the shore did shout,
To see us joyfully steaming out.
Another steamer got on shore,—
She never had been there before.

But for her then we could not wait,
And for the Foreland steered out straight;
And as we progressed on our way,
The band began to sweetly play;
And as we round the Foreland steered,
The music ashore was plainly heard.

We now repassed famed Margate's pier,
Our homeward way direct to steer;
It then came on so dark that night,
That we could scarcely see the light;
Our compass we'd to use and lead,
We could not see our way a-head.

The sailor at the lead cried out—
"By the mark three!' we heard him shout;
And as our rapid course we sped,
One cried out, "There's a light a-head!"
This light is proved to be the Nore,
And then we stood in for the shore.

Then up the river Medway went,
And every one seemed quite content;
And when we got to Chatham pier,
And spoke the friends who met them there,
They enjoyed it so, they all did say
They'd go again some other day.

THE IDIOT BOY.

I passed an idiot boy one day,
He looked at me with vacant gaze,
And was so childish in his way,
His antics caused me much amaze.
I thought on God whose guardian care,
Through all creation is displayed;
And wondered why a form so fair,
Without a mind should e'er be made.

I never passed the Asylum gate,
Where dwell the poor, the lost insane.
But thank my God for bounties great,
For intellect of heart and brain;
While thousands live who never can
Lift up their hearts and prayers above,
For God's great goodness shown to man,
The countless blessings of His love.

What mysteries all His works appear,—
  How little can the mind discern
Of God's Great laws and purpose here.
  The wonders found at every turn?
Good hast thou been, O God, to me!
  For reason's blessing to my mind;
Whilst others void of sense I see,
  I've felt Thy love, Thy mercy kind.

Reason, the greatest, noblest gift,
  That God has unto man bestowed,
That we to Him our souls may lift—
  Our voices raise in praises loud.
Wondrous to us when deep in thought,
  To think how soul and body blend;
The soul that life to Adam brought.
  Which God unto His clay did send.

What is our life without the mind,
  Where reason holds its mighty sway?
'Tis but a blank, to feeling blind,
  That withers and departs away.
We wonder how such things can be;
  As God o'errules the universe,
His wise intents we fail to see,
  In what appears to man a curse.

Thus earthquakes seem an awful blight,
  Destroying thousands in the earth;
The cholera too, midst human fright,
  Brings misery oft to many a hearth.
And fearful shipwrecks on the main,
  With howling storm's destroying rage;
While many a sailor brave is slain,
  Who on the sea his life engage.

We think of fields where thousands fall,
Throughout the battle's deadly strife ;
We think of tyrants crushing all,
And think how vain a thing is life.
Hush! mortal, hush! and learn to trust
In Him thou canst not understand;
And bow down humbly in the dust,
And learn how wise all nature's planned.

He guides the planets in their course,
All nature feels His sovering sway ;
The winds from Him receive their force,
And at His word they calmly stay.
His lightnings flash along the skies,
And through the earth His thunders roar ;
And when His works we'd oft despise,
They ought to lead us to adore.

His servant Job He told to stand
In front of Him, to charge his mind
That he God's works might understand—
But still 'twas little Job could find ;
Attached to nought in endless space,
The orb move round our glorious sun—
'Tis He appoints each one its place,
As through the air they quickly run.

Men must be idiots who'll not see
His power as shown in works below ;
'Tis He directs the things that be,
To man His love does richly show.
His works are all in wisdom made,
And glorious in our eyes appear ;
We see His goodness e'er displayed,
In bounteous harvest every year.

From Him we all our gifts receive,
The Benefactor let us own,
And may we to His glory live,
And bless and make His goodness known.
With solemn awe His works behold,
And view His reign in all supreme,
Adore Him and be of His fold,
While round us His rich mercies stream.

Forgive, O God! our prying thought,
That seeks in vain Thy paths to see;
O grant we ever may be brought,
Humbly on earth to trust in Thee.
O fill our souls with Thy rich love,
O let our faith in Thee abound;
Our finite minds Thy goodness prove—
The infinite cannot be found.

LINES ON HEARING THE BELLS RINGING ON THE SABBATH.

Hark! how the sabbath bells are pealing,
So sweetly o'er my senses stealing;
Mercy to man they seem revealing—
Blest Sabbath day!

To-day from myriads anthems rise,
To swell the music of the skies;
And God to man His love applies—
Blest Sabbath day!

God's children to His house repair,
And offer up their earnest prayer;
God's gracious blessing meets them there—
Blest Sabbath day!

Our souls mount up on wings of love,
To meet our glorious King above,
And there His heavenly presence prove—
Blest Sabbath day!

Hark! from God's houses all around,
The hallelujahs loud resound:
With prayer and praise they each abound—
Blest Sabbath day!

Blest day of rest to mankind given,
To fit his soul to dwell in heaven;
The best by far of all the seven—
Blest Sabbath day!

Each Sabbath brings us nearer home,
And soon His voice shall bid us come,
In eternal glories ever roam—
Blest Sabbath day!

We soon shall gain our portion fair,
Which Christ ascended to prepare;
To spend an endless Sabbath there—
Blest Sabbath day!

Press on, my soul! though rough the road,
That leads thee to that blest abode,
To dwell for ever with thy God—
Blest Sabbath day!

THE SAILOR'S GRAVE AT SEA.

He died far from home in the ship,
As she sailed o'er the watery main;
He has taken his last homeward trip,
To yonder bright heaven'y plain.

No parting fond words from his friends,
 No dear wife to wipe his fond brow;
Released, his soul soon ascends,
 Triumphant he dwells above now.

The poor sailor's for ever at rest.
 He sleeps low in some coral grave,
And the wild waves beat over his breast,
 No more the rough storms will he brave.

Though the place where he lieth be deep,
 To mortals for ever unknown,
Bright Angels watch over his sleep,
 The Omnipotent guardeth His own.

Though we cannot bend over his grave,
 Or hallow his dust with our tears;
Assured that he now is moored safe,
 'Tis that which allayeth our fears.

Moored safely from all this life's harms,
 Sleep tranquilly, thou sailor bold;
Through storms, winds, and peace giving calms,
 Through summer and winter's drear cold.

The wife as she walks the sea shore,
 And sighs for his loss morn and eve,
Thinks of him she will never see more,
 And mournfully doth her heart grieve.

There's a time thou sha't see him again,
 In that glorious dwelling above;
There they'll sing in a loftier strain,
 That God did all in His love.

LINES ON RECEIVING AN INKSTAND AS A PRESENT FROM A FRIEND.

To my table thou art welcome, new friend of my muse,
As the donor from whom thou art come;
A new link of friendship thy sight doth infuse,
That will gladden my heart and my home.
Thou remind'st me of one ever generous and kind,
Whose friendship is firm and sincere;
Who loves to do good with the stores of his mind,
With a conscience exalted and clear.
And while my poor verses in peace I indite,
While I study the learned and the wise,
Happy moments thy presence shall bring to my sight—
Thee, my Inkstand, I ever shall prize.

Beside thee my fond aspirations shall flow,
To the high, and the holy, and good;
As of old the bright vein of my muse shall o'erflow,
As through the night musing I've stood.
I'll think of those days when adversity's gloom
Cast the mantle of sadness around;
When sorrow and sickness o'ershadowed our home.
When solace nor peace could be found.
And then I'll regard thee with gratitude's gaze,
Whilst thankfulness beams from my eyes,
To think that I'm spared thus to write in the praise
Of him whose great friendship I prize.

What solace an object, though simple, may bring,
In our bosoms awaking a theme
That about the domain of our memory will cling,
Like the features imprest in a dream.
Associations will gather—the object around,
Though inanimate, calls forth our love;

The charms of a fond veneration are found
That will draw our affections above,
To loved ones departed whose presence we feel,
That we see in the object arise;
But between thee and me, in woe or in weal,
Thee, my Inkstand, I ever shall prize.

LINES ON HEARING THE REV. NEHEMIAH CURNOCH PREACH A JUBILEE SERMON,

JANUARY 17th, 1864.

Come, Christians, rejoice, and lift up your voice,
While the praise of Emmanuel we sing;
The glad dawn appears, and onward it cheers
Us to labour for God our Great King.
O, what hath He wrought in the multitudes brought
To accept of His gospel divine!
His banner's unfurled, and through all the world
With beams of effulgence will shine.

These are glorious days, which His goodness displays;
He is with us as onward we fight;
His bow spans the heaven, with promises given,
This earth shall be filled with His light.
God's heroes with toil have sown on each soil
The seed of His heavenly word—
It was watered with tears, and hallowed with prayers,
And great shall be their reward.

O, Father! we pray let Thy heavenly ray
Fill this earth, and claim for Thy Son!
Ride on with Thy sword, Emmanuel our Lord,
Till mankind to Thy sceptre is won.

May Thy spirit now fall on Thy servants all,
Like Elijah's mantle descend ;
May our Elishas be blest, with Thy Spirit imprest,
Bringing sinners to Jesus their friend

May each Church now awake, the kingdoms to shake,
In their beautiful garments now shine ;
Let their trumpets peal forth, east, west, south, and north,
Proclaiming the message divine.

Let them echo the tale, o'er mountain, through vale,
That the Jubilee morning arose—
That the gospel's blest word has won earth for our Lord,
And it blossoms again like the rose

May thy children soon see the great jubilee,
By patriarchs and prophets foretold,
When this world 'neath His sway, His word shall obey,
One family —one Shepherd—one—fold.

May Heaven-born bands unite in all lands
Their Hosannas to Jesus here raise ;
May all seek His love, and His kingdom above,
And this earth be filled with His praise.

O, come from above, Angel-heralds of love,
As he did on that glorious morn,
Proclaiming free grace to the whole of our race,
On the day that our Saviour was born.

Let the message of peace our joys here increase,
Through Thy mercy and love to us given,
And the bright glowing rays of millennial days
Unite all the nations with Heaven.

A WELCOME TO CHRISTMAS.

Here's a welcome to thee, Old Christmas!
  We will greet thy presence here;
Thou art come again to cheer us,
  At the happiest time of year.
This is our family gathering,
  And we'll join once more with glee,
To celebrate thy loved return,
  And a welcome give to thee.
        Chorus—Here's a welcome, &c.

Here's a welcome to thee, Old Christmas!
  While gathering round home's hearth,
And take our childhood's place again,
  And tell life's varied path.
How God through life hath blest us all
  With His great mercies here,
And brought us all together now
  To partake of Christmas cheer.
        Chorus—Here's a welcome, &c.

Here's a welcome to thee, Old Christmas!
  We will happy be at home,
Treat every one with kindness true,
  Both children and friends that come.
Thus we'll all rejoice together,
  All care and sorrow chase,
And bid them all be cheerful
  As we greet each welcome face.
      Chorus—Here's a welcome, &c.

Here's a welcome to thee, Old Christmas!
  Hang round the holly berry,
And raise the loving mistletoe,
  And let us all be merry.
Let gladness, mirth, and laughter,
  All bosoms warmly cheer,
And we'll wish that dear Old Christmas
  Came twenty times a year.

CHORUS.

Here's a welcome to thee, Old Christmas!
  We will greet thy presence here;
Thou art come again to cheer us,
  At the happiest time of the year.

LAUGH AND BE MERRY.

Let's laugh and be merry, in innocent mirth;
'Tis really a pleasure of infinite worth.
Indulge it then fully; we still may be wise,
With a radiant brow, and a smile in our eyes;
Then laugh and be merry, child, woman and man—
God's pleasure ordains it, so laugh while you can.

Let's laugh and be merry, 'tis good for the heart,
Though stoics and churls at our merryment start:
Heed not the poor soul who frowns at a straw,
Nor the pelf-scraping miser, e'er yearning for more ·
Then cast off for ever the unbearable ban
Of ill-natured feelings, and laugh while you can.

Let's laugh and be merry, and bury all gloom;
'Tis a pleasing companion, in every home,
Though lowly the dwelling, 'tis easy I'm sure
To live, love, and labour, in cheerfulness pure:
Then laugh and be merry, 'tis an excellent plan,
Though cares may surround you, to laugh while you can.

Let's laugh and be merry, no pleasure we find
In grief and desponding, they injure the mind;
Destroy all that's noble, that's manly and good,
Which have but to be felt to be well understood:
I know it, I've proved it, and thus as a man,
Say laugh and be merry, yes,—laugh while you can.

LINES ON THE DEATH OF MY PARROT.

My favourite parrot, I mourn thee now lost,
  Many hours I miss thee and know thou art dead,
A dear feathered friend, as I know to my cost,
  While tears of true sympathy o'er thee I shed.
Whene'er from my labours I entered my home,
  She well knew the sound of my footsteps and voice,
Would call out my name as I entered the room—
  Whenever she saw me she'd laugh and rejoice.

O death, how relentless! and couldst thou not find
  A creature less faithful to strike with thy hand?
It e'er seemed her pleasure to gladden my mind,
  To pearch on my shoulder, my arm, or my hand

But on my poor Polly must thou lay thy claw,
And take her away from my kindly embrace,
To fill thy most dread and insatiate maw,
And rob me of one of the best of her race?

How she would rejoice when released from her cage,
Would perch on my shoulder and chuckle with glee,
Then pull at my whiskers, my smile to engage,
Kiss my face like a child, for so loving was she;
Then fondly she'd kiss me, and whistle when done,
And talk in my ear too, like some faithful friend;
But death has stepp'd in and our friendship is done,
Her joys and her sorrows for ever must end.

But not so with us: for we ever shall live,
And every act of our lives shall be weighed;
An account at God's bar very strict we must give—
Solemn thought! that of sinning should make us afraid.
But many there'll be, at the judgements great day,
Who talents had here, but who them so absurd
In their day of probation did waste them away,
Annihilation will wish for as this cherish'd bird.

EVENING HYMN.

Shades of darkness round us hovering
And the sun sunk in the west,
The earth with sable mantle covering,
Invite our weary souls to rest.
But before we think of sleeping
We will kneel our vows to pray,
And bless God's holy name for keeping
Our lives from evil through this day,

Most mighty God, accept our praises,
  Which through Christ, we offer Thee;
Accept us in the act that raises,
  Poor fallen man, where'er he be.
O let Thy presence now o'ershadow
  Us who at Thy footstool bend;
Thy Holy Spirit send to hallow
  Our prayers that now to Thee ascend.

Father, give us Thy evening blessing!
  On us, Thy children, love bestow.
Help us onward to be pressing,
  Much more of Thy true love to know.
Guide us through life, we pray of Thee,
  And let Thy mercy clear our way;
Though rough and drear our path may be,
  From Thy side never let us stray.

May each day spent, as evening comes,
  Bring us more near our home above,
And family gatherings in our homes,
  Be types of Heaven's bright home above.
Then when the hosts of Heaven adore,
  And praise Thy name for mercies here,
May we united reach that shore,
  And all before Thy throne appear.

We shall rejoice there that Thy praise
  Did sound forth from our homes below;
When we in Heaven our voices raise,
  And our full souls with rapture glow.
O take us now into Thy keeping,
  To guard and keep us through the night;
Watch over us whilst we are sleeping,
  Wake us to praise at morning light.

LINES ON THE REVIVALS OF RELIGION.

What are Revivals, and what do they show?—
God's wonderful Love to mankind below;
For He hath the power if His churches will pray,
To save a whole nation in one single day.

The church is the light of our God on earth here;
The Bible the light by which His saints steer;
The Gospel the life-boat, to us sinners sent,
That Christ preached on earth wherever He went.

'Tis Christ's people's duty to preach it to all,
And sternly uphold it whatever befall;
A Christian that's idle, wherever he's found,
His duties neglects whilst men fall around.

But the church's opponents full often will say,
"What good is it for you to preach and to pray?
And why do you make this fuss and this noise,
The worldling to stop from carnal earth's joys?

Why not let him take all the pleasure he can?
For short is this life and contracted its span;
Then let him alone, and let him enjoy
The pleasures of life, if his soul they destroy..

Yes, let him alone! what is that, then, to you,
That about his great soul you make this ado?
It is nothing to you, that I know very well,
If he's journeying to Heaven or going to hell."

Mortal man, let us beg you—entreat you—take care,
Of slighting God's word I would have you beware;
The wicked he can consume with a breath,
And send them direct to eternal death.

But Christians must labour and sow the good seed--
What mortals may say he never must heed—
They must use their talents by God to them given
To rescue poor souls, and direct them to heaven.

To me, a good Christian's first duty appears
To fear God, and do good whenever he steers;
If he saves but one soul from sin's erring ways,
For ever that convert will show forth his praise.

What would be said of us, if when passing by
We heard from a river a piteous cry
Appealing to us a poor creature to save
From losing his life in a watery grave?

The world would say truly we were worse than brutes,
If we passed by unheeding on other pursuits,
And left a fellow creature to sink and to die,
With power to rescue him, but cared not to try.

God's churches in apathy ne'er should be found,
Whilst sinners are daily departing around;
But their duty to Him is to labour and pray,
That God His great mercy and power would display.

Thy Holy Spirit, O Father, from heaven now pour
On this city a full and benevolent shower,
Whilst for a revival Thy church lifts its voice,
O hear Thou their prayers, and Thy children rejoice.

Receive Thine own work in our land, we now pray,
And show Thine own power in a Pentecost day;
Throughout many lands Thy power has been shown,
And glorious showers have fallen on our own.

We bless Thy great name, where'er Thou hast trod,
Showing to man 'twas the work of our God,
All glory to Thee—all Thy churches shall tell
How much Thou hast shaken the shackles of hell.

Come now, blessed Lord, and show forth Thy sway,
And send us Thy blest Holy Spirit's bright ray,
And over earth's darkness shed wonderful light,
To fill all the world with thy presence so bright.

Soon may all the earth before Thy throne bow—
We know it will be, let us each see it now ;
Dispel, we beseech Thee, old Satan's dark night,
And over this earth uphold Thy blest right :

And then the whole world very clearly will see
All revivals whatever proceedeth from Thee,
As tokens they're sent of Thy fatherly love,
To prepare us to dwell in a bright home above.

BLESSED ARE THEY THAT MOURN: THEY SHALL BE COMFORTED.

"Blessed are the mourners," Jesus said,
"Who sorrow on account of sin,
In them my mercy is displayed,
And heaven they are sure to win."
Fret not, poor mourners, on the road
That brings you nearer to such bliss ;
Look upward to that blest abode,
Where end the heavy toils of this,

The blackest cloud to us displays
  The rainbow in its brightest form;
Reflecting God's own covenant rays,
  The bow of peace succeeds the storm.
So in the darkest storms of life,
  When rough waves nearly overwhelm;
Remember through this earth of strife
  That Christ is always at the helm.

Tried souls of Christ, with trusting mind,
  Doubt not His love, you are His care;
To lambs like you He calms the wind,
  And tells you never to despair.
'Tis He alone can guide you well,
  Through life if on Him you depend;
'Tis He your fears can all dispel,
  And prove life's best and faithful friend.

And He shall pilot your frail bark,
  Shall bid temptation's storm to cease,
And when it seems to you most dark,
  Will still the waves till all is peace.
The storms of life may round you war,
  And fill your soul with anxious fears,
You're journeying on and soon will soar
  Above this world of sighs and tears.

THE PRODIGAL'S RETURN.

Hark how the Prodigal cries,
  Borne down by grief and woe;
"I'll now in haste arise,
  And to my father go.

Sure he will hear my prayer,
And mercy grant to me,
Though I despised his care,
And love he showed to me.

To my father once more I turn,
And this shall be my prayer—
'Though unworthy, late I learn,
My conduct brings despair'
Unworthy to be his son,
I'll fall down at his feet;
My faults to him will own,
Repentant will him meet.

Long time on husks I fed;
Bitterly now I mourn,
That from his house I fled,
But home I will return.
O will he then me spurn,
Who once was fond and kind;
And say, should anger burn,
'In me no friend you'll find.'

I know I have done him wrong,
His counsel set at nought,
And wilful I've gone headlong;
His peace I ne'er have sought
My heart was filled with pride.
I thought myself secure;
I scorned to seek a guide,
Till hunger did endure.

Yet my father's men have got
Enough bread and to spare;
I'll with them cast my lot,
And take a servant's share.

How most wretched have I been,
  And wicked deeds have done ;
My garments torn and meam,
  Still I'm his youngest son."

The father sees him on his knees,
  And longs him to embrace,
And welcomes him again with peace,
  While tears fall down his face.
Thus the long-lost child returns,
  Receives affection's kiss.
As with love his bosom burns,
  And his are tears of bliss.

"O my poor repentant child,
  My mercy he shall know ;
He's wayward been and wild,
  Yet love to him I'll show.
Never can a father's love
  Turn from a repentant son,
And the best robe bring to prove,
  And let him put it on.

And the ring put on his hand,
  To bind him near my heart ;
Come now, and near me stand,
  And never more depart.
And bring the fatted calf,
  Let all again be joy,
And rejoice in his behalf,
  I see again my boy."

How oft do parents mourn.
  When loved ones go astray ;
They from their best friends turn,
  And will have their own way.

Such stubborn ones have brought,
Their parents' grey hairs low,
Who in the grave have sought
Belief from all their woe.

Some late repentant turn,
And mercy seek by prayer;
With love God's mercies burn,
And none e'er need despair.
He listens to their lays,
Who humbly to Him go;
God says, "Behold, he prays,
My mercy he shall know."

When stricken sinners plead,
And vile themselves confess,
Our God their prayers will heed,
And He their souls will bless.
Angels will tune their lyres,
And songs of praise be given,
For brands plucked from the fire,
And made the heirs of Heaven..

LINES ON THE OLD DEPARTED YEAR.

Hark! the solemn midnight bell,
Tells me another year has fled;
And to us all it says "farewell!'
How quickly has it from us sped;

Thou'rt gone for ever, past old year,
And all thy joys and cares are o'er;
That sounding bell reminds us here,
That year is past for evermore.

But oh ! what changes in the time
Have happened, of the last year's round ;
Some friends are in a distant clime,
And some lie in the silent ground.

And can we let the year that's past
Escape our memories like a dream ?
No ! rather let us view the past
As one more gone from life's short stream.

Some whom we here did fondly love,
Have gone and left us still below ;
They faded, died, then soared away,
And now a Saviour's love they know.

Hath worldly love engrossed our mind—
Ambition been our greatest aim ?
And tried in these our peace to find,
And sought nought else but earthly fame ?

If so, what broken cisterns we
Have hewn ourselves, that will not hold
The stream of life ; nor could we see
That life's allurements were not gold.

Still there are scenes that now are gone,
Our memories can with pleasure greet,
When souls to pure devotion won,
Together kneel at Jesus' feet.

'Tis gone and past, but each one shall
It meet, when at God's bar appear ;
To testify we lived it well,
May we improve each coming year !

LINES ON THE TALK OF INVASION BY THE FRENCH.

My country I love, and who is there dare
To invade its fair surface, so free and so fair ?
Whose sons are so hardy, so bold, and so brave,
Who would fight until death to protect and to save
Their homes and their children, their parents and wives,
For whom they would gladly endanger their lives.
The sons of old England will conquor or die,
And never were known to shrink or to fly ;
On sea or on land they've e'er held the palm,
And shielded our country from terror or harm ;
When war's crimson banner they've ever unfurled,
A terror they've proved and astonished the world.

Against them at Agincourt three were to one,
And yet soon the victory nobly they won :
King Henry the Fifth—the hero that day—
Addressing his army, thus bravely did say,—
" Is there one single man in my army afraid ?
Then let him go home—let his passport be made."

Not one of that valiant and disciplined band
But scorned to return to his fair native land ;
Like lions they fought on that fierce battle field,
Till the army of France was forced there to yield ;
By Britain's sons beaten, some few fled away,
And thousands were slain in that glorious fray.

And long o'er the sea England's sceptre has swayed,
Extended her commerce, religion, and trade ;
Trafalgar and Nile show the fame of her sons,
When they conquered their fleets and silenced their guns ;
The history of Britain most plainly doth show,
No reason has she to fear any foe.

And Waterloo showed how well they could fight,
How the legions of France they soon put to flight,
How nobly there victory soon they did gain;
And the British flag waves over every plain
Throughout every land, then who is afraid
Our foes will attempt our land to invade?

But if they are bold enough, then let them come,
They soon will be glad to return to their home;
With one hundred thousand riflemen brave
In England, would send them soon to the grave;
Should a hostile foe ever land on our shore,
They will all be destroyed and heard of no more.

LINES ON THOMAS FARMER, Esq.

Farmer, most worthy! my muse will rehearse
Thy deeds and thy virtues in this humble verse;
I'll endeavour a record of thy worth to raise,
That time may hand down to tell of thy praise.

What pleasure it must be to feel and to know
Thy bounty hath helped missionaries to sow
The seed of the gospel in every clime,
Like a good farmer waiting the harvest full time.

Throughout thy whole life thy deeds are all famed,
Of the faith of Christ's cross thou hast not been ashamed;
Thou'st done all thou couldst through the breadth of the land,
To help and to spread the great Wesleyan band.

And ofttimes with pity thy feelings o'erflow,
That our race so benighted does not Jesus know;
That a very large portion ne'er heard of his name,
Their bosoms so wretched ne'er felt his love's flame.

Farmer ! what love thou didst ever display
In sending the Gospel, whose life-giving ray
Shall in triumph dispel the gloom of all sin,
Every son of old Adam to Christ's fold bring in ;

When the heathen be given to our blessed Lord,
And from earth's widest bounds His name is adored ;
From heaven thou'lt see the seed thou hast sown
In tablets of life o'er this earth will be shown.

And though in a good Master's cause thou'rt grey,
Thy harvest thou'lt see in that blessed day ;
When all mankind then shall stand before God,
O glad thou wilt be for the path thou hast trod.

To see saints redeemed from each land and clime,
Through the blest works of thy life's sowing time ;
Through all thy remaining life may'st thou be found
Working for God, and with honour e'er crowned.

And thou sinkest when from earth fade away,
May thy soul then ascend to bright realms of day,
And join the pure host, redeemed now above,
From every clime singing of thy Saviours love.

LINES ON THE RAGGED SCHOOL.

It was not the rich scholars, and clean,
  That I saw at a school in one street ;
But the ragged and poor there were seen,
  With scarce any shoes to their feet.

Their clothes were all ragged and torn,
  And their faces all covered with dirt ;
And abject they looked and careworn,
  And many with scarcely a shirt.

Their hair was all matted and rough,
Seemed strangers to brush and to comb;
Quite hoarse were their voices, and gruff,
And cold and forlorn was their home.

If you only had heard in that street,
Their language, so wicked and wild,
You'd say as your ear it did greet,
"Oh! who is there cares for that child?

But there are some here with kind hearts,
Who have pity on children of sin;
In the Ragged School they take their parts,
Stray lambs of Christ's flock to bring in.

For the love of their Lord who once told
Peter his lambs all to feed;
And they try to bring home to His fold
Young children, who stand in much need.

Though rough and unpolished they are,
Like Jewels just dug from the mine,
These teachers prepare them with care,
As gems in Christ's kingdom to shine.

And the Scriptures do truly declare
Christ died for the whole of the race;
And their angels so bright and so fair,
In Heaven receive a blest place.

And it is their Father's blest will
That none of these young should be lost—
Then to save them, O try all your skill?
Redeemed as they were at such cost.

This fact is quite painful, though true,
  That thousands go down to the grave
Uncared for, and pitied by few
  Who've the power to endeavour to save.

Ladies, decked with their jewels so rare,
  And many earthly comforts beside ;
If they shrink from these labours to share,
  Can a part of their wealth put aside

To assist the kind teachers they go
  To labour in this noble cause ;
And to lessen much sorrow and woe,
  Save children from breaking God's laws.

And those who would patriots be,
  Who their country love to hear praised ;
Education's rich blessings must see,
  Is the lever by which it is raised.

Such patriots I very much doubt,
  Whate'er their fine works may declare,
If they coldly look on, and without
  A desire in these labours to share.

There's only one life to us each,
  So let ours be a well-written book,
That to others good morals may teach,
  As over its pages they look.

May none of the pages prove blanks,
  And those left behind us all own
We deserved all their blessings and thanks,
  For example we had to them shown.

And then when they look on our grave,
  They'll look on our dust with a tear,
And tell how he laboured to save
  Poor sinners while sojourning here.

ON SEEING A MOTH FLY INTO THE FLAME OF A CANDLE.

Poor helpless insect ! attracted by the glare,
Thou'st found how soon thou mayest be deceived ;
Thou'st fallen beneath that bright but dangerous snare,
That lay behind the brightness unpreceived.

And thus in life the gay alluring charms
Of pleasure's sound too often will ensnare ;
And late we find that sin and folly harms,
And to our lives bring many a saddening care.

The youth that roams through summer's sunny fields,
On the gaudy butterfly to lay his hold ;
Its gaudy plumage to him pleasure yields,
But to the insect pain and grief untold.

How often man the shadow but pursues,
With airy thoughts he sails along life's stream ;
With wild ambition oft his mind imbues,
As baseless as the shadows in a dream.

But there are some who, like the busy bee,
Extract some good from every balmy flower--
That cause delight when we their virtues see,
That bless mankind as with a genial shower.

And thus we may improve our life's short day ;
Do all we can to do our fellows good,
That when our vigour's power shall fade away,
We may regard the past as good men should.

And then our lives will not be spent in vain,
If to our race a blessing have been made ;
Thus to ourselves will surely be the gain,
And leave a name that time will never fade.

THE DREAM OF HEAVEN.

One night, worn and weary, I went to my bed,
With my sorrows and cares hardly prest,
When a beautiful vision came into my head,
And I drempt I was safe with the blest.
No cares or sad thoughts overshadowed their brow,
They rejoiced in full glory above ;
The light from the Lamb it did brilliantly glow,
All full on the saints of His love.

But how can I tell you the beauties of Heaven,
Revealed unto me in my dream ?
To mortals or angels it never was given
The power to describe the blest theme.
I'm longing to tell it but feel at a loss—
So wonderful 'twas and so grand ;
And all upon earth seemed but refuse and dross.
When compared to that far better land.

But if now my memory will serve me aright,
I will tell of my dreaming so fair—
Of the glory and beauty of that world so bright,
And the peace and the happiness there.
I saw the archangels with gossamer wings,
There did seraphs and cherubims raise
Their voices in rapture as each one he sings,
Whilst chanting their great Maker's praise,

I have seen the bright sun sink away in the west,
Like a flame of bright amber and gold ;
But that, when compared to the saint's happy rest,
Was as nought in compare to behold.
With rapturous awe I beheld all around,—
New glories kept meeting my sight ;
A stream of pure happiness constantly found,
In this beautiful Heaven so bright.

Its gates of rich pearl did in grandeur surpass
  Far more than my thoughts could conceive:
.ts streets of pure gold were like bright shining glass,
  More glorious than man could believe.
The high walls were studded with rich precious stones,
  Like sapphires and rubies they shine;
In brilliance and beauty so matchless they show,
  The architect was the Builder divine.

In amaranthine bowers, all clothed in white,
  On their brow was inscribed the new name,—
The white stone that glistens so lovely and bright,
  Were the saints with the emblems of fame.
On earth they were never ashamed of the cross,
  And conquered through Christ's mighty love,
All worldly-sought gain they counted but loss,
  And they reign now midst riches above.

And some I saw there who on earth were opprest,
  In troubles passed over life's race;
But in joy they arrived at the home of the blest,
  And were saved by the riches of grace.
Their clothes, soiled and ragged, were taken away,
  And white robes were supplied to each one;
In glory celestial, reflecting Christ's ray—
  In His image they shone like the sun.

I saw a clear river, so pure and so bright.
  That flowed on, refreshing all there,—
It dazzled my eyes as it steamed in the light,
  And, like crystal, resplendently fair.
The Lamb to this river of water did lead
  The flock He redeemed with His blood;
In lovely green pastures His saints He did feed,
  And His love comforts in that abode.

The blest tree of life it was there bearing fruit,
  Of its virtues rich all could partake ;
All blessings were there the righteous to suit,
  And those who had lived for Christ's sake,
Who'd accomplished some mission for Him upon earth,
  To bring others to love Him and praise ;
And lead them to seek for the Spirit's new birth,
  Who from death to new life did arise.

My soul seemed enraptured with holy sweet joy,
  Seeing myriads of saints walking there ;
In hymns of loud praises their time they employ,
  'Midst God's love in that region so fair.
On a throne of bright jasper the Almighty King
  Display'd the rich fund of His love ;
The rainbow illumine—the choirs loudly sing,
  And fill the whole Heaven above.

One I loved I saw there, with scars and with wounds ;
  Calm holy rays beamed from His face,
With loud hallelujahs His temple resounds,
  All His saints now rejoice in His grace.
Sweet music arose now from trumpets and strings,
  Flowing melody on my ear broke,
In praise of their Saviour and great King of Kings,
  While in ecstacy sweet I awoke.

HAD I THE MIND TO WILL MANKIND.

Had I the mind to will mankind,
  Each one to be sincere,
All tongues to tell with lofty swell
  The heart's emotions clear—

Bright bliss should beam in endless stream,
To warm each heart and hand;
What sweet relief!—how little grief
Should spread around our land.

The claims of right should rise o'er might,
And merit forth should shine;
I'd form a plan to measure man,
And worth should be my line.
I'd say to all—"Let nought appal,
Behold the pile of fame!
Advance like men—brain, arm, and pen,
And grace it with your name."

I'd strike a blow aside to throw
All envy from the world;
The lips I'd close where vice o'erflows,
And truth be wide unfurled
Then should we find, as God designed,
Our life become a boon;
And peace would reign on earth again,
Like Eden's brilliant noon.

THE RIFLE, THE VOICE, AND THE PEN.

When country requires all the aid of her sons
Its freedom and soil to defend,
Through its ranks a bright spirit of loftiness runs,
And warm aspirations ascend.
For the noblest of sentiment lighteth the soul
Of the patriot, where freedom is known;
He scorns the idea of ambition's control,
And burns for the land of his own.

'Tis our duty when Fatherland calls to the field,
To answer as Britons and men,
And grasp each the weapon he's fitted to wield—
The Rifle, the Voice, and the Pen.

Where confidence lives and ambition's unknown,
The Voice and the Pen may be strong;
But where the reverse is so frequently shown,
To repose upon these would be wrong.
That war is unholy—a terrible curse—
No one in his senses denies;
But serfdom of souls 'neath a despot is worse,
When the Angel of Liberty flies.
Then let's be prepared in all seasons and hours,
No matter our station or when;
Be armed with those weapons, akin to our powers—
The Rifle, the Voice, and the Pen.

O where is the land that can equal our isle?
Where the monarch—our pride and our boast?
Where the hearts who have reared so immortal a pile
Of glory and fame on our coast?
'Tis no wordy affair that dissolves on the lips,
'Tis no fanciful myth just to please;
We are rich, we have freedom, trade, commerce, and ships,
And a monarchy over the seas.

I hold then 'tis noble, deny it who may,
To regard our position as men,
And preserve our much envied pre-eminent sway
With the Rifle, the Voice, and the Pen.

THE WORDS OF THE WIFE.

My dearest love, despond not,
  Though cares our course assail;
O dearest husband, sigh not,
  Nor fortune's frowns bewail.
Come, raise thy spirits cheerly,
  And cease thee to repine;
I'll prize thee ever dearly:
  My heart shall e'er be thine.

It matters not to me, love,
  Though cold the world may stare,
Whate'er befalleth thee, love,
  With cheerfulness I'll share.
Have courage, I implore thee,
  For brighter days may shine;
The world is still before thee:
  My heart shall e'er be thine.

Be firm, and meet all crosses,
  And chase them from thy mind;
Let not our worldly losses
  Thy noble feelings blind;
O, smile! and dreary sorrow
  To oblivion consign,
For joy may beam to-morrow:
  My heart shall e'er be thine.

'Tis cowards only murmur,
  And sink beneath despair;
Our ills shall make us firmer
  To grapple every care.

Sore pains make ease the lighter,
To work our grand design;
And darkness light the brighter:
My heart shall e'er be thine.

Believe me nought can alter
The emotions of my breast,
Or make my fond love falter,
Or lower affection's crest.
In weal or woe my bosom
Around thy path shall twine,
Still full and fresh in blossom:
My heart shall e'er be thine.

And when old age o'ertakes us,
All senses fail and dim;
When health and strength forsake us,
In intellect and limb;
Thy worth and truth I'll cherish,
Through all our onward line;
Though youth and beauty perish,
My heart shall e'er be thine.

LINES ON MISS ELIZABETH C—— OF HULL.

With glowing beams Aurora decks the morn,
Like gold he tinges every radiant flower;
The fields and gardens choicely doth adorn,
And throws sweet beauties o'er each lovely bower.

The lark soars high with clear melodious song—
With lively voice he warbles forth his lay,
With hills surrounding echoing it along—
The glorious harbinger of opening day.

The hedges sparkle with the morning dew,
  Like diamond gems in brilliant lustre shine;
The violet peeps forth clothed in purple hue,
  Enriching the air like fragrant eglantine.

The blushing rose salutes the morning sun,
  In balmy fragrance seeks the monarch's aid;
The sunflower turns where'er his course is run,
  Gladdening upland, pasture, glen, and glade.

'Tis fit that I should thus call to my aid
  The richest beauties of each fragrant flower,
To describe so fair and beautiful a maid,
  Whose form delights in hall, or room, or bower.

Whose mind, with stores of learning's richly graced,
  With magic power glides in upon our heart;
In nature's finest mould each feature traced,
  It causes deep regret when we should part.

Thy life seems woven by some fairy loom;
  Sweet as the heather flower at early morn
With aromatic odour seems to bloom;
  O may it flourish free from every thorn!

May every year thy happiness increase,
  And time, as on it rolls its rapid course,
Bring nought to thee but happiness and peace,
  And may'st thou ne'er on troubled seas be tossed!

May truth and virtue shine around thy life,
  And sorrow flee for ever from thy breast;
Whether as maiden pure, or virtuous wife,
  May'st thou in every path of life be blest!

And may the poor around thee bless thy name;
  And memory, as it tells of good deeds past,
Give thee a title to a virtuous fame,
  And a bright Heaven for thy lot at last!

LINES TO MY WIFE ON OUR 21st WEDDING DAY, NOVEMBER 22nd, 1859.

Once more, dear wife, has time's incessant wing
Traversed the seasons, and returned to bring
November round, with winter's early ray:
This is the annual of our wedding day.

Years, twenty-one, their varied course hath sped,
Scattering joys and sorrows o'er our head,
Since love presented us at wedlock's shrine,
And Hymen bound thy hand and heart with mine.

Then, in the gay and blooming time of youth,
We pledged our vows of constancy and truth;
As age arrives we happy record bear—
Our plighted vows were mutually sincere.

Throughout my life, in restrospective view,
I've ever found my thanks to heaven are due;
Nor least of God's sweet thanks should I pray
For that blest one that cheered my wedding day:

When God to soothe my rugged path through life,
Sent me my faithful friend and loving wife;
And with her care by tender precepts charmed,
My mind has been with prudent counsel armed.

By whom advised in all things for my good,
In virtue's footsteps steadily I've trod;
A watchful guard, when dangers did surround,
In her a faithful counsellor I've found.

Highly esteemed, for prudent conduct most
She proves her husband's highest pride and boast;
To her my grateful thanks are always given—
I hope and trust her recompense is Heaven.

The nuptial cup by Providence prepared,
Of Sweets and bitters mixed, by all are shared ;
Our share of sweets thus far our thanks should call—
We have found the honey much outweigh the gall.

Though humble has our lot in life yet been,
We've happier been by shunning each extreme ;
Though riches we could never boast much store,
Hunger's grim wolf has ne'er approached our door.

By mutual striving for each other's good,
We've kept away that fiend, domestic feud ;
And may the future days we've yet to come
Still find us cheerful in our happy home.

And when arrives the inevitable doom,
May we find peace beyond the earthly tomb ;
Long as we hold our life's declining way,
Shall grateful memory bless our wedding day !

AN APPEAL ON BEHALF OF THE POOR.

Stern winter now, draws on with nipping cold,
With icy grasp throughout our land doth reign !
How many clothed in rags do we behold,
Worn down by sorrow, sickness, and in pain

Who seem to plead with those who can bestow
From their abundance, alms to cheer and bless :
And pleading hard that they will mercy show
Unto their fellows creatures in distress !

For the Saviour from His throne now sees
Your acts of love and charity ;
And says, "Whate'er ye do for these,
Ye do it also unto Me."

How racked their minds 'midst many earthly cares,
With hungry children crying, wanting bread!
For those who give they offer up their prayers,
That God will all His choicest blessings shed.
O you that are with plenty blest at home,
And ne'er experienced hunger's bitter pain,
Now benefactors to the poor become;
O do not let them cry to you in vain!
For the Saviour from His throne now sees
Your acts of love and charity;
And says, "Whate'er ye do for these
Ye do it also unto Me."

And you will thus enjoy your own the more.
Of widows think, and orphans you relieve!
You'll ne'er regret thus using from your store;
And for the wealth thus spent you'll never grieve.
When on the bed of death you come to lie,
With joy you'll think upon the time gone past,
When oft you've listened to the orphan's cry,
And o'er the widow rays of joy hath cast.
For the Saviour from His throne now sees
Your acts of love and charity;
And says, "Whate'er ye do for these,
Ye do it even unto Me."

O ye of wealth and fortune of our land
Have mercy, we beseech you, on the poor;
Your charity bestow, and firmly stand
The friends of those who wander to your door.
Think of your wealth as talents to employ
For other's good, when they are most in need;
'Tis in your power to make them sing with joy,
For you have plenty while the poor you feed.

For the Saviour from His throne now sees
Your acts of love and charity;
And says, Whate'er ye do for these,
Ye do it even unto Me.'

LINES ON S. GURNEY, Esq, M.P.,

TAKING THE CHAIR AT FOSTER STREET RAGGED SCHOOLS, APRIL 24TH, 1860.

Noble Gurney! accept this humble lay;
Let these few lines an earnest tribute pay
Of respect to one who dares be good.
We thee admire, whose taste refines,
In judgment chast, of polished mind,
As patron of ragged schools hath stood.

And in thy breast what constant pleasure springs
From doing good, what comfort e'er it brings
Into thy kind and generous heart!
Thou'rt happy in the treasures of thy mind;
In peace thy soul soars free and unconfined,
Still resolved in life to do thy part.

Through affluence surrounds thee with its beams,
Yet on the poor thy bounty nobly streams,
Desiring firmly their sad state to raise.
True patriotism this, to gladden those
Bowed down by sin, by poverty, and woes—
This shall redound for ever to thy praise.

Mayst thou of good the patron ever stand—
With noble Shaftesbury and a Christian band—
And a blessing to thy country prove!
And may Heaven its richest blessings shed,
While thou art living, on thy honoured head,
And fill thy worthy soul with heavenly love.

And when thy noble mission's done on earth,
May many records of thy truth and worth
To ages yet to come be handed down.
Then may thy noble spirit calmly rise,
To enjoy those blessed mansions in the skies,
And Christ give thee an immortal crown!

ESSEX HALL TEA MEETING.

At Johnson's house, called Essex Hall,
We met a friendly, Christian band;
And Christian ladies there did call—
A treat the owners there had planned.

For on the lawn we had our tea,
Beneath a mulberry tree, whose shade
Subdued the heat, and then with glee
A quiet sweet repast we made.

The roses with their sweet perfume
With fragrance filled the evening air—
Emitted from each bud and bloom—
The trees their luscious fruitage bear.

Of interest there were two bay trees
So fine, with shrubs and flowers around;
The richest incense filled the breeze,—
Rich nature's beauties there were found.

The evening sun we did behold,
Gilding the earth with radiant hue,
Tipping the hills like burnished gold,
The sky with bright celestial blue.

The peacock pranced about so gay,
  And showed his splendid spreading tail;
Birds carolled forth their evening lay,
  Borne on the balmy zephyr's gale.

Tea done, friend Johnson took the chair,
  And round him we ourselves did seat;
Aldous and West, and Taylor there,
  With others he did warmly greet.

And to us all he,did declare
  How God through Christ his soul had blest,
And how he now was journeying there
  To that high heavenly home of rest.

'Twas Waterloo's great annual day,
  Which ever calls to mind again
When our brave soldiers gained the day,
  And thousands of the French were slain.

Phillip Hardcastle told us there
  The regiments' movements in detail:
Of front and centre, van and rear,
  How the attack on Hugomont did fail.

And all exploits he did relate,
  Describing clear, he did it well,
From beginging to the last retreat,
  So animated did he tell.

Some more addressed the meeting there,
  Some poetry was also read;
And on the summer evening's air
  The praises of our God were sped.

A good bazaar was also there,
At which Miss Johnson did preside ;
And all seemed happy without care,
As onward time did gently glide.

And when the day was far, far spent,
We had to leave and meet the train ;
We thanked God for his blessings sent,
And Johnson hoped to meet again.

RETROSPECTION OF LIFE.

Life's meridian's past ! the future unknown !
I will try to review what I have here sown,
And what the next harvest is likely to be—
What eternity surely will prove unto me.

Solemn thought ! what a term of this life there is gone,
And a more solemn thought, how little I ve done ;
Much time I've mis-spent and my talents abused,
And little for God or for man have been used.

I stand quite amazed, when I look on the past,
And fear o'er my spirit a gloom hath now cast ;
Retrospection to me very clearly doth show
I have wasted my time greatcly whilst here below

O thou God of mercy ! let time ever past
Admonish me ; grant that it may be the last
In trifles consumed, or in vain worldly care ;
Made wise by the past, for the end I prepare.

I see nought within I surely can trust,
Of my own righteous works in no action just
And ofttimes I think I have lived in vain.
And wish that the past I could live o'er again.

But vain is the wish, and therefore I'll try
To live well the remainder before I shall die ;
As I look back in grief upon time vanished now,
To my mind it brings many a part broken vow.

Now lost I may be, and for ever undone,
Unless saved by mercy through God's only Son ;
Uncertainty's stamped on the lives of us all,,
For none know the hour that death may them call.

If we go to the churchyard there we may scan,
On the tombstones the different ages of man ;
How very few reaching a century lie there !
But children and youth a large portion share.

Many fathers' fond hope, or mothers' best joy,
In some beautiful girl, or fine blooming boy,
Have coused poignant sorrow their features to shade,
To see their dear treasured ones sicken and fade.

Some were in vigour, in life's fullest bloom,
Struck by fever and borne to a premature tomb ;
Others, unwarned, dropping suddenly dead,
The spirit from out its frail tenement fled.

Solemn thought ! if this should e'er be my case,
O where should I go ? and which be my place ?
What stern, solemn lessons these tombstones all teach !
A lesson which all our emotions should reach.

The time that's still left, O use with great care,
For the certain eternal world thyself prepare ;
Work while yet 'tis day, and do all you can
To accomplish salvation for each fellow man.

O Thou! whose great love still to me endures,
And mercy still unto my soul assures;
Now hear, O my Father! hear my vows to-day,
Forgive all my broken vows to Thee I pray.

I firmly desire now, with glad heart and free,
Myself and possessions to offer to Thee;
My weakness Thou knowest, then O guide my way,
That never again from Thy side I may stray.

But love Thee and serve Thee with patient heart,
Away from Thy precepts no more to depart,
Till landed I'm safe on th' eternal shore,
I will praise Thee and love Thee for time evermore.

LINES ON THE DEATH OF MY FRIEND. REV. G. B. STRANGWAYS.

Friend George is gone—from us he's ta'en his flight,
And winged his way to eternal realms of light;
His voice on earth we never shall hear more,
He's safely landed on the eternal shore.
Whilst here he in the paths of virtue trod,
And all his talents exercised for God;
He to reward him, sent a heavenly band,
To bear him yonder to that better land.

Cherubic legions at his bed-side wait
To bear him to the ever-blessed gate
Of Heaven high, in beauty to behold
Its pearly portals and its streets of gold;
And there arrayed in robes of spotless white,
The redeemed sees, now with their songs unite.
On his dear Saviour doth he fondly gaze,
And sing with joy his Maker's hymns of praise.

Poor invalid! while he was dwelling here,
Alternating long 'tween hope and fear,
How meekly borne by him the Saviour's cross,
Without which counting all things here but loss.
In judgement good, in taste was most refined
Serene and chaste his high and polished mind;
With glowing zeal and ever-earnest prayer
He laboured here for souls with yearning care.

On learning e'er his studious mind was bent—
To become a missionary his intent;
But while his studies hard he thus pursued,
Disease his sinking wasting form subdued,
And o'er his friends it cast a chilling gloom;
They grieved to see him hastening to the tomb.
He is now gone! as we look back we trace
His memory decked with every virtuous grace.

Most eloquent was he in Scripture's might,
To preach Christ's mercy was his chief delight;
His graceful manners all with love did blend,
Delighting all to know and call him friend.
Blest spirit! this accept, my humble lay—
The only tribute that I now can pay
For all thy friendship and thy love on earth,
Is to record just homage to thy worth.

And oft from earth my thoughts will upward rise,
To think of thee now blessed in the skies;
And looking forward to that blest reward,
Purchased for us by our Saviour Lord.
Following in thy meekly footsteps blest,
To attain like thee the promised heavenly rest;
United then our thankful voices raise,
And sing for ever in our Saviour's praise.

Now of eternal life hast thou made sure,
Thy happy spirit dwells among the pure ;
Any every falling tear is wiped away,
In those bright realms of everlasting day.
Cease mourning, friends! weep not for him again!
He is now freed from every care and pain ;
Wish him not back from forth his high abode,
He rests now in the glories of his God

LINES ON ALFRED HAMMOND.

DIED APRIL 20TH, 1858, AGED TWO YEARS.

The lovely flowers of spring are blooming round,
And nature smiles, all clothed in verdant hue ;
But Alfred's lovely form lies in the ground,
Awaiting the Resurrection, to arise anew.

The mother, as they lowly laid him down,
Wept at the thought of his once fond caress ;
No more will he on her fond bosom bound,
His happy spirit dwells among the blest.

O could his voice be heard from Heaven above,
He'd tell his parents now to weep no more ;
The little angel sings the song of love,
And joins with rapture the angelic choir.

"Rejoice, O father ! mother, shout for joy !
Give thanks that God away has taken me !
Praise the dear Saviour, with your darling boy,
That where I am ye both may ever be !

And when earth's scene for ever close with you,
And death releases you from every care,
As Heaven's bright gates unfold before your view,
To receive and welcome you, I shall be there.

And as the plains of Heaven we roam along,
We'll talk of Him and of His love we'll tell;
Sing loud hosannahs with the heavenly throng,
And shout, 'My God, Thou hast done all things well.'"

LINES AFTER HEARING A LECTURE BY THE REV. W. M. PUNSHON.

Great lecturer, and preacher, thou art inspired
With eloquence! thy tongue seems always fired,
And thousands listen to each glowing word
That pleasure to the minds of all afford.
From out thy lips the sacred force of truth
Inspires the mind of many a wavering youth;
Thy words hath caused them ever to leave sin,
And quick set out eternal life to win.

Into Christ's Church thou hast many brought,
To make all converts earnestly thou'st sought;
It is surprising, also nobly grand,
To see thee 'fore a crowded audience stand
And hear thy eloquent and flowing tongue
Enchant thy hearers, all both old and young:
They listen to thy powerful words intense,
Thy oratory chains both thought and sense.

Thou can'st before our minds such pictures draw,
To thee we listen with a breathless awe,
And wonder how it is thou can'st so bind
With potent spell the cultivated mind.
How didst thou gain those mighty thoughts sublime,
To bring forth in thy lectures every time,
To sway our judgments and our thoughts refine —
A masterpiece is found in every line.

Virtue in such forms thou canst pourtray
That makes us wish it ever held the sway;
That 'neath its spell our lives might all be brought,
Its peaceful sceptre o'er each act and thought.
And vice thou picturest with hideous glare—
Its base allurements which so oft ensnare—
That makes us tremble for the worldly gay,
Who shun truth's path and fritter life away.

How faithfully thy preaching doth reveal
God's love to man, and makes each conscience feel
Christ's saving grace to all thy flock convey,
Or warm with terrors of the judgment day.
Punshon! we bless thee, trusting thou mayest see
Saved souls above converted here by thee;
At Heaven's pearly gate may angels come
With heavenly greeting, "Welcome, brother, home."

And enter with them to thy Saviour's joy.
Through all eternity thy voice employ,
Which was thy pleasure ever here to raise,
So nobly in thy glorious Saviour's praise.
There may'st thou raise in far nobler strains,
And make it echo through the heavenly plains;
With thy seals of majesty—blest souls above,
Rejoice for ever in a Saviour's love.

ON UNBELIEF.

When Calvary's scenes were all past and gone,
With all its dark sorrows and sickening gloom;
Forth by His disciples the Saviour was borne,
And buried in silence within the cold tomb.

But when the third morning so glorious broke
  Calm o'er the earth, in its radiance bright,
Our Saviour from death's icy fetters awoke
  And soared high afar to the realms of light.

For Him His disciples full often would mourn,
  When together they met in that upper room;
To the sepulchre went but returned forlorn,
  Found Jesus not there, He was gone from the tomb.
Now as they are grieving a bright form appears,
  Though doors were all closed and barred secure,
Which filled every one with trembling fears,—
  The light of its presence could scarcely endure.

Some spirit they thought it must have been fled;
  Most affrighted they were to see it there come;
They supposed it a spirit arose from the dead,
  Permitted on earth again once to roam.
But when they all heard His kind gentle voice
  Speaking thus, " Dear children, have you any bread?"
It made every heart with gladness rejoice,
  As their dear Lord and Master once more with them fed.

But Thomas at this time was gone far away,
  When the others their new risen Saviour did see,
And when he was told the glad news the next day,
  He would not believe that such things could e'er be.
Although they affirmed no credence could gain,
  And all protestations were of no avail;
They told him their Lord He had risen again,
  Yet o'er unbelief they could not prevail.

But to them he said that he would believe,
  If Christ, his dear Lord, would to him appear,
And show him the wounds He did there receive
  On the Cross—that He did on Calvary bear;

Unless Christ before Him would once again stand,
And show unto him the wound in His side,
That into the hole he might thrust his hand,
To prove what they saw, he all there defied.

A week had passed by, when again He did stand
Among the disciples, and in the same place;
How truly delighted were that little band,
When again they all saw their dear Saviour's face.
Now Thomas was there and Christ to him said,
"Here, see in my hands the print of each nail:
Thrust now your own into my wounded side,
And over your unbelief let sight prevail."

Poor Thomas was filled with joy, and some fears,
When Christ unto him the sight did afford;
Then fast down his cheeks there rolled joyous tears,
He cried out with fervour, "My God, and my Lord!"
Christ said unto him, "Thou hast now believed,
But only believest because thou hast seen;
But blessed are they who by faith have received
Me, whose presence with them ne'er has been."

And how much like Thomas full often we've seen,
In doubts and in gloom our faith is quite lost;
To God's mercy and goodness how blind have we been!
In unbelief's sea how often been tossed!
But again we have gone with meek earnest prayer,
By trouble again to our Saviour been driven,
And while we were kneeling, beseeching Him there.
By faith we have gained a glimpse into Heaven.
The doubts and the fears we have often met here,
Have vanished away while praying we strove;
And Christ, in His mercy, did shining appear,
And filled all our souls with His perfect love.

Whilst others discern, we have been in the mount
  With Christ as in His bright image we shine,
Drawing streams of love from His blessed fount,
  Arrayed all in righteousness—clothing divine.

Save us, O Lord, when earth gloomy nears,
  Be then our strength when the loud trumpet roars,
Bid almighty faith smother all anguishing fears,
  And help us to look to the heavenly shores.
And while we now through this wilderness stray,
  Whatever may come of care or of grief,
Keep us, we beseech Thee! while in this our day,
  From ever being wrecked through dark unbelief.

LINES ON TEARS.

While passing through this earthly sphere,
Full often there is shed a tear;
The rugged path of life we know
Is wet with tears as on we go.

Here first we find the infant's tears,
When in the world it first appears;
Its helplessness the tear declares,
For it requires the mother's cares.

When into live begins to grow,
The mother's tears will often flow,
To hear her child in wailing strain,
Cry pitifully when in pain.

As onward then in life he goes,
He's subject to so many woes:
Sheds tears when he to school is sent,
Though done with parents' best intent.

And then in learning's path severe
Acquiring knowledge brings the tear;
Through life how oft 'tis clearly shown
No easy road to learning's known.

And then there are fond lover's tears,
Who often is depressed with fears,
When his desired and lovely maid
Smiles not on him and he's afraid.

He thinks some rival's gained her heart,
And from her he'll be forced to part;
There's jealousy within his breast,
The green-eyed monster breaks his rest.

He sees no sunshine in the skies,
He wants the sunshine of her eyes;
All joy and gladness from him go,
Love's passion makes his tears to flow.

And when in gentleness she turns,
With rapture his fond bosom burns,
And tears of joy by him are shed,
Invoking blessings on her head.

Soon partners they become for life,
Together blest as man and wife;
Together blending hopes and fears,
And sharing in each other's tears.

And there are too the mother's tears,
When near the close of life appears:
Her form his wasting fast away,
She feels her health and strength decay.

Then up to Heaven ascends the prayer,
"Oh, God! do for my children care!"
Around her couch she hears their sigh,
They for their kind good mother pray.

Her husband at her bedside stands,
With kindest words he clasps her hands;
Around her bed they all then kneel,
To show the love they for her feel.

They pray to God who always hears,
In broken words with sobs and tears.
Through Jesus' blood to give her peace—
To send her happy soul release.

For her to mount above the sky,
Whereat she never more will die;
Where her dear Saviour she will see,
And there for ever happy be.

Then for our friends we shed the tear,
Who meet with trials most severe;
And when we see they are bow'd down,
And fortune on them seems to frown—

When all against them doth appear,
'Tis then we shed soft pity's tear;
Nor can refrain when them we see
Borne down by want and misery.

'Tis no dishonour to the wise,
If oft a tear bedim their eyes,
For suffering virtue, when distress'd,
Down many cheeks a tear is press'd.

Or when we follow some loved form,
The burial ritual to perform,
Can we restrain when o'er his bier,
In friendship then to shed a tear?

All scenes like these will cause a sigh,
And draw the tear from many an eye;
Death touches our hearts' chords and brings
Cold sad vibration on its strings.

Then there are the poor widow's tears,
When thinking, in her fading years,
Of him who was her prop and stay,
By death from her now torn away.]

Her kindness lavished could not save
His life from hastening to the grave;
But where could he have found a friend,
Like his fond wife his wants to tend?

How softly through his room she goes,
And tries in vain to soothe his woes;
Ne'er of his fancies did complain.
Did all she could to ease his pain.

How faithful doth he find her now.
She gently wipes his fevered brow!
And as the vale of death he nears,
She leaves his bed to vent her tears.

His spirit takes its heavenly flight,
And wings its way to realms of light;
His widow leaves to mourn him here,
And o'er his corpse to shed a tear.

She thinks of happy days now past,
And o'er her mind a gloom is cast,
Some valued relic meets her sight,
Left by her loved one—taken flight.

Beholding it she sheds her tears,
Her comfort lost, no hope appears;
And fast the crystal drops o'erflow,
She's lost to all but care and woe.

Her heart seems breaking now with grief,
In tears she seeks her best relief;
She opens her Bible, finds it there—
God always hears the widow's prayer.

In trouble He will ne'er forsake,
Has always promised care to take
Of those who trust in Him with faith;
And to the widow, thus He saith:

"Come, trust in Me—all's for the best—
Thy husband's gone to heavenly rest;
Keep on awhile this war of life,
Soon you will quit this worldly strife.

You'll meet again on that bright shore,
For ever blest, to part no more;
Then throw off all thy gloomy fears,
Thou'rt going where there are no tears.

Then there are the penitent's tears,
Whene'er the wrath of God he fears;
When on his knees he's meekly found,
As they lift up their happy voice.

They shout aloud in highest Heaven,
"There is another soul forgiven!"
With joy the courts on high resound,
"The dead's alive! the lost is found!"

And now he feels he's blest indeed,
And from all punishment is freed;
By faith he views his Saviour nigh,
Can "Father! Abba, Father!" cry.

But oft he'll shed the repentant tear,
When far from Christ he'll wander here,
Whom he has vowed he ne'er will leave,
Or never more His spirit grieve.

But weak when dark temptation came,
And some there are deny His name;
They hear it treated oft with scorn,—
His name, who hath their sorrows borne.

They stray sometimes like wandering sheep,
Till Christ looks on and makes them weep;
And like Peter sadly mourn,
Who make His love so base return.

Then there's the desparing tear,
Of him who slights salvation here,
When with wan cheek and hollow eye,
He feels he is about to die.

He knows that he is near the grave,
And never tried his soul to save;
An awful task to look within,
And feel the cursed sting of sin!

He thinks of mercy oft despised—
The love of God he never prized;
Through life His counsel set at nought,
And now is to his death-bed brought.

His body's racked with pain and care,
His soul is filled with deep despair;
'Tis now he feels the bitter rod
Of a justly angered God.

His tortured soul would like to fly
Away from God's all-seeing eye;
His deep felt anguish who can tell?
Forewarning of the pangs of hell.

O may we never feel the smart
Or anguish of a broken heart!
To look back on a life mis-spent—
And lose the soul, for which twas lent.

O may we never have to trace,
As memory looks on life's spent space—
We have had more care upon the whole
To save the world, and not our soul.

While passing through this vale of tears,
And come at last to end our years,
May it through life have been our care
At last to have nought to despair

Our lives with trouble seem beset,
And bubbles everywhere are met;
But as our life thus onward rolls,
We here through Christ may save our souls.

But oft our minds are sunk in gloom
Man's history reads upon the tomb;
His birth and death the words declare,
His ashes now they moulder there.

But search the records of the earth,
For anything this man was worth
While in this world the life he led—
He might as well been with the dead

No good was known to do while here,
Dried orphans' nor the widows' tear;
No love did in his bosom burn:
His body moulders 'neath the urn.

Charity never known to give,—
No goodness in his heart did live;
He was a creature God did choose
To give wealth without the will to use.

Through all his life was pleasure's slave,—
Ne'er had the virtue to be brave:
No benefit to any one,
Except to point the course to shun.

And when before God's bar severe.
To give account of life spent here;
The talents he hath oft abused
And ne'er for good of others used.

'Twill be no use for him to say,
"The talents I have hid away!"
God then will mock the coward's fears,
And send him where there's nought but tears.

And there is the good Christian's tears,
When Calvary to his sight appears;
That scene by faith brought to his eye,
The Cross whereon his Lord did die—

To save his soul, the sinner's chief—
Good news almost beyond belief,
That thus the Son of God was given,
Poor fallen man to raise to Heaven.

O, glorious truth! for man He died,
And God's just claim hath satisfied;
That all poor sinners here might prove
The value of Almighty Love;

And feel on earth their sins forgiven,
And have their title made for Heaven.
I pray you fellow man believe.
Do not His Holy Spirit grieve.

Then tears of saints, they often flow,
As oft their hearts with true love glow;
And when advancing near their end,
They find in Christ a faithful friend.

They feel His blood hath power to save,
And over death they victory have;
Through Christ the spoiler's power defies,
To gain their mansion in the skies.

They wished they had Him better served,
And ne'er from such a Master swerved;
He's better been than all their fears,
And now for joy the saint sheds tears.

He good to them through life has been,
His mercy to them oft they've seen;
And now He calls for them to come,
Away to a glorious better home.

By faith he sees the better land,
And knows that there he soon will stand,
With the great redeemed hosts above,
To sing the wonders of His love

For on that glorious shining plain,
They sing a nobler loftier strain;
And no more tears they ever shed,
But crowns of glory deck each head.

Robed all in white the saints behold,
All hear him strike his harp of gold;
When he in that blest land appears,
Banished for ever is all his tears

The tears that fell on his death-bed,
The last tears that he ever shed;
From thence to Heaven away did fly,
Where God wipes tears from every eye.

Then let us follow Christ below,
Religious joys while here to know;
That when our Saviour shall appear,
We'll have no cause to shed a tear.

LINES ON THE HORRORS OF WAR.

What sounds are these that meet the world?
The blood-red flag's again unfurled;
Ambitious men their armies lead
In deadly combat fierce to bleed.

O, what a sickening thought, that man
So noble, should delight to plan
Destruction's horrors through the earth,
And life destroy as nothing worth.

All history's page presents to view
Foul scenes of carnage—ghastly true;
'Tis glory called where murder's done,—
And heroes those who've battles won.

They've headlong rushed 'midst fire and din,
With blood-stained steps the day to win,
And to their brows a laurel add,
No care for child or widow sad:

Ne'er thought upon the orphan's tear,
The brother or the sister dear;
And all the mourners left behind,
Who curse foul war that kills mankind.

When husbands fall amidst the strife,
And brothers in the prime of life;
Victims 'midst war's terrific sounds,
All covered o'er with piteous weunds.

How eager see! they meet the fray,
Press hotly on and clear the way;
And now they close as on they fly
For victory bent or nobly die

To martial music tramps each steed,
Their riders urge, some fall and bleed;
And for such strife the warrior's name
Is blazoned on the scroll of fame.

The cannon roars, the fight's begun,
Death flies from each exploding gun;
The grape-shot rush across the plain,
And spread the ground with warriors slain.

Still on they go till man to man
Engage in centre, wing, and van;
The rifle's aim is brought to bear,
Which causes death and deep despair.

While horses neighing rush apace,
Their riders bring in closer space:
Distinctly sounds the clashing steel,
As they the blows of death now deal.

They sound the charge with clarion shrill,
The trumpets sound trom hill to hill;
At each other's breast the bayonet's aimed,
Whilst red blood flows from dead and maimed.

Before the fight earth green appeared,
But now with purple gore is smeared!
O'er-covered now's the spacious plain,
With bleeding hosts of warriors slain.

Proud troops that came with haughty tread,
Lie number'd with the hosts of dead;
Their plumes that waved so proudly round,
Are trampled bloody on the ground.

Those hearts that throbbed to meet the foe
Are still—in death's embrace laid low;
That powerful arm, the warrior's pride,
Lies powerless by his breathless side.

That form the nation's flag that bore,
No flag shall ever carry more;
Perhaps some marble pile will tell
He fought for country—but too well.

But seek the house where once he lived,
Where the fatherless and widow grieved
For him, once happy in that place,
Amidst delight in every face.

His knee his children loved to climb,
And now they feel how long the time
Since father romped with them at home,
With mirth and laughter filled the room.

They to their mother oft appeal.
Whose heart does most acutely feel;
For well she knows their hopes are vain,
Their father ne'er will come again.

O no, for now that form is laid
Where war a charnal-house hath made;
He now lies buried 'neath the sod,
All unprepared to meet his God.

His soul is hurried thus away,
For pardon finds no time to pray;
Sent to his final last account,
No hope receives at Christ's blest fount.

What hellish fury urge them on!
All thoughts of life and home are gone;
'Midst pain they struggle, and the ground
Is red with blood from many a wound.

Whilst cannons roar, and horses fall,
Death shades the earth with funeral pall:
The warrior sleeps his last sad sleep,
Leaves comrades over him to weep.

But where's the host that in the morn,
Whose colours o'er the field were borne?
Each steed and rider now lie low,
All lifeless on this field of woe.

It inconsistent seems to me,
And little short of blasphemy,
For priests to call on God with prayer,
To bless these flags that cause despair.

'Twould better far befit their place,
To plead with God for special grace
To be poured out on all mankind,
In bonds of love all lands to bind.

The wars at sea, when each great fleet
Of ships of rival nations meet,
And from their sides the cannons roar,
Are dreadful as the wars on shore

Of each ship's crew it is the pride,
To crush each other side by side;
They board the foe at duty's call,
To win the prize, or dying fall.

But often sad we hear the tale,
Of Vessels foundering in the gale;
The crews all sunk in ocean deep,
In coral beds or caves to sleep.

Oft magazines of powder burst,
While ships blow up, death does its worst,—
Some hundreds fall, ships rent in twain.
Whilst fighting on the surging main.

They'll lie until the last trump sound,
The judgment summons shall resound,
Through earth and sea it will be heard,
When God sends forth th' Almighty word,

A noble boon are ships to man,
Whose intellect contrived the plan;
The bonds of peace they ought to bind,
And link in commerce all mankind:

But oft they're used for ends most vile,
To increase the bulk of mammon's pile;
The negro slavethey bear away,
Pent up like cattle night and day.

When father, mother, children, all,
'Midst shrieks that must all hearts appal,
Are torn from home and thrust on board,
Where none are near help to afford.

What hellish work! what fiends that can
Presume to sell their fellow man!
To scorch their flesh with brands to show
The preparations of their woe.

How long shall cruel torture last?
When, when shall tyrants' sway have passed?
How long, O God, wilt thou look on,
And see such monstrous outrage done?

Oh, righteous God! when shall this cease,
And earth exalt the Prince of Peace?
When shall the sword a plough-share be,
And man no war on earth shall see:

Oh, when will mankind learn and act!
The golden rule in heart and fact!
That tells "What we would have men do,
The same ourselves to them should show."

Not like the wretch who basely sold
His hopes of Heaven for love of gold;
But, like a righteous creature try
To point the way to bliss on high.

And who but must the tyrant hate,
Who'd crush the rights of every state;
O'ercome with might man's liberty,
Cause war, and crime, and misery?

To increase his own dominions vast;
And fetters round his fellows cast;
In bars of slavery to be bound,
And crushed in bondage to the ground.

We, Heavenly Father, beg of Thee,
To set Thy suffering children free:
By Thee we're made all of one blood.—
Direct all men to actions good.

Let's hope each ship will soon become
A house of prayer, Thy blessed home;
Thy Spirit light each sailor's heart,
That from Thy love he'll ne'er depart.

To the ignorant unfold the plan
Of thy great love to fallen man;
Thy word to preach, the world to raise,
Till every land resound Thy praise.

And may our soldiers here be found
To fight for faith on Christian ground;
And after death victorious rise,
To join blest armies in the skies.

And let us pray for country's peace,
That true religion may increase,
And ghastly war keep from our land,
By God's all-wise protective hand.

Till landed safely by His side,
For ever 'neath His care abide;
When war is hushed and conflicts cease;
In the land of happiness and peace.

ON DEATH.

Life's golden bowl's part broken
When its silvery cords decay;
They warn with solemn token
How we must pass away.
How quickly life hath flown!
It seems almost a dream;
To each of us hath shown
We hasten down life's stream.

Death hastens now to grasp—
On us will soon lay hand;
Our souls away must pass
Before God's bar to stand.
Then let us all now try
A Heaven, through Christ, to gain,
And then, when called to die,
Feel we've not lived in vain.

A KINDLY WORD FOR ALL.

How seldom mankind stay to think,
Or, thinking, care to feel,
The power possessed by kindliness
The pangs of woe to heal!
How carefully ought we guard the tongue,
Considering well withal,
To have always upon the lips
A kindly word for all.

Pure kindliness, by narrow minds,
Too oft is laid aside
As something lowering to their state,
Their dignity would hide;
But pitiful must be those hearts,
Who thus ignobly fall
Before false pride, and cease to hold
A kindly word for all.

Tell me, ye connoisseurs of joy,—
Ye searchers after bliss,—
Who roam the world in pleasure's quest,
The cheeks of peace to kiss:
Tell me, I say, do there exist,
Throughout gay pleasure's hall,
Bright gems that equal souls that breathe
A kindly word for all!

But as the noblest minds on earth
Have shown and lead the way
To live and love in truth and peace,
Our homage let us pay
To each warm heart where goodness finds
An echo at its call,
Who ever does as sacred hold
A kindly word for all.

Though harshness may confront us oft,
With cold relentless stare.
Let's still be wise, and calmly show
How man can breathe, "forbear,"
In whispered accents to himself,
That nought can e'er appal;
Christ's path he treads, and, like Him, has
A kindly word for all.

LINES ON THE LOSS OF THE SHIP, "ROYAL CHARTER."

Friends mourn for the lost on the dark rocky coast
Of the rough Moelfra's bay,
For shipwreck'd there were the brave and the fair,
Where the ship "Royal Charter" did lay.

We feel for those left, of their comforts bereft,
The loss of their sires and their sons;
We would banish the fears, and dry the sad tears,
Of the widows and fatherless ones.
'Twas here the rough surges howled funeral dirges
Of sailors both hardy and brave;
And as the ship creaks heard the passengers' shrieks
As they sank to a watery grave.

How solemn the thought! this noble ship brought
Many so near to their home;
Then with awful shocks, was dashed on the rocks,
There soon a wreck to become!

The ship was well known, and her speed it was shown,
In each voyage so quickly she sailed;
Each heart beat with glee, as they put out to sea,
Hoping England quite soon would be hailed.

But how little we know, while dwelling below,
What ills are about to befall,
When we leave the fair shore no friends to see more
Till the last congregation of all.

Some had laboured for wealth, and sacrificed health,
To spend it in comforts at home,
They thought of the place, and each smiling face
With welcome to meet them would come.

But on came the gale—they reefed in their sail,
And strove to make everything sure;
In tatters they blowed, and could not be stowed—
Unable the storm to endure.

They the anchor let go 'midst confusion and woe,
To keep the ship off from the shore,
But the wind rent in twain the stout massive chain,
And we have her loss to deplore.

One Rogers a sailor bold, worth all his weight in gold,
With daring ashore he did swim;
The rough waves he braved, and some, by him saved,
For life are indebted to him.

We cannot now see why such things should be,
And often may think them all wrong;
One day God will prove He did it in love,—
Such mysteries to Him belong.

They now praise each hour His love and His power,
They're now free from every snare;
Where time is no more on that happy shore—
Eternity's fullness is there.

LINES ON HAPPINESS.

Is happiness nought but an empty sound?
And our whole lives do they abound
With nought but sorrow and pain?
Must toil and labour our portion be,
And we on earth no pleasure see,
And ne'er contentment gain?

Is there on earth no magic ground
Where peace and happiness can be found?
Oh, where is this sweet place?
Through every race and tribe of man
Are any known who have a plan
To cheer the human race?

Exists there a sequestered spot
Hid from us, and we know it not,
Amongst us here below,
Where favoured friends together meet,
Enjoy true happiness complete,—
Say, who doth this place know?

Is it found 'midst sunbeams bright,
Or 'neath the silvery moon's pale light,
At all around the world?
Shall we seek it in the silent glen,
Away, afar from haunts of men,
In still seclusion furled?

Or shall we seek where violets grow,
Or where the fragrant roses blow
In gardens' lovely bowers?
Is it found in earthly friendship sweet,
In worldly love do we it meet?—
Thorns grow on earthly flowers!

Or doth it dwell in the palace gay,
Or in the lowly cottage? Say
  Where, O where is it found?
In the parterre where gay flowers bloom,
That shed around their sweet perfume,
  Or on some enchanted ground

Shall we seek it where the ocean roars,
Dashing their waves on the island shores,
  All sparkling in the sun?
Or seek it by some rippling rill,
Meandering gaily down a hill,
  As glittering crystal run?

Shall we seek it where the hawthorn blows,
Or where the rich sweet-briar grows,
  That scents the evening air?
Or in the ball, 'midst fashions gay,
Where mirth and pleasure hold the sway,
  Where dance the young and fair?

And is it found in music's strains?
In the fair one's glance that thrills the veins
  And chains the lover's heart?
Or search the miser's heart so cold
For happiness, while hoarding gold,
  And from each comfort part?

O seek for it in none of these
They wither as the autumn trees.
  The storm the sunbeams hide.
The violets' perfume's waft away
By zephyrs breeze that o'er them play?
  Day throws the moon aside.

The full rich rose that glads our eyes,
When plucked, it withers fast and dies—
Fit emblem of our sphere.
In love and friendship bright and gay,
Though oft in life we own their sway—
True happiness is not here

In the palace high, and humble cot
The gem you'll seek but find it not;
It dwells in higher ground,
Where Faith and Hope and Charity
With pure religion's light we see:
There happiness is found.

And Thou, great Father! who surveys
This earth and man, teach him Thy praise;
To soar with heavenly wings;
Inciting his best thoughts to rise
To happiness beyond the skies,
Above all earthly things.

ON GOD'S LOVE TO MAN.

Come, Holy Spirit, my soul inflame
With love divine—my sense inspire;
Help me to magnify His name,
And fill my soul with hallowed fire.

Thou great Almighty King! who reigns
Supreme through heaven and over earth;
Stupendous Majesty, who deigns
To bless men's souls of priceless worth.

My daring muse would try to fly,
And mount the blest abode of God;
With eagle pinions soar on high,
To mark the footsteps He hath trod.

Vain, vain desires! my grovelling sense
  Can never trace His wonderous ways;
The glories of Omnipotence
  Are far beyond my feeble lays

Yet I would trace His wonders here,
  In every tree, and plant, and flower;
The lovely beauties of our sphere,
  Are emblems of Almighty power.

These gifts to man all clearly show
  He still is loved, though he hath strayed;
If love supreme you wish to know,
  In His own Word 'tis best pourtrayed.

There in full mercy it is seen
  What has been done for fallen man;
Although rebellious man hath been,
  For him's devised a saving plan.

His own dear Son a ransom gave
  For the fallen sons of Adam's race;
And gave Him up their souls to save,
  And freely offered all His grace.

'Tis here our God His love makes known,
  'Tis here we view Him as our friend,
'Tis here His mercy best is shown,
  'Tis here we see Him condesend.

And though we can His goodness trace
  In all earth's beauties round us spread;
His love shone bright on Jesus' face,
  When on the Cross His blood He shed.

All nature shows His care and love;
  What glorious gifts around we find;
'Bove all He sent His Son to prove
  He wished the good of all mankind.

Most mighty God! was this for me,
For wretched me, by sins undone?—
The Saviour died to set me free,
For me God gave His only Son!

Oh, wonderous love! how my heart glows
When thinking of Thy love divine;
Oh, wonderous love! how rich it flows
Throughout the earth in fullness shines.

And still shall shine throughout all time,
And shower its blessings on our race,
Till every soul, in every clime,
Are subject of His saving grace.

LINES ON THE ANNUAL WESLEYAN MISSIONARY MEETING AT EXETER HALL, APRIL 30TH, 1860.

They come from all quarters to this favoured land,
To the meeting at Exeter Hall, in the Strand;
To advocate missions all over the world,
The Cross of their Saviour—their banner unfurled.

They meet all united in solemn conclave,
To use their best efforts the heathen to save;
From the Wesleyan body has gone forth the sound,
And is spreading its glories the whole earth around.

True patriots of men, with love their hearts glow,
Pioneers of salvation wherever they go;
Their delight and their glory while sojourning here,
Is to preach Christ a Saviour without any fear.

The Excelsior motto of Wesley reads thus,—
"The best of all is, God is working with us:"
And still will work with us if faithful to Him,
Who died on the Cross the whole world to redeem

Glorious sight! see the learned and wise,
In Christ's vineyard labour to gain the high prize,
Converting poor souls with the water of life,
And sowing blest peace in this world of strife.

O band of blest warriors! nobly thy cause
Extends the great blessings of God's holy laws;
How happy thy labours to bring to His fold
All hearts sunk in darkness and horrors untold.

Glory be to His name, the morning star beams.
And over this earth is diffusing its streams;
May earth's darkest parts be restored to the light,
And beam in its fullness the gospel so bright!

May the Missions' good seed so abundantly sown,
Made mighty by Thee, all idols dethrone;
May every god Dagon before Thee decay,
And Christ be exalted our worship to pay.

We thank Thee for light to the wretched Fejee,
Thou hast caused many there Thy mercy to see;
The cannibals once who each other would eat,
Now in their own mind sit at Jesus' feet.

May the millions of China enveloped in sin,
To the great Christian family soon be brought in;
May India, Japan, and the whole human race,
All soon be made heirs of Thy kingdom of grace.

Banish all the false systems invented by man,
Make bare Thy right arm in Thy own blessed plan;
For well we do know 'tis Thy changeless decree,
That earth shall be filled with the knowledge of Thee.

Let Thy glorious truths still brilliantly shine,
And fill all mankind with Thy love divine;
Let Christ be exalted and His people see
His love cheer the earth, wherever man be.

Haste forward the time for the whole earth to be
With righteousness covered, as earth by the sea;
May Wesleyans prove the light of the age,
In war against sin as they boldly engage.

May sin vanish where their doctrine's unfurled,
And Methodism prove a light to the world;
Sun of righteousness! rise, dispel all the gloom
That over this earth as a fog seems to loom.

Girt Thy sword on Thy thigh, victorious King!
Ride prosperously on, and to Thy feet bring
Man, through the uttermost earth to Thee given,
And lighten this earth with glory from Heaven.

LINES ON THE ROSE.

Beautiful rose, broken from thy parent tree,
  How sweet thy fragrance falls upon our sense;
The balmy odour we inhale from thee
  Brings our thoughts to Scripture's frankincense.

Though, fragile flower, thy life is very short,
  Thy beauties fade and wither all away,
And vanish like a dream of passing thought:
  Thy lovely blossoms wither and decay.

And such is life, with all its varied cares,
  Short and transient like the dew of morn;
And all our paths are oft beset with snares,
  Surrounded like the rose with many a thorn.

Although the rose be crushed, it will not lose
Its sweet perfume, though withered it may be ;
Sweet on our ear will fall the voice of those
Whose lives were spent in works of charity.

All those who strive to do what good they can,
Though death may come their names shall ever live,
And they shall leave behind to living man
A fragrance lasting far beyond the grave.

LINES ON "BODIES."

Some folks there are who can with ease
Twist words and meanings as they please ;
But let their taste be what it may,
On "bodies" now I'll weave my lay.

How many curious things we hear,
Take place around us everywhere !
And some we find so lost and weak,
Against all other bodies speak.

And you would think, to hear them rail,
Their slander vile about retail,
That to please them none where able,
Like the ass and old man in the fable ;

Who tried all ways to please each one,
But left off worse than he begun,
As nothing found he, but abuse,
To try to please he found no use

But still to please some friends I'll try,
And to the task my thoughts apply ;
Of bodies earthly in this sphere
I'll write, as often they appear.

On learned bodies I'll not dwell,
Of such 'tis nought I know to tell;
But human bodies is my theme,
With some odd ones my muse shall teem.

There are some very silly noddies,
Who think that they are "everybodies;"
But men discerning often find
They've shallow heads and little mind.

Some bodies think that they inherit
All that's in this world of merit;
Determined in their own dear mind,
Of others every fault to find.

Above all men they'd set their sense,
And boast with lordly consequence;
No good or use are such on earth,
Devoid of manliness and worth.

They look on others with a frown,
And run their fellow creatures down;
To feed and sleep seems all their aim,
And slander every good man's name.

They say the world in which we live
Is the best in which to lend or give;
But if you want to beg or borrow,
'Tis, "Go away, and come to-morrow."

Others there are, who every day
Style all "nobodies"—'tis their way;
Some such in every town we see,
Who seem to say, "Look up to me."

In topmost seats they take their place,
Which often sadly they disgrace;
Such when in power and in their pride,
Cause better men to stand aside.

Men sometimes doubt their sanity,
To see their pomp and vanity;
Their ignorance most men confound,
To see them puff and strut around.

And then their learning is so great,
They're constantly so large in state,
To show their great authority,
Ears tingle with their oratory.

But "nobody" is a term most used,
A word that's often much abused;
As oft when in derision made,
Or of the poor contemptuous said.

But who did ever "nobody" see,
Though everywhere he's said to be;
A scapegoat whereon all is laid,
Both faults and sins of every shade.

There are "somebodies" who let you know it,
And every pains they take to show it;
Now lifted up from want's low door,
By the sweat and labour of the poor.

Once low now raised up to be great,—
Forget who gained them their estate;
On th' labourer look with scowling brow,
They want not his assistance now.

And there's another body of note,
Mr. Anybody, who all will quote;
A queer sort of fellow is always found,
All hours of the day on every ground.

But ask him your way to direct,
Of business you wish to effect;
Says "anybody will show you the way,
And by such you are led astray.

And there are "bodies" who ne'er can find
Anything good enough for their mind;
And if you ask such to do one good,
With all their possessions which they should;

You soon will find you have made a mistake,
No trouble for others these persons will take;
Anybody may do it for what they care,
Still of the credit they'll take a large share.

If you ask for their alms in any good cause,
They Hem! and they Ha! and make a great pause,
And tell you they'll not be able to live,
If always to every one something they give

They seem to say with pride all elate,
"We now are become men of wealthy estate,
We have a right to tyrannise over others,
To treat with oppression our now poorer brothers."

But thanks, now, education hath shown
Man is not a slave, on him is bestown
Great culture of mind, which he can display,
Such as oppressors can ne'er take away.

In learning's pursuit we seldom are slow,
The germs of improvement doth rapidly grow;
And though some may think we're poor and slipshoddy,
We steadily move and care for nobody.

And in spite of all their jeering and scoff,
The taxes on knowledge are all nearly off;
A tax on intelligence never would pass
Without strong opposition from every class.

A moral purpose I have here to serve,
And thus from the right I never will swerve:
Some men there are, and not only a few,
To whom much praise is justly their due.

They speak the best they can of us all,
Dispensing the honey and sparing the gall;
At sunk humanity they never will sneer,
Do all they can poor creatures to cheer.

Good deeds, for slander, they often return,
With charity bright their warm bosoms burn;
To dwell with such men I always would love—
Their principles holy come down from above.

Let's think we're links, all of one chain,
Our mission is peace, to lessen all pain;
Thus each should endeavour his mind to improve—
To all to show forth the power of true love.

I hope I have made this moral quite clear,
To do good as a duty whilst sojourning here;
Despising nobody whoever they be,
And love all mankind sincerly and free.

THE TRACT DISTRIBUTOR.

In many towns and villages we meet
Christians with little books, who kindly greet
Each passer-by, and offer them a book;
Receiving which how pleasantly they look.
And why is it that Christian's time thus spend?
They ever hope to be the sinner's friend,—
Lead men to seek for Christ's redeeming love,
To fix their hearts on better things above.

The love of Christ do their own souls possess;
That love the principle that rules their breast,
The reigning passion leading them to good,
To exalt Christ's cross, as all good Christians should.

Sin to dispel, with all its blight and gloom,
And righteousness in place thereof to bloom;
This is the way all Christians ought to shine,
Which proves they are endowed with love divine.

Hail, Christians all, who in this work engage!
In doing good fill up your life's short page;
Your Saviour knows of all your arduous toil,—
And will repay you for each weary mile.
Still labour bravely for your Lord on earth,
And be assured He will reward your worth;
For it is known by many as great facts,
Thousands have been saved by reading tracts.

Great sovereign Lord! how we Thy mercies bless,
When Thou hast granted us the least success;
'Tis Thy blest work that we desire to know,
And Thou art with us in the way we go.
But we beseech Thee in Thy glorious power,
Bless tract distributors with a glorious shower
Of Thy great Spirit high; and may we see
We are sure to prosper, if we trust in Thee.

O grant that tracts their influence may prove
To all a boon, and lead them all to love
Their Saviour Christ, and every mercy find,
Through light divine, e'er beaming on the mind.
May tracts dispel sin's gloomy paths of night,
And shed o'er all the beams of Gospel light;
Tract dissemination is a glorious plan,
To reach the hearts, and bless the homes of man.

Many by them blest, once had a wretched home,
Till the tract distributor dispelled the gloom,
And left a tract, a means by which they found
Our Saviour died for all mankind around.

They read it o'er till they for mercy cried,
The merits pleading of Christ crucified;
And soon by wrestling was God's mercy shown,
In pardoning them, through Christ Himself made known.

And thousands now, in Heaven's high glorious plain,
Know well that tract diffusion's not in vain;
Their minds by Heavenly influence was imprest,
They saw salvation, and in Christ they rest.
They'll ever bless those Christian men who took
To them that priceless glorious little book;
Bright instruments were they on earth's cold sod,
To lead them forth to Heaven and to God.

We see them oft, from house to house they go,
'Midst scenes of wretchedness, of sin, and woe;
As home Missionaries 'tis their joy to tell
The powers of Christ, to save all soul's from hell.
All worldly frowns and sneers they boldly brave
And strive all guilty sinners' souls to save;
They laboured in the vineyard of their Lord,
Who'll give His labourers a rich reward.

AFFECTION.

Could true love tell its simple story,
  Full oft romantic it would seem;
Rough clouds will often dim its glory,—
  Shut out emotions tenderest beam.
But there is a power imparted—
  When affection's placed aright,
On the loving, and true-hearted,
  Which render life a scene most bright.

Its sunbeams fall on youth and maiden,
Despair's dark clouds soon pass away,
Though with threatening tempest laden,
Beneath affection's sparkling ray.
'Tis sweet to draw from forth its fountain,
Love's nectar, rich to sweeten life,
To make affection like a mountain,
On which to climb through every strife.

Ah! for its rays upon us beaming,
While through this life we travel on,
Around our path its glory streaming,
To cheer the heart that's lone and wan;
It brings a brighter bliss unfading,
A hallowed light throughout all time,
To lead us where no clouds are shading,
Right onward towards the Heavenly clime.

A SINNER SAVED BY GRACE.

Behold a man of sinful race,
Redeemed by Jesus' Love Divine!
A sinner, rescued by God's grace,
Behold him! in His image shine.

Though born in sin—a child of woe,
Yet by the Spirit's power imprest,
Is brought by Christ's own love to know,
And on this Rock, to build for rest.

He felt himself a sinner lost,
No merit of his own could find,
Then turned to view the Saviour's cross,
And found th' Redeemer of mankind.

His mind with sacred truths he stored,
The Bible is his map and chart,
The promises of his gracious Lord,
Bring consolation to his heart.

Strong in affection's faith and love,
'Tis his delight to search and trace—
The wonders wrought from Heaven above,
The heights and depths of sovereign grace.

And in this world he lives to prove
The goodness of his changeless friend;
His Heavenly Guide he lives to love,
Who will preserve him to the end.

His head is here with glory crowned,
Strong in Jesu's power and might.
Th' Redeem'd one now with joy is found,
And travelling towards the plains of Light.

He'll fight through life, and victory win,
His armour soon he will lay down;
He has proved the conqueror over sin,
He will receive a Heavenly Crown.

THE VOW.

O Lord, my God, Thee will I love!
Who sent Thy Spirit from above,—
To change my sinful heart.
No more from Thee my soul shall stray,
No more I'll walk in error's way,
And never from Thee part.

Let me in all devoted be
To Him, who lived and died for me,
His love my heart constrain
O Jesus! Thou hast bought my soul,
I vow that Thou shalt have me whole,
Thy love in me shall reign.

Lord I have broken many a vow,
But I'm resolved to love Thee now,—
With all my heart and soul
Let me in sorrow to Thee fly,
On Thy Almighty aid rely,
Thy Spirit me control

Who have I loved in Heaven above,
That so deserve my earnest love?
And Thou shalt have it all.
Who have I Lord on earth but Thee?
Thou shalt be all in all to me,
Then I shall never fall.

No other power but Thine alone—
Shall share with Thee Thy rightful Throne,
In my imperfect heart.
But sanctified by power divine,
Shall in Thy glorious image shine,
No more from Thee depart

Whilst I on earth shall dwell secure,
And of Thy favour shall be sure,
By Thee be richly blest,
Shall run my course with even joy,
My talents in Thy praise employ,
Then gain Thy promised rest.

LINES ON OUR BELOVED QUEEN'S JOURNEY TO LEEDS, TO OPEN THE TOWN HALL.

Great sovereign lady, forgive my muse so bold
I'll humbly try thy virtues to unfold,
  And write in praise of England's noble Queen.
My pen requires a more than magic art
To tell how nobly thou'st performed thy part,
  As the best of monarchs England e'er hath seen.

What blessings 'neath thy sway do we enjoy!
Thy every care, thy talents to employ
  For all our good that we may happy be.
A boon to all thy people dwelling here,
To be well governed, and to have no fear
  Of tyrants' will—and dwell in liberty:

When those who govern do it all by love,
And in their movements all their actions prove
  They seek the happiness of all around;
And those beneath them gratefully doth show
They value those who govern, for they know
  They try to do them all the good they can.

Beloved Queen! all this thou triest to do,
Pursuing virtue with a courage true:
  That path alone which happiness will make,
With Queen or subject seeking it aright,
In all things act as if in God's own sight,
  Who will a righteous people ne'er forsake.

Thy court so chaste above all other lands,
Where virtue e'er is prized, and love commands,—
Wisdom and uprightness guard the throne
Thrice happy soil! what land is blest like thee?
With warriors brave and senators so free,
Thy people happy more than any known.

Where'er she journeys 'tis a cheering thing
To hear her subjects make the welkin ring,—
They pray for blessings on her head to fall:
Which shows she is to every heart most dear,
With honour all her movements they revere.
A welcome homage she receives from all.
At Leeds town hall full thousands her did greet,

All glad in heart their much-loved Queen to meet,
For Leeds it was a most auspicious day;
The Queen then made a kindly-worded speach,
Which to her subjects' hearts did quickly reach,—
She Fairbairn knighted in a queenly way.

Her noble heart, no doubt, with rapture beat,
When marching forth Her Majesty to meet
Were thirty thousand ruddy children seen,
From Sunday schools of which the town is proud,
And sung with voices clear, in strains so loud,
"God bless and save our most illustrious Queen!"

Their song was wafted high into the air,
The King Almighty listened to the prayer
That called down blessings on her noble head:
And from our hearts I'm sure we all can pray
With pure affection, every one can say,
"O Lord, on her Thy choicest blessings shed!

May her children all be precious in Thy sight.
Her family blessed with every virtue bright,
Where'er their home, be blest with peace and love.
And after she has finished reigning here,
May they again meet in the heavenly sphere,
And reign with God eternally above."

THE CHRISTIAN'S WARFARE.

How brave the Christian warrior stands,
Clad with the armour of his God!
The Spirit's sword is in his hands,
His feet are with the Gospel shod.

In Truth's great panoply complete,
Salvation's helmet on his head,—
With Righteousness, a breast plate meet,
And Faith's broad shield before him spread.

He wrestles not with flesh and blood,
But principalities and powers;
Rulers of darkness—like a flood,
Nigh, and assailing at all hours.

Oft Satan's darts are at him hurled,
And sometimes slightly scathe his breast,
Which bends his thoughts towards the world,
In glittering vice, and falsehood drest,

Above the din of war he hears
His Great and High Commander's voice,
His arm it nerves, his heart it cheers,
And make the warrior's soul rejoice.

And thus undaunted on he goes,
With giant skill, and valour here,
Through Christ he conquers all his foes,
And weilds his weapon of all prayer.

With prayer's omnipotence he moves,
From this sin's-alien armies flee,
Till more than conqueror he proves,—
Through Christ, who gives him victory.

Thus strong in his Redeemer's strength,
Sin, death, and hell, he tramples down,
Fights the good fight, and wins at length,
Through mercy an immortal crown.

LINES DEDICATED TO THE TEACHERS OF SUNDAY SCHOOLS.

Dear teachers press on, in this great cause of truth,
To enlighten the souls of our ignorant youth;
Up! Rise and be doing, in this sowing time,
Your works shall bear fruit, throughout every clime;
Sow your seed in the morn with tenderest care,
Spread it well o'er the surface, now barren and bare,
Let it feel the blest Gospel's magnificent light,
Chase sin from the soil, with its withering blight,
And glorious your harvest shall be.

As the blade rises, tend with a diligent hand,
The thorns of vice clear from the face of the land,
The trenches of Truth making plain to the eye,
Water well with the Spirit, the seed that are dry,
And thus in the Sabbath School labour ye still,
Your mission of love to the young to fulfil;
Train their minds to the Lord, as the seed from the sod,
To be members of Christ, and children of God,
And glorious your harvest shall be.

In pure christian love, and with earnestness plead,
The lambs of Christ flock with the blest Gospel feed,
Lead them tenderly on to the throne of His Grace,
To view the sweet beams from Immanuel's face.
Blessed Jesus looks down from His Kingdom above,
Invites you to show forth your honour and love,
In his vineyard to toil, and sow the Sweet Word,
He promises peace, and a lasting reward,
And glorious your harvest shall be.

And when at the Throne of His mercy you stand,
And behold a glorious and sanctified band,
Who will welcome your presence with gladdening strain,
And show you your labours have not been in vain;
Inscribed with your name, in Heaven there'll be—
Monuments no mortals their grandeur can see.
And Heaven to you shall be doubly blest,
For bringing lost souls to the heaven of rest;
And glorious your harvest shall be.

A PRAYER ON MY BIRTH-DAY.

O Lord God Almighty! I am this day fifty-one years old. I know not how many years I may yet be spared, by Thy Infinite mercy, still to live: but, whether they may be many or few, I desire again on this day, to review my covenant with Thee, and to consecrate myself again to Thy service. It has been a blessed service where I have been faithful, but alas! for me, in looking back on the past, I see in myself much unfaithfulness; so many mercies disregarded, so many opportunities for doing good unimproved, so many sins committed against Thee, that I am constrained to say, "It is of the Lord's mercy, that I am not consumed." "Enter not into judgement with thy servant O Lord, for in Thy sight, shall no flesh living, be justified." "Let Thy goodness lead me to repentance." "May I humble myself in the dust, in confusion and shame of face, for having sinned against such a God of Mercy, and Love." And fly once more to the blood of Christ. that cleanseth from all sin, and find my pardon in the Great Atonement, and be led by the Holy Spirit for the future, to give myself up, unreservedly to Thee. May the love of Christ constrain me to live not unto myself, but for the glory of Him who died for me, and for the Salvation of others. Grant O Most Merciful Father, that the year upon which I have just entered, may be more fully and entirely devoted to Thee, than any year of my past life! may I become more humble – more prayerful, and more watchful against sin, so that my life may be pure and holy. "Guide me O Thou Great Jehovah, pilgrim, through this barren land. I am weak, but Thou art mighty, guide me by Thy powerful hand" And so teach me to number my days that I may incline my heart unto wisdom, till I shall come to Thine Eternal joy, and dwell with Thee for ever, and sing with the glorious host of Heaven, unto Him who loved me, and washed me, in His own blood: to Him be glory and dominion for ever. Help me to live that I may be able to look to Heaven as my future home,—to the Father's House of many Mansions, and give all diligence, to make my calling and election sure to gain it. May nothing earthly be able to prevent me from attaining to Thy everlasting joy. May I hold fast that whereunto I have attained, that no man take my crown. May I each day, have hallowed communion with Thee, till Thou shalt see fit to call me from this state of being, to a far higher land, brighter, and glorious sphere. And when the summons comes, may Jesus be with me, and His everlasting arm of mercy around me, that I may have Him for my Friend and Guide, through the dark valley of the shadow of death: so that my spirit may have nought to fear, but to clap its glad wings, and soar away, and mingle with the blaze of day. O Lord, God, let this prayer be ratified, that I may dwell in Thy House, for ever to behold Thy beauty, and Thy Glory, and Thou shalt have all the Praise, Amen, Amen.

OUR BRAVE OLD GREENWICH BOYS.

The naval frame of Britain stands
  Supreme throughout the world ;
Her hearts of oak, and dauntless hands
  Still hold her flag unfurled
Our sailors' noble deeds of yore,
  No lapse of time destroys,
Their fame resounds on every shore,
  Our brave old Greenwich boys.

Our sea-girt home they've held secure
From dark invasion's dread,
They've kept our envied freedom sure,
And sounds of terror spread.
Those staunch old hearts I love to sing,
Who midst the battle's noise
Have victory borne on honour's wing,—
Our brave old Greenwich boys.

Their hoary locks I love to see,
And hear their tales of war,
Of stirring scenes of strife at sea,
And listen to their lore.
Their veneration for their chiefs
One hears, and oft enjoys,
They boast of guns, and yards, and reefs,—
Our brave old Greenwich boys

All honour to our nation's name
Who noble deeds allaud,
While grateful to her sons of fame,
Forgets not to reward.
When strength and health wi h age decays,
Where nought their ease alloys,
A home they find to end their lays,—
Our brave old Greenwich boys.

O, may this monument so grand
Benignly near its head,
An honour to our native land,
When years on years are fled.
And may Old England's rising worth
Maintain her glory's prize,
And emulate the pride of earth,
Our brave old Greenwich boys.

LINES ON CLASS MEETINGS.

DEDICATED TO MR. C. CORNELL, TWELVE YEARS MY LEADER.

In reading God's blest Book of truth,
We find the history there of Ruth;
An example good is set us there,
That we should with God's people share,
And boldly each take up his cross,
Decide for Christ come gain or loss.
"This people shall be mine," she said,
"And from their God I'll ne'er be led;
Nor from Naomi, she's to me
A mother been in misery,
When my young husband, struck by death,
Departed and gave up his breath."
She could not now Naomi see
In trouble, without sympathy;
She'd lost both son and husband dear,
And for them oft had shed a tear:
Now journeying towards her native town,
With grief and sorrow stricken down.
But faithful Ruth still cleaved to her,
No troubles could her mind deter
From following thus her faithful friend,
On whom she could in truth depend,
And whom she knew would kindly guide
Her through the shoals of life's rough tide.
She'd battled hard with life's rough storm
And trials great, yet did perform
Her duties all with patient hand;
She looked to God his help to find;
Though lost were husband dear and son,
She said, "O God, Thy will be done."

And Ruth's example I will show,
Is what we want our young to know;
(There's something wanting oft I fear,
Our scholars losing every year,
From Sabbath schools just at the age)
When first they in life's walks engage.

We lose sight of them for a time,
Now see them in their youthful prime
In classes, that the Church may throw
Her shield around them here below;
And having raised them in good ground,
In th' Church we love to have them found.

To see them labouring for the Lord,
With joy our leaders aid afford,
To improve and light each other's mind,
For this class meetings were designed;
To tell God's love to our own souls,
His mercy teach as on time rolls.

Some think we go there to confess,—
To speak of our own wickedness;
But I would ask of such to say,
If there are not in this our day,
Good Bible classes, young and old,
Where ministers attend each fold.

With Christ's love many have been warmed,
And good associations formed,
Where Christian youths oft seek their peace
In Christ, their happiness to increase,
To withstand the evils of the world,
When at them Satan's darts are hurled.

John Wesley with his keen foresight,
Felt sure class meetings would work right;
Established them a boon so great
To worshippers of every state;
To impartial Christians all they show
That countless blessings from them flow.

And thousands now in every land,
Led on by God's protecting hand.
Have oft acknowledged their great good,
When there they've met as Christians should;
To tell God's goodness and to raise
Their voice in solemn songs of praise.

The leader then with pious care,
Pleads for his class in earnest prayer,
That God his little band will bless,
And on their hearts His truth impress,
To make them wise, and seek the way
To abandon sin, and watch and pray

For Him to guide them by His hand,
To seek the better heavenly land;
And then from every heart doth raise
Prayer, God's holy sacrifice;
Our faith is raised to bliss on high,
And truth divine beams on faith's eye.

Our lives are here of sterling worth,
A heaven we here enjoy on earth;
While blessings through the spirit flow,
That bring us joys no earthlings know;
Bright charm divine! we're on the road
That leads us to our gracious God.

In the Prophet Malachi we read
Of some of God's own chosen seed;
How oft they to each other spoke,
And from their grateful hearts oft broke
Expressions of their love; 'tis clear,
To offend Him was their greatest fear.

"And these shall be mine" saith the Lord,
"Who love delighting in my word;
Within my book their names I'll write,
For righteousness is their delight;
And in that last great day of mine,
Bright in my kingdom shall they shine.

"I'll spare them as a dearest son,
And say to each 'thou hast well done!'
The reward receive of all thy trials,
For ended now are thy self-denials;
The starry crown thou shalt receive,
In happiness for ever live."

O Father! while on earth we stray,
Be thou our guard, and guide our way;
O keep us in the paths of right,
And hold us by Thy power and might;
And help us still to be Thine heirs,
To cast on our best Friend our cares.

We can raise our Ebenezers then,
And tell what good Thou hast done for men;
Believing all is for the best,
To bring us to Thy endless rest;
Heaven's glories soon beam on our sight,
To behold the pearly gates of light.

Come with us, friend, we'll do thee good,
For the Wesleyan cause has nobly stood
Persecution's test; in history's page
It stands the glory of the age;
The gauntlet through the earth has hurled—
'Tis destined to convert the world.

TRIAL BY JURY.

England, beloved country! whose just laws
Uphold the right of truth and honour's cause;
Trials by jury prominently stand
A lasting honour to our native land.

The noblest scheme that ever man devised,
And by us all it should be highly prized;
Oppressors rich, however great in might,
Can never trample on the poor man's right.

An English jury never will be sold,
They value honour dearly, more than gold;
And English judges like Sir Matthew Hale,
Impartially will balance Justice's scale.

Those who uprightly their decision give
Among their fellows, honoured men will live;
A star of liberty to leave each son—
The Magna Charta which their fathers won.

An heirloom right securely handed down,
A brilliant jewell rare in freedom's crown;
The right of Englishmen supremely free,
That girt our island like the mighty sea.

To other lands a pattern through all time,
If copied 'twould bless every other clime;
Till slavery, wherever it may be,
Would break its chains, and every man be free.

O haste that time, thou God of nations! bless
Those patriots good who never will oppress
Their fellow man, but striving all they can
For freedom's rights to every race of man.

THE RIFLE VOLUNTEERS.

Our native soil so blest, so free.
First nation of the world,
Whose standard fair on land and sea,
Is ever wide unfurled.
Whose every son would yield his breath,
Than lose one spot of ground:
Where loyalty in life and death,
With every rank is found.
When foes designed against our shore,
And raised the nation's fears,
Uprose a new and ardent corps,
Our rifle volunteers.

Though doubts and obstacles at first,
Were scattered in their way,
Nought damp'd enthusiasm's burst,
And loyalty held sway.
In face of resolutions strong,
Opponents changed to friends,

And now united march along,
  And bright success attends.
High emulation lights each breast,
  Excelsior is the word,
They all contend with manly zest,
  Whilst friendship's voice is heard.

Whene'er they meet their presence calls
  Forth loud and hearty cheers,
In spacious plain or stately halls—
  Our gallant volunteers,
And may the day be distant far,
  When duty's voice shall call
To scenes of deadly strife and war,
  Our country to appal.
For peace has been our joy for years,
  With commerce, art, and trade ;
But woe betide him who appears,
  To bring invasion's shade.

And should a base invader's tread,
  Once press upon our shore,
Our arms would make them flee with dread,
  And dare to come no more.
And show that Britons, every man,
  Are jealous of their right ;
Alive to every means and plan
  To assert their country's might.
Then let us join with heart and voice,
  And give three loyal cheers,
For Queen and country let's rejoice,
  And our brave volunteers.

LINES ON THE RESURRECTION.

When the tragic scene of Calvary was o'er.
The Saviour's body from the Cross they bore ;
'Midst balm and spices, and fine linen round,
His body, ready for the tomb, was bound.

They bore His body then to that new tomb,
Which Joseph gave—in the dark rock of gloom ;
And when His weeping friends at length were gone,
Unto the sepulchre they rolled a stone.

And Roman guards around the tomb did pace,
And then a seal upon the stone did place,
With every care, to make the whole secure,—
To keep Him there they thought they had made sure.

For they said, ' This Deceiver told us plain,
Within three days that He would rise again ;"
For they had seen His miracles, and knew
The wonderous works that He had power to do.

His power, again, called Lazarus from the grave,
And showed His might the widow's son to save;
The mourner poor He cheered with Gospel light,
And at His word the blind received his sight.

He made the lame to walk, the deaf to hear,
The leper from disease he rendered clear ;
The tempest's raging wrath His voice could still,
Subdued the sea, and calmed it at His will.

His life in doing good on earth was spent,
To bless mankind about each day He went ;
And in return for good that he had done,
They crucified God's own beloved Son.

They scoffed at Him, and on Him basely railed,
When on the cross to suffer He was nailed ;
They jeered Him, saying, "Thou didst others save,
Why not preserve Thy body from the grave—

And from the cross come down, and we shall know
Thou art the Christ—and we'll believe on you !"
But though, poor sinners, they did thus deride,
And knowing not 'twas for their sins He died.

His poor disciples, to, they also feared
He might not be what He to them appeared;
"We hoped He would save Israel,' they said,
"And rise the third day, now we see Him dead."

And when the third eventful day did dawn,
Christ rose triumphant early on that morn ;
When to the sepulchre disciples run,
They saw the angels brighter than the sun.

Arrayed were they in robes of spotless white,
Which shed around a pearly radiance bright ;
The disciples learnt their glorious Lord had risen,
And burst the barriers of death's gloomy prison.

The angels told them He had gone on high,
To reign triumphant ever in the sky ;
And had the power o'er death's cold earthly gloom,
To raise men's dust eternally to bloom.

Though infidels at resurrection sneer,
They see new resurrection daily here;
Year after year this earth by winter bound—
All fruit seems dead within the frozen ground.

But when the sun shines forth with cheering beams,
It warms the earth, and melts its ice-bound streams ;
All nature quickly feels its influence mild,
Up springs a garden from the desert wild.

The trees begin to bud, the flowers to bloom,
Raised by the sun from out their wintry tomb;
And all around seems plainly then to sae,
That Spring is Nature's resurrection day,

And is it harder for Almighty God
To raise our bodies from the earth's cold sod?
God forbid the thought! we will depend
On Him for joys we know will never end.

When the patriarch Job was in great pain,
Said he was certain he should live again,
Tho' decay and worms might his flesh destroy,
Yet his Redeemer he should see with joy.

And though his body was so much diseased,
God could refine it whensoe'er He pleased;
Give Him a body that would ne'er decay,
To live throughout an everlasting day.

But Sadducees in every place there be,
Denying almost all they cannot see;
Many a one now living in our day,
Laugh at the future—"There is none," they say.

Should we allow that argument, what then?
Would their opinions help their fellow men?
And should we not our own foundation lose,
By thus adopting vile pernicious views?

If Christians' highest hope they take away,
What in return they give us as our stay?
For no equivalent can any give
That we may rest upon e'en while we live.

And then, most awful, when we come to die,
They'd have us trust in an accursed lie,—
That death would be our last and final doom,
With nought beyond the cold and earthy tomb.

What can it be that thus possess their mind?—
Like moles of earth they try their way to find!
Where can the wiseacres knowledge get?
On what philosophy are their senses set?

In sin they burrow, knowing not God's Son,
And when too late they find themselves undone;
But earnest Christians, with their hearts elate,
Expect a happier and a blest estate.

Which, then, has the advantage of these two,
Christian or Infidel, when death's in view;
The unbeliever has no hope at all—
The Christian, he can on his Saviour fall.

Who conquered death and victory obtained,
O'er hell and death His mighty power maintained;
To all His saints His love will e'er be shown.
When they shall gain their everlasting crown.

Begone our doubts, away with all our fears.
Nature's resurrection every year appears,
That proves God's power our sinful dust to raise
To heavenly bodies, ever Him to praise.

LINES ON MISS A. B. COUTTS.

Most noble Lady; though not of the titled great.
  Thy deeds of charity exalt thy name,
And tell of worth's benevolent estate,
  United with thy good and virtuous name.

Thou'rt one amongst us of the pious few
  Whom wealth hath favoured, ever doing good
To soothe the ills of life with love so true,
  And cause religion to be understood.

Home missionary, we hail thee in the cause ;
  Thy country's welfare ever near thy heart,
To uphold the honour of its righteous laws,
  Thy wealth and talents with the needy part.

Honoured is thy name throughout our land ;
  In every humble school in England's realm,
With ragged and with Sunday schools shall stand
  Till chaos comes, and all the world o'erwhelm.

Open is thy hand to those who need,
  To lend thy succour to the poor distress'd ;
Thy bounty often hungry souls doth feed,
  When by poverty they're sore opprest.

Columbia's sons shall hail the noble deed
  That gave the means a bishop there to send ;
To the good Shepherd many souls to lead,
  That proves how great thy wish to be a friend.

Thy talents for thy Lord thou dost employ,
  In mercy's path thou dost perform thy part ;
The widow's heart thou dost make leep with joy,
  Whilst cheering up the orphan's sorrowing heart.

Go forward, lady, in the way thou art,
  Nor heed the titles of the great and vain ;
As a Christian heroine perform thy part,
  The time will come to meet thy acts again.

No marble shrine shall be required then
  To spread thy deeds or chronicle thy fame ;
Thy virtues here historians will pen,
  And tell to those unborn thy virtuous name.

ON PERFECTION.

Absolute perfection ! none can, I fear,
Presume that mortals can obtain it here,
The very noblest acts of best men show
'Tis not obtainable while here below .—
A state that's found in God's own works alone,
Wherein alone perfection's light is shown.

Yet unto Abraham our God did say,
"Now walk before me in a perfect way ;"
And Abraham his firm obedience proved
By offering unto God the son he loved ;
By faith and works he ever strove to be
What God desires his children all to see.

For He would have mankind all daily prove
The high and glorious traits of perfect love ;
That love which always casts away all fear,
And makes us all His still small voice to hear ;
Our hearts to be His own Love's blest abode,
Bright temples pure of love to man and God.

And God Himself delights each hour to bless
His children all with perfect holiness ;
To fill their longing souls with Love Divine,
And make them all in His bright image shine ;
To make their souls a calm abode of peace,
And make their happiness and love increase.

O sanctify, great Lord, Thy people here,
In seeking holiness make all sincere ;
And may we ne'er within ourselves gain rest,
Till of this blessing we are all possessed :
And ever try, in every way, to prove
We love our Maker with a perfect love.

HAIL THE BLEST HARVEST AGAIN.

The spring has departed and summer has come,
  The corn is all full in the ear,
The birds are all singing, the bees gaily hum,
  And ripe fruit in abundance appear
Let us lift up our hearts and our voices in praise,
  For this plenty's all-bountiful reign,
To the God of Creation as thankful we gaze,
  And hail the blest harvest again.

The husbandman looks now, with pride and delight,
  On the fruitful reward of his toil;
The sun in rich brilliancy dazzles the sight,
  And gladness o'ercovers the soil.
The provisions thus sent by the Almighty hand
  Will remove all discomfort and pain,
And rouse every soul in our much favoured land,
  To hail the blest harvest again.

The reapers all joyously hie to the field
To bring in the year's luscious store.
Unto every dwelling subsistance to yield,
And banish distress from the poor.
What a glorious treasure our earth, yielding food
Like a beautiful gold spangled plain!
While our praises arise to the Author of good
We will hail the blest harvest again.

The God of our being, the great God of nature,
Transcendant in mercy, in bounty and love.
Every moment provides for the wants of each creature
And nourish their souls for the bright home above.
O, let not His bounty and Fatherly care
Be extended so largely to mortals in vain,
But still His great goodness in thankfulness share,
And hail the blest harvest again.

LINES TO SARAH STODDART WILLIS, ON HER SIXTEENTH BIRTHDAY.

Dear maid, to thee I try my muse again,
In lines of poetry my song will make:
Thy natal day in friendship's joyous strain,
Shall be the subject for my mind to take.

Sixteen years have rolled their annual round,
And thus to thee each birth-day fully brought;
Thou shade and sunshine many times hath found,
As after happiness thou hast often sought.

How oft in infancy thy mother kind,
Has, like a guardian angel, watched her child,
And as thou'st grown in years informed thy mind
Of holy things, in accents soft and mild.

How oft thy light elastic step rejoiced
Thy parents' hearts ; they have been glad to see
Thy merry gambles, as thy happy voice
Sounded through the house in cheerful glee.

Thy parents round thy path with kindly care
From dangers thou hast saved, by filial love,
Who looked with pride upon their daughter fair,
To see her midst the youthful circle move.

Thy father's care how oft has been bestowed—
To his loved child how many gifts has made—
As she advanced, how many symptoms showed
His love in various ways would be repaired.

She fondly loves her parents, for she sees
They have been guardians of her infant years ;
Had it not been for such kind friends as these,
Her rising path might have been strewed with tears.

And may thy spring of life thus happy prove,
In virtue's path may'st thou for ever tread ;
And all thy friends around have cause to love,
And pray for blessings on thy youthful head.

And when thy youth is, like a sunbeam, flown,
And age, like summer, follows after spring—
May buds of early life in fruit be shown,
And to old age its virtues comforts bring.

And as old Times keeps on its annual race,
Thy birth-days, ever joyous, still increase ;
May fond affection, twined with every grace,
E'er lead thee on in virtue's path of peace.

And when, beloved by all, old age may come,
While round the friends in number still increase,
And happines be written on every page,
And after life have everlasting peace.

ON INDECISION.

How many and great the ills that flow
From indecision, which often show
Man blest with large and powerful mind,
In all good works far, far, behind;
By want of proper courage shown,
To take the right path to them known.

How many live in this our day.
Who love to walk in error's way;
They, when admonished by some friend,
Their path will in destruction end,
Like Felix, say "Let conscience be.
And when convenient I'll seek thee."

'Tis strange man should be such a dupe,
And let his mind so lowly stoop;
Like th' drunkard hark to virtue's strain,
Admire its truths, but fall again;
To drown his conscience vainly tries,
Unhappy lives and wretched dies.

The gambler knows the wretched fate
His lawless deeds so oft await;
He knows his wicked course must tend
To bring a dark untimely end;
But still presists and risks his all,
By his own hand at length doth fall.

And oft we find the forward child
Pursues his course, unchecked and wild;
Oft good advice falls on his ear
From parents kind, whose love is dear;
He still pursues his wicked ways,
Till ignominy ends his days.

And many a daughter, brought up well,
Spurned good advice—she sunk and fell;
Her mother's counsel heard with scorn,
By vice and folly onward borne:
She thought she could all conscience brave
Her end has been a self sought grave.

We might go on, of numbers tell,
Nought could induce them to live well
Passed undecided all their days,
Resolving still to mend their ways;
By death they undecided fell,
Their lives but paved the way to hell.

They might have lived and loved the right.
And left a name both pure and bright,
Their good deeds handed down to fame,
A pure life, and unsullied name;
To lead the minds of rising youth
In duty's path, midst love and truth.

Dear friends, one life is all you have,
Probation time your soul to save;
If life's allowed to pass away
All reckless, 'midst the worldly gay;
You'll surely find that, to your cost,
That Indecision your soul hath lost.

LINES ON HEARING A BLIND YOUNG LADY, MISS SCOTT, PLAY UPON THE PIANO.

Dear maid! and is thy sight for ever fled?
To seeing hast thou bid a last farewell?
Is nought but memory left to thee instead?
In darkness now art thou consigned to dwell?

Again no sun can ever cheer thine eyes,
  Or nature's chaste and beautiful array;
Not once again shall bright meridian skies,
  Their brilliant glories to thy sight display.

Ne'er more beneath the radiant beams of dawn,
  Thy bosom warm with ecstacy shall heave;
Farewell to all the blushes of the morn,
  The silent twilight of the lingering eve.

Farewell the sweet and opening buds of spring,
  And nature robed in mantle pure of green;
The shining flowers their fragrance sweet will bring,
  But for thee they'll pass away unseen.

Thy friends with wrinkles may wax dim and old,
  And all their former beauty wither'd be,
And all such changes thou wilt ne'er behold
  And age will still be beautiful to thee.

Yet with thy fingers gentle sound can wake
  The glowing music dwelling in our souls;
When the piano's tuneful notes you shake
  In chastest melody thy sweet voice rolls.

May time, thus pleasing gently pass away.
  The approach of age upon thee softly steal;
May'st thou ne'er feel the wane of life's decay,
  Be ever blest with holy joy and weal.

And may the sun that gilds thy memory's field,
  Dispense to thee a bright perpetual day.
The springs of roaming fancy never yield
  To dreary winter's cold and barren sway.

And may the flowers that once so bright appeared,
  Long live within thy memory's early bloom,
And those thy musing fancy since hath reared,
  Gild all thy path approaching towards the tomb.

And may thy life, like one short fleeting dream,
  When closed in Death's cold mortal earthly night,
Expand and reach the bright eternal stream,
  And wake to lustrous brilliant heavenly light.

When Heaven's high beauties spread thou shalt behold,
  What glorious wonders then shall meet thy gaze;
Rich beauties dazzling shall that time unfold,—
  May'st thou rejoice for ever in its rays.

Those things to us our Saviour will explain,
  Which here our souls have times and oft opprest;
Then we shall shout with loud and rapturous strain,
  And tell that God hath done all for the best.

LINES TO MISS SOPHIA MADAMS.

OCTOBER 9TH, 1858.

You have asked me, Miss Sophia, to write,
That for your album I'd indite,
  Which I will endeavour to do.
Thrice happy the task to write in your praise,
And in your favour my poesy raise—
  So with pleasure I'm writing to you.

With every virtuous grace you're arrayed,
And modesty decks your features, fair maid
  And youth with its loveliest charms.
They seem to display the morn of your life
In richest contentment, without any strife,
  And free from all cares and alarms.

And thus through life may you ever pursue
All virtuous objects, and ever renew
  The vows unto Him you have raised;
And all vice-alluring shadows forsake,
And hold of the life-giving banner now take,
  Which shall for ever be praised

May your forthcoming life ever bring you sweet peace,
And day after day your joys may increase
Through life's charming varied round;
May God the great giver of all blessings new,
Who sends the fair rainbow with dazzling hue,
Your friend for ever be found.

And when old age cometh creeping apace,
When nearly done is your now earthly race,
May you view that heavenly land,
Where saints and angels all joyously sing
The glories of God, the heavenly King—
May you join that heavenly band.

LINES ON THE DEATH OF MR. DAVID HAMBLIN, AT MADRAS, JUNE 30TH, 1858.

Alas! my husband for ever now is gone,
His spirit's fled away to happier spheres;
His earthly course and race on earth is run—
His helpmate's fate we mourn with bitter tears.

In a foreign land my dear beloved died,
Far, far away from all the friends he loved;
At Madras his life waned in its ebbing tide—
His soul has mounted up to joys above.

His wife with kindly hand could not attend
The partner of her life, nor wipe his brow
From the cold sweat that told full well his end—
Strange hands performed the act of kindness now.

No monumental marble marks his grave,
O'er his remains perchance some wild flowers bloom,
And shows where rests in peace the sailors brave,
Waving with wild luxuriance o'er the tomb.

Borne away by strangers to his rest,
Who paid to him the last sad funeral rite;
As the sun in golden lines sunk in the west,
Gilding the earth with beams of golden light,

If any stranger wanders near that spot,
  And o'er the dust in pity drops a tear,
His wife and children from his humble cot.
  Shall offer up to Heaven an earnest prayer.

How little thought he when he left his home,
  The town of Ipswich, his dear native place,
That back from India he would never come,
  His wife and children fold in fond embrace.

But as his vacant chair now meets our view,
  Where oft he sat with smiling happy face,
It causes tears of love to flow anew,
  Though hope reminds he's in a happy place.

O, Hamblin! how we sorrow for thy loss,
  And friendship mourns thy sad and early doom;
The deep regret of frien s, although too late
  That thou shouldst go so far away from home.

His children, as they mark their mother's tears,
  Say, "Oh! will father never come again?"
Widow and fatherless, pray chase away your tears—
  Father and husband roam the heavenly plain.

The wind God tempers to the new shorn lamb,
  To the widow husband, and father to the child;
Then put your trust in Him and love His name,
  And find in Him a friend both kind and mild.

And could his voice be heard by those he loves,
  'Twould say, "Dear wife and children weep no more;
With cherubim and seraphim I sing above,
  And join with rapture in the angelic choir.

But there's a time will come we'll meet again,
  And partings there shall be for ever o'er;
And we shall greet each other on that plain,
  Where death and pain will ne er be thought of more."

THE VILLAGE CHURCH.

Our village church with ivy mantle crowned,
  Whose tapering spire points upward to the skies,
As though to whisper, "Peace may here be found,"
  A hallowed place from whence our praises rise.
Dear is the spot, a holy charm pervades,
  With solemn feelings as I tread the place,
The spirit whispers, and my soul upbraids,
  Because so cold in seeking for His grace.

A solemn joy, sad, yet sublimely sweet,
  Steals o'er my feelings as I linger here;
The Saviour and the sinner seem to meet,
  And words break forth of solemn, earnest prayer.

'Midst all around a death-like stillness reigns,
The lettered tombs record of those whose breath
Forsook earth's cares for Heaven's eternal gains,
And proved victorious through the hand of death.

Perchance the mind reverts to by-gone days,
When youthful health in full and lovely glow,
Would smile around us in benignant rays,
To bless life's course and make it happy flow.
When dear companions then in joyous glee,
Would mingle with us in each well-known game;
And we were happy as the young can be,
And through life we e'er should be the same.

I view the grave-yard, read each mouldering tomb,—
One name I mark who used to labour here,
Who sleeps beneath the aged yew tree's bloom,
Who in this church had oft engaged in prayer.
How calm he rests, the holy, reverend sire;
The voice is hushed that once its precepts gave,
But there are those his precepts did inspire,
And led to seek a home beyond the grave.

'Twas not ambition lured him in his toil,
'Twas not to gain a worldly sounding fame;
For souls' salvation laboured here awile,
And others left to gain an earthly name.
We think of former years for ever fled,
How fervently he tilled midst hopes an fears;
We show respect for him, the worthy dead,
His grave we reverence with our silent tears

In memory fancy paints his saint-like smile,
When God in mercy did his labours own,
In gratitude his voice rang through the aisle,
As ripening were the loving seeds he'd sown.
'Twas his delight God's mercy to declare,
The sacred truths revealed in His word,
The village flock engaged his earnest care,
While on he taught the love of Christ his Lord.

The village poor could of his labours tell,
  How oft he hastened to the bed of pain,
Pointing to Him who loves the sufferer well,
  And Heaven will prove he laboured not in vain.
For many a sinner, by his teaching blest,
  Sought after mercy from the Lord of love :
And now they've gained the everlasting rest,
  And with the Saviour dwell in peace above.

The flaggy greensward covers rich and poor ;
  Death spares not wealth or title on his way,
Though sculptured arms record great deeds of war,
  Beneath the turf all sink beneath his sway.
There's no distinction now 'tween high estate
  And humble poverty within the grave ;
The unknown mound is equal with the great,
  From which a soul may rise for Christ to save.

The rustic porch vibrates a hollowed sound,
  Wherein we feel in contact with the dead ;
The faintest whispers through the place resound,
  The sun's bright rays are through each window shed.
There is a something in a holy place
  That falls upon our senses fixed and keen,
And holds us firm engaged in thought's embrace,
  And fills our souls with loftiness serene.

For ages past the dear old pile hath stood,
  A beacon mark to souls now passed away ;
Who first in childhood sought the fount of good,
  And tottered there in age's last decay.
The bells' familiar tones recall to mind
  Old scenes and faces now for ever fled ;
Who up the path to Hymen's court would wend,
  But now they sleep among the silent dead.

REPENTANCE.

Oh that past days of probation
  On earth were allowed me again,
The oft slighted gifts of salvation
  No more would I treat with disdain.
For sins never more would I barter
  My soul to which gold is as dross;
I would fly to the great gospel charter,
  And humbly bow down at the cross.
In vain should the arms of frail beauty
  Allure me to pathways of shame,
Nor pleasure entice me from duty,
  Till dishonour had branded my name.
The cup with its liquor should never
  Spread over my soul its dark spell,
From my Maker to cause me to sever,
  And hasten the horrors of hell.

O Father, it is thy compassion
  That hath spared the poor sinner so long,
When heedless and blinded with passion,
  I joined in the drunkard's lewd song.
And now as in mercy thou'st spared me,
  And not in thy wrath cut me down,
I will grasp at thy offer of mercy,
  And seek for a heavenly crown.

Arise, O my soul, there is beaming
  On Calvary's summit a dome,
The prodigal starts from his dreaming,
  And speeds to his father and home.
The father, his prodigal viewing,
  All rags, and in desperate plight,
His love to his lost one renewing,
  It brings him increasing delight.

Bring forth the best robe and put on him,
  On his finger the loving ring place
And shower all affection upon him —
  He hears the sweet message of grace.
The welcome glad tidings of peace
  Descend to his soul from above,
'Tis mercy that grants him release,
  Receives his bewailing with love.

Thy sorrow, repentance, and tears,
  Are weighed and found wanting, but, lo!
Jesus' blood in the scale now appears,
  That washes all whiter than snow
Mercy smiles on the penitent's grief,
  The sign of redemption doth raise;
A look to the cross brings relief,
  And sorrow is turned into praise

SCENE FROM LONDON LIFE.—TWO CHILDREN

Poor Hannah Southgate told her griefs
  To little Fanny Moore,
One Monday night as Fanny stood
  Beside her mother's door.

In touching accents spake the child,
  With sense beyond her years,
I overheard each word she said,
  Her eyes were filled with tears.

Now Hannah was a thoughtful child,
  All free from sinful guile,
Her countenance was always sad,
  It never wore a smile.

Still no complaining passed her lips,
In hope she seemed to dwell,
Though hard her lot, her sorrows keen,
She bore her burden well.

Her little friend had often asked
What made her always so,
And strove to cheer her drooping heart
And chase away her woe.

This night her little face assumed
An almost ghastly hue ;
The gaslight burning in the street,
A pa ler o'er her threw.

'O Fanny dear, did you but know
What cause I have to fret,
The dreadful sights I see at home,
You never would forget.

That poisonous, foul, accursed drink,
Brings all our want and pain.
Makes father like a madman rave,
And wholly turns his brain.

All yesterday my father toiled,
And mother did the same,
Though 'twas God's holy Sabbath day ;—
Now was it not a shame ?

And I was dirty all the day ;
Not like you, Fanny dear,
Your parents love the house of God,
My life is allways drear.

No comfort have I in my life,
Have blows and kicks beside ;
I often wish I d gone to heaven
When brother Jimmy died.

At night all unwashed as they'd worked.
  They went across the road,
Got quarrelling at the gin-shop's bar,
  While we were wanting food.

A cry of murder there was raised;
  A crowd drew round the door;
I ran and saw my mother lay
  All bleeding on the floor.

'Twas now the gin-shop's closing time,
  There rose a general shout,
'Midst which the landlord bawling cried,—
  "Come, turn these drunkards out."

Her eyes were blackened, and her face
  Was fearful to behold,
Which showed the landlord how accursed
  The poison that he sold.

Said little Fanny, "Hannah dear,"
While tears ran down her cheek,
  And sobbing choked her utterance,
Till she could scarcely speak,—

"I am so grieved I cannot tell,
  A cruel fate indeed,
To see a tender heart like yours
  So sorely made to bleed.

A lady will be here to-day,
  I'll tell her of your case,
She is a pious Christian soul,
  And blessed with mercy's grace.

She knows and works hard for a home
  Where children are received,
Brought up in truth and cleanliness,
  And all their wants relieved."

Said Hannah, while her eyes grew bright,
"Pray Fanny speak for me,
If I cou'd only live in peace,
How grateful I should be."

The lady came, her case was told,
And she to School was sent;
Her parents kept on drinking still
And all their money spent.

The father died a maniac,
The mother's corpse was found
One winter's morn, all stiff and cold,
Half naked on the ground.

LINES ON THE VISIT OF THE NEW ZEALAND CHIEFS TO THIS COUNTRY.

Awake, poetic muse! and with thy earnest lays,
Tell of Old England in her ancient days;
When her sons lived in rude barbarous style,
And naked danced around the burning pile,—
They immolated victims to Woden's heathen god,
The idol then of Britain, our then benighted sod:
For midnight darkness then rested on our land,
Before the Roman army landed on its strand.

But Britons then preserved their ancient valour good,
For years the Roman army gallantly withstood;
At length, o'erpowered by numbers, they suffer'd a defeat,
And to their native woods they mostly did retreat;
But some were taken prisoners and sent away to Rome,
Leaving for a time their sea-girt native home.
Caractacus, their chief stood there and gazed around,
Astonished at the buildings he in that city found,

Exclaimed: "O why—O why should such a mighty nation
Bring to our English shores the fire of desolation!
With all this splendour round them, with all their pomp and
pride,
They could not leave in peace our island to abide.
Surely such a people, blessed with wealth so great,
Could never wish to envy our poor and rude estate?
And surely they must see there's nought for us to gain,
Then they desire to bind us within a captive's chain?"

Such were the feeling words of this brave warrior chief:
He made his feelings known in hopes to gain relief.
Soon after this the Emperor made him free, once more
Returned this noble Briton unto his native shore.
Glad tidings soon were spread, when St. Augustine's band
First brought Christianity into our goodly land;
The Tree of Knowledge planted upon the British soil,
From which such endless blessings have flowed upon our isle.

And men have gone from England to many a foreign shore,
To propagate the Gospel among the heathen poor;
To each benighted land who've lived in darkness long,
The lamp of life is lighted with its all-joyful song.
The labour of our missionaries have been greatly blest,
And ope'd the way for thousands to find the promised rest;
And now throughout the world their sacred anthems ring,
In praise of blessed Jesus, our Sovereign Lord and King!

New Zealand now has heard the Gospel's joyful sound,
And thousands there rejoicing in Jesus now are found;
And from that distant land there hourly doth arise
Praises loud and earnest ascending to the skies.

And soon shall come that bright and long-expected day
When all the earth shall bow before His mighty sway!
Shall all acknowledge Him, and to His sceptre bend,
And shout their songs of praise unto the sinner's Friend!

Once Lord Macaulay said, "that it may be the doom
Of England to decay and sink in shades of gloom;
That in that day a traveller on London Bridge may stand;
Sketching from the ruins of St. Paul's Cathedral grand;
And on this fine old City may rise another race,
And build a greater city on London's ancient space.'
But that will never be long as the Gospel stands,
God's bulwark to protect all favour'd Christian lands.

For on the English nation our God hath set His seal,
Bestow'd His blessed Gospel, His servants to reveal;
Increased our nation greatly in dignity and might,
To send to heathen lands the Gospel's precious light.
And if we're only faithful unto His blessed cause,
Ever striving to uphold the honour of His laws,
Beneath His high protection at enemies we'll smile,
For God is sure to guard our glorious Christian isle.

Many battles have we fought and made our foes retreat,
Or bow down in the dust, most abject at our feet;
While empires great have faded and fallen to decay,
That time hath all destroy'd and swept them all away.
The desert now resounds with sad and bitter wail,
Its funeral dirge is heard upon the midnight gale;
Idolaters there were, but now their time is past,
While England's Christianity ever more shall last.

And over all the nations Christ shall reign supreme,
And all mankind shall drink salvation's healing stream ;
For we have seen New Zealanders from their own native shore
Their chiefs arrived in England and His great name adore.
Once they were but cannibals, but now they've learnt the way,
To sing the songs of Zion, before Him kneel and pray ;
On Southwark Chapel's platform meekly they did stand
To tell the wonders God had wrought within their native land.

And our beloved country shall more and more increase,
If faithful to proclaim the blessed word of peace.
"Excelsior" be our motto—higher and higher still,
Whilst the blessed message sounds aloud from hill to hill ;
We'll firmly serve our God and have no cause to fear,
For He shall bless us all, and all our labours cheer :
Where'er the flag of England in freedom is unfurled,
Our Christian principles may prove a blessing to the world.

Then listen, noble patriot, who loves thy country dear,
Its noble Christian principles throughout thy life revere ;
Those precepts ever cherish that make thy country great,
And everything debasing O chase away with hate !
Then shall our favoured country, with all its power and might,
Bless the whole wide world with all its Christian light ;
With heavenly pointing flame her pioneers shall shine,
Until the whole world's filled with love and truth divine.

SPRING

Hail, hail, lovely spring! we greet thee again,
With thy offerings of beauty and flowers;
Thou appearest to gladden and cheer us once more
In this beautiful dwelling of ours.
Sweet nature her tributes of gratitude brings
And empties her lap at thy feet;
Through mountain and valley sweet melody rings
With the songs of thy warblers so sweet.

To soothe and to cheer us, and banish away
The dark clouds of gloom and despair;
Thy face woos the sunbeams to gladden the day,
And the sweet flowers to perfume the air;
The scenes of our childhood, life's earliest spring,
In memory we wander them o'er,
And remembrance displays the sweet days of our youth,
When we drank from each spring's joyous store

But changing is life like the seasons of time.
Or like the gay rainbow it fades ;
What is brilliant and gay at the dawn of the morn,
Ere evening's all tinged with deep shades :
Then as all things below are subject to change,
And rapidly time from us flies.
Let us build upon Christ, our unsearchable friend,
Till He pilots us home to the skies.

LINES TO THE REV. DANIEL PEARSON.

On his leaving Richmond, as a Missionary to the British Army in India, October 15th, 1859.

Farewell, dear Richmond, I soon shall pass away
From thy Institution dear, and every lovely scene ;
Farewell for many a long and far off distant day,
To all thy dear sweet valleys and all thy meadows green.
Yet shall my memory still dwell upon the past,
The many happy hours I've spent while staying here ;
But now to climes away my lot in life is cast,
To labour for my God in a far distant sphere.

Long time shall pass away e'er I shall stray again
Across thy flowery meads, or by thy rippling streams ;
Or roam at dawn of morn, along thy lovely plain—
All scented with sweet hawthorn—as the morning beams.
Full often I have mounted up thy verdant hills,
And gazed with fervid rapture on thy river bright ;
Now happiness and health my glowing bosom fills
But I must now depart where other scenes invite.

Yet often shall my memory conjure up the name,
The countenance and form of some beloved friend,
With whom I've often studied, or enjoyed some game
When o'er the verdant fields our wayward steps would wend.

Oh! blessed are the scenes where memory loves to rove,
And bring before the mind the scenes of early youth;
Some angel's, sister's voice, or dear fond mother's love,
Who ever strove to lead us in the path of truth.

And long as memory holds her seat and power with me,
I'll love to think of those that I have left behind:
And when'er, Miss Wylde, my thoughts shall turn to thee,
I ever shall remember that thou hast been most kind:
For thou hast e'er been anxious, as a mother would,
To make me always happy with each kind gentle plan;
Conducing to my comfort with feeling kind and good,
To render me through life a happy, useful man.

For governors so kind and true 'tis hard to part,
And all my brother students whom I dearly love;
And while I bid adieu with sorrow-swelling heart,
I feel a consolation I shall meet them all above!
But if with health and strength we boldly labour on,
All winning souls to Christ, and each one ever tries
To do his best to serve God's dear and only Son,
We shall then increase the army of the skies.

Glad then shall we be that our life had been spent
Within the Wesleyan College, which we all love most dear;
Of learning gained while there we never shall repent,
But try to use it always poor drooping souls to cheer.
And when each one hath run his mortal earthly race,
And having preached through life the blessed Gospel Word,
The glad sound he shall hear, "Come, and take your place;
Enter, faithful servants, the joy of your dear Lord!"

THE OLD COVENANTERS.

O long be remembered thy patriot band,
  Who scorned thy religion to yield,
And set at defiance the monarch's command,
  Left home for the mountain and field.
Strongly thou'st fought against darkness and blight,
  Though oppression laid heavy on thee,
And borne the blest Bible, thy armour of light,
  Thy sons and thy daughters to free.

And thou didst fall along the dark moor,
  Yet the blood that then hallowed the soil
Struck a blow from the freedom of Albion's shore,
  Shed a light to illumine our isle.
Though thou wert cut off in the midst of thy days,
  Yet thy deeds have enkindled a flame
That shall burn through all time in thy patriots' praise.
  All Christians revering thy name

Such brave men as thee are a boon to the earth,
  Thy lives and thy virtues shall shine,
Proclaiming such men from heaven had birth,
  To establish the Kingdom Divine.
Thou art the men that bid conscience soar free,
  Spite of monarchs' and tyrants' command;
'Tis such as thou wert, though oppressed they may be,
  Who're the glory and pride of our land.

LINES

On hearing the REV. JOHN S. WORKMAN Preach from Job, 37th chapter, part of the 21st verse: "And now men see not the bright light which is in the clouds."

How numerous the clouds that darken our course,
  As we journey through life on our care-bestrewn way;
That will threaten at times to shade with remorse,
  And o'erwhelm our existence in gloomy array.
But although they may threaten we will not despair,
  And cheerfully through all their terrors will roam;
For each cloud has a lining of silver so fair,
  That will guide every Christian on safe to his home.

The clouds of our childhood when parents' hopes waver,
In fear lest the beautiful bud should decay;
While appealing to Heaven for merciful favour,
To remove the dark cloud that endangers our way.
'Midst paternal affection, and hearts fill'd with gladness,
They watch the last shade of the cloud that departs;
Now the bright lining glistens and chases their sadness,
Bringing rays of sweet peace and delights to their hearts.

The clouds of our youth, when the storms of temptation
Encircle our footsteps our souls to enthrall;
That darken the road to eternal salvation,
'Midst scenes and transactions enough to appal.
But through the dark shadows a kind hand extended,
Disclosed the beams of brightness and love;
By pastors' kind teaching our lives are amended,
And cloudless we view the bright mansions above.

When faltering in manhood, in worldliness waging,
The clouds of backsliding embitter our path;
While mammon and pride all our thoughts are engaging,
Thinking nought of God's mercy, His justice, or wrath.
At length comes an hour when sickness and sorrow
The latent spark kindles and fans to a flame;
The cloud flies away, and we're brought ere the morrow
To supplicate mercy, and call on His Name!

What clouds will come o'er us when friends prove unfaithful,
What temptations of evil encircle our mind,—
When our bounty relieved them in the times most needful,
They've proved most ungrateful and vilely unkind.
But, oh! when a true friend once gladdens our dwelling,
Who proves in his heart and his dealings sincere,
How soon the clouds vanish, our pain all dispelling,
And our heart's best emotions in fulness appear.

The clouds of calamity gather around us,
When grieving to part with a dear treasured friend,
To whom the sweet ties of affection have bound us,
As over their last parting moments we bend.
But, oh! what a halo of brightness surprises
And chases for ever the dark clouds of gloom,
When we feel that the glorious spirit arises,
That the earthly alone is consigned to the tomb!

Dark clouds chill the frame as the aged decayeth,
When affliction with tottering steps may be seen,
As the brink of death's river the spirit approacheth,
With a slight single thread of existence between.
But how the cloud changes from shadow to sunshine,
When memory can bring no remorse for the past;
When the last term of life spent resignedly praying,
In calmness awaiting the bliss that shall last.

Thus 'tis only when life has been frittered away,
While the bright clouds of mercy have ever been near,
And the world's poor allurements have firmly held sway,
That death shows the clouds of desponding and fear.
No clouds chill, or bleak or darksome soever,
In the breast of the lowest that treads the earth's sod,
Can terrors awaken, or confidence sever,
Who walks all his life in the favour of God.

None ever need fear, for God is e'er near us,
He rides on the clouds and the wings of the wind;
Sends the beauty of nature and plenty to cheer us,
With a Father's benevolence loving and kind.
If clouds for a season seem darkening above us,
And complaining essays in our bosoms to dwell;
Cast away the foul tempter, there's brightness before us,
Be sure that our Maker doth everything well.

God's promise is faithful His goodness unswerving,
To all who will seek Him and trust in His word;
Through the clouds of deception His eye is observing,
The true Christians' pleading is sure to be heard.
Think not to deceive Him by faithless pretending,
The clouds of men's falsehood He pierces all through;
But rather press on to salvation, transcending
The brightest of happiness mortals e'er knew.

Let preachers and people now all work together,
The black clouds of Satan and sin to dispel;
Till all shall rejoice in the bright coming weather,
Where the host of redeemed in paradise dwell.
With earnestness meekly proclaiming salvation,
To cheer on the suffering, the toil-worn, and poor;
Till all erring souls in our much favoured nation
March onward with gladness to reach the blest shore.

Then vain all the clouds that come over our being,
The side of their brightness alone we shall see;
In sanctified radiance before the All-seeing,
A crown with the blessed our portion will be
Again let's remember whatever may sadden,
What clouds may come o'er us as onward we roam,
Each cloud has a lining of silver to gladden
And shed a bright light over every sad home.

WELCOME TO GARIBALDI.

Hail, hail, noble patriot, a heart proffered greeting!
Humanity welcomes and blesses thy name;
Every soul in our island receive thee with gladness,
All honour thy virtue, thy worth, and thy fame.

Not alone for the mighty exploits of thy daring,
All standing unrivalled in brilliant relief,
That have borne their fair banner of freedom unsullied,
And immortall'd thy memory as liberty's chief:

'Tis the pure sterling truth of thy stedfast devotion,
That rouses our country to honour thy worth,
And moves the whole soul and the voice of our nation,
Thy presence to greet as the noblest of earth.

Thy love for thy country inspires veneration.
And blessings warm freely shower down on thy head;
In thy advent we bow at the shrine of true freedom,
Whilst tyranny trembles and shudders with dread.

With hearts overflowing we feel in thy presence
Emotions no language hath power to pourtray,
The path that thou tread'st seems invested with goodness,
The sun's line of truth seems to hallow thy way.

Garibaldi, thrice welcome! the prayer of thy brothers,
Whose chains thou hast broken and bid them be free,
Of the captives once dying in tyranny's dungeon,
In gratitude rises to heaven and thee.

The babes of thy country in lisping sweet accents
'Neath mothers' fond teaching shall prattle thy name;
Historians and poets shall count it an honour,
To bear thy renown on the annals of fame.

O long may thy life, still surrounded with grandeur,
Be spared to partake of the fruits of thy toil,
To see thy dear country united in freedom,
No foreign oppressors to darken her soil;

And Italy rise once again in her beauty,
Send her sons and her daughters to gladden the world;
Again may her hearts and her muses still flourish
Beneath the bright banner of freedom unfurled.

CHARITY.

Hail, glorious work ! Jehovah views thy toil,
And mercy wafts each echo to the skies;
Thine alms dispensing throughout Albion's Isle ;
Let thy good works as holy incense rise,
Do all thou canst to benefit the poor ;
The widow's mite was welcome to the Lord,
He saw her heart, He knew her scanty store,
And bade her mite receive its God's reward.

The rich man's barns were full, on Him bestowed
To feast himself, but not the poor refuse ;
Yet unto Lazarus no charity he showed,
To him refused the crumbs he could not use.
Self was his God : he bade the wine cup flow,
But poison lurked within the fatal bowl,
And death was hovering round this feast below,
And God that night sent for his selfish soul.

Not so the gentle Saviour of mankind,
He sought the wretched but to soothe each sigh ;
Bade children in his heart sweet peace to find,
And owned them cherubs for His court on high.
Take Christ's example all friends of the poor :
The bread ye cast upon the waters now,
Though small, shall be unperishing in store,
And meet you when at Jesus' throne you bow.

Then shall those who did your bounty feel,
With tears of joy around their Father's throne,
Your deeds of love and mercy there reveal,
And hail thy entrance into bliss unknown
There too shall mercy stand with humid eye,
And blot thy sins away with tears of joy,
And sign thy passport to the realms on high—
Where bliss eternal reigns without alloy.

COMMUNION WITH GOD.

My Father God! I call on Thee!
And Oh! in mercy answer me,
Oh! Let me feel Thy Spirit's power
  When Death assails, and faith is small,
  O hear me when on Thee I call,
Be with me—in each trying hour.

My Father God! Thou knowest all
That in this world will me befall,
O grant that I may feel
  Secure while resting in thy love!
  In Christ thy Son on earth to prove,
Thy love to me reveal.

Thou knowest that life's a thorny road,
And sin oftimes our souls doth cloud;
Thou my protector be.
  When enemies surround the sod,
  And try to lure my soul from God,
Draw me, O God to Thee!

Dispel the mists that darken life,
And help me in this earthly strife
In thy communion still;
  All evil thoughts by Thee removed:
  May I walk with Thee,—Best Beloved,
Preserved from worldly ill.

And when upon me though shalt call,
May I be ready then to fall
Into thy arms to rest;
  In death let me feel mercy's beam,
  And taste the everlasting stream,
And be for ever blest.

A WELCOME TO GARIBALDI.

Dedicated to JOHN RICHARDSON Esq., C.C., mover of the freedom of the City of London to GARIBALDI, and Hon. Sec. and founder of the GARIBALDI Reception and Testimonial Fund.

Here's welcome to thee, GARIBALDI,
  Thou bravest of the brave
The friend of glorious liberty,
  Liberator of the slave!
As Freedom's sons through England's Isle,
  We hail thy coming here;
And give thee a glowing welcome
  With heart and soul sincere.

Thou patriot pure and noble,
  Unrivalled on the earth;
For thy virtues true and lofty,
  We love thee for thy worth.
In bright and sunny Italy
  Thou'st made her children free;
Mankind through various nations
  Their homage pay to thee.

Bright as a beacon-light of freedom
  Where'er thou hast appeared;
Thou hast riven the chains of slavery,
  Thy fettered brothers cheered.
'Tis not for thy own self-grandeur
  Thou hast fought thy way;
No, 'twas for thy suffering nation
  Thou battled through the fray.

It was for grand religious liberty
  Thy bravery has been displayed;
Opening the Inquisition prisons
  Where captives long were laid.
Thou opened each dark dungeon,
  The prisoners thou didst release,
And bid them go and serve their God
  With freedom and in peace.

And 'tis such noble men as thee
 The great pioneers have been,
As foremost ranking with the free,
 Best friends the world has seen;
Who opened the way for the Bible
 And its glories to display;
May all the sons of Italy
 Be cheered by its brightening ray.

Let no narrow-minded bigots' creed,
 Or church zeal, however right,
'Twixt God and man ever interfere,
 Let his conscience be free as light;
Let that be free as heaven's pure air,
 Blessing each benighted sod,
His right is freedom everywhere
 In his own way to worship God.

In vain shall despots' minions voice
 Be raised to cause thy fall;
For Freedom's sons shall thee sustain,
 Defiant to them all.
Of thy fair glory all shall hear,
 It flies from pole to pole;
While British hearts all bless thy name,
 Fear fills each tyrant's soul.

And all whose deeds forth nobly stand—
 The great, the wise, and good—
Shall hail thee as a kinsman true,
 In lofty brotherhood.
They'll hail thee great among them all,
 And warmly grasp thine hand;
And give thee a brother's welcome here,
 To our free native land.

And England now will gladly greet
 The man whose dauntless toil
Has planted Freedom's banner oft
 On many a blood-stained soil;

Whose efforts all unswerving firm,
  Whose every scheme and plan,
Where formed to crush all tyranny,
  And free his fellow man.

All hail thee, liberator great!
  With pure affection greet;
With warmest hearts both small and great,
  Come forward thee to meet.
Thy self-denying lofty soul
  Leads thousands to aspire
To emulate thy brilliant fame,
  And freedom to desire.

Foremost thou in every battle,
  Thy powers swayed the fight;
Ever in the cause of justice
  Firm to uphold the right
Thy soldiers all to thee devoted,
  A faithful, loving band;
Well they helped thee win thy laurels,
  And free their native land.

What crown of gems however bright,
  Is meet to grace thy brow;
Gold and diamonds all would fade,
  Thy glories forth to show.
The granite pile, or marble reared,
  Would fail to show thy worth;
Long as man shall value freedom,
  Thy fame will live on earth.

May Heaven's abundant blessings
  Rest on thee, hero brave!
Whose soul, fired with devotion,
  Risked life to free the slave.
Thine has been a bright example
  Of deeds most nobly planned;
And Italy may well be proud
  Of the hero of her land.

May peace be thy happy portion !
  And free from battle's strife,
Around thee gather all good men,
  And angels guard thy life !
May thy glorious bright example,
  Thy actions nobly done,
Fire the patriotic bosom
  Of each Italian son ;
Let all tyrant despots tremble,
  And hate thy honoured name ;
But all the sons of liberty
  Shall hand it down to fame.
Thy virtues they will emulate
  Through every land and clime,
And GARIBALDI's name shall last
  Till earth's remotest time.

EVER BE CHEERFUL.

Ever be cheerful, 'tis good for the mind,
With a countenance beaming with tenderness kind
Be ever forgiving, delighting to show
How lovely the streams of affection will flow.
Let no evil feelings disturb your career,
Pursuing your duties with consciences clear ;
Ever be cheerful, and hold to the truth,
'Tis the charm of our childhood, our manhood, and youth.

Ever be cheerful, encourage all good,
And smoothen the sorrows we meet on our road ;
To leave the world better let all of us try,
That we may be cheerful when summoned to die.
Let our lives be all free from dishonour and guile,
That reflection may ever return with a smile ;
Ever be cheerful and open as day,
And banish all sorrow and frowning away.

Ever be cheerful, and trusting in Him,
Who passed through the grave with its terrors so grim,
To atone for our sins, with the life He had given,
And open the portals of mercy in Heaven.

Keep steadily treading the hard narrow path,
For the broad one allures to destruction and wrath;
Ever be cheerful, life soon will be past,
You will gain the bright diadem promised at last.
Ever be cheerful, no terrors hath death,
For the saint who in Jesus resigneth his breath;
Where reflection and conscience together will blend,
His pillow to soften with peace to the end.
When a smile decks the features now soaring away
To the realms of an endless celestial day;
Ever be cheerful, and banish all doubt,
For Heaven will open with welcoming shout

TRUTH SHALL CONQUER ALL.

Through all life's varied passing scenes,
Deception haunts our way,
And o'er the world's designing craft
We stumble day by day.
For falsehood's made to look like truth,
The memory to enthrall,
Though baseless proving in the end,
For truth shall conquer all.

The gaudy surface often hides
A spurious thing beneath;
As gilding cloaks the counterfeit,
And covers base deceit,
That will not bear the honest test,
But into fragments fall,
Which fills the false heart with dismay,
For truth shall conquer all.

A single hour scarce pass away,
But cause have we to find
That to escape from falsehood's snares
Requires a subtle mind.
For lies will stare us in the face,
Behind our backs will crawl,
Our names and honour to destroy;
But truth shall conquer all.

One half the bulk of Mammon's wealth,
That glitters all so bright,
Is gained by means, if rightly traced.
Would shrink from honour's light.
Duplicity and wrong oft lie
Beneath its gilded pall;
When death approaches, conscience stings;
Thus truth shall conquer all.

THE SECURITY OF ENGLAND IS HER CHRISTIAN RELIGION.

If war should come to mar our peaceful land,
And cause the orphans and the widows" tears to flow,
Still that firm base on which secure we stand,
Shall bid defiance to each mighty foe:
And for our faith have martyrs bled and died,
Strong in the power of Him who made them free,
His presence with them, they have death defied,
And champions been of glorious liberty.

And Britain then would from the flame rise out,
And nations hear her powerful voice once more;
With freedom's voice again her sons would shout
Religion's voice re-echo to each shore.
Ten thousands thousands liberated bands,
Whose sires feudal bondsmen born to be,
Would rouse the world and rise their loosened hands,
And aid great Britain's power the world to free.

The traitor foul might rear his serpent crest,
Unfurl the blood-stained revolution's flag,
And try the sceptre from her grasp to wrest:
Before the face the tongue of scorn to wag.
Yet lofty would her dauntless spirit tower,
With freedom's flag triumphantly unfurled,
And laugh at every haughty tyrant's power,
And shake her stainless trident o'er the world.

Her faith shall blossom till the end of time
  And 'neath her flag shall never dwell a slave ;
Her rule shall men admire in every clime,
  And her religion's power their souls to save.
In the cause of liberty we've forward stood
  And from her path all obstacles have hurled ;
A fadeless title built, approved by God,
  And deeds have wrought to magnify the world.

For God and true religion on we roam,
  This, this our motto for each soul shall be,
For faith we'll fight that blesses hearth and home,
  And makes us all so happy and so free.
And ne'er will we our birthright sell for aught,
  But worthy followers of our fathers prove,
Who with their blood this precious freedom bought,
  Till we join them in glory's walks above.

THE RETROSPECT.

The retrospect of former days,
  Is solacing and sweet employment,
It makes our providential ways—
  Both food for profit and employment.

I muse in silent ecstacy,
  On many a happy friendly meeting ;
And while I feel a lively joy,
  I mourn to prove those joys were fleeting.

No! not fleeting—their still sweet breath
  Remains o'er time and change victorious ;
Their odours shall receive in death,
  And make eternity more glorious.

Hope dies not while at Jesus' feet ;
  Our faithful spirits hold communion,
And by anticipation sweet,
  Look forward to eternal union.

Though hid the ways of Providence,
 We'll acquiesce in calm submission,
We walk by faith—by sight, nor sense,
 And bow and bless His wise decision.

We know our Father's hand controls,
 We trust He will approve and love us;
On Christ we build our faithful souls
 Nor from this rock shall aught remove us.

Past hours of social intercourse,
 Are fraught with many a bright reflection,
And though we often mourn their loss,
 They fondly cling to recollection.

And while we take a calm review,
 We feel a sacred consolation,
The hand that's guided hitherto
 Will end the glorious consummation.

And as we view His gracious care,
 In adoration meekly bending,
Ascends to Heaven our grateful prayer,
 Like incense to the Throne ascending.

It rises to yon sapphire Throne,
 Where Heaven's High Priest appears before it,
And mingles with our prayers His own,
 And breathes sweet holy incense o'er it.

He brings it in His hands to God,
 The Holy Spirit o'er it hovering:
Points to His wounds and streaming blood,
 And all sin's cleansing fount discovering.

The heart it moves of God on high,
 The hosts of Heaven are all in motion;
The love that sent His Son to die,
 Fills all their souls with deep devotion.

The countless company are there,
 There with the blest they hold communion;
Departed is all earthly care,
 With Christ they're joined in endless union.

Who would not here then bear His cross,
And ask for help here to be given,
To count no sacrifice a loss,
To gain a brilliant crown in Heaven.

How happy then the man whose life
Can bear a retrospect unflinching,
Where truth's gems shone through ills and strife,
And all the snares of earth unquenching.

LINES ON THE PULLING DOWN OF AN OLD CHAPEL AND ERECTING A NEW ONE ON ITS SITE.

Thy days are all numbered, for Time's iron hand
Lies heavy, old chapel, on thee;
But long be remembered the patriot band,
Who braved even death and each monarch's command,
Till they won for their children the boast of our land,
That man's conscience should ever be free.

But though thou must fall, from thy ashes shall rise
A more costly and beautiful shrine,
Where our children may worship Jehovah, and prize
The memory of those who to yonder bright skies
Have been called for their worth from all earthly ties,
As stars in His presence to shine.

When the chosen of old, to their Maker would rear
A temple wherein to adore;
The rich gold of Ophir they held not too dear,
Nor the wealth of their kingdoms, His name to revere,
Of Him who in visions had deigned to appear;
They deemed all an offering too poor.

Then let not our dwellings be decked and arrayed,
With grandeur and pride to behold,
When houses of God are imploring our aid,
When time-honoured structures have sunk and decayed;
If you give to His cause you shall be repaid,
And become the bright sheep of His fold.

Cast fearlessly, then, on the waters thy bread,
And He who sees all with His eyes,
Ere the days of thy life shall have vanished and fled,
Shall return in bright blessings tenfold on thy head,
And thou through life's valley in safety be led
To thy glorious home upon high.

THOUGHTS ON SEEING CHILDREN AT PLAY.

Dear children play on, 'tis thy joyous time now,
Thy young hearts are strangers to guile,
For the finger of care hath not passed o'er thy brow,
Nor sorrow yet clouded thy smile.

All is pleasing and fair to thy innocent eyes,
No grief can thy pleasure destroy;
For the tear that one minute thy sorrow supplies,
In a moment is changed into joy.

But I think of the days of thy manhood to come,
When each scene shall be chequered with care,
And the visions of childhood, and loved ones at home,
Are passed like a bubble of air.

Like phantoms departed, and left but their name,
Our memories' page to enshrine;
Still the bright beams of Hope on our hearts have a claim,
Too dear for us e'er to resign.

Reflect on thy pleasures though passing away,
Thy frail bark is launched on life's sea;
Take Christ for your pilot o'er earth's rocky way,
He your guide to the heaven shall be.

And oh, when the storms of adversity lower,
May the clear beach of reason arise,
And faith grasp the helm—till sin's luring shore
Is passed—and hope beams from the skies.

In adversity's hour, when sorrow and pain
Wring thy heart, may it still find a balm
In God's pages of truth till life's stormy reign,
Is exchanged for eternity's calm

CONSCIENCE.

Man's conscience is his monitor,
  A mirror just and true,
Where every action of his life
Is placed before his view.

In characters effaceless stamped,
  No sophistry can hide,
Or self-deception dim its light,
  Nor stem its searching tide.

And why? "Tis God's own gracious means,"
  Is sternly written there;
It every shade of vice condems,
  But loves the just and fair.

Amidst the pleasures of the world,
  Men oft seem gay and bright,
And every thought and care beyond
  Seem banished from their sight.

But 'tis not so! for conscience holds
  Its empire ever near,
Bring consolation to the just,
  The worldling fills with fear

He's forced to hear the warning voice,
  Though racking heart and brain;
Though hard he strives to still reproach.
  His striving's all in vain.

Forewarned and checked is every man,
  Who meditates a crime,
The monarch or the ragged thief,
  In every land and clime.

There's no escape, no gold avails,
  For conscience none can cheat;
The criminal fears at every turn,
  The avenger's hand to meet.

But to the just a comforter,
  Will conscience ever prove;
Its admonitions, when obeyed,
  Bring peace, and joy, and love.

Then, oh, let conscience be our guide,
Let's cease to be unwise,
And shun the path where ruin lurks
So plain before our eyes.

CHILDHOOD.

O childhood, childhood! happy stage!
How oft does fancy roam
Amidst the cares of riper age,
To trace on memory's faithful page
The scenes of boyhood's home.

When doom'd in other lands to dwell,
Through scenes all strange to roam,
'Tis then we feel the magic spell
Steal o'er the soul, and fondly tell
Of boyhood's happy home.

Though pomp and splendour call me guest,
Beneath ambition's dome,
A hallowed grief assails the breast,
The weary spirit sighs to rest
Again in boyhood's home.

Though wealth may crown the exile's schemes,
And monarchs seek his smile;
Yet the brightest of his earthly dreams
Are those, when fancy's golden beams
Those happy dreams beguile.

If sorrow or dismay arise,
To blight each earthly tie,
The wanderer turns his weary eyes,
To those bright scenes and sunny skies,
With longings there to die.

Though tyrants drag the swarthy slave,
Far from his darling plains,
Behold the dangers he can brave!
The felon's doom, a nameless grave,
To burst his galling chains!

O'er pathless wilds and burning sands,
Untiring will he roam
Through hostile tribes and stranger lands,
Until amidst those scenes he stands
Of happy boyhood's home.

Home! home's the watchword. home's the prayer,
Where'er our footsteps roam,
The bright, the beautiful, the fair,
In vain may spread the gilded snare,
We turn from lordly halls to share
A humble cot at home.

CANDOUR.

I love the man whose open heart
And countenance the rays impart
Of sterling truth and worth:
Who scorns to flatter or deceive;
And fears not those who disbelieve,
Where cringing ne'er had birth.

'Tis he, I mean, who never shrinks
From telling plainly what he thinks
Our faults' or merits' due
In whom we can our thoughts confide;
Who sternly will our case decide
Impartial, just and true.

Pure candour ranks a virtue high:
'Tis formed the mind to dignify,
Alike with friends and foes,—
It throws a halo round our path,
Courts no forced smile, shuns no man's wrath.
But dwells in calm repose.

Though little favoured by the world,
And oft about as worthless hurled,
From grasping love of gain:
It still preserves its priceless fame,—
Sets honour's signet on each name
That grace its noble train.

Home's peace for years is oft destroyed,
With pain and sorrow life's alloyed,
By hiding trivial things;
Which when discovered oftimes lead
To words, and even blows indeed,
And sin and misery brings;

That had the truth at once been told,
By mean deception uncontrolled,
Had led to peace and love.
The light of truth our path will cheer,
And candour banish dread and fear,
And life's firm guardian prove.

Then let us strive with manly grace,
To meet the world with honest face,
And no man's favour buy:
A course straightforward still pursue,
Keep honour's landmark e'er in view,
And scorn to breathe a lie.

What comfort else can spring from life?
How much we find of cruel strife,
Where men the truth disguise,
But O, how loveable are those
Who candidly their hearts disclose,
How good, how great, how wise!

HYPOCRICY.

The innocent and trusting heart,
How oft 'tis lured away
By simulating sanctity
That fills life's busy way—
That brings sharp scandal's daggers forth
Against God's Holy Word;
And 'neath its foul envenomed dart
The scoffer's tongue is heard.
Among the blackest evils known,
That haunt the walks of men,
Is heartless base hypocricy
Emerged from Satan's den:

With fulsome words and aspect sleek,
  It works its loathsome snare.
Then leaves its victims to repine,
  And die in cold despair.
For thrown upon a heartless world,
  When virtue thus hath flown,
Without a friend or succour near,—
  Scorned even by their own.
Houseless, foodless,—wanderers now,
  Cold, frantic, and forlorn;
Stalk life-like fiends, and curse full oft
  The day that they were born.
'Tis true! 'tis true! alas, too true!
  Such things we daily see;
The effect of that dark monster fiend,
  Man's vile hypocricy.
How well the Scriptures such describe
  Their actions dark and mean,—
"Like ravening wolves they're inwardly,
  Though in sheep's clothing seen,"
How guarded ought we then to be,
  Against this baneful thing,
Where 'neath the honeyed flattering tongue,
  There lies a poisonous sting;
That fires its venom forth and blasts
  'Neath friendship's seeming guise,
An unsuspecting honest name,
  With meanly whispered lies
But shows a surface all the while,
  Of cordial genial care,
And throws its victims off their guard,
  And hides the hateful snare.
Beware, and know, and mark the man
  Who'll praise you to your face,
And coincide with all you say
  With meek approving grace.

This truth you may believe,
His plaint manner's but a cloak,
The better to deceive;
But rather trust that diamond rough,
Who'll challange your ideas;
Contest with firmness for his own,
Unbought by smiles or fears:
Who hates a hypocrite like gall,
Suspects each canting word,
And from whose lips unvarnished truth,
Though rough, is ever heard.
Confide not ought in such a one,

——

OUR CHELSEA PENSIONERS SO BRAVE

When wars have passed and peace returned,
And sounds of joy have filled the land.
And patriots' hearts for country burned,
And gladness beamed on every hand:
When victory's wreaths have crowned our arms,
And Briton's fame abroad hath spread,
And stilled the rush of war's alarms,
And strife and dark invasion's dread:—

Our thought revert, with sorrowing pride,
To those brave heroes on the field,
Who died for country side by side,
Than shrink, or to dishonour yield.

With grateful hearts we see again
The maimed and lamed in battle's strife;
Their wounds we soothe and ease their pain,
Although disabled now for life.

A noble home our veterans find
As age creeps on and strength decay,
Where solace dwells for heart and mind,
Where life in peace is passed away.
The whitened locks of soldiers here.
Have calmly gone down to the grave,
With every care their last to cheer,
Our Chelsea pensioners so brave.

The glorious liberty we boast,
By British arms hath been preserved,
Who've rendered safe our sea-girt coast,
Our love and gratitude deserved.
Compare our free and happy land
With many a tyrant-trodden soil,
Where mind is crushed by despot's hand;
Like beasts of burden, sons of toil.

Where no man's home is free from spies,
Where plots and secret murders rage,
From which the exile patriot flies,
And in our midst in life engage;
Where priest-craft dark in bondage holds
The minds and consciences of all,
Their weak impostures to uphold,
With terrors that men's hearts appal.

No civil wars distract our isle,
No frightful carnage here we see,
No slaves against our laws revile,
And freedom smiles where'er ye be.
And glorious beams of liberty,
Swell British hearts on land and wave,
And who the men who've kept us free?—
Our Chelsea pensioners so brave.

REJOICE, O MY SOUL.

Rejoice, O my soul! the glad dawn now appears.
The bright Son of Righteousness comes and he cheers;
'Tis the wrath of His presence that here I now feel.
While mercy and love His rich goodness reveal.
'Tis my shepheard now leads me to drink of the stream,
'Tis His life-giving blood, I am happy through Him;
'Tis His blood that has washed me whiter than snow,
Which now makes me love Him, and makes my heart to glow.

'Twas on Calvary's cross that He suffered for me,
Salvation was gained when He died on the tree,
He with grief bowed His head, "'Tis finished!" He cried,
For my soul's salvation He groaned there and died.
I grasp at the mercy thus purchased and given,
And my soul seems warmed with bright beams from heaven;
The Covenant of promise, the bright bow above,
I see and rejoice in the fulness of love.

Thus shall I go on through Jesus my might,
My strength and my guide and my glorious light;
His grace to me given will lead me to prove
His gracious salvation in bright realms above
There I with raptures His goodness shall tell,
And acknowledge how here He did all things well;
Then bow down before Him amidst the great throng,
Redeemed by His mercy to join Heaven's song.

LINES ON THE BIBLE,

DEDICATED TO THE JUVENILE BIBLE SOCIETY.

Glorious old Bible! The Best Book on earth,
It showeth how great is the souls precious worth;
'Tis a gracious charter where we may all see
God's mercy and goodness to all men are free;
A lever whereby man is helped to arise
And seek for a mission of bliss in the skies;
For a patriot band are those noble youths.

This is the book that has made England great,
Dispelling our ignorance, raising our state;
Given to England to spread through the world,
Diffusing its truths where our flag is unfurled;
And if we desire true freedom for man,
We shall give all our aid to this glorious plan
For a patriot band are those noble youths,
Who seek by all means to publish its truths.

Sometimes we hear enemies talk of this land—
They tell us that armies will come on our strand;
But true to the Bible we may at them laugh,
With God our protector we'd beat them like chaff;
If faithful to Him, we'd invaders defy,
Yet will send them our Bible—to serve them we'll try.
For a patriot band are those noble youths,
Who seek by all means to publish its truths.

Go on then, young friends, in this work engage
For the glory of God and the light of the age:
Do all that you can God's love to reveal,
Make your lives glorious, and labour with zeal
To spread the blest Bible wherever you can,
And be benefactors of perishing man.
For a patriot band are those noble youths,
Who seek by all means to publish its truths.

And be well assured if you work for the Lord,
Your labour and zeal He will early reward;
And He'll be your guide through all the world's strife,
Will bless you with favour through this earthly life;
And after you've done with this mission of love,
Will call you all home to His glory above.
For a patriot band are those noble youths,
Who seek by all means to publish its truths.

ONWARD AND UPWARD.

Our lives are great and noble,
If we live for deeds sublime;
And thus impress our footsteps,
Upon the sands of time.

And while we run our earthly race,
Work well in God's great plan;
And be a valiant Hero,
For the benefit of man.

'Tis thus the noble hearted,
Pass on through every strife;
Labouring for the oppressed,
And consecrate their life.

They love the cause of freedom,
And round her altar's fire,
They raise their voices high,
With heaven's enraptured choir.

For peace and home and duty,
They lift their thoughts above;
For Religion in its beauty,
To bless this earth with love.

When tyrants are oppressors,
And do the people wrong;
Their voice is raised against them,
Bold, faithful, earnest, stroug.

'Tis thus the reign of darkness,
Is banished from our earth;
And flowers of glorious freedom,
Thus bloom with heavenly birth.

'Tis thus that earth's great temples,
With beauty shall be crowned;
And peace and liberty with joy,
Through the whole world abound.

Thus men of noble valour,
Armed in the cause of right;
Do battle with the evil,
And for the good they fight.

Thus do these blessed heroes,
Win for themselves a name;
Bequeathing to posterity,
A bright and lasting fame.

Each year of theirs is passed,
But they noble triumphs win;
Trampling down oppression,
Conquerors over sin.

And they shall gain the crown,
Promised by their Lord:
For their valiant fighting,
And Heaven be their reward.

"THY WILL BE DONE."

My Father, God, to Thee I humbly bend,
Convinced in Thee I've ever found a friend;
Parent I live by Thy power supreme,
And grateful love still shall be my theme.
To Thee I bow at the evening hour,
To praise Thy goodness and extol Thy power;
Thou art my Friend and I have lived to see
Thy gracious bounty shower'd down on me.

Oh! help me now with grateful sense imbued,
To offer up to Thee my warmest gratitude;
Thou art Love, Thy nature does reveal,
And Thy benevolence I daily see and feel.

Oh! keep me in the narrow path I pray,
Leading me on in Thine appointed way;
Save I beseech Thee through Christ Thy only Son,
Help me to gain the plaudit of well done.

Help me each day Thy mercies to rehearse,
In songs of love, offer up each verse;
Take from me all that feeds my pride,
Help me to cleave to Thy loving side.
Help me by Thy good Spirit trained,
In Thee to find my Paradise regained;
Help me in every trial through Thy Son,
To say I am my Father's, and His will be done.

I WILL NEVER LEAVE THEE.

Hast Thou said Thou will not leave me?
Oh! thou God of truth and love;
Hast Thou promised Thou will ever,
Faithful to that promise prove?
Not to me alone Thou speakest,
Oh! Thou gracious loving Lord;
But to all in Christ—the weakest,
Thou proclaim'st the wonderous word.

I will never leave thee, never!
I thine all efficient Lord;
I thy shield and buckler ever,
Thy exceeding great reward.
I can well preserve thee ever,
All thy foes and dangers see;
And will suffer nought to sever,
Thy confiding soul from me.

Lord thy goodness thrills my spirit,
'Tis enough Thy word so passed;
I thy presence shall inheret,
Long as eternal ages last.
Thou wilt never leave me, never,
God of love on whom I call;
God, my God and mine for ever,
And for ever all in all.

HEAVEN OUR HOME.

Blest thought to have a home above,
  Where all is joy, and peace, and love;
To have a home among the blest,
  And in our Father's mansion rest.

This mansion, christians all survey,
  And keep in view through life's rough way;
The blessed end they keep in view,
  Which cheers them all their journey through.

Blest home when at life's journey's end,
  From earth triumphant to ascend
Then all life's cares and battles o'er,
  They strive to gain the heavenly shore.

And oh! what wonders meet their sight,
  The glorious city dazzling bright;
The Throne—the Saviour—God is seen,
  Without a ray of cloud between.

No sickness there shall e'er invade.
  Nor sorrow cast its gloomy shade;
But in that home so bright and fair,
  Peace and love dwell ever there.

Oh ! let me keep this home in view,
Whilst I life's journey still pursue ;
Press on my road to reach the shore
My home above for ever more.

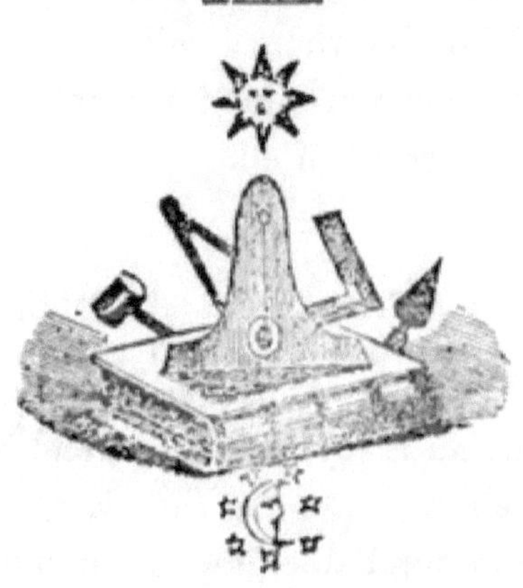

ESSAY ON FREEMASONRY.

(Written to please a friend of mine, who is a Mason, and Captain of a ship.)

MAN was never intended in the all-wise dispensation of God to be an isolated and solitary being, but he was formed with an intellect and capacity to improve his fellow man, and faculties to glorify God Wise men with a desire to do good, and to get good form themselves into sects and societies, and amongst the different societies or companies in this world, Freemasonry occupies the first position, and stands out boldly pre-eminent a benefit to mankind; and some of the most noble men that have ever lived in our world and who have done a vast amount of good in it, whose desire has been to glorify God and to be a benefit to their fellow men have been Freemasons. It would be a long line of worthies we might select from the masonic scroll of fame, but as the task would be herculean, we must leave that and turn to its general principles, and the good it is doing in our world.

After the great deluge of the world by water for man's wickedness, it was thought by men if they could combine together and build a tower whose height should almost reach the heavens, that then they could defy Omnipotence, and if a second deluge were to take place, they could run into this strong tower and be safe. But God in his infinite wisdom frustrated their designs and confounded their language, so that men have gone abroad into all the earth but have different manners, customs, and languages. But still there are links in the great chain of society, whereby men are a benefit to their fellow men, and are endeavouring to carry out the golden rule of loving their neighbours as themselves, and like true philanthropists, are endeavouring to do good in their day and generation, and seeing they have only one life to live, are desirous of handing down to posterity an unsullied name; and if perchance their survivors should look upon the stone that marks their last resting place, they may be enabled to say, "there lie the ashes of one whom I knew to be a good man, and who in acts of benevolence was always doing his fellow creatures good."

Men in all ages have congregated together, society of the right kind being the best thing to polish man, and rub off that roughness and ignorance that men have been found to possess who did not mingle with society. Man's pursuit is after happiness—from infancy to old age he pursues different plans that he thinks will most conduce to the gaining of the object of his pursuit—but experience discloses the fact that unalloyed happiness is not allotted to man in this world, inasmuch as health is constantly liable to be disturbed by sickness, joy with sorrow, hope by disappointment—the calm and content of mental delight by the tortures of anxiety, and the ordinary course of mortal happiness, destined to be eventually extinguished by death. Some have thought that they could serve God best and their fellow men best, by isolating themselves and shutting themselves up in a monastry away from their fellow men, but this has always proved a great mistake, a man to do his duty must mix with society, and must take care that he carries about with him and shows to others those principles that shall do good to others, and leaven the mass of society in which he mixes, and raise not only his fellow man who comes in contact with him, but should like a good patriot and lover of his country, disseminate those principles that should like a moral lever raise all who come in contact with him, and that the world may have to say after he has passed his three score years and ten, that he lived to some purpose and did some good while he lived among mankind.

There are several societies bound together by laws formed among themselves for their own good, and known to each other by different signs, known only by themselves, and of all the different societies that have ever been formed, none stands so forward—so proudly preeminent among men as the Freemasons, who are known to each other all over the world; and it would be difficult in any part of the world not to find a Freemason, from the burning plains of India, to the snowy regions of Liberia, you will find Freemasons, and whenever a man is in distress, in any part of the world, if he is a Mason he will find some good brother ready to lend him a helping hand, and though I am not a Mason myself, yet I believe it to be a general benefit to those who are, and I believe if their principles were carried out, mankind would be generally benefited by them : and surely it needs in this world that we should do all that we can to promote the peace of mankind, and endeavour to link them together in unity, especially when we look back on the past history of man, and see what war has done to desolate our world—when we think of thousands of men meeting each other in deadly conflict, and of the horrors that war entails upon man. It seems to me that any man or any society that would try to bind men in the bonds would be general benefactors to any land or country, and would be carrying out the golden rule "whatsoever ye would that men should do unto you, do ye even so unto them :"—and again, as the Bible unfolds to us there is to be a time of universal peace under the reign of the Messiah, all who endeavour to bring about this glorious time for the benefit of the human race, must be considered as benefactors in their day and generation, and will leave their footprints on the sands of time that can never be obliterated, but shall help swell the grand chorus of the angelic host, who ushered into this world the Prince of peace in the song of ' Glory to God in the highest, on earth peace, and good will towards men '

I shall endeavour to show in this little treatise some of the benefits of Masonry to man. In the first place the art of building among men is one of his greatest blessings and comforts, and we are often led to think of men who live in a city according to the buildings of the city. Masonry has been in all ages a science tending to elevate the ideas of men, and has been sent down to earth unto men's minds by the Great Supreme and Almighty Architect, who by His wisdom laid the foundations of the earth, and by His power upholds, guides, and governs all the planets in their different courses. I believe architecture has been greatly improved by Freemasonry—many a noble building we gaze upon with its exquisite sculptured stone work its massive pillars, capitals. cornices, corbets, and pinnacles—owes something of its beauty to Freemasonry.

The mountains and hills, the valleys and mines have brought their marble and granite, and silver and gold, and the forest its trees; but it is in the mind of man to design the goodly edifice, and to bring forth by his energy and perseverance the noble temples of art and science, and out of the rough materials of nature to bring forth beauty, order, and harmony.

The majesty and beauty of nature is wonderful, and shows the power and wisdom of God—but His love is manifested to man in the gift of His dear Son—He is a living stone, the sure foundation—He is the living stone and those that love Him are living stones also. The foundation—the rock of ages, and these who by skilful masonry build upon that rock—growing up into a living temple whose builder and founder is God And to His creature man alone has He given those exalted talents to improve his mind and made him what he really is—the mighty master-piece of His vast creation.

I cannot help stopping here to notice what some men with debased intellects have affirmed, that man is only a superior order of the brute creation. I for one pity such weak minds, and would simply ask such men—what has the brute ever done to better his condition, they still live in caves and dens of the earth as they have always done since they were first created, and have done nothing towards improving their condition; but man with his gigantic intellect is continually improving his condition and the wonders of science he is continually bringing to light must be a matter of surprise even to himself. When we think of the genius of man, that he can employ steam as he does to propel mighty ships, and also to the most minute machinery—when we think of his mighty intellect devising and carrying out plans whereby the electric fluid carries his messages to the distant parts of the earth, under and above water—we almost wonder there is any men so debased and wilfully ignorant as to say and assert such a vile and pernicious opinion—but men who assert such things are generally infidels, who do not believe in a Supreme Being who governs and directs all things in infinite wisdom—how I pity such men, and am led to look back to what such men do for the benefit of their fellow men, and must candidly confess I cannot find they do any good in their lives, and when they come to die they generally turn coward and abjure their principles and call upon God to have mercy upon them: but the man who takes the word of God for his standard—and I am thankful to say, masonry like a beautiful edifice is built upon this standard—is doing good to his fellow man and erecting noble and benevolent institutions, and is endeavouring to employ the talents God has given him—to alleviate the sorrows of others, and often causing the widows' and orphans' hearts to sing with joy—this I believe masonry does in an eminent degree and thousands have great cause to be thankful after having experienced its benefits, and thousands more will I feel assured till the latest posterity, have reason to bless the benefits of Freemasonry.

I am not sure I am right in thinking masonry took its first rise from the building of the Tower of Babel; I have been informed it was at an earlier period, and may be traced to the garden of paradise when our first parents sewed the fig leaves together and made themselves aprons, and from them may be traced onward in the march of time, through Seth, Enoch, and Noah to the flood. Then onwards through Shem and Japheth to the time of Abraham and Sarah his wife, where the distinction was made between the slave Ishmael and the free born son Isaac. But it arrived at its greatest glory in the days of Solomon, who, assisted by the king of a neighbouring country, erected that glorious temple at Jerusalem for the worship of Jehovah, which for splendour and magnificence has never yet been equalled; and according to the scriptural account of it I think impossible ever to be surpassed.

There are in the world multitudes of noble Masons, doing good in their day and generation, and leaving their footprints on the sands of time—squaring their lives by the square of righteousness, and sounding some of the depths of human misery by the plummet of love. They have noble institutions for the poor orphans, which are open to the inspection of visitors, and I am sure any one whether a mason or not. if he has right feelings will feel his heart swell with delight to see the children trained in these institutions—trained in the knowledge and precepts of the Bible—to lead them to the grand lodge of heaven to meet their parents. Then there are the asylums for the aged and decayed Freemans and their wives, where they may dwell together in peace and comfort and spend the remnent of their days in preparation for the Grand Lodge above. Then there is the Annuity Fund for those Brethren and Sisters who may require it. Then there is the Fund of Benevolence, to which I am informed no distressed brother if he was worthy, ever applied in vain. These I think are abundant proofs that they love like brethren, and that it is a great advantage to belong to the noble ancient fraternity.

From my heart I wish that Christians had some means to distinguish each other, surely they might be proud to acknowledge their Christian brethren. I regret to see such conformity to the world and wish some of those who are ashamed of Christ—had to exhibit the standard of the cross in some way that could not be misunderstood

> "Ashamed of Jesus, yes I may,
> When I ve no sin to wash away."

There may be some Masons that are no benefit to the Lodges, as well as some Christians who are no benefit to the Churches; but I again say I wish the Christians had some sign that they could distinguish each other by, so that a brother meeting them in a railway carriage, or on board ship or anywhere, might take counsel together instead of passing their time unprofitably. But I feel assured a good Mason must be a good man, as Freemasonry teaches him how to live and how to die—it leads him to contemplate the final destiny, and enables him to triumph over death and to trample the king of terrors beneath his feet, and to await with a hope that maketh not ashamed the morning of the resurrection. Thus: Freemasonry may become to some the handmaid of Christianity, and lead its great Architect's works to be admired, and its possessor to make one of the great lodge above and dwell in the happy abode for ever.

Then it is a noble theme for the mind of man to endeavour to elucidate the beauties of science, and to bring to light its mysteries to improve the condition of mankind. Such an employment is a right one and worthy of his most exalted talents, and it is a service of happiness to himself that his Maker has given him the talents, and he is improving them for the good of others. Then I believe that Masonry is calculated to make man happy, wise and good in an eminent degree; and we must all know and feel and acknowledge there is misery enough in the world, and anything tending to alleviate the sorrows and woes of man should be encouraged, and men of learning in all ages have incontestably proved that man is a being peculiarly formed for society, and that he is entitled to all the pleasures and benefits that flow from society, and draws a vast amount of happiness in life from the pleasures of true friendship. And he also improves his moral and intelectual condition, by mixing in society that has for its object and pursuit the glory of God and the benefit of his fellow man—in such pursuit alone real happiness is to be found, and I assured masonry is calculated to improve and cultivate the understanding—men who enter it have to go through their regular degrees as an apprentice and workman before they can arrive at the elevated position of grand master; and it must make men more wise as they pass through this ordeal, as masonry comprises within its ample circle every branch of useful knowledge and learning There is no science however deep that is not known, or knowledge however profound that it does not grapple with and lay hold of, and the minds of those who belong to masonry will never want for lofty themes to study, as they are all contained within its mighty grasp, from the mechanic and artificer up to the most profound philosopher, there is something for each one to study and contemplate The builder and architect may learn plans of wisdom and beauty, and compass in his mind vast and useful improvements in the art of building. The geometrician may plan his problems and trace the points, the line, the angles, and the circles, till he arrives at perfection and is capable of giving to the world solutions of the most difficult problems. The geographer by the use of charts and maps may travel seas and compass continents, and explore empires; and is enabled to trace the history of bygone days—the rise and fall of empires—and the history of his own beloved country. Astronomers who delight in beholding the planetary system, and looking up through nature to nature's God, will find masonry assist him to investigate the wonders of the sun—that great luminary of vast size and matchless grandour, round which the planetary orbs perform their annual revolutions, delighting and astonishing the most gigantic minds with wonder and astonishment at the amazing velocity and regularity of their courses: shewing to man a portion of that great Being's works who stoops to call the good man his friend, and promises in His word that all things shall work together for good to him that loves his great Creator, and endeavours in all things to do his will and please him; and there is nothing that will tend to elevate the mind of man and make him do what is right, more than the conviction that God is always present with and beholding his every action—and the lodges of Masons I am informed have plenty inscriptions from the best of all books—the Bible—and it is impossible when in a lodge with all those noble inscriptions around him, but that his mind must be improved by them. Then again there is the brotherly affection with which all are greeted when at their lodge, or if they meet in the street, causing those who witness them to exclaim, "Behold how good and pleasent a thing it is for brethern to dwell together in unity:" and they are preparing daily for that glorious heavenly world, to which all the most splendid scenes on earth is as nothing to the glories which are to be revealed to them that love God.

Solomon's temple was perhaps the most glorious place that was ever built upon earth, but how humbly did he dedicate that splendid piece of masonry to God. I almost think in my mind that I hear him exclaim—"But will God indeed dwell here—the heaven of heavens cannot contain him—how much less this place which I have builded." And then when we put in comparison with this what is revealed of the new and heavenly Jerusalem how all earthly buildings sink in comparison as we read of its gates of pearls, its walls of precious stones, and its street of gold; of the happiness of its inhabitants, and its never ending duration—all things here are passing away, and man is passing with them.

The preparatory character of human life which is founded upon scripture invites man to use every possible effort to fit himself for that exalted state of existance to which he is authorized by revelation to direct his hopes and aspirations—in his exertions with this object in view he must be guided by his thoughts, words and precepts, and the animating promises revealed in the Bible—and from this source he must learn with a view of practicing—first his duty to his Maker, and then the several moral duties which he owes to himself and to his fellow creatures; and his duty to his Maker can only be fulfilled by strict obedience to His Divine will. Permit me then as a friend to wish you may pass your life usefully here, squared by the square, and ruled by the plummet of your masonry—till God sees fit to call you home to your reward in heaven—where I hope to meet you and your Brother Masons in that better world, where we shall be clothed with the white robe and have the crown of gold and the beautiful harp—to sing the praises of the Divine Architect for ever and ever. Amen, and Amen. This is the humble prayer of

Yours very respectfully,

GEORGE JOSEPH WILLIAMSON.

H. G. Savage, Steam Printer, Sutton Street, East.

www.ingramcontent.com/pod-product-compliance
Lightning Source LLC
Chambersburg PA
CBHW022022110726
47901CB00006B/1630

9783337401566